Asda Tickled Pink

uniquely supports the work of the UK's two leading breast cancer charities **Breast Cancer Now** and **Breast Cancer Care** helping to provide life-saving research and life changing support to anyone affected by breast cancer.

For over 22 years, colleague and customer fund-raising, along with incredible pink products on sale, has generated **over £60m** to support the vital services and research for anyone affected by a breast cancer diagnosis.

You can find out more on our website **https://www.asda.com/tickled-pink/**

Breast Cancer Now is a registered charity (charity nos.1160558, SC045584, and 1200) via BCNTL
and
Breast Cancer Care is a registered charity (Charity Nos.1017658 and SCO38104) via Breast Cancer Care Trading Limited (company no: 2681072)

 Penguin
Random House
UK

MAKE SURE YOU STAY BREAST AWARE BY REGULARLY CHECKING FOR SIGNS AND SYMPTOMS

One in eight women in the UK will be diagnosed with breast cancer in their lifetime

'LOVE YOUR BREASTS, BE BREAST AWARE'

- Breast cancer is the most common cancer in the UK.

- It's important to know your breasts whatever your age. There's no right or wrong way to check, it's about looking and feeling regularly.

- It's not just a lump. Make sure you know all the signs to look out for.

- Most symptoms won't be cancer but tell your doctor about any new or unusual changes.

Readers love Lucy Dillon . . .

'An extraordinary book. I cried so many times
reading it . . . my new all-time favourite'

'A lovely heart-warming book that is full of
creativity, friendship and self-discovery'

'A sheer delight to read . . . I laughed, cried
and fell in love with all the characters'

'Uplifting, joyous, bittersweet and completely inspiring'

'Loved this book, I didn't want to put it down'

'Beautiful, just beautiful. Had me sobbing buckets!'

'An excellent book with great characters,
both human and canine!'

'A wonderful book full of honesty, beauty, love
and forgiveness. You'll need the tissues!'

'A beautiful, heart-warming story which
had me sobbing at the end'

By Lucy Dillon

Where the Light Gets In
All I Ever Wanted
One Small Act of Kindness
A Hundred Pieces of Me
The Secret of Happy Ever After
Walking Back to Happiness
Lost Dogs and Lonely Hearts
The Ballroom Class

For more information on Lucy Dillon and her books, please visit her website at www.lucydillon.co.uk

 www.facebook.com/pages/LucyDillonBooks

 @lucy_dillon

 @lucydillonbooks

Unexpected Lessons in Love

Lucy Dillon

BLACK SWAN

TRANSWORLD PUBLISHERS
61–63 Uxbridge Road, London W5 5SA
www.penguin.co.uk

Transworld is part of the Penguin Random House group of companies
whose addresses can be found at global.penguinrandomhouse.com

Penguin
Random House
UK

First published in Great Britain in 2020 by Black Swan
an imprint of Transworld Publishers

A CIP catalogue record for this book
is available from the British Library.

ISBN 9781784162108

Typeset in 11.75/14.1 pt Adobe Garamond by Jouve (UK), Milton Keynes.
Printed and bound in Great Britain by Clays Ltd, Elcograf S.p.A.

Penguin Random House is committed to a sustainable future
for our business, our readers and our planet. This book is made
from Forest Stewardship Council® certified paper.

MIX
Paper from
responsible sources
FSC® C018179
FSC
www.fsc.org

1 3 5 7 9 10 8 6 4 2

For anyone who's ever heard that little voice
in their head – and had the courage
to take its advice.

Prologue

Brooklyn Bridge, October

Jeannie was walking with Dan's hands over her eyes but she wasn't worried. Right now, here in this delicious champagne bubble of a moment, she was wrapped in a bliss that she'd never believed you could feel in real life.

So far their long weekend in New York had been one romantic surprise after another. Dan had planned it in secret, but he'd chosen everything Jeannie would have chosen herself: a morning spent browsing the vintage shops at Chelsea Market, then an afternoon crunching through copper leaves and sipping hot chocolate in Central Park. Cocktails and oysters, yellow cabs and multicoloured Times Square lights, sneaky kisses as they rode the crowded subway: every second had felt as if the two of them were starring in their own movie.

The hotel was so gorgeous Jeannie could have happily spent the whole weekend in their tiny super-chic room, with its soft rugs and even softer lighting. And of course, with Dan. Just thinking about Dan's tanned skin against the crisp white bedlinen gave her a hot rush of happiness: there were *some* highlights Jeannie wouldn't be sharing with her mum when she got home.

Today, their last day, had started with eggs and coffee

at a deli counter, then they'd joined a downtown walking tour around the haunts of Jeannie's eighties' pop heroes, where Dan had patiently taken selfies of them outside Blondie's rehearsal rooms, and Madonna's *actual flat*. Sure, it was just bricks and windows, but to Jeannie, these streets were where the soundtrack of her life had bubbled up out of nowhere, from musicians who'd once struggled just like her. Her soul had lifted when the tour guide talked about their setbacks and successes, and she'd kissed Dan with grateful love, wondering if he knew how much it meant to her that he'd obviously heard the things she *hadn't* said.

Now they were on Brooklyn Bridge, and Dan was promising her the view of a lifetime if she just kept going, one, two, three more steps.

'There,' he said, but he didn't uncover her eyes straight away. Jeannie put her own small hands, neat enough to fly across the fretboard of her ukulele, over Dan's long fingers. He had clever, strong vet's hands, hands that treated injured dogs and birthed calves. A chilly breeze was blowing off the river below, but between Dan and Jeannie, there was a rose-gold glow.

She leaned back into his body, not wanting the moment to end. The light was just fading from the sky, and Jeannie's whole soul rang with music, like euphoric birdsong surging through her veins. Her best friend Edith had assured her that happiness like this was impossible in real life. But for once, Edith Constantine was wrong. *So* wrong.

'Ready?' There was a slight tease in Dan's voice; suddenly she hoped he hadn't taken her to the edge of the bridge. Jeannie wasn't good with heights. She scrabbled to remember if she'd told Dan that – there were moments when she forgot they hadn't yet reached the boring 'user manual' stage of knowing each other. Allergies to marzipan, fear of crows, stuff you only mentioned when you'd run out of interesting things to talk about.

'Ta da!' Dan pulled his hands away and she gasped as the glittering Manhattan skyline rose in front of her, a black and silver collage of lights and towers that sparkled out of the dusk.

'Wow!' Jeannie turned within the tight circle of his arms so she was nose to nose with him. Dan was handsome from any angle. The breeze flipped his blond hair into his eyes, unusual deep denim-blue eyes, and Jeannie had to remind herself that this was actually her life. It felt too perfect, too romantic, to be real. Yet it was. This was love, at last.

'I'm so happy!' she blurted out and, to her amazement, Dan's eyes glistened just like hers. He blinked, as if he couldn't quite believe how perfect this moment was either.

And then it happened. In what seemed like slow motion, Dan unwrapped his arms from around her, stepped back and dropped to one knee. There were people walking across the bridge; some stepped around him with a tut, but others saw what was going on and stopped, indulgent smiles forming on their lips.

Jeannie blinked. No, wait. Was this … what she thought it was? Her heart thudded against her ribs. Was Dan going to propose? She hadn't even dared imagine this moment, and now she was in the middle of it. A proposal … that was a moment that only happened once. In your whole life.

Suddenly Jeannie felt dizzy, as if Dan *had* taken her to the edge of the bridge.

'Jeannie McCarthy,' Dan was saying, and now the passers-by had stopped, gathering into clumps along the sidewalk. 'I know we've only known each other for five months, but they've been the happiest five months of my life. Will you marry me?'

Manhattan rose behind Dan like a second, bigger crowd of well-wishers, smiling at the lovers, twinkling its lights like stars. Phone cameras were surreptitiously raised; breath was held. Jeannie felt as if all New York was waiting for her response.

Dan gazed up at her with those melting blue eyes. He was gorgeous, intelligent, and he'd flown her to New York to propose. Jeannie shook herself. What more could she ask for? What more did she want?

Her mouth opened before she had time to answer that in her head.

'Yes!' she said, and everyone on the bridge applauded.

Chapter One

Jeannie McCarthy was twenty minutes and four miles away from Longhampton Town Hall when she had the first thought about her impending marriage that she couldn't push to one side.

That thought was: *I can't breathe.*

To be fair, the claustrophobic sensation in her chest was partly down to the dress she was wearing. Jeannie's wedding gown was a corseted fairy tale of a frock, with tulle underskirts that whispered with every movement and delicate ivory roses swooping across the satin sweetheart bodice. Not something Jeannie would normally have chosen – her style was more harem pants and/or Docs, depending on the weather – but she'd so been startled by the vision of elegance facing her in the mirror that the decision somehow felt out of her hands. She looked *right* in it, like a real bride. The boutique assistant had covered her mouth with her white-gloved hands, while the owner rushed over to the fitting room, congratulatory flute of Prosecco at the ready. 'That's the one,' she'd breathed, nodding reverentially. 'Trust me, darling, that's your dress.'

It seemed like Fate that Jeannie had found Her Dress,

5

first off the rails. But then it had felt like Fate when Dan was the first person who messaged her the night she gave up on finding Mr Right the old-fashioned way and jumped reluctantly into online dating. From there, just a year from first date to wedding date. Not a single minute wasted. Or, as the shop owner put it, with another reassuring nod, 'When you know, you know.' It had all happened so fast. So very, very fast.

Of course, the other reason for the tightness in Jeannie's chest was the growing realisation that she was about to make a massive mistake.

Jeannie tried to take another, deeper, breath, and nearly choked. The rigid lacing stopped her from filling her lungs more than half full, and she was pretty sure lack of oxygen was starting to affect her brain. She hadn't taken a full breath since she'd been laced into the corset back at the bridal suite, and now her head was swimming. The chilly glass of champagne thrust into her hand before she left hadn't helped. 'Just to relax you!' the hotel owner had said with a smile. More booze. Her dad had finished it off for her.

Mrs Hicks. Jeannie Hicks.

It sounded like a stranger. It sounded like a *hiccup*.

By three o'clock, she'd be Mrs Jeannie Hicks for the rest of her life. Jeannie McCarthy, singer-songwriter, teacher, daughter, would be . . . someone else.

Panic rocketed up into her throat, leaving a bitter space-dust trail behind it. Jeannie swallowed but the scorching sensation didn't go away. She shot a sideways glance at her dad, Brian, sitting next to her in the back of the car, but he was gazing out of the window, mouthing his speech to himself, pausing and smiling intermittently, angling his head in acknowledgement of the imaginary laughter.

It's nerves, Jeannie told herself. It's just nerves. It's natural, it shows you're taking the concept of marriage seriously, all the blogs said that. The commitment. The lifetime commitment to one person, for better or worse, richer or poorer, etc, etc.

She leaned back against the leather seat of the county's one and only Rolls-Royce Silver Shadow and tried to draw oxygen as far down her lungs as the corset would allow. It was only a sip of breath. Like the nibble of scrambled egg at the hotel. The blink of sleep last night. Not enough of anything to deal with the iceberg of humiliation looming towards her.

Jeannie made herself focus on what was happening right now at the town hall. Dan would be waiting for her, welcoming the people who'd already arrived with his confident smile. She pictured him: freshly cut blond hair gleaming in the sunshine, neat and lean in his new suit – bespoke, dark blue, matching waistcoat. He'd be saying something funny to every guest while keeping his mum calm and the photographer moving, because, unlike Jeannie, Dan could do about fifteen things at once and thought so many moves ahead that she sometimes wondered if he was psychic.

He would have no clue she was thinking this, though. A chilly sensation swept through her. What *was* he thinking? Was he having doubts too?

Jeannie stared out of the window at the passing hedgerows as the car took her closer and closer to the town hall. *I wish I could turn the clock back to this morning, and start again.*

No, yesterday morning.

That wasn't long enough.

This time last week?

I wish I could go back a whole year, Jeannie wished frantically. And then I wouldn't be about to hurt so many people.

But the thought of never meeting Dan at all . . . Her stomach flipped. What was she supposed to do?

'OK there? Bit bumpy, these old cars, eh, love? Are you worried about your hairdo?' Her dad's hand reached for hers, and the comforting grip of Brian's big fingers made tears well up into Jeannie's throat. 'Soon have you there. Not long now.'

She turned gingerly towards him, unable to move her head too sharply in case the grips holding her tiara in place drove any further into her scalp. That was another thing she hadn't expected to be wearing on her wedding day: a tiara. Jeannie had always assumed she'd wear a flower crown, and get married on the family farm in Dumfries, under an oak tree, with a ceilidh band. And yet here she was, on her way to the register office in the town she and her husband-to-be had only moved to the previous week. Dan had a new job at the local vet's. Easier, they'd decided, to organise a wedding and a house move in the same place. Their fresh start together, a bold leap into the unknown, holding hands.

None of this is like I'd imagined it'd be, Jeannie thought, with a floaty detachment. Not one thing. Apart from her dad, and this car. He'd always said he'd take her to her wedding in a Rolls. That only seemed to make it worse.

'*Is* everything OK, love?' Brian turned to look at her.

His lanky frame was swimming in a suit that looked as if it belonged to someone else. Jeannie couldn't remember the last time she'd seen her dad in a suit. She'd only seen him wear a tie once, and that was when his champion tup, Decker, met the Countess of Wessex at the Royal Welsh Show.

'I'm fine!' The words came out stickily, the petal-pink gloss on her lips making a clacking noise.

'You sounded as if you—' He stopped, and frowned, confused.

Say something, yelled the voice in Jeannie's head, but she couldn't speak. Her head felt stuffed with cotton wool, unable to process this overwhelming urge to stop, stop, *stop everything*.

A small girl on the side of the road spotted the wedding car, and waved at the shiny black Rolls with the white ribbon fluttering from the silver mascot.

Brian waved back with the special enthusiasm he reserved for children. 'Ah, look at the wee girl there! Come on, Jeannie, she's waving at you! She thinks you look like a princess!'

Dutifully, Jeannie lifted her hand, waved and tried to pull her mouth into a smile. It only deepened the worrying feeling that she was *playing* a bride. That this wasn't really her wedding. That this wasn't actually happening.

'Doesn't seem ten minutes since you were that age!' Brian said, with a sigh. 'Making up funny little songs for us on your ukulele. Singing all day long. Not much has changed, eh?'

Jeannie fixed the smile on her face, pressing her lips together, keeping her wild thoughts in as she saw a sign: 'Longhampton 3 miles'.

They were nearly there. *Nearly there.* What was she going to do?

'Jeannie?' Dad was looking concerned. 'Are you all right?'

'I . . .' She pushed the words out. 'I'm . . . just so . . .'

To her despair, Brian didn't take the bait. 'It's normal to be a bit nervous, love. Uncle Charlie had to do my buttons up because my hands were . . .' He waggled them in front of her. 'Your mother was late – I thought she wasn't coming! But she'd laddered her tights, hopping into the car too quickly.' He sighed, the memory softening his eyes. 'Bet it's hard to believe, looking at us old goats now, that we were once just like you and Dan! But we were, you know.'

Jeannie's heart stopped. It was the worst thing Dad could have said, because it forced her to confront the thought she'd been trying to avoid for weeks: that, actually, she and Dan *weren't* like her parents.

She had a sudden flash of her mother, Sue – small and strong, always busy – and automatically pictured Dad in his overalls next to her, whistling some country tune till Sue begged him to stop. It was impossible to imagine Brian and Sue separately. They laughed and joked and drove each other mad at times, but their real communication was wordless: a language of pauses and glances shaped by the years that followed Sue's freak accident, when all the McCarthys had had to learn a new way to be a family. That's what in sickness and in health *means*, thought Jeannie. For better and for worse – it wasn't a cliché, it was real. Life had hammered Mum and Dad's love like a red-hot horseshoe, but it was stronger for each blow. It couldn't have survived otherwise. *They* couldn't.

A hollow sensation ballooned inside her. How could she promise that to Dan? She didn't know him well enough. She didn't know herself well enough.

With that realisation, Jeannie felt unexpectedly weightless, as if her head might detach from her body and float away. But how *did* you stop something like this now, minutes away from the ceremony? She couldn't. Too many people were involved. And Dan! How could she do this to Dan?

The thought of hurting Dan made her sick. He didn't deserve this.

Jeannie took another shallow breath, and another, and another. None of the air was reaching her brain. The pearls she'd borrowed from her mum were going up and down on her chest; her bosom was actually heaving, she noted, randomly, like a hysterical duchess in *Downton Abbey*.

The Rolls-Royce turned off the main road, and Jeannie spotted another sign: 'Longhampton 2 miles'. Only minutes away now. Literally minutes.

'Dad.' Jeannie didn't know where the voice was coming from; it was forcing its way out of her crushed ribs. 'Can we . . . can we stop somewhere? Just for a moment?'

Brian shot out his left arm, and made a big show of looking at his wrist. He'd put his father's gold watch on, in honour of the occasion. 'I don't see why not, we're ahead of that schedule of yours, aren't we?'

He leaned forward and rapped on the window, sliding it to one side. 'Excuse me, my friend. Would you mind pulling over for a moment when you get a chance? We're running a little early and my daughter doesn't want to beat the groom to the door!'

There was a lay-by coming up on their side of the road, shaded by trees with an overflowing litter bin and a sign pointing towards a footpath. Jeannie had never been so grateful to see a lay-by in her life. The chauffeur indicated, parked under a tree, and turned off the engine. A dusty silence filled the car.

I've got to do it now, thought Jeannie, but she didn't know how to start.

That had always been her trouble: speaking up for herself. It had been a joke when she was little (*Speak up, Jeannie!*), an issue at primary school (*Jeannie? Are you awake?*), but not a problem since her teens, thanks to her best mate, Edith, doing the talking for both of them. At moments of stress, Jeannie's mind went completely blank. Edith's never did.

To her relief, Brian cleared his throat awkwardly. 'Now then, I'm glad we've stopped,' he said. 'There's something I've got to ask you. Don't take it the wrong way – I read it in one of those wedding-etiquette books your mum had out from the library.'

He took both Jeannie's hands, this time with a sweet gravity, and it was such an old-fashioned gesture she couldn't look at him. Her heart was hammering.

'If you've got the smallest doubt about marrying Daniel,' Brian began, 'even the smallest doubt, then say so now. It's not too late.'

Wind rushed in her ears: a powerful surge of bright white panic.

And relief. The sheer relief of hearing Dad say that. How did he know? Had he read it in her face? He knew her so well.

They stared at each other, and Brian's gentle expression

12

abruptly warped with shock at the unexpected gratitude in Jeannie's eyes.

'Jeannie?' he faltered.

And then her brain caught up with her heart. It was one thing for Dad to say that, but how could she call it off now? Forget everyone they knew arriving at the town hall right this minute – what about the money they'd spent on the reception? In the garden room of the hotel, caterers were already plating up smoked salmon; champagne was chilling in the ice bucket. The mobile disco man was driving down from Birmingham, her labour of love playlist programmed in, with their first dance ready to go. God, the cake! The three-hundred-quid cake! The thought of how much this had cost her parents, and Dan's mum, plus their own savings, made Jeannie's armpits prickle with sweat. They'd tried to budget but it had still run into thousands of pounds.

'Jeannie?'

Dad's voice was a couple of tones higher than normal. He clearly hadn't expected her to stay silent, but he was having to go with it now.

Slowly, she dropped her chin and lifted it again. The slowest nod she'd ever made, one simple gesture that would ruin someone's life. It made her feel queasy and giddy and relieved all at once.

She heard her dad, who never swore, say something under his breath that almost made her laugh. He sounded petrified.

'You're nodding . . . because you're sure about marrying Dan, or because . . . you want to call it off?'

'I can't marry Dan.'

As the words left Jeannie's lips a lightness opened up

inside her. Done. It was done. And it felt completely right. Awful, shameful, daunting – but right.

'Oh, bloody hell.' Brian let out a long breath. 'Can I ask . . . why?' He was well out of his depth with these emotional questions, but Jeannie knew he never shied away from grim tasks. Particularly when it involved the people he loved.

She paused, trying to pin down her slippery thoughts as much for herself as for her father. 'Dan's wonderful.' The words felt empty. 'It's nothing he's done, Dad. But . . . those vows are for ever. And I've only known him a year.'

Really? When you put it like that, it sounded ridiculous. Didn't you think of that before you said yes? That's what everyone would say. The truth was, there hadn't been a lot of time to think before she said yes, not on Brooklyn Bridge, at the height of their romantic weekend when she felt drunk on happiness. No time at all afterwards, when the congratulations cards started arriving and Dan's mum Andrea posted her a wedding planner book.

'It's not always about how long you've known someone, love.' Brian's forehead creased, as if he wasn't sure whether he should be reassuring her or not. 'Your mum and I, we'd only been courting a few months before I popped the question. I know it's been a bit of a whirlwind, but things are different these days with this internet business – maybe it's better, if you two chose each other out of all those millions on that website . . . ?'

'I don't know how to explain it, Dad.' Her throat was dry. 'I wish I could. I really wish I could.'

The voice in Jeannie's head told her she'd better try to,

and fast. She'd have to give *some* reason why she was humiliating Dan. Was it better to fake appendicitis, like that time she'd tried to swerve Guide camp? Please God, she thought, strike me down with appendicitis right now. Or something minor but definite, something that means Dad's got to run me to A & E instead of the register office.

As she thought it, shame crawled over her skin. She was a coward, too.

The chauffeur coughed, discreetly, to remind them of the time, and Jeannie covered her face, overwhelmed. 'I'm sorry, Dad. Forget what I've just said. It's just nerves! I'll go ahead with it, and then if isn't just nerves, we can file for a divorce when we—'

'No!' Brian was horrified. 'No, you can't make vows you don't believe in! It makes a mockery of the whole thing. And how will Daniel feel, knowing you're lying in front of everyone?'

They stared helplessly at each other, two people wading across a river with no idea how deep it might get but with no option other than to keep wading now they'd started.

'Do you love him?' It was a simple question.

Jeannie swallowed. A few months ago, she'd have said yes, without a second thought. Dan was her proof that love at first sight existed, but as the weeks went on, she couldn't help feeling that there was something missing, some private corner of his soul he wasn't sharing. Not his plans for their future, he was very open about those, but . . . his fears? His flaws? The parts of his past he wasn't proud of? Ironically, she and Dan knew lots of random facts about each other, thanks to the long online chats they'd had before they even met in real life – tea or coffee? Cats or dogs? – but Jeannie sometimes wondered what she *didn't* know about him. He barely talked about the past, and since the proposal their weekends had been so full of cake testing and seating plans that there was never time for moments of Sunday-night boredom when glimpses of the human being underneath the date-night persona slipped out. Jeannie held nothing back; she didn't know how to. But she'd realised lately that Dan had a sweet smile that he turned on when he didn't want to talk.

Her dad was still waiting for an answer. *Did she love him?* Could you honestly say you loved someone if you didn't know them inside out?

An unhappy voice came from somewhere outside of herself. 'I don't know.'

There was a long pause. Three small words, to create so much chaos.

'You're absolutely sure?'

Jeannie nodded.

'Jeeze . . .' Brian rubbed his eyes, then braced himself. 'Well, let's sort this out. Do you want me to tell him on the phone? Or do you want me to drive over there and speak to him?'

What would Dan do? Would he cry? Would he be angry? Jeannie realised she didn't know; she'd never seen him deal with bad news before.

'I'll call him.' Brian was thinking aloud. 'I'll say I need to talk to him, give him a chance to get away from his mother and the ushers, then I can ring back and explain how you feel. And when we've got that out of the way, we'll phone your mum and get on with . . . sorting everything else.'

'No, Dad.' Jeannie sat up straight and the corset nipped the soft skin under her arms. 'I've got to do this. I'll phone Dan, ask him to go somewhere quiet so I can speak to him. Then I'll . . . tell him.'

Brian started to protest, but stopped as Jeannie shook her head, begging him not to smother the fragile flame of determination. He sighed, sadly this time, and squeezed her hand. 'I wish you'd talked to us about this sooner, love, but if you're not sure, this is the right thing to do. You can't marry with doubts. You should only ever promise the future to the person you can't live without.' He kissed her head. 'Always best to be honest.'

Jeannie didn't feel honest. She felt like an absolute cow. 'I'm so sorry, Dad.'

'What for?'

'For wasting this money, and the embarrassment and . . . and the fuss of everyone coming and . . .'

'What? There's no one at that wedding who'd see you marry a man you didn't love, just for the sake of a good lunch.' Brian let out a long breath then said, 'Right, so, let's get this over with.'

He struggled with the door mechanism and as it swung open, Jeannie breathed as deeply as she could. Not very deeply, because of the corset, but it felt like fresh air for the first time that morning.

'Everything OK?' called the chauffeur as Brian helped her out.

'Yes, fine! Fine!' Her voice croaked. 'Just checking something with the venue!'

Why was she still lying? This had to happen more often than you'd think, surely? She wouldn't be the first person round here to call off a wedding.

Not on the morning of, though. Not at the church door.

Brian held her tiny pearl-encrusted wedding clutch while Jeannie extracted her phone. It was jammed in between the brand-new lipstick and powder compact and hairclips and breath mints. She flinched at her lock-screen image: the selfie of her and Dan laughing into the camera, with Manhattan glittering behind them and their golden future rolling out in front; then she touched his contact details and put the mobile to her ear.

Her head echoed with emptiness as the phone connected at the other end. Someone had shoved a crisp packet into a gap in the hedgerow. Salt and vinegar. Jeannie had no idea how she was going to start this conversation.

There was a microscopic pause, and her heart stopped – until she realised Dan hadn't answered: it was going straight to voicemail. Panic swept through Jeannie's brain, wiping away any words or thoughts.

His recorded voice was there in her ear, familiar, friendly and ever so slightly posh.

'Hi, this is Dan Hicks. Sorry I can't take your call. Please leave a message after the tone.'

The enormity of what she was doing made Jeannie dizzy. Everything would change after whatever words came out of her mouth next. Everything. Now. Say something.

'Dan, it's me, it's Jeannie.' Her voice sounded weak, more Scottish than normal, not hers. 'Can you call me as soon as you get this? I need to talk to you about some-thing important. I don't . . .' She squeezed her eyes shut. 'Just ring me, please.'

Then she jabbed at the screen with a trembling finger,

and hit the red icon on the second or third attempt. It was done.

Jeannie turned to see Brian watching her. His forehead was furrowed under his shock of white hair, but he tried to smile encouragingly. It wasn't a successful combination. 'All done, love?'

'I left a message.'

'Good girl.'

Maybe it was better like this, Jeannie argued with herself. A message gave Dan time to prepare, and it gave her time to come up with a better reason than 'something just doesn't feel right'. She stared at their blurry reflections in the car's gleaming paintwork. Was it too late to claim she had food poisoning? She certainly felt as if she could throw up any moment.

'So what now?' Brian cleared his throat. 'Will we . . . wait here till he rings back?'

'I suppose so?'

But what if Dan's phone was turned off, ready for the ceremony? He wouldn't see she'd left a message. He'd be standing there, waiting for her to arrive, and she'd have to do this again – outside the town hall. In front of everyone.

'I'll try again,' said Jeannie, 'just in case he was on another call.'

'What if he rings back?' Brian started, but Jeannie was already dialling before this last shred of courage ran out. She didn't want to humiliate Dan. She truly didn't want that.

The phone went straight to voicemail again, but the beep made her start speaking automatically. 'Dan, it's me. Please don't go to the town hall. I can't go ahead with the wedding today. I'm so sorry. I'm so *so* sorry. Please call me as soon as you get this.'

Should she have left the second message? Too late now, anyway. Jeannie's stomach churned with a mess of emotions – fear, shame, panic – but a voice was telling her that she'd done the right thing. It didn't make her feel much better.

Brian nodded towards the car. 'Might as well wait in comfort, eh?'

She clambered awkwardly into the back while her dad had a discreet word with the driver.

I'm a jilter, she thought as a paralysing numbness spread through her. Jeannie the Jilter.

'Jeannie?' Brian murmured as he got in next to her. 'Have you a number for the best man? We should call him if Daniel doesn't ring soon.'

'Yes, I've got it on my phone. Owen, he's called. Owen Patterson.' Jeannie opened her ridiculous tiny clutch but as she pulled her phone out it started to ring. Her pulse rocketed up, but it wasn't Dan calling.

Owen, it said.

'It's him. It's the best man.' She stared at it, dully. 'Why's he ringing me?'

'Do you want me to take it?'

Jeannie realised what her dad meant: was this the best man phoning because Dan had heard her message and couldn't speak? She went cold. What she'd set in motion had started. 'No . . . I'd better.'

She steeled herself, and touched the screen with shaking hands. 'Owen?'

'Jeannie! Where are you?' She didn't recognise the voice; she'd only met Dan's best friend briefly, the previous night at the rehearsal dinner.

'We're in the car. We stopped because we were running

a bit early . . .' They weren't early now, though: they were five minutes late. That would be why Owen was ringing.

'Thank goodness for that.' He sounded relieved. 'Now, please don't panic, but don't go to the town hall. Something's happened. I've told the registrar and she's going to send the guests on to the reception.'

'What? What's happened?'

Brian grabbed her hand but Jeannie was filled with unexpected euphoria: Fate had come through after all! Her imagination raced: what act of God had materialised to save her? A flood at the town hall? A power cut? She didn't care. She was off the hook! There was time to fix her mistake . . .

'Jeannie, I'm afraid there's been an accident.' Owen's voice was careful. She could hear raised voices in the background, a siren. 'But everything's going to be fine, I promise.'

Chapter Two

'It's going to be fine. It's going to be absolutely fine, don't worry,' Owen kept saying, over and over, but each repetition sounded less convincing. The only thing Jeannie could think was: *What's* going to be fine?

Her breath was coming in shallow unsatisfying gulps. It wasn't the corset squeezing her chest now, it was adrenalin pumping her heart too fast, and underneath that, a dark relief that the wedding couldn't happen now.

Jeannie's skin crawled. *Relief?* But it was true. She was relieved.

Brian's hand covered hers and took the phone; she didn't stop him.

'Owen, this is Brian McCarthy.' He fumbled with the door handle and got out of the car a second time, more urgently now. 'So, tell me what exactly's happened?'

Jeannie watched him step away towards the hedge, one hand shoved in his white hair as he frowned and nodded. A sudden, stomach-turning thought occurred to her: the message! What if she hadn't needed to leave that message for Dan after all? Maybe they could postpone, indefinitely – or at least talk . . .

Brian turned back to look at her, and with a jolt Jeannie realised it wasn't a power cut at the town hall, or a flood. It was something much worse.

'OK . . . I see. I see. Right.' His voice was calm, but the rapid, stunned blinking made Jeannie's blood run cold. 'If you could do that . . . Yes, I'll tell her.' He glanced over at her again. 'She's . . . Well, we'll be there as soon as we can. Thank you, Owen. Good man.'

He didn't even speak to her first. He went round to the chauffeur's window and muttered new instructions to him, low and serious. She heard the driver groan as her dad gave an address in town, and then Brian got back into the car.

'Dad?' She could barely form the words. 'Dad, what's happened?'

Brian took her hands in his, and Jeannie realised she was shaking. 'I'm afraid Daniel's had an accident. He was hit by a bus just round the corner from his hotel in town.'

Dan was in the accident? Jeannie stared, unable to take it in. 'He was hit . . . by a *bus*?'

'The driver said he stepped into the road without looking – poor chap didn't have a chance to stop. Daniel was . . . Well, he was on his phone.'

No. Jeannie's hand flew up to her mouth as if she could force her catastrophic words back in. 'Oh my God. That was *me*! That must have been when I called!'

'Now we don't know that, love.'

But she did. Guilt rushed through her, dark and staining. 'It was my fault! This is all my fault.'

'Jeannie, come on, deep breaths. The ambulance is there; Dan's going to be fine.' Brian cupped her face in his big gentle hands. 'Come on, breathe in, and out.'

She clung to her dad's wrists, keeping her eyes locked on his as if she was drowning. He gazed back, unable to disguise his anxiety.

What have I done? Jeannie thought as the car moved off again, less serenely this time. *What have I done?*

Dan and the ushers were staying at a hotel at the far end of the town, where the Victorian terraces turned into the dull grey of the outlying industrial estates.

Long before they reached the scene of the accident an ambulance overtook the Rolls-Royce in a blur of blue lights and sirens, followed by a police car. And another one. Brian gripped Jeannie's hands: they were holding each other's tightly now, as if they were about to make a skydive together. He said nothing.

The chauffeur had to slow down as they got nearer; the road had been taped off and traffic was being stopped and rerouted by two policemen, a process hampered by the obvious rubbernecking of the passing motorists.

Jeannie sat rigid in her seat, terrified to look at the scene ahead. There were crowds of people, too many to see through. Dan was in there somewhere. Until she saw him, it wasn't happening. It was a mistake. A dream. A really, really bad dream.

'I can't get any nearer, love.' The chauffeur was bright red, and apologetic. 'I think it'll be easier if you get out here? I'm sorry. I really am, but no one'll let me through and I'm not sure it's . . .'

He trailed off but she knew what he meant. It was a horrible mental image, the bridal car forcing its way towards an injured groom. But it wasn't as if she could approach discreetly, not in this enormous dress.

'Absolutely right. Stop here, good a place as any.' Brian opened the door and helped Jeannie out.

'Do you want me to wait?' the driver asked.

'No, you're fine; we'll manage. Thank you very much. You've been great.'

It was a surreally polite conversation to be having, thought Jeannie.

She staggered on her brand-new heels as she got out of the car, and as she started walking, her legs felt elastic and strange. Her steps were too fast, faster than she intended, until she was almost running to keep up with herself.

Two ambulances were parked at an angle across the road with their doors open and their stretchers and kit laid out. A number 14 bus had pulled over to one side, the passengers half-disgorged to get a better look, some staring from the upper windows. The driver was slumped against the door, speaking to a policeman; he was ashen, rubbing his eyes as if he wanted to rub away what had just happened. Jeannie heard the ambulance crew talking, the back and forth of diagnosis and instructions. She could hear the crackle and bark of the police radio, the bleep of equipment, and then, in the distance, the heavy thudding of a helicopter.

In all this, there was no trace of Dan. No cries, no words. Nothing.

'Let me through,' she heard herself say, 'let me through, I'm his girlfriend!'

As Jeannie pushed past, she heard a new sound over the clicking of her own heels, a rustling hush of curiosity and shock.

It's the bride it's the bride it's the bride.

Behind her, her dad's voice, polite but firm. 'Let us through, please. Thank you, excuse me.' The crowd, parting like the Dead Sea, to reveal a smaller crowd: five paramedics surrounding a motionless man, his body only visible from the waist down.

The socks. Jeannie stopped. Dan was wearing the socks she'd given him for his last birthday present: red with tiny white Westies. It made everything suddenly sharper, more real. She stared at them, remembering how he'd unwrapped them over dinner, his uncomplicated smile of delight as he put them straight on in the restaurant, despite her embarrassed protestations. They'd been so happy that weekend.

What have I done?

Jeannie's eyes stayed fixed on the socks; she dreaded the paramedics moving to reveal his injured body, even though she needed to see Dan was all right. He'd always laughed at how squeamish she was, the way she covered her eyes even at James Bond films. Where was the blood? Was there no blood? If there was no blood maybe it would be OK. Maybe he'd just get up, with bruises.

Someone else was by her side now, a dark-haired man in a green kilt and a white rose buttonhole. His face was round and boyish, and he was clearly concentrating hard to maintain his air of calm.

'Jeannie, I'm Owen.' He touched her arm awkwardly, then added, 'We met last night. Briefly, at the dinner. I'm *so* sorry.'

'Why?' Something in the way he said it made her freeze inside. 'Is Dan dead? Is he going to die?'

'No, no . . .' Owen stepped back, shocked. 'God, no! He's just . . .'

The air ambulance had been getting nearer as they spoke, and whatever Owen said next was drowned out by the heavy whump-whump as it landed in the empty car park opposite. Blossom from the trees around the hotel lifted and swirled in the backdraught like confetti, sticking in hair and eyes.

More paramedics arrived now, running across the road, calling out to their colleagues. As the first crew stepped away to let them take over, Jeannie caught sight of Dan and she stumbled forward, almost slipping in her haste to get near him.

He was lying on the road, his eyes closed, with only the dried blood down his neck to suggest he wasn't asleep. Livid red grazes showed where he'd hit the kerb; an invisible fist punched Jeannie square in the chest as she noted ruby speckles of blood on the soft skin on his neck, still gleaming from the Turkish barber's lotion – the morning's wet shave, the treat he'd planned for his ushers. There was more thick dark blood coagulating on the road surface, though, and a dark smear on the edge of the pavement. Dan's left leg was strapped into the paramedics' equipment, his beautiful face cradled in a massive brace. Jeannie dragged in tiny breath after tiny breath, trying not to gag as she knelt by his side.

Should she take his hand? The thick net under her skirt was cutting tiny squares into her stockinged knees. She wanted to touch him, just to let him know she was there, but maybe she shouldn't move his arm? The way the medics were talking about keeping him still, getting him stabilised . . .

Owen crouched behind her. He smelled of fresh aftershave, of dry-cleaned jackets. 'We're with you, mate, hang in there,' he was saying. His hands moved jerkily in the air too, as if he wasn't sure whether it was safe to touch Dan either. 'Come on, stay with us. Stay with us, Dan mate.'

A paramedic appeared at Jeannie's elbow, steering her away as the air ambulance team unwrapped sterile equipment and fixed stretchers. 'Is it Jeannie? Jeannie, this is what's happening. The team are intubating Daniel and we're getting him comfortable so they can monitor him on the way to Birmingham.'

'But the hospital here's nearer! It's just down the road, we passed it on the way . . .' Jeannie gesticulated back towards the town. 'Why do you have to fly him to *Birmingham*?'

'It has an ICU. Daniel's suffered a head injury, and he's going to need urgent assessment, and specialist care.' Even the unflappable paramedic's eyes were sympathetic. 'I'm so sorry, on your wedding day. What a nightmare for you. But Daniel's in good hands, I promise.'

Jeannie flinched. She didn't deserve sympathy. All she could see was Dan, stepping in front of the bus. Distracted by her call, thinking about her, attention glued to his phone.

'So what can we do now?' Owen was addressing the paramedic. 'Is there room for Jeannie to go with him in the air ambulance? If you want to, of course?'

He turned to her with his thick brows knitted together in a question, and Jeannie scrabbled to make the moment feel real. The paramedic was talking, explaining about limited room and extra equipment and her dress, but the words floated around her head.

It's not a dream, Jeannie, she told herself, this is really happening.

Owen seemed to read her lost expression, and turned back to the medic. 'No problem, I can drive Jeannie. My car's right here.'

'And I'll get a taxi, pick up your mum and follow on,' said Brian.

'Don't worry about a taxi, Mr McCarthy, I'll call Mark; he drove the ushers down there an hour ago.' Owen pulled out his phone and started scrolling through the contacts, then stepped away, one discreet pace. 'Mark? I need you to do us a favour . . .'

The ambulance crew was lifting Dan, strapped to a stretcher and surrounded by stabilising padding. Jeannie went to touch his exposed fingers. They were cold.

'I'm coming, Dan.' He had an oxygen mask over his face now, and a red line of blood strapped to his bare arm. The strong, tanned arm that had wrapped around her waist in bed, the night before last. His face was unresponsive, shockingly pale. Bloodless. Jeannie wanted to scream *I'm sorry I'm sorry I'm sorry*, but her throat was dry.

'Cheers, Mark. I'll update you when I can. Yes, absolutely.' Owen was back. He slipped his phone away and put a hand on Jeannie's shoulder. 'Mark's on his way. Five minutes.'

Jeannie couldn't remember which one Mark was. She'd heard a lot about Dan's ushers but hadn't met them: most of them had arrived too late the previous evening to make it to the rehearsal dinner. Even Owen, the best man, had arrived at the same time as the cheese and port, blaming a work crisis for his delay. That was why she hadn't recognised him, Jeannie realised: he wasn't wearing his glasses now. He'd had thick tortoiseshell glasses last night. Jarvis Cocker glasses.

'Let's get going. Always feels better when you're in motion, doesn't it?' Owen was guiding her away from the scene, where the police had moved into the space left by the ambulance crew, and towards the hotel. The crowds parted as if by magic as they approached, staring at the bride in a very different kind of way to the one Jeannie had imagined, as little as one single hour ago.

Owen had an old Mercedes full of papers, files and empty crisp packets, and he drove it quickly. Even with the deep seats, Jeannie's petticoats fluffed up around her like a nest, but she managed to find an angle which let her breathe almost comfortably; timing her breaths was a convenient distraction from the haunting image of Dan's waxy face.

They didn't talk. Owen's attention was focused on the road ahead; he didn't turn his head to look at her once. That suited Jeannie: she was terrified of what might be written on her face.

Mark the usher called while they were on the motorway, and established that the McCarthys were now following on behind. Owen put him on speaker so Jeannie could hear but she had no desire to join the conversation, even if she'd been able to find words.

'You'll let me know, won't you, soon as you hear anything?' Mark sounded on the verge of tears.

'I will, mate.'

'Tell Danny how much we love him. Stupid idiot, getting run over on his wedding day. And give our love to Janie. Anything we can do, anything at all?'

Owen glanced across at Jeannie. 'Jeannie's right here.'

'Oh God, *Jeannie*, Jeannie, sorry.' There was the hubbub of raised voices. 'Look, I've got to go; we're just sorting out the caterers. Mrs McCarthy's made us a list, so tell Janie everything's under control, OK?'

'OK, Mark. Will do.'

Jeannie wondered, in a detached way, how often had Dan spoken about her to Mark that he couldn't remember her name. But then people got her name wrong all the time. She'd had Jenny, Janey, Jessie . . . Edith might have hated her own 'old lady' name but at least no one ever forgot it.

Edith. She closed her eyes: the word in her head sounded like blonde corkscrew curls and striped tights, not old ladies. How could something as massive as this be happening and Edith not know? There hadn't been any wedding-morning text from her. Maybe she was waiting to send a 3 p.m. congratulations one. Maybe she was too busy having lunch with Florence Welch.

'Sorry about that.' Owen ended the call, embarrassed. 'Mark's never been great with names. He's an optician, normally has a piece of paper in front of him with your name on it.'

'Mark. Was he the one who . . . ?' She was struggling to remember which one Mark was. Her mind went blank.

'The one with the glasses,' said Owen, helpfully. 'And half a beard?'

That didn't narrow it down. Dan's friends looked pretty similar.

'He was the one who started crying before we left, and made that speech about how Dan got him through his A-level Maths exam and how he owed his whole career to him. And he wasn't even pissed.'

'Oh, him.' Now she remembered.

'You'll get to know everyone soon enough. Great bunch of lads.'

'Seems so,' she replied blankly. That had been one of the difficulties about her and Dan's long-distance relationship, him up in Newcastle, her in Bristol; every moment of their weekends had seemed too precious to spend on getting to know anyone other than each other. Dan talked about Owen quite a lot – 'the best bloke in the world' – but he'd always said there was plenty of time to meet his mates.

Plenty of time in the years and years and years they had together.

Owen slowed down; they'd hit weekend traffic. Above them, another helicopter skipped over the lanes of stationary cars, backed up on the motorway like ropes of silvery beads, and Jeannie felt despair wash back over her at the sound of the rotor blades. Who was in there? Were they dying? Had Dan landed? Was he in theatre yet?

'Do you want to listen to some music?' Owen asked, as if he could hear the fear crashing and banging round her brain. 'Might stop you thinking too much?'

Jeannie shook her head.

'Dan said you were in a band,' he went on, determined to fill the silence. 'He played me some of your songs – they were very good.'

'Thanks.' Owen was polite, if nothing else. She was pretty sure, going by the CDs scattered around the car, that he wouldn't be into the sort of music Edie's Birdhouse played: classic eighties' covers, mainly, delivered with Edith's deadpan irony, plus their own – *Jeannie's* own – acoustic pop songs. She guessed Owen was thirty-one, like Dan, but his taste was more like her dad's: the Smiths, the Who, Led Zeppelin. Jeannie could never stop herself checking out people's playlists. Owen wasn't cool, clearly. But he liked music.

'Are you . . . recording anything at the moment?' He pulled a face. 'Not sure if it's still called recording, is it? Don't laugh at me. I still have CDs, as you can see.'

She took a deep breath, as deep as she could, anyway. 'I'm not actually in a band any more.'

'Oh?' Owen turned his head, distracted by the unexpected bitterness in her voice.

The bitterness had surprised Jeannie too. 'We broke it up. We . . . went in different directions.'

'Musical differences?' He was really trying. 'Or personal ones? Like Oasis?'

'Something like that,' said Jeannie. 'Actually, very like that, as it happens. You know what? Can we just listen to the radio? Sport, not music.'

'Fine with me.' Owen turned on the radio and let the sound of a tedious cricket match between two counties Jeannie didn't even register scribble over the silence between them as they both sat, worrying about Dan.

The receptionist at the hospital didn't react to the sudden appearance of a bride plus a kilted man in a waiting area full of Saturday sports injuries and grumbling children, but a sudden hush fell over the whole main area as Owen leaned on the counter and explained their situation.

'He arrived by air ambulance, from a road traffic incident in Longhampton? Daniel Hicks, H, I, C, K, S,' he was saying, but Jeannie wasn't taking in any of the responses. Her attention had snagged on the clock behind the desk: one second, two seconds, three seconds. She stared at it, mesmerised. That was all it had taken to flip the day from the picture-perfect spring wedding to this. One short message; one step into the road. By now, they should be eating cake and listening to speeches. Instead they were here.

A nurse appeared in navy-blue overalls, wisps of blonde hair escaping from her bun. She couldn't quite hide her double take when she saw Jeannie in her wedding dress.

'Mrs Hicks?' she asked.

'No,' said Jeannie automatically.

'He was . . . on the way to the wedding,' Owen murmured.

The nurse looked genuinely horrified. 'Oh, excuse me, I do apologise. I'm Amber, the ICU ward sister. I'm so sorry – you must feel as if you're in a nightmare.'

People kept saying that. *A nightmare. A nightmare.*

'How's Dan?' asked Owen. 'Can you tell us? Is he in theatre?'

'Let me take you up to the ward and we can talk there,' said Amber, and Jeannie felt everyone's eyes follow them down the corridor towards the lift.

They were the only people in the side room Amber took them to off the critical care ward. Four horseshoe-shaped sofas offered space for four stunned families to huddle together, and a television showing an episode of *Judge Rinder* filled the silence. Owen sat by her side, his bare knees large and round under the kilt. A kilt and a wedding dress, she thought, the wrong sugar-paste figures from the top of the cake.

'I'm afraid I don't have any definite news for you yet,' Amber said, 'other than that Daniel was taken to theatre as soon as he arrived. The neurosurgical team operated to reduce the pressure on his brain, caused by the swelling when he hit his head. They're fitting an ICP – a monitor to keep track of the pressure in there – and he's going to stay under observation in a medically induced coma until the doctors feel it's safe for him to wake up.'

Jeannie's breath stuck in her throat. 'He hasn't woken up?'

'No, and please don't be alarmed by that. We're monitoring everything. He's stable, which is good.'

Owen's phone beeped, and he looked down. 'Sorry, lots of people trying to get in touch. Should I have turned this off?'

'Fine in here,' said Amber. 'But not on the ward, please.'

'Has someone told Dan's mum where we are?' Jeannie looked at Owen. How had she and this stranger ended up in charge? Surely parents were meant to be here to cope with stuff like this? Adults. 'Is someone looking after Andrea? She'll be . . .'

She didn't want to say *hysterical* in case it sounded rude. Owen knew Dan's mum better than she did. She'd only met her mother-in-law-to-be three times, and though they'd got on well, Jeannie sensed Andrea's emotions were very . . . close to the surface.

She caught a flicker of apprehension in Owen's expression before he pulled back his shoulders. 'Of course. I'll find out what's happening. Back in a second.'

He stepped out into the corridor, and Jeannie shivered. She felt as if she was balancing on the very edge of her nerves, with a sheer and terrifying drop on the other side. Whatever the next few hours brought – good news, bad news, worse news – her life had now changed, for ever. Hers, and Dan's.

Chapter Three

Time stood still in the side room, but nowhere else. Jeannie's phone vibrated in her clutch like a trapped wasp, but she couldn't move her hands to pop the clasp, even if she'd wanted to answer it. Which she didn't. Owen reappeared, in between urgent calls, with a plastic cup of tea for her – 'Three sugars, you need the glucose, Jeannie' – but he had no news. He brought her another tea twenty minutes later, and frowned at the first in surprise, as if he'd never seen it before.

'They're down here? That's great, thank you so much, thank you.'

Jeannie heard her mother's voice before she saw her through the window: a strong, clear Yorkshire accent that rang out with confidence, and felt her heart lift for the first time since the accident. Mum was here. Mum would know what to do.

'Oh yes, here she is . . . Oh, Jeannie, come here, pet!'

Sue McCarthy burst in, followed by Brian, who was carrying a holdall and a Tesco carrier bag that probably held 'emergency food'. Neither of them had changed out of their wedding outfits in their haste to get there; Brian's tie was undone and he'd ditched his too-big jacket, and Sue had slipped on some comfy red trainers under her Jacques Vert trouser suit.

Just the thought of that morning – her mum fussing about her new court shoes, borrowing blister plasters from the hotel owner – pushed Jeannie over the edge.

'Oh, Mum!' she managed, then burst into tears.

'We're here now, darling!' Sue flung her arms around Jeannie and hugged her tight, rocking gently. 'We're here now.'

'So we are.' Brian stood back for a moment, but emotion overwhelmed him too, and he wrapped his arms round them both, burying his face in Sue's hair.

For a few minutes, the shadows swamping Jeannie retreated as she breathed in her mum's familiar smell – White Linen, special occasions only – and let their comforting murmurs wash over her. It would be fine. There would be news soon; doctors were miracle workers; Dan was a strong young man . . . Then she heard a noise outside, the sound of skidding heels and hiccupping sobs, and it was as if pain itself was running down the corridor towards them.

'Where are they? In here? Oh, thank God!'

The McCarthys sprang apart as Dan's mother rushed in with Owen following close behind, checking his phone. His brave face had temporarily slipped and he looked younger, and crumpled.

'Oh, Jeannie!' Andrea Hicks grabbed Jeannie's wrists, her small mouth twisted in distress. The room felt even more airless, as the waves of pain rolled off her. Then she blinked hard, as if she'd just noticed Jeannie's beautiful wedding dress. 'Oh! You look so . . . !' Her huge blue eyes filled with new anguish.

'How are you, Andrea?' Sue touched her arm. 'Can we get you anything?'

'Me? No, no . . . I just don't understand how on earth it could have happened!' Andrea shook her head in disbelief, and the feathery fascinator perched on her blonde bob trembled. 'That bus driver – has he been arrested yet? How could anyone *not see* a man in wedding clothes? I mean . . . was he *drunk*?'

By the door, Jeannie caught Owen glancing towards her dad, shaking his head imperceptibly, and her dad meeting the look with a nod. Let her get it off her chest, their eyes seemed to say. It wasn't the right time to tell Andrea that Dan was the one who'd been at fault.

But it's my fault, screamed a voice in Jeannie's head.

'How about a cup of hot sweet tea?' Sue's voice was gentle, but firm. 'The surgeon's going to come and brief us as soon as Dan's back on the ward.'

Andrea sank on to the plastic sofa and put her hands over her mouth, her eyes so wide Jeannie could see white around the blue of her irises. Her nails were flawless: a glossy shell pink, the colour of ballet slippers, to match her elegant knee-length shift and kitten heels. Andrea's outfit had been planned with great care over the past few months. Dan and Jeannie's wedding, she'd told them, more than once, had given her 'something nice to look forward to for the first time in years'.

'I'm so sorry, Andrea!' It burst out of Jeannie; she didn't know why.

Andrea glanced up, surprised. 'It's not your fault, sweetie! How on earth could it be *your* fault?'

Sue picked up the holdall. 'Right, Jeannie, while we're waiting, why don't we get you into something more comfortable?' She stretched out a hand. 'You don't want to spill tea on your lovely frock.'

Too late. There were tiny pinpricks of blood on the ballerina skirt, from where she'd knelt next to Dan on the road. Dark marks and fragments of grit trapped in the net.

'Danny didn't even see your dress!' Andrea's voice vanished in a gulp.

'He did,' said Jeannie, then realised Dan *hadn't* seen her. She'd seen him, lying in the road. He might never see her again. She raised her eyes to her mum, shaken.

'Come on, Jeannie,' said Sue, and herded her away from Andrea's sobs.

In another empty room further down the corridor, Jeannie stood still as her mother began loosening the corset strings running down her back. It wasn't easy. It had taken both Sue and Jeannie's sister-in-law Teri to get her into it, and the constant pressure of her struggles to breathe against the bindings had tightened the knots into hard pearls.

'Shall I find someone to help?' Jeannie asked over her shoulder.

'No.' Sue blew out her cheeks. 'I'm nearly there. It's just . . . I've been on my feet all day. Those daft shoes! But I'll be fine!'

Jeannie stared ahead. She knew better than to say anything else. You wouldn't guess, looking at Sue McCarthy, that twenty years ago she'd nearly died, crushed under her own horse out riding at home. Jeannie had been nine, her brother Angus eleven. Now Sue carried herself exactly the way she did before the accident – with the height and force of a Viking warrior queen, despite being just over five feet two – but she

40

still suffered chronic pain from the injuries she'd suffered. Her right leg had been saved thanks to a specialist visiting the local hospital, but her right arm was shattered and even with years of physio, had never regained its strength. Sue's worst scars were the ones no one saw: disorientating memory blanks, and bouts of depression that knocked her for six, but she refused to let any of it show. Jeannie knew Dad hid Mum's slumps for her. As she'd got older, she'd realised Dad hid lots of things for the woman he'd worshipped for over thirty years, including his own fears.

'Mum, cut the laces. Please. I need *out*.' The claustrophobia was swarming up Jeannie's throat. The nurse could be back any moment with the neurosurgeon. 'Call a nurse; they're bound to have scissors.'

'No! It's too nice to cut. And you'll want to wear it again, won't you? For when Dan's better. Want to keep it perfect' – *tug* – 'for that special day!' A harder tug.

Jeannie squeezed her eyes shut. She was glad her mum couldn't see her face. Another reason to get out of this thing. Her fraud felt even worse while she was dressed like this.

'I know it's hard to imagine now,' Sue went on, struggling with the laces, 'but give yourselves something in the future to focus on. That's what got me through rehab, making plans with your dad.' She yanked at the knot as if she could make everything right by undoing it. 'Your father had a holiday booked for us in Ireland and he said, "You'll be on that ferry, Susan", and we were. Not that actual ferry, but eventually . . .'

Eventually, thought Jeannie, staring at the poster outlining meal times and nurse visits. Four years of tears and struggles and determination later, Mum had got on that ferry. And so much pain, the sort that either bound a couple together for life, or drove them apart, broken by the changes and the arrival of a partner they hadn't reckoned on. Will I need to be there for Dan, like Dad was for Mum?

Sue stopped pulling. 'I'm sorry, darling. Would you rather wear a different dress next time? Of course you would. You don't want to be reminded of today.'

There's not going to be a next time, thought Jeannie. Then she suddenly realised what this meant – Dad hadn't told Mum what had happened in the car.

Jeannie dug her nails into her palms and thought, I should tell Mum what I did. But she couldn't bear to let her shocking secret back into the light. She couldn't bear to think of what people would say, if they connected Dan's accident with something as selfish as her last-minute cold feet.

It didn't matter now. All that mattered was Dan. Jeannie just wanted to see him wake up, to open those beautiful dark blue eyes and look at her, say her name. A sob hiccupped out from somewhere deep inside her soul.

'Oh, love, I'm sorry. Wedding talk isn't what you need right now, is it?' Sue hugged Jeannie, resting her chin on her bare shoulder. 'It's a scary time, but Dan's in the best possible place. We're here for you. We understand what you're going through.'

I've got to tell her, Jeannie thought. 'Mum, I . . .' she started, then stopped.

'What, love?' Sue had honest eyes, like Jeannie's; they were bright and brown like a bird's, set in a strong-boned face that had been lifted up to the sun, and the rain, and more than a few glasses of wine. Sue embraced her wrinkles and didn't cover her silvery streaks, because she was too happy to be alive to care about getting older. Even today, on her mother-of-the-bride best, she'd only given Andrea's make-up artist – 'my present to the girls!' – two minutes before she was out of the chair, and back chatting to everyone. Long enough for a swipe of mascara, and some blush, most of which had now worn off.

'Do you really think Dan's going to be OK?' Jeannie felt treacherous for asking, but her mum was realistic, in a way Dad never was. 'Honestly?'

'I do.' Sue nodded. 'He's young, he's strong, and, most importantly, he's got you. Knowing your dad was there by my side made everything that bit easier to face. That's what marriage *is*. Never having to face life's ups and downs on your own.'

A cold blade ran through Jeannie's heart.

'But we haven't even spoken to the doctor yet, have we? Let's not assume the worst. Now then, I've nearly got this knot undone,' Sue went on. 'If you could just take the strain of the corset while I use this pen here to get . . .' – *tug* – '*inside* the knot . . .' – *tug. Tug. Tug.*

Jeannie obediently deflated her lungs, and relaxed herself into the ruthless grip of the bodice, fighting down the urge to explode as hard as she could.

Black dots danced in front of her eyes.

'There!' There was a moment of exquisite relief as the pressure finally slackened on her ribcage and she took a gasping breath, deeper than she'd expected, like a swimmer coming up for air. She staggered, unbalanced by the rush of oxygen to her head, and when she turned round, her mother was looking at her strangely.

'What?'

Sue pointed at Jeannie's shoulders. 'You've got marks all around your back where it was cutting into you. Didn't it hurt?'

'Really?' She twisted her head. 'I stopped noticing after a while.'

'Too much else to think about.' Sue busily unzipped the skirt, motioning for Jeannie to step out of the petticoats so she could fold everything up. 'Now then, you get yourself changed, and I'll find us a cup of tea.' She hugged her quickly, the puffy net of Jeannie's discarded dress squashing between them. 'It'll be fine, pet. You'll see. It'll all be fine.'

The overnight bag smelled of home as she unzipped it. Jeannie tugged on her jeans as fast as she could, then her favourite shirt, a bell-sleeved blouse from a second-hand shop, embroidered with butterflies. Her cramped toes wriggled with relief in her cool Converse, and she pulled the pins out of her hair, running her hands through it until the crispy hairsprayed curls disintegrated into her usual chestnut waves. She breathed in, and out, and her clothes didn't try to stop her.

The spell of her wedding dress was broken, and Jeannie was unsettled by how much the morning's preparations already felt as if they'd happened to someone else.

She stared at her reflection in a window. Did her eyes look guiltier? Forget the phone call now, she told the pale face staring back at her. No one knows; no one needs to know. Just worry about Dan.

By the time Jeannie found her way back the gathering had swelled by two more, and the room was looking distinctly crowded. Her brother Angus had arrived with Teri. He was shoving a canapé from the Tesco bag into his mouth, while Teri was easing her swollen feet out of a pair of silver sandals. The apricot chiffon of her bridesmaid's dress strained over her bump; the website Jeannie had bought it from had been adamant that it would 'skim curves' but that had been before Teri and Angus had found out it was a bump for two.

'I don't mind stepping down,' Teri had said when they found out, but they both knew that there wasn't much choice, or much time to find a replacement. Edith, Jeannie's first-choice bridesmaid was miles away geographically – and much further than that in other respects.

Angus jumped up, brushing crumbs off his trousers. 'So? What's happening?'

'I don't know,' said Jeannie. 'Hasn't anyone been in since we left?'

'No, no one!' Andrea sniffed. 'It's been ages!'

'It means there's nothing to tell us, love.' Brian gave her a reassuring pat on the knee. 'If there was bad news, we'd have heard by now.'

'Are you sure you won't have a canapé, Mrs Hicks?' Angus asked, offering the bag. Some quick-thinking soul at the reception had boxed up the canapés that should have been circulating with champagne. 'We could be here for a while, and you need to take care of your blood sugar.'

Andrea smiled wanly and took a mini Yorkshire pudding with roast beef shavings. She suffered from various conditions that needed regular monitoring, as most of the immediate family now knew after the previous night's dinner, since half of it had had to be taken back and replaced with ingredients Andrea wasn't allergic to or avoiding for dietary reasons.

'Where's Owen?' asked Jeannie.

'Outside,' said Angus, making a phone gesture with his hand. 'He's dealing with the reception people. He's very organised, isn't he?'

As he spoke, Teri's phone pinged, and so did Brian's.

'Auntie Barbara says to let her know if there's anything she can do,' said Teri at the same time as Brian said, 'Your grandma's thinking of you.'

'Thanks,' said Jeannie automatically.

'Anyone fancy a cup of tea?' Angus asked, but before anyone could say no, the consultant finally appeared at the door, followed by the ICU ward sister. He was tall, bald, and if he was surprised to see a waiting room full of a bridal party, he was too professional – or too tired – to let it show in his expression.

'Daniel Hicks's family?' He processed the notes on the file the nurse handed him, saw Jeannie and then extended a hand towards her. 'Ah, Mrs Hicks.' She took it uncertainly. 'I'm *so* sorry, what a day it's been for you.'

Andrea had leaped to her feet at the sound of 'Mrs Hicks'. 'Doctor? What's the news? Can we see him?'

'Andrea is Mrs Hicks,' said Jeannie, moving her forward. 'She's Dan's mum.' Andrea's distress deserved more attention. Jeannie wasn't trembling like Andrea. Other than a rising nausea in her throat her body felt almost too normal now. It was her mind that kept racing round and round.

'What's the news?' asked Brian, firmly, before she could say anything else. 'Is Daniel awake yet?'

The surgeon looked between them. 'It's good news and

bad news, I'm afraid. First of all, my name is Roger Allcott and I'm a neurosurgeon. I specialise in brain injuries.'

Andrea drew in an audible breath. Jeannie dug a nail into her palm to make herself focus.

'Daniel had a CT scan on arrival, which shows he's sustained a serious head injury, along with a hairline fracture to his left leg, and some minor cuts and scrapes. He hit his head on the kerb when he fell, and that impact has caused a bleed on the brain, and some related swelling. The pressure on his brain's under control, but the swelling needs to go down, things need to settle, before we can diagnose further. The important thing is that he's as stable as we can hope for at the moment.'

Andrea breathed out, a long shudder. 'But will he be all right?'

Mr Allcott nodded slowly. 'We'll have a clearer picture in the morning. For now, Daniel's being monitored extremely carefully and if anything should change, it'll be picked up immediately.' He paused, acknowledging he was only raising more questions. 'I'm sorry I don't have something more specific to tell you but we'll know more when he's regained consciousness.'

Will he be all right? Andrea's unanswered question echoed around the room.

'Can we see him?' asked Jeannie.

'Of course.' The doctor glanced around the room: Jeannie, Andrea, Brian, Sue, Angus, Teri . . . 'The ward is very small, so maybe just two of you for now. Mrs Hicks? Jeannie?'

Andrea had gathered up her clutch bag and jacket and was at the door before Jeannie had even got to her feet.

*

Dan was in a corner of the ICU, cradled in a high-sided cot surrounded with machines and drips and monitors. His head was bandaged, leaving tufts of blond hair sticking out, and a plastic breathing mask covered most of his face. Red tubes, green lights, flickering LEDs pulsing blood and fluids into his unresponsive veins. Jeannie swallowed a rush of horror. Her handsome, energetic boyfriend, floating in a world she couldn't reach, his powerful athlete's heart only beating because a machine was pulling each breath through him.

Now it felt real. Now it felt *very* real.

At the sight of Dan's motionless body, Andrea let out a sob and lurched towards the bed. 'Oh, my baby! My baby boy!'

Jeannie's shoulders slumped. Dan, she wept inside her head, Dan, please come back. I'm so sorry.

The nurse who'd let them in put a comforting arm around her. 'I know it's upsetting to see Daniel breathing with the ventilator, but it always looks worse than it is, the first time you see it. He's stable, and he's very strong. I'm guessing he's a sporty guy?'

Jeannie nodded. 'Tennis. Football. He's a vet.' She couldn't drag her gaze away from Dan's face. The Dan she knew never stopped moving – his sharp eyes, his ready bark of a laugh, his dark brown eyebrows that quirked flirtily, a constant stream of energy flooding through him, animating everyone else. In the early days, in their first WhatsApp messages, texts and emails, his words had leaped off the screen with exclamation marks and smileys, every line accompanied by that familiar icon photo – Dan celebrating in front of the goal mouth in his university football kit, head thrown back, arms raised in triumph.

'Is he in any pain?' she asked in a cracked voice.

'None at all. He's sedated; that's the drip there. There's a nurse here twenty-four/seven, checking the monitors, making sure he's comfortable.'

'Does he know we're here?' Andrea was kneeling at the bedside, and she clutched Dan's limp hand in hers, squeezing it tight, then laying her cheek against it. 'Can he hear us? Danny?'

'We always assume the patients can hear us.' Jeannie noted the nurse was called Kate. She had freckles, and three gold studs in her ear. 'We chat away to them while we're doing our checks – only fair to keep them in the loop, I always say! I'll give you a moment while I grab his notes . . .'

Kate drew a curtain around the bed as she slipped away. There were three other beds in the ward concealed behind curtains, and from the beeps and murmurs, it sounded as if they were occupied. Other nightmares, thought Jeannie. Other normal days wrenched off their rails, struggling loved ones, fears too big to look at straight on.

'We're here, Danny,' said Andrea, gripping Dan's hand. 'Mum and Jeannie. Your best girls. We're here for you.' Her words dissolved in a surge of tears, and she turned to Jeannie, her eyes begging for her to take over.

Jeannie slipped on to the spare chair, getting as close as she could to the bed. Her throat was dry and she hesitated before crouching down to whisper in Dan's ear. An ear she'd tucked a flower behind, just days before, a bright yellow gerbera from a bunch he'd given her 'because it's Wednesday!' Dan smelled of hospital now, not warm skin and cologne and energy.

49

'I'm here,' she managed. 'It's Jeannie, Dan. Hang on.'

And then tears washed away her voice too, and she and Andrea sat on either side of the bed, holding Dan's hands, as the machines hummed and whirred and kept him alive.

Chapter Four

The hospital seemed completely different when Jeannie stepped out of the ICU and back into the bright strip-lit corridor outside. Night had fallen while she'd been holding Dan's hand, listening to the machines, and now she had no idea what time it was. The day had folded in on itself.

Andrea had slipped out some time ago and not returned, and now Jeannie's parents were the only ones left waiting for her in the side room. Or rather, Brian was snatching forty winks, his head tilted backwards and his mouth wide open, while Sue was on her mobile, her pen poised to cross something off a long list on the chair next to her.

'. . . so I've sorted the caterers and you'll speak to the hotel in . . . Oh, you're a star. Ah, Owen – she's just coming out! I'll speak to you later, pet, bye now!' She stood up, not quite masking a wince of stiffness. 'Jeannie! Come here. How is he?'

'Sleeping.' Jeannie hugged her mum and looked over her shoulder at the list: 'Reception. Caterers. Insurance? Honeymoon. Flowers to hospice. Overnight bag. What's been happening?'

'Nothing you need to worry about. Everything's under control. Owen's taken Andrea to buy some bits and pieces – she's staying here tonight. The hospital's got emergency accommodation, but there's only one bed left. I thought you should have it, since it's your wedding night, but they allocated it to Andrea as next of kin, and she says she'd feel happier being close by.' Sue's markedly neutral expression suggested she didn't completely agree with that, but had been talked down. 'We've booked you a room in a hotel down the road – but you can come back with us, if you prefer?'

Jeannie flinched. Back to the honeymoon suite with the rose petals on the four-poster bed? And all the guests asking her how Dan was, comforting her . . . not knowing they'd narrowly escaped a scandalous no-show?

'I'll stay here, Mum,' she said.

'You'll be all right on your own?'

'She'll only be there a few hours, Susan. It's nearly nine now.' Brian's frown had deepened; Sue was clearly way past the limits of her energy, but she was pushing on, ignoring the warning signs of pain lining her face. 'Owen says he'll drop you off, then come back for you in the morning. Try to get some sleep, love. Speaking of which, Susan . . . it's time we got back ourselves or we'll be no good to man nor beast tomorrow.'

Sue flashed him a quick, loaded glare. 'I'm *fine*, Brian. Don't fuss.'

'Well, I'm not. I'm cream-crackered and it's an hour's drive,' he replied. 'Is there anything you need before we go, Jeannie? Some chocolate from that wee shop, maybe?'

He smiled encouragingly, as if she were a sweet-toothed nine-year-old again, and a Curly Wurly could make everything better.

'Good idea, Dad,' said Jeannie, because she understood

how hopeless he felt right now – and also because she needed to get him on his own.

Brian and Jeannie joined the other shell-shocked relatives doing the rounds of the shelves, sleepwalking through a nightmare of a hospital visit shopping list – toothpaste, face wipes, Lucozade, *Yours* magazine.

'Is that enough?' he kept saying, stacking bottles of water and overpriced chocolate into her hands. 'You sure you don't want a Twix? They have the giant ones here.'

'Yes, a Twix would be nice,' said Jeannie. She checked over her shoulder to make sure her mum was still on her mobile in the foyer, then said, 'Dad, did you tell Mum about what happened in the car? Before . . . before the accident?'

Brian's hand froze on the Twixes. His gaze slid towards the foyer too. 'No. I haven't had a chance.'

'Well, please don't.'

'Don't tell her? Why not?'

'Because it's just not important now, is it? Not compared with *this*.'

'Jeannie, your mum would understand . . .'

'It's not that – I don't want anyone to know!' she whispered urgently. 'If Andrea finds out I was about to stand Dan up at the altar she'll be devastated. Does she need that, on top of what's already happened? I just want to forget about it.'

Even as the words left her mouth, Jeannie could hear what a stupid thing she'd just said. How could she forget about it? That irrational feeling in the car of physical panic, that powerful, blood-racing knowledge that she was about to shatter someone else's life, just to get herself free – if it was so important, she *shouldn't* pretend it hadn't happened.

'Your mum and I don't have secrets.' Brian looked aghast. 'We never have done. I'm not a good liar, Jeannie, you know that. I couldn't even get you to believe in the tooth fairy.'

'I'm not asking you to lie to Mum, *just don't tell her.* Why would she even ask?' Jeannie's pulse was racing again, too fast, too hard. Talking about it was bringing that alien emotion back, like a nightmare popping back into her head in broad daylight. Had that really been her, in the dress, in the car, holding the bouquet?

Brian carefully put down the fistful of chocolate bars. 'Listen to me, Jeannie. Yes, you left it later than you should have done to make that decision, but *no one* should go ahead with a wedding if it's not right. Your mum would be the first to tell you that. And I'm sure Daniel wouldn't want to marry someone who didn't—'

Jeannie couldn't bear to let him finish. 'Please, Dad,' she begged. 'Let me just get through the next few days, until we at least know Dan's going to be all right.'

'He *is* going to be all right,' said Brian automatically. He tried, but he couldn't quite maintain his reassuring expression, and fear crushed Jeannie's chest. If Dad couldn't look reassuring, a man whose resting expression was Comforting Dad, then things were out of their control.

'We don't know that,' she said, and her voice broke.

'Oh, love,' said Brian, and hugged her, right there in the shop, in front of the emergency toothbrushes and nine kinds of tissues. Neither of them had to say anything more.

*

Brian and Sue left, and Jeannie retreated to the deserted coffee shop in the foyer with the pile of leaflets her mum had collected for her from the Patient Liaison office. Reading through head injury facts did nothing to loosen the hard knot in her stomach, and after a while, she gave up, and got her phone out to scroll through selfie after selfie of her and Dan.

Today, their wedding day, was a special anniversary. It was exactly one year since their first contact – the last-minute availability at the town hall had seemed fated for them. They lived three hundred miles apart, so their paths shouldn't even have crossed, but fate and algo-rithms, Dan's smile, and Jeannie's 'intriguing' profile had conspired to bring them together.

'I found you,' Dan always said, as if Jeannie had been hiding from him all her life. 'And you found me.' He said the most romantic things, but so sincerely they never sounded cheesy.

One year ago, Jeannie's photo stream was exclusively guitars she wanted, cute dogs in the pub she worked in, gigs she'd played, and close-ups of her and Edith's special glittery stage make-up. Almost overnight, it changed. Suddenly it was Jeannie and Dan, heads together form-ing one heart, sharing the selfie space. As she scrolled, Jeannie could see herself blossoming, shyly, in the sun-shine of Dan's confidence. Her crooked smile slowly became as wide and fearless as his.

She stopped at her favourite photo of the two them: starting the New Year with a kiss. The background was blurry with snowflakes, and Jeannie's chest ached at the memory of Dan's lips resting on her cold nose. It was like a movie poster: Dan's long lashes dark against his cheek, a few chestnut curls escaping from under her navy bob-ble hat as she lifted her face to his. Eyes closed, heart bursting with love and champagne. She'd been so happy that night. Happy like Christmas Eve as a little girl, when the fidgety excitement at what was to come was somehow even better than Christmas Day itself. Jeannie remembered the chilled softness of Dan's down jacket as she rested her head against his shoulder, listening to Big Ben and feeling as if she was shimmering with light inside and out. Maybe there *was* something in astrology, she'd thought, smiling up at the milky moon, if the dir-ection of her life could shift so unexpectedly from her quiet nights alone and her dead-in-the-water career to adored girlfriend with a future full of romance and coun-try cottages and glossy wedding magazines.

And yet . . . A funny void pulsed in the back of Jeannie's mind as she gazed at the image, and was gone before it formed into a thought.

She *had* been happy, yet something had changed. What's wrong with me? Jeannie wondered, as her eyes filled with tears. What did I do to spoil it?

'Jeannie? Mind if I join you?'

She sat bolt upright – Owen had appeared round the corner of the café.

'Um, no.' She wiped her eyes. 'Course not.'

There was a screech of metal on tiles as he lowered himself into the chair opposite her. 'That you and Dan?'

'Yup. New Year.' He was tilting his head to see, so she turned the screen to show him.

'Ah, the famous New Year's Eve in London!'

'Yes.' Jeannie looked up. 'Did he tell you about it?'

'Um, not exactly. We usually get the whole gang together

in a cottage and this year . . . well, I guess Dan preferred to see in *this* New Year with his fiancée!'

'He did spend Christmas on call.' Jeannie wasn't sure why she felt so defensive. 'We barely saw each other because of his shifts, so Dan booked a last-minute deal in London as a surprise.'

'Not criticising.' Owen raised his hands. 'Why wouldn't he want to spend it with you? He's done his fair share of playing beer pong with us lot. Is that the London Eye? It looks very romantic.'

'Uh-huh. It was amazing.' Dan was generous with his weekends away – to make up for his long hours and frequent drawing of the short straw over holiday shifts. 'So normally there's a big get-together at New Year?'

'Yes, but I wouldn't read anything into that. Dan probably thought if you saw how competitive he gets at Pictionary, you'd call the wedding off. Ha ha! Anyway, how is he? Any news?'

'No. The nurses said he's stable, which is good but . . . I don't know. He's so pale.' They were so helpless, all of them. How could anyone tell what was happening inside Dan's brain? Even the doctors?

'Yeah, sorry. That was a stupid question.' He eyed her uneaten sponge cake. 'You having that?'

Brian had bought two slices as the café was shutting, as if the sack of chocolate under the table wasn't enough. Jeannie shook her head. 'Have it.'

Owen picked up one slice of cake and half of it vanished in a single bite. A few crumbs stuck to the corners of his wide mouth. He suppressed an involuntary *mmm* noise.

'You've got . . .' Jeannie pointed at her own lips.

Owen frowned like Paddington Bear surprised with a marmalade sandwich. 'What?'

'Around . . . here? Crumbs.'

'Oh, right.' He swiped at his face, dislodging the flecks of cake. 'Thanks.'

'You're welcome.'

He finished off the remainder, then paused, raised his eyebrow at the second piece in a hopeful sort of way.

'Go for it,' said Jeannie. 'They're just small pieces.' They weren't.

She suddenly thought about the showstopper wedding cake she'd been looking forward to tucking into so much. One tier of carrot (hers), one of chocolate (Dan's), one vanilla, topped with sugar-craft couple, dogs and cats and tiny ukuleles. Who was eating that? Had it been binned? Jeannie was surprised how little she actually cared, beyond remorse at the money wasted. The hours she'd spent on things like the portionability of carrot cake, when she should have been asking herself much harder questions.

Owen picked up the second slice and dispatched it in the same ravenous manner. 'Sorry,' he said thickly. 'Haven't eaten since breakfast. I usually pop something in my sporran for later but obviously I didn't have time.'

'Like what?'

'Couple of biscuits. Mars bar. Amazing what you can fit in there. Usually a lot of waiting around at weddings, before you get to the canapés. I've saved more than one groom from acute hunger with a well-timed Dairy Milk.'

Jeannie finally realised what had been niggling her all day about Owen: his accent didn't match his outfit. She'd been teased at school for her 'weird' accent – a blend of Borders Scots and her mum's northern English, garnished with nuggets of Dad's Northern Irish slang – but Owen sounded definitely south of the border. 'If it's not a rude thing to say, you don't sound very Scottish for a man with a dagger down his sock.'

'To be fair, I'm not.' Owen picked up a paper napkin and carefully dabbed his mouth for jammy debris before she could point it out. 'My family's from down the road – I'm a Brummie. But my mum's from Inverness.'

'And you *choose* to wear a kilt at weddings?'

'Ha! Funnily enough, it was Dan who suggested I got myself a kilt – back when we were at school.' Owen folded the napkin, creasing it into a paper dart, suddenly self-conscious. 'He said you can always strike up a conversation in a kilt. I've never been the greatest at small talk, not like Dan. Well, you know that. He did his best to help me out when we were younger, but . . . you know. Reckon he thought the kilt would step in when he wasn't around.'

Jeannie understood the exact mix of affection and self-deprecation in Owen's half-grin. He wasn't unattractive – he was the sort of average bloke you'd struggle to describe unless he always wore red jumpers – but standing next to athletic, sociable Dan, Owen must have vanished. Tallish, darkish hair, medium build. He had kind eyes, though.

'I know what you mean,' she said suddenly. 'My best mate does the talking for both of us. Did,' she corrected herself.

'Was she here today?' Owen asked. 'Was she your bridesmaid?'

'No, that was Teri, my sister-in-law. My best mate's the

one I was in the band with. The one I'm not speaking to any more. She was so good at talking she talked herself into a dream job in London while we were at a festival, hence the band breaking up. Her name's Edith. Edith Constantine.'

Owen raised his eyebrows. '*Edith*. Wow. And I thought Murdo was bad.'

'Your real name's Murdo?'

'No, it's my middle name. Mum's choice.'

'Ah, well. In that case, you've paid the dues on the kilt.'

They exchanged a reluctant, weary smile. Kind eyes, and easy to talk to, Jeannie amended.

'So, go on,' he said, nodding at the head injury leaflets. 'What do we need to know?'

Instantly, the stark reality of the situation returned to the table. Jeannie looked down and wondered how to tell Owen his best friend could easily be paralysed, or brain-damaged. Almost certainly scarred in some way. Her vision blurred with tears. Dan could still wake up and be fine, she reminded herself. He could still be *fine*.

A fat teardrop plopped on the leaflets, and Owen reached silently for the pile.

He worked his way through the information, humming and twisting his face as he read, and slowly a sense of relief spread through Jeannie's aching body. Owen knew Dan, and Andrea, much better than she did. He'd know the right thing to do, and he seemed happy to shoulder the responsibility of Andrea's distress. Mum seemed happy to make lists with Owen, and she was usually very slow to rely on anyone other than Dad.

Although if Owen knew what she'd done, would he be

so kind to her? Jeannie shivered, and bit her lower lip to stop herself making a noise.

No one knew about that, and no one would. The secret was trapped between her and her dad, like a spider under a glass. But it hadn't gone away.

Forget it, she told herself. Forget it ever happened.

'Jeannie?'

Her head snapped up. Owen had finished with the leaflets and was looking at her, as if he wasn't sure how to frame a question. She had a horrible instinct that he was going to ask about Dan's mysterious phone call. 'What?'

'Nothing. I was just . . . wondering if you were ready to go? Don't want to rush you away.'

'Oh, um. Yes. Are you staying at the hotel too?'

'No, I only live a few miles from here.' He picked up the overnight bag her mum had brought and slung it over his shoulder. 'Another reason I was delighted to hear Dan was moving so close. I was looking forward to spending more time with him. And with you, of course,' he added quickly. 'Not that we still won't! It'll just be . . . delayed.'

Jeannie managed a weak smile. 'Thanks for everything you've done today. Not quite the best man's duty you were expecting, eh?'

'Dan's been my best mate since I was eleven. I've learned to expect the unexpected.' Owen stopped, and though he smiled bravely, Jeannie felt the slump in his broad shoulders. 'I'm just glad I can help him out for once.'

There was no change in Dan's condition the next day, or the next, or the day after. No miracle awakening, no terrifying green flatlining on the machines. Just a constant, monotonous beep from the monitors, a ripple of nervous conversation from Andrea, Owen's solid note-taking presence, and the constantly alternating surges of panic and guilt inside Jeannie's head.

Mr Allcott came regularly to check Dan's progress, and reassured them that the team were as satisfied as they could be with his responses. They were 'through the most critical period' – which Jeannie interpreted as 'he could have died but he hasn't' – but beyond that, the neurosurgeon was cautious.

'I'm afraid we have to take it day by day,' he said as Kate the nurse updated the records at the foot of the bed. 'We're monitoring the pressure on Daniel's brain, that's the key thing, but other than that, there's not much we can do until he wakes up.'

'And when do you think that's likely to be?' asked Jeannie.

'Usually coma patients regain consciousness of their own accord within twenty-four hours or so, but Daniel doesn't seem ready to do that just yet.'

'What if he doesn't? Wake up of his own accord?' The words came out more baldly than Jeannie had intended, and she felt Andrea's hand reach for hers, gripping it tight.

Mr Allcott didn't flinch. 'If Daniel doesn't show signs of regaining consciousness independently over the next few days, we'll attempt to wake him up. He's heavily sedated right now, and we'll reduce that sedation, very carefully, of course. Depending on how he responds, it'll give us a good steer on where we go next.'

'Right.' That sounded positive. Sort of. Jeannie wrote it down in the notebook Owen had brought to keep by Dan's bed, to record everything the doctors told them.

There were so many technical terms, so much jargon, that she knew she'd forget; and besides, every time Andrea left to go to the loo, she quizzed Jeannie anxiously on her return about any minuscule change or comment from a nurse. It helped to show her that, honestly, there was nothing.

'But will he be all right when he wakes up?' Andrea's fears vibrated in her voice. 'Will he remember the accident? Will he be able to tell us what happened?'

Jeannie's body tensed, and the nurse, noticing, patted her shoulder sympathetically.

'It's impossible to predict anything with complete certainty at this stage, Mrs Hicks.' There was some shuffling from the medical students, which made Jeannie think Dan was a more interesting case than they were letting on. 'Physically Daniel's body has suffered a massive shock, in addition to the brain trauma. We need to give him time to recover from that.' He paused. 'And of course, *you've* had a big shock too.'

Oh, that was it, she realised, her heart sinking as she cast a glance at the young medics: *we're* the interesting case. The bride, the groom, his mother and a coma.

When Mr Allcott had left, taking his flock of students with him, and Andrea had gone for yet more tea, Nurse Kate pulled back the curtain round Dan's bed and crouched by Jeannie's chair.

'Listen, why don't you go home and get some rest?' She had a kind face and a comfortingly unfazeable attitude. 'Reading between the lines, it sounds like Mr Allcott doesn't think Dan's likely to wake up today. Even if he does, he's going to be very confused, and we'd contact you immediately to come back. You've done a great job, being here for him, but Mr Allcott's right, you need some self-care to get over *your* shock. Have a long bath, find some clean clothes, sleep the night in your own bed – I'll update your book for you with anything that happens.' She patted Jeannie's arm. 'Go home.'

Where was home, though? They'd only moved into the house they were renting from Dan's boss the week before the wedding – they'd barely unpacked. Dorothy Cottage wasn't 'home'. The flat she'd shared with Edith in Bristol had been home. The McCarthys' ramshackle farmhouse with its dog baskets, and ancient kitchen that Dad was always about to replace, was home.

'I've said the same to your mother-in-law,' Kate went on. 'She's going to stay tonight, and have some time off tomorrow when you get back. Take it in turns, that's the best way. Owen's said he'll drive you home if you want.'

Owen had dropped her off at the Travelodge every night, and collected her at exactly eight thirty the next morning, thoughtfully soundtracking each journey with the local news, so she didn't have to listen to any music that might remind her of Dan.

Everyone was so kind. Owen. Kate. They were all looking after her, trying to make up for her wedding day. If only they knew. 'Thank you,' said Jeannie, and felt like an utter fraud.

Chapter Five

Dorothy Cottage was down the lane from Four Oaks, the Victorian villa where Dan's boss George Fenwick lived, which itself was next door to his wife Rachel's dog rescue centre and boarding kennels.

It was just a temporary base, Dan had promised, until they got to know the town well enough to find their own place, but when Owen pulled up outside, and Jeannie looked at her new home through the arch of honeysuckle crowning the gate, her heart clenched in her chest. Under any other circumstances she'd have felt beyond lucky to be coming home to such a pretty house. The climbing roses had bloomed around the door since she'd left it on Friday, and the red brickwork was now splashed with ivory- and honey-coloured petals.

Owen yanked on the handbrake, but he didn't turn the engine off. 'So, I guess I'll see you back at the hospital tomorrow?'

'Yup. Thanks for bringing me home.' As she said it, Jeannie wasn't sure how she *was* going to get back to the hospital in the morning. Dan's car was in the garage, but she wasn't covered to drive it. It had been on their list of things to do, but in the rush of moving in and finalising wedding arrangements, they hadn't got round to phoning the insurers. Jeannie wished they'd done that instead

65

of spending a whole afternoon renegotiating a seating plan to fit in two unexpected plus ones and a baby. Could she do it in the morning? Would Dan need to speak to the insurers? Which of the hundreds of still-sealed boxes were his documents in, anyway? Her head started to ache.

'You've been amazing,' she added. 'Thank you.'

'It's good to be able to do something practical.' Owen fidgeted with his square glasses; the contact lenses were long gone. 'Hard, isn't it – just sitting there, watching those nurses and doctors buzzing about, not knowing what the hell they're doing.'

'I'm sure Dan knows we're there.'

'Irony is, he'd probably be fascinated by everything that's going on, if he was conscious. Driving them mad with questions!'

They shared an exhausted smile, that wasn't really a smile. More an acknowledgement. She and Owen had been strangers four days ago; now they'd lived through something that had altered them both. Dan hovered invisibly between them, even in Owen's car.

They sat without speaking for a moment. Although Jeannie desperately wanted to be alone, she dreaded it at the same time. That house, full of plans for a life that should have started now. Dan there, and not there.

'Have you got a long journey home?' she asked, then remembered he'd said he lived nearby. 'Sorry, did you tell me where you lived? My mind's not taking anything in.'

'I didn't, exactly. I'm in a village about ten miles from the hospital. My office is one mile in the other direction so I'll drop in on the way back, see if there's anything . . . Oh. Speak of the devil.'

Owen's phone was ringing. 'I work with my dad,' he

explained. 'Family business. We've got a haulage firm; head office is down here. I'm the logistics manager. Not as glamorous as saving kittens and puppies, but someone's got to move stuff from A to Waitrose.'

It sounded like something he'd said a million times, as if he was used to deflecting jokes about his boring job. Jeannie didn't know why he was being so apologetic: it sounded great, being able to get home in ten minutes.

'It worked better when I could say A to BHS,' he added, wryly.

'Do you get to drive the wagons?'

'I wish I did! Ha!' He drummed the wheel with his forefingers, a reasonable paradiddle. 'It would make life easier sometimes. Anyway, I've got to get this. Nothing else you need?'

'No, you've done enough. I'll see you tomorrow.' Jeannie grabbed her bags and got out of the car before she could think about how empty the house would be.

The first time Jeannie had crossed the threshold of Dorothy Cottage had been in Dan's arms. He'd insisted on carrying her in, even though her protests were real; she hadn't wanted Dan to start his first week in Longhampton with a slipped disc. But he'd insisted. He loved the romantic gestures, and she loved him for making them.

Jeannie tried not to think about that as she unlocked the front door. There was a thick pile of post to step over on the doormat, mainly pink and white wedding cards, and an unpleasant cloying scent coming from the kitchen. She dumped her bags at the foot of the wooden staircase and went to investigate.

The kitchen was the only room they'd properly

unpacked, since coffee and food were non-negotiable even in the frantic last days of wedding planning. On the table, next to a pile of place cards she'd forgotten to take to the reception, sat a dilapidated Marks & Spencer's flower box, damp spreading up its side. That was where the smell was coming from.

Jeannie ripped it open: a sad bunch of wilted roses and pollen-stained lilies slumped out. Water had drained out of the plastic bag, and soaked into the wrapping. She fished out the sodden note but the envelope had turned into papier mâché and there was no way of opening it, let alone reading the message.

She sank on to the chair, shaken by the ugliness of the dying flowers. They'd be from Dan. He sent her flowers almost every week when they couldn't be together, and this would be his final bouquet for her as his girlfriend. Delivered, presumably, to the Fenwicks by mistake, and brought down here by Rachel, the only other person with a key.

With a sob, Jeannie picked up the soggy bouquet and rammed it in the kitchen bin. It wouldn't shut but something made her keep crushing the lid down anyway. Her head throbbed and she gave up, stumbling back on to the chair. Her joints felt weak, as if they might give way any moment. Jeannie ached, and the silent house echoed back at her.

Come on, she thought, thinking of Nurse Kate's comforting advice to take care of herself. Run a bath. Everything feels better after a bath.

It had been one of the first things Jeannie had loved about their new cottage: its deep bathtub, big enough for two. She'd barely had a shower since the morning of the wedding, and the prospect of a long hot soak pushed her up the narrow stairs with her last shreds of energy.

She turned on the taps and poured in a generous dollop of her good bath oil, then went into the bedroom to find a towel. Dan had been the last to leave the house the day before the wedding, and the intimate traces of his final movements stopped Jeannie short. His red dressing gown, flung over a chair; his cod liver oil capsules on the bedside table next to her song-ideas notebook. This was their first shared room. It still felt strange to see Dan's things mingled with hers. But she was here and he . . .

Jeannie squeezed her eyes shut, told herself it would be fine, then grabbed a towel and went back to the bathroom.

The oil had frothed up into delicious bubbles, and she dipped her fingers in the foam to check it wasn't too hot. But the bath was stone cold.

What? Jeannie shoved her hand under the hot tap, gasped at the cold water and suddenly remembered – Dan had turned off the hot water before he left, on account of them being away on honeymoon for a fortnight, and she didn't know how to turn it on again.

And now Dan wasn't here to ask. He might *never* be here to ask.

Everything wobbled. Jeannie slid down against the bathroom wall, finally out of energy. She covered her eyes with her clammy palms, trying to block out everything apart from her heartbeat.

Someone was knocking on the back door but she ignored it. She couldn't face talking to anyone, even if they were trying to be kind. Especially if they were trying to be kind.

The knocking stopped. The door opened – Jeannie wasn't surprised, she'd lived in the countryside most of her life – and a woman's voice shouted, 'Hello? Hello, Jeannie? It's Rachel. I didn't know if you had any milk for tea. I can leave it on the step if you want?'

It was Dan's boss's wife. Her landlady. Sue's voice popped uninvited into Jeannie's head and said, Don't be *rude*, Jeannie.

She dragged herself to her feet and went downstairs.

The back door opened from the kitchen out on to a small lawn; beyond that, a footpath ran up to the big house one way, and down through the open fields into the town the other. Standing on the step was a woman with dark hair interrupted by a silver streak at one temple, and behind the woman was a very, very old dog. A Border collie with blue eyes, so old that his black and white coat had faded to a pale grey all over. He was staring at her with an intensity that didn't match his cloudy eyes. He looked sorry for her too.

'I am *so* sorry to disturb you,' said Rachel apologetically. 'But I saw the lights on in the kitchen, and I thought if you were back you might need something to make tea.' She lifted up a milk bottle, a packet of biscuits, and a loaf. 'I know what it's like, you'll want to be on your own, so I'll drop these off and let you get on with it. I'm just sorry I didn't leave them earlier – I popped those flowers in, they were on your doorstep on Saturday morning, but . . . Oh no, Jeannie, I'm so sorry.'

Jeannie wiped roughly at her wet face. 'I keep thinking I've got no tears left, and then . . .'

'I'm going to make you a cup of tea, then I'll go. If you want.' Rachel put the bread on the table, and rubbed

Jeannie's arm. 'You don't mind if Gem comes in, do you?'

Jeannie shook her head and watched as the collie tip-toed through the kitchen after his mistress, his paws soundless on the tiles. He tipped his head, sniffed the air, then skulked over to the sofa in the corner, next to the red Aga. He hesitated, judging the height carefully, then leaped up and curled himself into a ball. The leap was an effort for his old bones, but the dog still made no sound. He was his own ghost.

'How long have you been back?' Rachel hunted through cupboards for teabags. 'Have you got our numbers? I did tell your mum that you should call us if you needed collecting from the hospital.'

'They're in Dan's phone.' Jeannie stopped short. That was a point. Where was Dan's phone? Did Owen have it? An ominous anxiety swirled up in her stomach.

'Call us whenever you need us, and I mean *whenever.*' Rachel found some junk mail and started scribbling on the back. 'You know vets, we're used to phones ringing any time of day or night. Please don't tell me you got the train home tonight?'

'Owen brought me back. Dan's best man.'

'Have you eaten? Proper food, I mean?'

'Um, not recently.'

The kettle boiled and Rachel made the tea, then turned to look at Jeannie, hands on her slim hips. 'You can say no,' she said, gently, 'but won't you come up to the house and let me make you something to eat? And what about clean clothes? Can I do some washing for you?'

Jeannie shook her head. Her clothes were still in a

suitcase somewhere, sorted into outfits for sight-seeing and cocktail nights. Her mind was still in the hospital, ever alert for changes in the bleeps and lines. Her heart . . . where was that? She felt like a magician's assistant, head over here, torso over there, sword through the middle.

'I tried to run a bath but there's no hot water . . .' She waved, defeated, in the direction of the stairs. 'I just . . .' She felt her mouth trembling. 'I just really wanted a bath.'

Rachel understood. 'Drink your tea. Then come up to the house with me and let someone look after *you* for a bit.'

Jeannie had only met Dan's new employer and his wife briefly the day they moved in – to add to the complications, the Fenwicks had had to leave for a rare holiday the day they arrived: their fifth anniversary minibreak.

Rachel had shown Jeannie round their new home while George was introducing Dan to the surgery, the locums and the nurses. She was an efficient talker: in the space of ten minutes, Jeannie had learned how Rachel had inherited the dog rescue after working in London *and never owning so much as a cactus*; that their ten-year-old son Fergus was staying with his friend in town while they were away, and that Jeannie should buy *some non-fashion wellies*, and throw away her black clothes immediately, on account of dog hairs. Which would *get in places you wouldn't believe.*

'See you at the wedding!' Rachel had yelled, leaning out of her window as George revved the engine and muttered about being late. 'Call if there's anything you need and don't, whatever you do . . .'

72

Whatever Rachel's words of advice had been were lost as George accelerated away in a cloud of gravel, but Jeannie had found a bunch of flowers on the kitchen table, arranged in a vase so she wouldn't have to open up a box to find one, with a card from both Fenwicks, wishing them happiness in their new home. Rachel was kind. She'd also filled the fridge with beer.

'Here we are, excuse the mess,' said Rachel, pushing open the front door. 'We've had a lot of comings and goings this week so I'm behind with my housework, and to be honest, it's always a bit of a tip. First things first, let's get that nice hot bath going . . .'

Jeannie looked round the airy hall, which smelled of polish and toast. A vase of white lilies filled an oak sideboard, and several pairs of green wellies stood in size order in the porch. The walls were lined with photographs in modern black frames, leading up a magnificent oak staircase: Rachel, George, a young boy, presumably Fergus, lots of pets from dogs to horses to guinea pigs, mixed up with old sepia family portraits, framed in the same style. It had the effect of bringing the whole clan together to peer at visitors down a distinctive long nose.

'Mainly my lot.' Rachel threw out an explanatory hand as they ascended. 'Auntie Dot, Mum and Dad, my sister Amelia – you can tell by the Mossop schnozz. It seems to affect the women more than the men . . .' She pointed at a family group of blond giants in checked shirts, beaming in unison at the camera with identical toothy grins – apart from one teenage boy who was glowering. 'The Fenwicks circa 1980. Very fertile, great teeth. The ideal farming family. Apart from their inability to tan.' She went up a few more steps, then paused next to a black and white portrait. 'Oh, and that's us. Me and George. On our wedding day.'

It was a beautiful image of two people in love. The photographer had caught the newly married couple off guard outside the church: Rachel, looking as dark and angular as she did now but polished into striking elegance, was leaning her forehead against George's shoulder and holding his hand, while he gazed down at his wife with an expression of tender disbelief, as if he couldn't believe his luck. The love between the two was palpable.

'That's the most beautiful wedding photo I've ever seen,' said Jeannie.

Rachel touched the gold frame. It stood out in the shoal of black frames. 'Thank you. I think it's very . . . us.' She sighed. 'Anyway . . . What, Gem? Oh, and this is his family, obviously.'

The elderly collie had silently followed them up. Jeannie noted there were several portraits of collies amidst the human family. The dogs all looked identical to her, but obviously not to whoever had framed them.

'I'll get you some towels,' said Rachel, pushing open the bathroom door. 'I had an enormous water tank installed when we renovated this place, my treat to myself, so run a good deep bath. It's the nearest I get to a hotel bathroom these days.'

'I won't be long,' Jeannie started. Her conscience reminded her she needed to bathe, get dressed, eat, then phone Andrea to see how Dan was. Then work out how she was going to get back to the hospital in the morning.

'Be as long or as quick as you want! Fergus is in his room, he's got food and a book so that's him sorted for hours, and George is finishing up at the surgery, some emergency with a cat. So you won't be disturbed.'

The door handle was an old brass bulb; it felt solid and calming under Jeannie's fingers. The whole house felt calming, despite the family mess and Rachel's scattergun conversation.

'Give me a shout when you're done and I'll make you something to eat. Oops!' Rachel yanked a pair of Y-fronts off the radiator where they were drying. 'Sorry about those. Married life, eh?'

Jeannie closed the door and set the taps running. The water was hot and soothing, and when she slid into the fragrant bubbles (Rachel had a well-stocked toiletries shelf) it was all she could do not to drift into a grateful sleep.

There was no sign of George or Fergus when Jeannie ventured downstairs to the kitchen in the yoga kit Rachel had left outside the bathroom. Rachel herself was standing at the Aga with her back to the door, stirring a pan while conducting an animated conversation on her mobile.

'. . . so I brought her home for tea, poor girl. She's going through absolute hell and she's on her own . . . Yes, I know you're on your own at the surgery too but it's hardly the same thing, is it? You're not the one facing brain damage or life in a wheelchair or God knows what . . .'

The toast was burning under the Aga lid and as Rachel tucked the phone under her ear and reached out to flip it, she saw Jeannie there and her dark eyes widened in embarrassment.

Jeannie made to back out of the room, but Rachel waved her in, pulling out a chair at the big table and sweeping away a pile of magazines, copies of *Vet Times*, clothes catalogues and old *Longhampton Gazette*s. She dumped them on another chair and a tortoiseshell cat sprang out of nowhere with a furious yowl, which in turn woke up Gem, who was napping on the window seat.

Jeannie sat down. In her haste to clear the table, Rachel had missed a local paper. She turned it over and read the front page, and her throat tightened when she read the headline.

'Air Ambulance in Wedding Horror Crash'. There was a photograph of the air ambulance, and she caught the words 'bridegroom' and 'wedding' and 'rapid response'.

Rachel turned back with the toast, saw what Jeannie was reading and snatched the paper off the table, making 'I am so sorry' faces as she waltzed round and dropped it into the recycling bin, all while still on the phone to George.

'Oh, oh, darling? While you're in the surgery, can you bring me some medicated shampoo? Freda says those Westies won't stop scratching, poor mites.' Her straight eyebrows drew together in a frown and she rolled her eyes. '*Yes*, I'll pay for it. Take it out of the rescue accounts. Well, take it out of our joint account, then. George, come on, one shampoo, it's not going to bankrupt you . . .'

Underneath the apron that said 'World's Worst Cook', Rachel was wearing pale chinos, rolled up at the ankle to the exact perfect length, with a pair of gold plimsolls. It was the kind of effortless summery style you saw in magazines. It said something about Rachel, Jeannie thought, that she managed to keep the chinos unstained around the collection of animals and family evidenced by the kitchen. She wondered if she could retrieve the newspaper from the bin while Rachel's back was turned, and then decided she didn't really want to.

Rachel was simultaneously dishing up the eggs and finishing up her call. 'Fine, I'll see you in half an hour. Thirty minutes. Love you,' she added, but it sounded a bit automatic.

'Don't worry,' she added to Jeannie, seeing her reaction. 'George'll be ages yet. You'll be tucked up on your own sofa in peace before he's even got his scrubs off.' As she spoke, she stepped over towards the door and roared up the stairs. 'Fergus? Supper!'

The bright yellow scrambled eggs Rachel had dumped in the middle of the table looked tempting, and the smell of the toast reminded Jeannie that she hadn't eaten a proper meal since . . . since the breakfast she'd forced down on the morning of her wedding. Four days ago.

'Eggs are my limit,' explained Rachel, filling a plate and offering it to Jeannie. 'George is the chef in this family. Or Fergus. Fergus likes experimenting. It's his way of ensuring he gets his eight thousand calories a day.'

As she spoke a tall boy sloped into the kitchen. Jeannie would have put him as older than ten, from his height. He had Rachel's nearly black eyes and strong nose, but, curiously, blond hair the colour of wheat. He was wearing a Longhampton Young Farmers Pantomime T-shirt with a very bad cartoon of a cow on the front.

'Jeannie, this is Fergus. Ferg, this is Jeannie. She's moved into Dorothy Cottage with her . . .' Rachel hesitated, struggling for the right word, then said, smoothly, 'With Dan, who's come to work with Dad. Dan's in . . .'

Fergus gave her a cautious look from under his fringe. 'Yeah, I know, my friend Connor's mum was on the bus? She saw you in your wedding dress, with the police and the ambulances and everything.'

'Ferg!' Rachel looked aghast – but not completely surprised. 'That is *enough*. Bit of sensitivity, please!'

Fergus grabbed his plate and a fork. 'Sorry, didn't mean to be rude. I hope he's all right and everything?'

'Honestly . . .' Rachel touched Jeannie's shoulder. 'I'm sorry, Jeannie. He's painfully to the point. Like his dad.'

'And you,' muttered Fergus.

'It's OK,' said Jeannie. If Connor's mum had seen it, then everyone had seen it. And everyone would be talking about it if it was in the paper. It was just something she'd have to get used to. 'The good news is Dan's stable and everyone's really positive.'

'That's great,' said Rachel, still flustered. 'Do you have anything more cheerful to share, Fergus?'

'Dad says some loony is poisoning cats with antifreeze in Hartley,' he replied, and reached for the butter dish.

'Why don't you eat your supper upstairs?' Rachel gave Jeannie a mortified glance. 'I'm so sorry,' she said. 'Welcome to Longhampton.'

Chapter Six

Rachel drove Jeannie to the station the next morning, and when she arrived at the ICU just after ten, the scene was exactly the same as she'd left it.

Dan lay in the bed, his face partially obscured by the tubes and drips, while the forest of machines pulsed around him. The Get Well cards on the side table had doubled overnight, and now threatened to spill over in a glittery heap of positivity.

Who were Adam and Erin? Jeannie wondered, reading the nearest. Or Lydia, Larry, Oliver and Phoebe? They called Dan Danny, which suggested they were family friends, not university mates. Andrea would tell her. It would be something she could ask her later.

She sat down on the chair nearest the bed, and cautiously stroked his neck with the back of her finger. Kate had said it was fine to hold his hand, to let him know she was there, but there was so much delicate machinery detecting every minute variation in Dan's condition, that Jeannie was terrified of disrupting the vital sensor monitoring the pressure on his brain.

'Hello, Dan,' she said softly. 'It's me. How're you feeling?'

She held her breath, simultaneously scared and hopeful that Dan's eyes might flicker open at the sound of her voice. But there was no response. Not even a variation in the monitors.

'Kate said that music might help you while you're asleep,' she went on, 'so I've made some playlists of our favourite songs. Something to listen to, instead of me droning on the whole time. Bet you're sick of people chatting, aren't you? When you can't join in? Must be driving you mad!'

He didn't respond. Obviously.

'This one is to remind you of that weekend we had in Rome. Our first holiday away together.' Jeannie waved her phone in Dan's direction, just in case some miracle had occurred and he could now see through his closed eyelids. 'Do you remember? Walking round the Vatican Museums, and that room full of animal statues? You said the dogs looked like they had Addison's disease, and that French lady told you to shut up.' She paused. 'And then she asked you what Addison's disease looked like and it turned out her dog had it. Do you remember? She ended up being quite nice in the end . . .'

Jeannie paused. She was waiting for Dan to jump in with his own favourite bits of that weekend away, which were the guided Roman food tour around the Trastevere with a family of Canadians and two nuns from Dublin, and the bar they'd found down a side street where they'd people-watched till way past two in the morning. Dan attracted interesting people like a magnet, and he made Jeannie feel as if she was one too; it sounded corny but that was something she'd never really felt before.

They'd been happy in Rome, Jeannie knew that for certain. Dating, falling in love, exploring each other as if they were tourists in each other's hearts – these were happy memories and she clung to them.

She turned the volume right down, so as not to disturb the other patients, and tucked the phone close to Dan's ear. The first track on it was 'Perfect' by Ed Sheeran and the opening notes made her chest cave in with nostalgia for a moment that already felt another lifetime ago.

Jeannie closed her own eyes and listened. Music was an anchor for her, fixing a moment in her heart so she could always return to it, no matter how many years and tides of emotion swept over it later. The exact falling-in-love sensation that had filled her head that weekend rushed back over her now. She and Dan must have heard 'Perfect' five or six times, busked in several different languages, until it became a running joke – which language would they hear it in next? The long weekend came back in flashes: the Airbnb near the Pantheon with the shuttered windows and the linen sheets, the tingling, shivering energy in their fingertips and lips, the excuses to take selfies in front of landmarks – and underneath, her bewildered joy at knowing Dan felt exactly the same as she did. They were flying, flying through every second towards a future that was suddenly more than Jeannie had ever imagined. Brighter coloured, intensely romantic. A love she'd been waiting her whole life to find; a love that Edith had scornfully told her didn't exist in reality.

The memory was so exquisitely painful that Jeannie reached to stop the song, but she told herself she needed to feel this, and *Dan* needed to feel this, and she let the kisses, the Aperol spritzes, the smell of the city night stream through her mind on the melody.

Jeannie gazed at his beautiful sleeping face, and wondered if the same memories were firing behind Dan's eyelids. She'd only had a handful of chances to watch Dan sleeping, and one of those times had been in Rome. She'd lain on her side, watching the morning light pass across his smooth skin, thinking he looked like one of the marble sculptures in the Vatican Museums. Was this music pulling him back, leading him to consciousness like a rope in murky water?

'How we doing in here?' Kate put her head round the curtain. 'Ah, great idea, some music. Did you see Andrea on your way in? She's popped out for a tea.'

Jeannie shook her head, and turned down the volume until it vanished. She wasn't sure she wanted to share the music with Andrea. It felt too personal. 'No change overnight?'

'No, but he's stable. Recovering in his own time. You know what some people are like. Eh, Dan?' Kate quickly checked Dan's unresponsive pupils with her tiny torch, a clinical detail Jeannie still had to turn away from. 'Could you be a love and pass me that clipboard?'

Jeannie reached over to get it, and spotted a pile of papers hidden underneath: they were internet stories about miracle recoveries – patients who'd been in horrific accidents and lain in comas for months, then woken up absolutely fine, apart from a new Welsh accent or the ability to smell apples from twenty miles away. Loads of them, from all over the world, with the same end result: 'We thought we'd lost Brad/Maureen/Rajeev/Dad, and the doctors said they'd done everything they could but one morning s/he was sitting up in bed right as rain/talking Spanish/asking about the Test match.'

Jeannie felt uncomfortable. Andrea had been collecting evidence of miracles while she'd been googling long-term damage from head injuries. She wanted to share Andrea's optimism, but her own mother's long road to recovery had taught their whole family that it was better to hope for the best but prepare for the worst. It made the smallest improvements feel like triumphs.

'Does this happen?' she asked the nurse, showing her the printouts. 'Is there a chance that . . . Dan might wake up as if nothing had happened?'

Kate stopped filling in Dan's notes, and considered her response carefully. 'It does happen, but it's rare, especially if the patient's been in a coma for more than a few days. Which isn't to say impossible, of course!' She gave Jeannie a bright smile. 'Dan's showing positive signs. Let's keep focused on that.'

She left, and Jeannie turned the music back up on the phone, wanting to fit in one more song before Andrea came back. It was 'Ho Hey' by the Lumineers. Again her heart plunged: the lyrics somehow said everything she felt about that few months of falling in love, realising that the real life she'd been waiting for was finally here, with Dan. She'd been so happy. They'd both been so happy.

So when did it go wrong? Jeannie gazed helplessly down at Dan. Where had that magic gone?

Andrea appeared at the ICU door, carrying a cup of tea and a magazine, and waved at her.

A penny dropped in Jeannie's head. It was when I started reading wedding magazines, she thought. When we started wedding planning. That was when Dan and I stopped asking each other real questions, because it seemed a bit too embarrassing to ask your *fiancé* whether he believed in heaven, or what his favourite season was. Instead we just talked about chicken vs salmon, and first dances.

The day Dan proposed was the day they stopped learning about each other. Five months after they'd met.

Jeannie's mind raced as Andrea tiptoed down the ward, mouthing her hellos.

But now she had a chance to put that right. There was time to talk to Andrea, to talk to Owen, to think of every question she wanted to ask Dan, and herself. *They* could answer them. She could fill in the blank spaces in her heart before he woke up, and maybe that suffocating panic at the thought of marriage to a man she didn't think she knew would go away, and they could start again.

Jeannie reached for the phone under Dan's ear, carefully slid it back into her bag and leaned over to pick up the Get Well cards from the table.

'Hello, Andrea!' she said, smiling as his mother approached. 'So tell me – who are Adam and Erin?'

And from the delighted expression on Andrea's face, she couldn't have asked a more welcome question. There wasn't anything in the world that Andrea liked more than talking about her Danny.

Jeannie bought some sweet-scented spray roses from the flower stall at the station before she caught the bus back home. She wanted to give Rachel something to say thanks for letting her use about a fiver's worth of really expensive bath oil – and for the six hours' blissful sleep she'd had afterwards.

The bus stopped just outside the sign for Four Oaks

Kennels and when Jeannie wandered into the yard, she saw Rachel standing by a Land Rover, talking to a much shorter grey-haired woman in a red fleece. Rachel was clearly upset about something, and the other woman kept rubbing her arm, trying to calm her down.

As Jeannie got nearer she could hear a faint howling coming from the back of the Land Rover. It was a sharp, fearful sound that ran through her and set tears rising in her throat.

Rachel swept her hands through her dark hair, making the silver strands sparkle in the sun; her face was blotchy with angry tears. 'What is *wrong* with people?' she was saying. 'I just don't understand how a human being can be so cruel.'

'That's why the police were there. Not to nick that sod, to stop me doing what I'd like to do to him.' The other woman's expression was fierce. 'But come on, we've got them out, he's down at the station, and this is a new start. Let's get them washed and fed, and things'll feel better.'

'Rachel? Rachel!' Jeannie hurried over the yard. 'Is everything all right?'

Rachel spun round, trying to make her expression normal. 'Oh, hi, Jeannie. This is Debbie – Debbie, Jeannie, Jeannie, Debbie – she's a rescue co-ordinator. We've just come from a farm near the border that the police have raided with the council.'

'What kind of farm?'

'Unlicensed puppy farm. I've got a boot full of puppies and their mums.' Debbie nodded towards the Land Rover. 'We brought what we could fit in the crates. There's another load gone over to the pound at Much Harlowe.

85

One of our other vets came out with us, and he said it was one of the worst cases he'd seen in years. He had to put down a couple of the dogs there.'

'What?' Jeannie was horrified.

Rachel shook her head, pressing her lips together. 'It was awful, Jeannie. Filthy. Debbie's brought rescue litters here before but it's the first time I've actually seen it for myself. If you saw what this man was promising on his website, then saw where the puppies he was selling actually were . . .'

'He'll get what's coming to him,' said Debbie shortly.

'So . . . what can I do?' Jeannie wanted to hug Rachel; she looked so distraught. 'How can I help?'

'Oh no – no, you've got *more* than enough to worry about.' Rachel turned to Debbie. 'Jeannie's boyfriend is our new vet, Dan – he's been in an accident, he's in hospital—'

Jeannie interrupted her. 'And that's exactly why I'm offering – I need something to take my mind off the fact that I can't do a thing to help *him* right now.' She turned to Debbie. 'What can I do? It sounds like you could do with an extra pair of hands.'

'Well, we've got about twenty dogs in there, and they need to be washed, dried and fed,' she said briskly. 'We can worry about shots and things later.'

'Where will they go? Is there room here?' Jeannie had sudden visions of Rachel commandeering the cottage for overflow dog accommodation. Was that part of the tenancy deal for vet partners?

Rachel pulled herself together. Her strong jaw re-asserted itself, and Jeannie caught a flash of the stern older woman in the photos on the Fenwicks' staircase.

'We'll make room. We're full, technically, but we always manage.'

'Good girl.' Debbie patted her approvingly, as if she were a big dog. 'I don't know what we'd do without you. She's been an amazing help to us, has Rachel,' she added to Jeannie. 'Rehomed hundreds of dogs since she took over here. She's a star.'

The whining was getting louder. 'I should have been doing more. *So* much more.' Rachel stared at the ground, then shook herself. 'I just had no idea . . . Come on, I need to be doing something to take my mind off things too.'

The dogs that came out of the back of the Land Rover were like no dogs Jeannie had ever seen before. All she could make out were dull, terrified eyes in a mass of filthy, greasy hair.

There were three crates full of smelly dogs, some big but mostly very small. They stank of undigested food and urine and fear. The mothers – breeding machines, Debbie told her bluntly – were scrawny and scared, as if they'd barely seen humans before, and those they'd seen had given them good reason to cower. The puppies had been given spray-painted dots by the vet, to identify them in litters. When Debbie and Rachel tried to lift the wriggling puppies, the mothers howled and tried their best to stop them moving the pups, but they were weak and jumping with fleas themselves. There was a tiger-striped, broad-headed Staffordshire bull terrier, a bedraggled poodle, and a Border collie that was a mass of hip bones and knots.

Rachel dealt with the dogs gently but efficiently, but

when the collie came out, Jeannie noticed her shoulders sag. She reached in to touch the dog's matted coat with a tender hand, even gentler than before, then crouched down to whisper in her twitching ear.

'We'll do them one batch at a time, starting with the Staffies,' said Debbie, opening up a shed opposite the kennels that Rachel used for washing dogs. 'Make sure Mum can see them, otherwise she'll be climbing out of this sink.'

They held the squirming Staffie in the deep Belfast sink and washed the filth off her with warm water while the puppies wriggled in a laundry basket lined with newspaper. She trembled under their touch, her tail held submissively underneath her saggy teats. Debbie thought she'd only just stopped feeding; the pups were probably about four weeks old but 'the vet'll have to check for us, because they're not what they should be.' Jeannie stroked the Staffie's head and murmured as comfortingly as she could while Rachel washed her skinny body and cleaned out her stinking ears; the dog never took her liquid brown eyes off the basket the whole time, even when Rachel carefully checked her over for injuries.

'Jeannie, can you go into the office and bring out whatever recovery diet we've got in there?' Rachel fished around in her back pocket for the key. 'She needs feeding up, poor girl.'

'Recovery diet?' Jeannie felt out of her depth. 'Will it be marked?'

'Um, yes. It's in the food cupboard; George gave us some damaged stock from the rep. And some bowls? If there's none I'll go up to the surgery and get it myself. This is an emergency.'

'No problem.' Jeannie was glad to see Rachel recovering her energy, and she was even gladder to get out of the grooming room. It wasn't so much the stench of the unwashed dogs as the fear in the bitch's eyes, and the thought of what she and her pups must have suffered to be so terrified of human contact. Her submission was more heartbreaking to see than any aggression.

When Jeannie came back, piles of supplies stacked up in her arms, the air smelled fresher, of hot water and medicated shampoo. Rachel and Debbie had finished drying the dog and put her in a metal crate while they cleaned up the puppies in the sink, two at a time.

'Good girl,' said Rachel, and Jeannie wasn't sure whether she was talking to her or the dog. 'Jeannie, can you put some food out for her? We'll let her eat in here, so she can see the pups.'

Jeannie forked the tinned food into the bowl and put it down, and the Staffie nearly exploded out of the crate to get it. She ate quickly, glancing side to side, as if the bowl might be taken away at any moment, but kept looking over to the sink where her pups were.

'Poor little girl, don't you even have a name?' said Jeannie. Even Debbie, who had a compassionate toughness about her, was blinking against angry tears in her eyes.

'How old, did the vet reckon?' Rachel asked.

Debbie rubbed her cropped silvery hair. 'Not two. And this isn't her first litter, by any stretch. A baby herself.'

The horror of that sank in, and they stood without speaking, watching the dog lick the bowl clean, shunting it round the stone flags to get every scrap.

'Well, she's safe now,' said Rachel. 'This is where her life starts properly. And her name is Sadie.'

'Lady Sadie,' said Jeannie. Because she looked like one.

In an hour, Jeannie and Debbie had bathed all the puppies, while Rachel cleaned up the shivering collie mother, carefully snipping out the knots that were too tangled to comb. She murmured softly the whole time until Jeannie thought she saw the dog start to lean into Rachel's side, very, very cautiously. Or maybe she just hoped she was.

They moved the families into makeshift kennels: the Staffies into towel-lined crates in the office, the collies nearby in the grooming room and the poodles in a quiet boarded-off corner in the main kennel. There were twenty dogs altogether, less than a third of the dogs the council had seized from the breeder. Luckily, Freda and Ted, the volunteers who'd been out walking the other rescue dogs, had returned, and were dealing with the poodle's matted coat, since they 'knew poodles'. Freda was bathing the puppies as best she could, but Ted was proving to be a dab hand with the scissors, gently removing the worst of the knots so the mother could be washed.

'What are you going to do with them?' Jeannie asked as Rachel filled in some paperwork in the office. 'Will you rehome them?'

'It's not always that straightforward.' Rachel chewed her lip and ticked some more boxes. 'We've had breeding bitches dumped on us before, and the poor things . . . they've always got issues. No socialisation, petrified of men, no idea about leads, some with physical problems from lying in a stone shed their whole lives . . .'

The crate full of Staffie puppies in front of them was a squeaking mass of pot-bellied cuteness, with their mum watching over them from the relative peace of an adjoining cage. With another small meal inside her, Lady Sadie still seemed exhausted.

'Won't it be easier, finding homes for puppies?' Jeannie asked.

'Absolutely, yes, people always want puppies.' Rachel laughed hollowly. 'They'll recover quickly enough but they'll need supervision and socialisation and worming and proper food until they're ready to go to new homes. The mums will need spaying, and feeding, and George will need to check them over to make sure there are no bigger problems . . .' She sighed and jabbed the biro against the side of her head in frustration. 'It's expensive. We're always running at a loss. But what can you do? I'd never turn them away. I'll just have to beg George for another favour.'

'It's great that he's so supportive,' said Jeannie. 'Dan told me that part of his job would be volunteering a few hours a week here – and you know I'm happy to volunteer too.'

'Yes, George's always been incredibly good to us.' Rachel sighed. 'But . . .' She stopped.

'But what?'

'Nothing.' Rachel frowned at her laptop, then tutted at herself. 'George is a saint, he's been bailing out Four Oaks Dog Rescue since before my time, God bless his grumpy soul. It's *my* fault we're always needing bailing out. But we'll find a way to manage.' She looked up. 'I guess that's the thing about marriage – it's for better, for worse. And, in our case, Four Oaks.'

Chapter Seven

Two things were getting Jeannie through the slow days by Dan's bedside: unlimited chocolate sent from her parents, and Owen's steady wrangling of the information snowstorm that swirled around them.

The latest example of Owen turning chaos into neatly cross-hatched data was the spreadsheet he'd WhatsApped her, putting their visiting duties on a rota.

I know, I'm a boring office nerd . . . he'd added, self-consciously.

> *But Andrea keeps texting me in a flap that Dan will wake up with no one there, so this is to set her mind at rest. Obviously you can be there all day long if you want, but the nurses told me, on the quiet, that Dan needs a bit of space too. Don't want him to get earache on top of everything else!*

They had a Dan WhatsApp group chat with Andrea but Owen had sent her this privately. Jeannie knew why: Andrea didn't respond well to anything she considered 'negative' news, and it was sometimes hard to have a straightforward conversation about Dan's daily progress with the nurses. Jeannie sensed Owen needed to know the truth, whatever it was, and despite her normal squeamishness, she realised she felt the same.

Andrea wasn't 'due' in until the afternoon, according to Owen's rota, but when Jeannie arrived the next morning, just after the ward round, she was already there holding Dan's hand. Her face lit up when she saw Jeannie approaching.

'Danny, Jeannie's here!' she said. 'Ooh, what have you got there?'

As Jeannie had left the house, she'd grabbed a few framed family photos from a packing box in the sitting room, one Dan hadn't yet unpacked: Mr Allcott had suggested bringing in photographs to talk about, in case Dan could hear them, and since Jeannie barely knew Dan's family she thought it'd be a good way of filling in some blanks herself.

Andrea was more than happy to talk about the first: a silver-framed picture of her and a teenage Dan in matching tennis whites. 'Oh, I remember this! Danny and I were a great doubles team – so sweet of him to play with his old mum!' she said, then admitted, when Jeannie pressed her, that she'd been a county player herself in her youth. It wasn't a surprise to hear Dan was a tennis prodigy; Jeannie was more interested in Andrea's modest revelations about her own youthful successes. The stories tumbled out as if she hadn't thought about them for years.

'The funny thing is, I was always much better at doubles than singles,' she concluded wistfully. 'Do you play?'

Jeannie shook her head.

'We must teach you!'

They both gazed at the photograph. Dan had been a cute teenager, she thought, a bit like a young Prince William: longish blond hair flopping into his eyes as he squinted in the sunshine, golden skin, long athletic legs.

He wasn't smiling; Andrea was, though – under her white Chris Evert sweatband, her heart-shaped face was bright with pride, and also with the light glinting off the massive trophy they'd just won.

'Tennis captain for his school *and* captain of the cricket team,' Andrea added. She glanced down at Dan's sleeping form, dropping her voice as if she was afraid he might hear. 'He had to board, after Malcolm and I separated and I . . . I had to move away. Danny had such lovely friends there, like darling Owen, so I knew he was happy. But I missed him. Malcolm would have sent him at eight but it was the one thing I put my foot down about.'

Jeannie snapped to attention. Dan never talked about his dad. All she knew about Malcolm Hicks was that he'd made a stack of money in property, and then he'd walked out on Andrea and emigrated to Canada to start a new family when Dan was still at school. The one time she'd asked, early on, he'd told her the bare facts, then said, 'I try not to think about Dad,' and changed the subject. He didn't seem sad, though; his jaw had tensed.

But Andrea had introduced the topic of her own accord, and Jeannie wondered if maybe she'd had the same middle-of-the-night thought she'd had: if Dan was seriously, life-changingly injured, surely his father would want to know? Should they tell him? Dan hadn't wanted to tell him about the wedding, but this . . .

'This is fun! What else did you bring?' Andrea asked brightly, and Jeannie handed her the next photograph. She flinched as Andrea's forehead wrinkled instantly: it was Dan and his dad.

'Sorry, I just grabbed a few from the top of Dan's sitting-room box,' she said. 'I didn't really look . . .'

'I didn't know Danny had this.'

It was taken on the sandstone steps of a school building. Malcolm Hicks, tall and smart in a pinstripe suit and panama hat, was standing with his hand on a younger Dan's shoulder, looking straight into the camera with a charming half-smile. Dan had his mother's pale blonde hair, but the deep blue eyes and dark brows were his father's. So, by the looks of things, was his easy confidence.

The lightness had drained from Andrea's expression, tightening the lines around her throat. 'Speech day,' she said, smiling with an effort.

Jeannie was painfully aware that she didn't really know her mother-in-law very well at all. It was awkward without Dan there to help them along.

'I'm so sorry, Andrea,' she said, and reached to take it back. 'It was just in a box. I don't even know if Dan had it out anywhere . . .'

'Malcolm was not a good man,' said Andrea, measuring the words with care. 'But Danny won three prizes that day and his father was very proud. That's why Danny kept the photograph, I should think. Malcolm walked out on us about a week after that was taken.'

Oh God. Jeannie kicked herself inwardly. But this was the minefield she was tiptoeing through: she didn't know Dan well enough to start opening his packing boxes without him there, let alone handle his mother.

She braced herself. 'Does Malcolm know about . . . ?'

'No! No, he doesn't. It's the last thing Danny would want, his father turning up here to bully the nurses. Or worse.' Andrea laid a hand on her throat and Jeannie saw a scared, smaller woman appear in her face. 'I'm sorry,

Jeannie, I'm afraid even talking about that man makes me feel . . .'

'Are you all right?' Andrea seemed to be hyperventilating. 'Do you want me to get Kate?'

'I'm fine, sweetie. Fine. I always say that man gave me a wonderful son and several anxiety-related medical conditions,' said Andrea. She didn't look fine, though. 'Do you have any pictures of you two there? Danny sent me a lovely one of the day you got engaged . . .'

She was as good at changing the subject as Dan was. Reluctantly, Jeannie looked in the bag but the third photograph she'd grabbed was of Dan's university football team. 'Oh. No. But I have some on my phone?'

'Show me, please!' Andrea leaned over. 'And I want to see some of this pop group of yours! Danny's so hopeless with details; I need to hear more about it. Ooh, is that you? What fabulous glitter! Is it in fashion again?'

Jeannie felt a sudden warmth towards her almost-mother-in-law. Andrea seemed so keen to talk, to tell stories and hear them. They were only halfway through the New York selfies – Andrea needed to know *all* the details – when a familiar step came clicking down the ward towards them, followed by more feet behind.

'Ah, I'm glad I've found you two here! Is this a good time to have a word?'

Their heads snapped up as Mr Allcott appeared at the foot of Dan's bed, followed by Nurse Kate. Kate had a sheaf of leaflets on top of her usual clipboard and Jeannie's heart rate stepped up a notch. What was the consultant here to tell them?

'Hello! We were just chatting,' she said, putting her phone in her bag. 'Well, Andrea and I were.'

'Ha, ha! Very good.'

'Have you got news?' Andrea asked straight away. 'Are you ready to bring Dan round?'

'Yes, and no, I'm afraid.' Mr Allcott settled himself in the chair on the other side. 'I've had a meeting this morning with the other members of Dan's medical team, and I wanted to update you on what we've discussed.'

Jeannie's stomach tensed, and she reached for the notebook on the table.

'As you rightly remember, Andrea, we spoke early on about trying to bring Dan round if he didn't regain consciousness independently,' the consultant began, and Andrea leaned forward, only to slump back when he added, 'but after some exploratory tests we've decided to put that on hold for a little longer.'

'Oh.' She looked bereft.

'Why?' asked Jeannie.

Mr Allcott began to outline the complex reasons: possibility of blood clots, pressure on his brain, technical terms that made sense while he explained them but which Jeannie knew she'd have to look up again in the café later. It was surreal, having this conversation over Dan's motionless body, she thought. She and Andrea on one side, the consultant on the other, Dan in the middle. His future – *their* future – under discussion.

'. . . so, is there anything else I can tell you while I'm here?' he finished.

'I have a question,' said Andrea.

'Fire away.'

'Will he . . . will Danny recognise us when he wakes up?' Her wide eyes pleaded for reassurance.

'Patients often lose short-term memory following head

trauma – it's to do with the different areas of the brain where long- and short-term memory are stored. But longer-term, *repeated* memory's much harder to wipe, and we haven't detected any damage to that part of Daniel's brain, so . . . I'd say it's more than likely he'll know you two, but he might have little recollection of the days leading up to the accident.' Mr Allcott turned to Jeannie. 'I'm afraid he probably won't remember much about your wedding day, but at least the dress will still be a surprise!'

What? Jeannie blinked: she'd managed to put the wedding out of her mind for a few hours.

Andrea grabbed her hand, squeezing it so tight she could feel Andrea's rings cutting into her skin. 'I can't lie, it's not what we wanted to hear, but as long as Danny's recovering I suppose we just have to be patient.'

'We're still very positive about his recovery, Mrs Hicks. As soon as we have anything to tell you, I promise you we will.' Mr Allcott checked his watch, then slapped his knees and got up. 'I'm sorry to run in and out but I'm due in theatre – another RTI, unfortunately. I know it's a lot to take in, but if you've got any more questions, jot them down and let Kate know.'

Jeannie was watching Kate's expression and she detected a more guarded reaction in the nurse's eyes.

Jeannie rang Owen with the update on the train home. He was, as she'd expected, pleased but wary.

'Sounds like they're doing all they can,' he said over the beeping sound of lorries reversing. 'I hope he's blanked out his stag night when he comes round. Lucky him – wish I could . . .'

Jeannie fidgeted with her coffee cup. The consultant's comment about her wedding dress had set off a niggling chain of doubts about Dan's memory loss. How much would he remember about the wedding day? Would he remember her messages? Might he blurt out her shameful secret in front of Andrea – and Owen? Surely he wouldn't. Surely that was exactly the immediate memory that would be lost.

Stop thinking about yourself. Worry about Dan.

Owen was talking again. 'What are you up to tonight?'

'I'm going to get on with unpacking. The house is still full of boxes.' Jeannie didn't want to, but she was running out of clothes. She'd imagined herself and Dan unpacking together, in a montage of amusing 'I never knew you had one of those!' moments, set to a Belle and Sebastian soundtrack. Huge pepper grinders, comedy sombreros, roller skates. That sort of thing. It felt wrong to do it alone. Especially Dan's boxes: it felt intrusive, somehow. 'I thought maybe I could bring some of Dan's things in? You know, familiar clothing, more photographs to talk about. I'd love it if you could explain who all these people are in his school photos . . .'

Owen didn't reply. Jeannie wondered if the lorries had reversed over him.

'Owen?'

'Yeah, um. Maybe leave that, till he's back?'

'How do you mean?'

'Well, better to focus on the future, you and him. You don't want to spend your time off going through Dan's junk – what about taking in a wedding present? Talking to him about that?'

'I don't think he's going to be brought out of a coma by

a *saucepan set*.' She frowned. Owen's tone was definitely strange. 'Owen?'

'Oh, nothing, forget it.' The lorries were beeping again. 'Listen, I've got to go, I'll speak to you tomorrow.' And he was cut off. Or run over.

Jeannie looked at the phone, confused. Owen seemed like a sensitive bloke; maybe he'd sensed her reluctance to start delving into Dan's private boxes. Maybe he was right.

But why did he feel the need to say so?

Jeannie told herself that it was her duty as a tenant and sort-of-employee to update the Fenwicks on Dan's condition, but the truth was that she wanted to see how the puppies were getting on. Helping Rachel had given her a rare few hours of feeling useful, and she didn't mind offering her time when Rachel had been so kind to her already.

She was turning the corner leading up to the kennels when the sound of raised voices stopped her in her tracks. The tone wasn't that of a light chat, either. Jeannie hung back, to give whoever it was time to finish, then realised that the female voice was Rachel's.

'. . . what was I supposed to do?' She sounded more furious than distressed. 'You saw the state they were in!'

'I'm not saying you should have turned them away, just that you can't assume we can pay for it all! The rescue can't keep running at a loss, Rachel. You *know* how tight things are this month – not just this month, for the last *six* months. And we'll have to find another locum to cover for Dan . . .'

'Won't the insurance cover that?'

'Sometimes I find it hard to believe you ever worked in a business environment. No, it won't.'

'Well, it should! It was an accident! And, anyway, that's only money – it's nowhere near as bad for us as it is for Jeannie. I can't imagine what she's going through. Can you?'

'I'm not equating the two things. I'm just saying I can't magic up a couple of thousand quid like . . . that.' A snap of the fingers. 'For twenty dogs. *Twenty*, Rachel.'

'Oh, don't do your finger-snapping thing, George. You know it goes straight through me . . .'

There was a volley of snapping.

Jeannie felt bad for eavesdropping but in a way, she was glad she'd overheard that because Rachel and George were far too polite to be honest to her face. Of course Dan's accident had affected the business. And she was living in the cottage, not paying rent . . .

'It's just the inoculations and the spaying,' Rachel was saying, and it sounded as if this conversation was into its fourth or fifth round.

'Just. *Just*. No. You used to do great fundraisers – you can do another.'

'George . . .'

'Don't *George* me. I'm not in the mood, Rachel.'

Jeannie strained her ears to hear Rachel's response but they'd moved away. As she was leaning round, but not so far that she could be seen, she felt something cold touch her arm and she jumped back with a squeak.

Rachel's collie was standing behind her. Jeannie blinked at him in shock. How the hell had Gem got there without her noticing? He stood motionless, fixing her with his strange pale blue eyes.

'Gem? Gem? Where've you gone?'

Jeannie didn't want Rachel to walk down the path and realise she'd been listening in, so she scrambled to her feet and walked around the corner. The dog followed her, silently herding her towards the house.

Rachel was coming the other way, striding so fast she nearly bumped into Jeannie.

'Ah, Jeannie!' A clutch of silver bangles jangled down her wrist as she pushed her hair off her face. Rachel didn't look herself: her eyes were disappointed, and her nose seemed even sterner. 'Everything all right?'

'Yes, I was just . . .' Jeannie's gaze drifted to the solid form of a man in a checked shirt, striding just as fast as Rachel but in the opposite direction. George. She could see now where Fergus got his height from. In a few cross movements, George reached the house, bleeped open the 4 × 4 parked outside, threw in his bag and drove off in a flurry of stone chippings.

'I never met a man who drove crossly till I met George,' Rachel observed. 'He gets through tyres like nobody's business. I'm guessing you heard our frank exchange of opinions? Sorry about that. We try to take our arguments away from the dogs. They don't like raised voices.'

'I wasn't eavesdropping.'

Rachel shook her head and motioned for Jeannie to follow her back to the kennels. 'To be fair, it wasn't really an argument. More a lecture.' She pushed open the door to the kitchen area where the Staffie pups were wide awake and squirming over each other in their crate. 'He's put his foot down about these dogs. Says I've got to stop treating him like a piggy bank and get off my arse and raise some money – for a change. Ha! As if,' she muttered to herself. 'Living in my house . . .'

'Is there something I can help with?'

'Oh, probably.' Rachel got two mugs out of the cupboard and flicked on the kettle. 'I mean, it's not as if we *don't* fundraise. We've got a charity shop in town, and George is conveniently forgetting that we *did* have a dog show this spring. We raised enough for the annual spaying budget. But costs have gone up a lot this year, and this is the summer for the town's carnival so it's not going to be easy to do something at short notice. People are committed. We need the money now.' She stared down at the puppies and her face darkened.

'Are you all right?' asked Jeannie. 'It must have been horrible, what you saw.'

Rachel let out a breath and shrugged. 'I can't forget it. It makes me want to do so much more.'

Jeannie crouched by the crate to let the puppies sniff her fingers. Gem was stationed at the door, far away from the puppies but clearly watching over them while the mother dozed nearby. When Jeannie reached towards them, he stiffened as if he could sense her movement in the air.

The kettle boiled and Rachel reached for the tea caddy. 'Have I told you the Gem story?' she asked in a more upbeat tone.

'No.'

'He was Auntie Dot's own dog. She left Gem to me along with the house and the rescue. Some dog walkers found him as a puppy, left to freeze in a bag with the rest of his litter. They brought them up here to Dot, the crazy dog lady, and she nursed them by her Aga. She chose Gem for herself – or he chose her, whichever – and Gem looked after Dot until she died. When I came here a decade ago, feeling about as lost and unwanted as he'd been, Gem looked after me. I think Dot told him to.'

Jeannie looked up, surprised by the unexpected rawness in Rachel's voice.

'I wasn't in a good place,' Rachel admitted. 'But that's for another time.'

'How old is he now?'

'Seventeen! George says he's the oldest collie he has ever known. I don't know what I'd do without him. But I'm going to have to start thinking about that soon. And I really don't want to.'

Rachel's shoulders slumped; then she pulled herself together. 'When I first came here, I thought Dot was ancient and a bit tragic, but I'll be fifty soon and look at me!' She gestured in horror towards her dungarees as if she'd only just realised what she was wearing. 'I look like Tinky Winky's grandma! And I didn't even know who Tinky Winky was till I moved here. I had a subscription to *Vogue*. I had standards. I had *highlights* . . .'

She suddenly stopped, widening her eyes. 'Oh God, shut up, Rachel. What am I wittering on about? What news of Dan? Is he ready for visitors? Although I'm not sure seeing his boss by the bedside would get anyone better, especially not in George's current mood . . .'

Jeannie shook her head. She'd have preferred to carry on hearing about this mad aunt or why Rachel had been in need of rescue herself, but she was getting self-conscious about how she 'should' be reacting to Dan's situation. Did people expect her to be devastated about the wedding – or not to care?

'Or,' said Rachel, seeing her awkwardness, 'we could just play with some puppies in the name of socialisation?'

'That'd be nice,' said Jeannie.

Rachel handed her the mug of tea. 'It's good for them,' she said. 'Good for all of us.'

Chapter Eight

When Jeannie called her parents with her daily Dan update, Sue responded with a wave of positivity so strong Jeannie could almost see the smile through the telephone line. She knew exactly how her mum's eyes would be crinkling up; she'd be nodding encouragingly, just as she'd nodded encouragingly about their exam results (up and down), and Angus's football team (useless), and Edie's Birdhouse's first tentative SoundCloud releases (brilliant, obviously). It was a running family joke: tell Mum some news – any news – and watch her start nodding like the Churchill dog.

Jeannie hoped her own voice sounded more positive than she felt.

'Hang in there, my darling.' Sue's voice was warm and comforting, like hot sweet tea. 'Dan could turn the corner any moment.'

'I know, Mum.' She got up and wandered round the kitchen, opening cupboards that she knew held nothing much, then closing them. She didn't want to eat anyway. She just couldn't bear to sit still in the empty house.

'How's Andrea coping?' Sue asked. 'Is she still sleeping in the hospital?'

'No, Owen found her an Airbnb not too far away. He's

been doing the evening visits this week – he lives down the road.'

'What a sweetheart that boy is. I'm so glad Dan's got good friends to look after you. How's *he* dealing with it all?'

'He's fine. I think. He's very organised.' Jeannie thought of the bedside notebook, the three different sets of handwriting recording Dan's surprisingly busy days. Andrea jotted down every twitch and 'smile'; Owen recorded medical details, the nurse's observations, new tests in a clear, helpful set of lists; Jeannie doodled.

'Is someone supporting *him*? A girlfriend?' Sue didn't beat about the bush.

'He hasn't mentioned anyone.'

'Well, maybe you should find out. Poor Owen. It's his best friend in that hospital bed too, don't forget. Men are terrible at asking for help. Thank goodness your father's never been one to hide his emotions . . .'

Jeannie made a non-committal noise. Owen didn't talk about himself much: she'd have remembered if he'd made any reference to a girlfriend. She closed the cupboard and opened the fridge instead. Empty, apart from two jars of marmalade and a lone can of Guinness, sitting slightly apart from each other, like unintroduced party guests.

'How about food?' Sue went on, as if she could see down the telephone line. 'Can I send you a supermarket delivery? Do you need a bit more money to tide you over?'

'Mum, I'm fine. People have been really kind. My doorstep's like some kind of harvest festival donation point – I've got two casseroles in the freezer already and so much jam.' Word had evidently got round the kennels about Rachel's tenants' bad luck, and her team of rescue volunteers had dropped off many edible gestures of sympathy.

'Well, I hope you're eating it. It's so important to take care of yourself, so you can take care of Daniel.' Sue paused. 'Are you making some time for your music?'

'When? If I'm not *at* the hospital, I'm going there, or coming back . . .'

'I'm not talking about putting on a show, just getting your guitar out and playing for ten minutes. You can't worry about Daniel round the clock. You *mustn't*. I know what I'm like when I can't get out to ride, I go a bit mad, and I know you're the same with your music, pet . . .'

Jeannie stared out of the kitchen window over the fields, glad Sue couldn't see her face. Her guitars and ukuleles were upstairs in the spare room, untouched. It wasn't because of Dan either: the truth was, since Edith's dramatic betrayal she'd felt blocked. Dan didn't really get it, but she didn't expect him to. She couldn't explain her complicated relationship with the music in her head either. Its sly disappearance hadn't mattered when they'd had the wedding occupying every spare moment, but now that she needed the release of playing, the thought of picking up a guitar and finding nothing scared her.

'. . . is there a village choir you can join? Or a singing-for-fun group?' Sue sounded like she'd made a list.

'Mum, can I ask you something?' Jeannie turned away from the window and braced herself to ask a question she didn't necessarily want to know the answer to. 'About . . . *your* accident?'

'Of course, darling. Anything.'

'Did you have any memory of what happened when you woke up?'

Sue laughed, then sighed. 'God, no. One minute I was riding across a field on Captain Jack, the next I was in a hospital bed. I thought I'd died. Everything was white like heaven, then I heard your dad crying, and I realised my leg was in plaster and I couldn't speak. Dad's idea of heaven, maybe! Why do you ask? Are you worried Dan will remember being hurt?'

'Sort of.'

Jeannie closed her eyes and let the worst fear form in her head. *I'm worried he'll remember I was going to jilt him, and I still can't give him a good reason why.*

She was horrified by her own selfishness. Her mind didn't feel like her own any more. Thoughts that absolutely shocked her kept popping up, making her bite her lips to keep them in.

Of course she wanted Dan to wake up, and to be fine. Of course she did. Just because she didn't want to *marry* him didn't mean she didn't love him. It didn't mean she didn't want him to be well, and happy and . . .

'Well, don't worry. The human brain's very clever. It'll have blotted that out,' Sue said, comfortingly. 'Things might come back, eventually, but it's a slow process. Don't think about that yet. Do you want a word with your dad? He's just outside doing the lawn.'

Dad. Suddenly Jeannie was back in the airless Rolls-Royce, and her throat closed up. Dad was bound to ask if he could share their awful secret with Mum, and she couldn't deal with that now. She just couldn't. If Dan couldn't remember, then she was prepared to blank it from her mind too. It had never happened. None of it.

'No, it's OK,' she said. 'Don't disturb him. Give him my love.'

'I will,' said Sue, and Jeannie felt a terrible yearning to be home, in the middle of their familiar love. 'We're always thinking of you. Now go and do something nice for yourself, all right?'

'Yes, Mum,' said Jeannie, and wondered if it was a good thing or a bad one that her mum could read her like a book.

Jeannie poured herself a glass of wine, and sat down to tackle the pile of post that had mounted up while she'd been at the hospital. Mum had told her side of the family what had happened, and nipped any attempts to 'help' in the bud – but there were several wedding cards containing cheques and gift vouchers from people whose names meant absolutely nothing to her. She felt like a trespasser in her own home: complete strangers wishing her and Dan happiness and love without having even met her. One card was even addressed to 'Dan and Jessica'.

Jeannie blinked back lonely tears. This wasn't her romantic dream; it didn't even feel like her *life*. Dan was lying in a hospital bed, maybe paralysed, maybe brain-damaged, and she was here, in a house she hadn't chosen, trying to make sense of a future she didn't understand.

And someone else was knocking at the back door. Again.

Jeannie hauled herself up and went to answer it. If it was another casserole, she'd have to come clean and tell them she was a part-time vegetarian.

A blonde woman was standing on the step, barely

holding on to the three terriers who were jumping up and down on top of each other with glee.

'Hope I'm not interrupting but I wanted to leave you these and introduce myself!' The woman thrust a Tupperware box at Jeannie and tugged the dogs back in line. 'I'm Natalie – I help out at the kennels. Hi!' She raised a hand attached to a lead which was attached to the smallest terrier, and waved it as far as she could without lifting the dog off the ground at the same time.

'Thank you,' said Jeannie.

'I was so sorry to hear about your . . .' Natalie hesitated on the word 'husband', then ploughed on. 'Dan's accident. If you ever need a lift down to the station, please give me a ring – I have a café in town and I'm often up here, especially now we've got all these puppies to deal with.'

Jeannie seized the chance to talk about something other than herself. 'Oh, I was just up there, playing with them!'

'Brilliant! The more people they meet, the better. Do you fancy coming back with me for half an hour, if you're not busy?' She nodded towards the big house. 'It's nearly suppertime, and Rachel's got a job on her hands stopping fights breaking out!'

'You know what,' said Jeannie, 'that'd be really . . .'

The phone started ringing in the hall. Was it Mum ringing back, or Dad wanting to talk to her? Or Andrea? Immediately the medical tang of the hospital swept back into her throat.

'Sorry, I should get that. It might be the hospital.'

'Of course.' Natalie tilted her head sympathetically. 'Look, we'll be there for a while if you want to wander up. And enjoy the biscuits. No dog hairs, I promise.

Come on, you lot!' She hauled the terriers away and set off up the lane.

Jeannie managed to grab the phone before it stopped ringing. 'Mum? What did you forget?'

But it wasn't her mother. The caller had hung up just as she answered. And when Jeannie checked to see who it had been, the number had been withheld.

She stared at the phone for a numb moment and waited to see if the caller had left a message. But there was no message, no number. And she was too relieved it wasn't the hospital to care more than that.

Sue's words popped back into Jeannie's mind when Owen unexpectedly turned up in the middle of her daytime visiting 'shift' the next day. She was in the shop buying yet more chocolate when his shaggy head appeared in the huge revolving door at the entrance, trapped in the middle of a slow-moving family of visitors. He was wearing his dark blue work suit, and although it was a bit tight around the thighs, his shirt was neatly ironed and his shoes were polished. Jeannie couldn't detect the presence of a female influence in Owen's outfit, although she guessed her mum would be able to.

'Hello,' she said when he finally made it into the foyer. 'Did the rota change? Wasn't expecting to see you during daylight hours.'

'I'm out tonight so I thought I'd drop in while I was passing,' he explained.

'Ooh, hot date?' said Jeannie and instantly kicked herself. *Why did you say that?*

Owen flushed. 'No, my niece's ballet-school concert. My sister's making the whole family turn up to support.

I've got a meeting with the accountants to get through first – not sure which I'm looking forward to more. Shall we go on up?' He gestured towards the stairs.

'Dan's with the doctors for another half hour, if you've got time to wait?'

He checked his watch. 'I have, just about. You find somewhere to sit and I'll grab us a coffee.'

Jeannie nodded, and sat down at a table while Owen went to the counter; he soon returned with two coffees and a slice of chocolate cake with two forks.

'I thought you could help me,' he explained, so dead-pan she didn't realise he was joking at first.

They chatted for a bit about the new tests the medical team were running, and the baby photos Andrea had brought in. Owen smiled as Jeannie talked, letting her ramble on, and she wondered if she was being boring. He was extremely easy to talk to, but today, unusually, he wasn't saying much.

'You've only eaten half this cake,' she pointed out. 'Are you feeling all right?'

Owen pressed some crumbs into his fork, then looked up at her. His brown eyes were wary. 'Jeannie, I'm sorry to ask you something that might bring back bad memories but . . . have you got Dan's phone?'

'No, I thought you had it.' Her heart gave a strange skip.

'I don't. One of the nurses gave me a bag with everything he was wearing when he was admitted but the phone wasn't there. I've got Dan's watch, and his wallet, his speech, his lucky panda – don't ask – and his signet ring, but no phone. I wondered if someone had given it to you.'

Jeannie put her fork down. There was something in the way Owen was asking that made it sound as if there was another question, hidden underneath the obvious one. 'I don't think I've ever seen it.'

'Your dad didn't pick it up?'

'Not as far as I know.'

'I wonder whether the ambulance crew took it?' He frowned. 'Surely they'd have handed it in when he was admitted. Or maybe the police picked it up, for evidence?'

'Does it matter where his phone is?' Jeannie snapped. The word *evidence* made the hairs prickle on the back of her arms. Owen's natural desire to impose order on chaos wasn't making her feel very reassured now.

He met her gaze. 'Well, it's going to have a lot of personal information on it, so yes, I think it'd matter who's got it. And he's going to want it back at some point.'

'I just . . .' Jeannie felt obliged to justify herself. Her passionate outburst floated on the air between them, like smoke after fireworks. 'I just . . . Knowing Dan was on the phone when the bus hit him – *that phone* is why he's in hospital now. I don't care if I never see it again, to be honest.'

Owen made a sympathetic noise but carried on looking at her as if he was weighing up his thoughts. His eyes bored straight into hers, and Jeannie felt a nervous dancing in the back of her chest.

Oh my God, what does he know?

'Well, that's what everyone says, isn't it?' The words were jittering out of her mouth, even as her brain was telling her to shut up. 'That he was on the phone, and didn't see the bus?'

'He was, yes. That's definite, I'm afraid.'

Jeannie's mind raced, trying to imagine that morning from Owen's point of view. *Moments before the wedding, Dan tells Owen he's got a missed call from Jeannie, that he needs to step outside to listen to the message . . .* Did Owen want the phone so he could find out what that message had been?

'So . . . it's fine if it's been lost.' Something else occurred to her. 'It'll be locked anyway. If someone finds it, they won't be able to open it. I don't even know Dan's passcode. So . . . let it go. I hope it's been run over.'

Owen blinked a couple of times, thoughtfully, then nodded. 'True,' he said. 'But if it turns up, just give it to me, eh?'

Their eyes met over the table, and this time Jeannie felt as if affable Owen was trying to break into *her* head. She fought to put up a glass screen in her mind, over the secret she didn't want anyone to know, least of all him.

'Why do *you* want it?' she said.

He took a second too long to answer. 'Because there are things I don't understand about Dan's accident that I think his phone might explain.'

A chill ran across Jeannie's skin, colder than the air conditioning outside the ICU.

'Like what?' she managed.

He shook his head, and stared down at the floor for an agonising moment. 'I'm not sure,' he admitted. 'I shouldn't have said anything. I'm sorry.'

'But you think . . .' She covered her mouth with her hands, unable to stop the words coming out.

Owen reached across the table, mistaking her reaction for distress. 'I'm sorry, Jeannie, I really didn't mean to upset you.'

They both looked down, at his hand touching her shoulder, and he pulled it back. 'Sorry, forget I said anything,' he went on quickly. 'There's something else I wanted to talk to you about, something I read on the coma support website.'

'Go on.' Jeannie's heart was still banging far too fast.

'We're talking to Dan as if he can hear us, which is great, but obviously it's hard trying to come up with conversation on your own. This site suggested getting friends and family to record their favourite memories to play to the patient – it quoted research that shows hearing familiar voices and stories increases neural activity, which might help Dan wake up sooner.'

'That's a great idea!'

Owen seemed relieved. 'Oh, good. I wasn't sure if you'd mind hearing boring stories – well, we don't think they're boring, obviously – from people you don't even know.'

'Why would I mind?' In fact, Jeannie was secretly pleased he'd suggested it; listening to Dan's friends recounting favourite anecdotes would give her a chance to fill in some of the uncomfortable blanks she had about his life before they met.

And then what? demanded a voice in her head. You'll fall in love again and stay? So you can commit to another wedding when he wakes up?

Tension clamped her temples like a tight band.

'Jeannie?'

She shook herself. 'Sorry. I'm so tired. No, I think it's a lovely idea. I've really enjoyed listening to Andrea's stories about Dan. I've got to know her so much better, as well as hearing a few things he's never told me.'

'Ha! I bet she told you the *Blue Peter* badge story, didn't she? I knew she would . . . It's helped *her* a lot too, having you there to listen,' said Owen. 'I honestly don't know how she'd have coped without you.'

'What? Me?' Jeannie felt awkward, taking any credit for Andrea's fragile state. 'I've barely done anything. You're the one who sorted out her hotel, and done the running around . . .'

'Just logistics. I do it all day at work. You're giving Andrea the emotional support she needs. It must be tough when you're going through hell yourself. She recognises that, you know. She's been singing your praises, telling everyone how patient you are, how sweet you are with Dan . . .'

'Has she?'

'She told me only yesterday that she thought Dan had done very well for himself.' Owen pretended to look stunned. 'You have no idea what high praise that is.'

He was trying to make Jeannie feel better, and she did for a second. But Andrea wouldn't like her so much if she knew what had nearly happened on the morning of the wedding. She dragged on a smile. 'Really?'

The cake was still half-eaten between them, and Owen had relaxed enough to start attacking the remainder with his fork. 'Absolutely! And that's not something I ever thought I'd hear her say, believe me.'

'Why? Did Andrea have a problem with Dan's previous girlfriends?' Jeannie was genuinely curious. Dan never talked about his exes, and had never asked about hers. There wasn't much to reveal on her side, anyway. Two uni boyfriends, a drummer called Ted who'd dumped her when he found out she was better than he

117

was, and an ill-starred fling with a 'cocktail curator' that Edith had written a song about. 'Martin the Martini Man.' It had a particularly spiteful – and catchy – chorus.

Now Owen was the one squirming in his seat. 'Ha! No. Well, I'm not sure whether I'm supposed to answer that. Ha! What's the right answer?'

'Was there anyone serious? I mean, I'm assuming there was. It's fine, you can tell me.' Her breath quickened, because she wasn't actually sure it *was* fine.

'Some . . . I don't know. If Dan hasn't talked about it, I'm not sure it's up to me.'

There was a hint of evasion in his voice. More than a hint. Jeannie tried to catch the ambiguity in Owen's expression before it changed but he smiled, and the gentle best friend was back. Gentle, and discreet.

'All that matters is you and Dan and the future,' he said firmly. 'Speaking of which, won't the doctors be finished with him by now?'

Jeannie nodded in agreement, and they made their way to the stairs. Owen was too loyal to spill any beans, but who knew what stories his other friends might have to tell?

Chapter Nine

Jeannie had just walked in through the front door that Friday night when Natalie knocked on the back door to see if she fancied some dinner – and if so, whether she wouldn't mind helping her and Rachel with their fund-raising brainstorm at the same time.

'We're trying to come up with some new ideas to help pay for the puppies' jabs and to sort out some issues with the mums,' she explained. 'George is out with Fergus at lads and dads cricket, and my other half's got a PTA meeting at school, so it's just us and a bottle of wine and some pizza. We could do with some fresh ideas. And I could do with someone new to break it to Rachel we can't do Longhampton's Got Talent again.'

'Why not?'

'Because despite what Mrs Rachel Fenwick might like to think,' said Natalie glumly, 'her Border collie *cannot* sing. And neither can she.'

The brainstorming was fun, especially when Rachel opened the second bottle of wine and Natalie started throwing out more and more random suggestions to raise cash. For every suggestion they wrote down as a possibility – auction of favours, karaoke, charity dog bath ('no one likes bathing their dog . . .'), charity nail clip ('*no one* likes doing nails . . .'), charity anal gland squeeze ('seriously . . .') – there were plenty more outrageous and downright weird ones that didn't make the cut.

'I'm not saying I don't want to *do* a nude dog-walker calendar,' said Rachel, waving her glass of wine in response to Natalie's suggestion. 'I'm just querying who is going to pay actual money to have Ted and Freda posing on their walls, with only an extending lead and a bag of liver sausage to protect their modesty?'

'I'd have one,' said Jeannie.

'I'd have two,' said Natalie. 'One for me, one just to see Johnny's mother's face when I gave her it for Christmas. There you go: there's three sold already.'

'You two are weird.' Rachel helped herself to another slice of pizza. 'I still say, what about a concert? Longhampton's Got Talent?'

'Please, Rachel . . .' Natalie put her head in her hands.

'No, but this time Longhampton *has* got talent!' Rachel pointed at Jeannie. 'We have our very own professional musician! Could we persuade your band to perform, Jeannie?'

Your band. Edie's Birdhouse – which had never been *her* band, apparently – seemed part of a different life, and yet their last official gig had only been a few months ago. Jeannie realised she might never get up on a stage again, not on her own. She was just a ukulele teacher and a barmaid now.

'Sorry to disappoint you, but I don't have a band any more.'

'Why?' Rachel refilled her glass. 'Didn't Dan tell George you were in a band with your friend?'

'I was. But my friend' – it was hard to say that word – 'got chatting to a producer at a festival last year who needed a lyricist. Edith's lyrics are really good, to be fair. He offered her a deal to move to London and work in the studio with a writing team. She couldn't say no. It's a great opportunity. I don't blame her for taking it.' Jeannie shrugged but she knew it probably wasn't hiding the sense of betrayal gnawing at her insides.

She had also missed out a few key details. One, Edith hadn't told her that Amir had been in touch. Two, Edith hadn't even tried to negotiate a job for her. And three, Edith's parting shot had been, 'If you wanted it so much, why didn't you talk to him?' As if she hadn't known for twenty years that 'just talking to someone' wasn't something Jeannie had ever been able to do.

'Oh, that's crap,' said Natalie immediately. 'She didn't say we come as a package?'

'No. Well, the project they're working on is a very different kind of music to the sort I write. More . . . dance-y.'

'I bet you wouldn't want to do it anyway.' Rachel lifted her chin, getting it. 'Well, sod Edith. She sounds like a selfish cow.'

She said it with such relish Jeannie felt momentarily better. Dan's opinion was along the same lines, but he'd never liked Edith, or had the faintest idea what her lyrics meant, so it hadn't felt quite as satisfying as Rachel and Natalie's spontaneous disgust.

'You don't need her to play, though,' Rachel went on. 'Could you do a solo set?'

Jeannie shook her head. 'I'm taking a break from the whole thing. I'm not . . . in the right place at the moment.'

The truth was actually scarier than that: Jeannie was afraid the music in her soul had gone. Even before Dan's accident, a dark void had gradually expanded inside where music used to blossom and bubble and flow, all day, every day, since she was old enough to hold her first ukulele. Worse than that, she didn't even want to play. Her guitars and ukuleles were still in the spare room, where she'd carried them the day she moved in. She felt as if she'd let them down but she couldn't bear to pick them up and feel nothing.

'Of course not, with Dan too . . .' Rachel frowned at herself. 'God, I'm sorry. You've got more than enough on your plate . . .'

'So, no concert.' Natalie crossed it off her list with a subtle 'you've done me a favour' wink at Jeannie. 'We're back to auctions and a swear box in the pub.'

'We need something bigger than swear boxes.' Rachel sank her hands into her hair, exposing a tiny white tattoo on her inner wrist, a paw print. 'George presented me a spreadsheet last night, with all the rescue's accounts on it in different colours so I could understand. It came with a free lecture.' She stared up at the ceiling. 'He hasn't lectured me in ages. I hadn't told him what a patronising git he is in ages either. It's just like the old days, but with less sexual tension.'

'What about a car boot sale?' Jeannie suggested. 'My parents are always doing them. It's surprising how much you can raise by getting rid of stuff you don't need. Clothes you don't wear any more, books you've read, that kind of thing.'

'We are the decluttering queens,' said Natalie. 'How do you think our charity shop gets so much stock? I personally invented the term "autumn purge", to get a second bite of the "spring clean of junk" cherry. There's barely an attic in town we haven't plundered for unworn gladrags.'

Rachel had started the last slice of pizza, but suddenly put it down and narrowed her eyes at an unseen thought.

'Rachel?' Jeannie turned to her, then to Natalie. 'Did I say something?'

'She's thinking.' Natalie refilled their glasses. 'Don't disturb her. But don't speak, Rachel, if your next suggestion is going to involve me singing or dancing or doing anything involving anal glands.'

The evening was broken up shortly afterwards by the arrival of Natalie's husband, Johnny, who'd come to collect her on his way back from Longhampton High School PTA meeting.

'Don't tell me!' he said, standing at the door in his parka. 'Longhampton's Got Talent! Now, I'd like to volunteer my services as—'

'It's a no from *everyone*, Johnny,' said Natalie with a despairing backwards glance over her shoulder, and she pushed him out.

Jeannie was looking forward to hearing what stories Owen would shake out of Dan's friends over the weekend. She was also intrigued to see which memories Owen himself would choose to coax Dan back to consciousness, stories that might shine a light on their unlikely friendship. What had they got up to, golden boy Dan and his Paddington Bear-ish friend? And how had they made friends in the first place?

In the meantime she had a few memories of her own to share with Dan, printed out and tucked in her bag: the long WhatsApp conversations they'd shared in their early days. Glancing through them on the train had made Jeannie's eyes well up, and her heart beat faster, and she hoped their tentative flirting might set some emotions dancing across Dan's slumbering mind too.

As she walked into the ICU, there was quite a bit of activity on the ICU ward, centred on a new patient in the other bed.

The man's visitors, his parents and girlfriend, had arrived at the same time as she had, and although they hadn't spoken in the lift, she recognised them – and also the crackle of tension that hung in their silence.

She slipped her fingers around Dan's hand, taking care not to dislodge the cannulas, and spoke in a low voice. Jeannie was conscious of the other family, who were now talking so loudly she couldn't help picking up details.

The man's name was Tyler. He'd been in a motorbike accident, three days after his twenty-fifth birthday.

'So, I've got something for you!' said Jeannie, unfolding the first set of printed sheets. 'I've got our messages from that night we first chatted. That was quite an evening, remember? Just you, me, and the overnight ward.'

There was no response from Dan, but Jeannie heard Tyler's girlfriend crying, and the mother telling her to get a grip.

'*Hi, HoarseWhisperer!*' she read self-consciously. But they wouldn't be listening. They had other things to focus on. '*Thanks for your message. You read right – I play the uku-lele. But no, I don't clean windows or lean on lampposts. I'm in a band, but you probably haven't heard of us unless you go to very small festivals. Why the name – have you got a cold?*'

Jeannie couldn't help overhearing the conversation as

she paused for breath. It hadn't been Tyler's fault he'd gone under the lorry. All lorries should be more aware of bikers; everyone knew what bastards they were. Hadn't Ty always said that? Yes, he had.

'*Hi, NotNowBono,*' she went on. She could hear Dan's voice in her head, and as she spoke his words aloud her voice automatically tilted more towards his Home Counties accent. '*How do you know I haven't heard of your band?! Tell me about it! I don't actually whisper hoarsely or otherwise – I'm a vet who's not great at puns. I'm on night shift right now, hanging out with a Labrador who ate two socks and a thong yesterday.*'

'*But she's OK?*'

'*She's looking a lot better than the socks.*'

Hannah needed to stop crying right now because it wasn't helping anyone. Least of all Tyler. When was that nurse coming back? If Hannah wanted to make herself useful, she could go and find the nurse. Get some information for everyone. And tea. Four sugars.

The clatter of Hannah's feet almost running down the ward made Jeannie bite her lip. It sounded like someone running away from a situation she couldn't get her head around and Jeannie knew how that felt. She focused on the printed conversation in her hand. The paper was trembling.

'*What does night shift involve?*' she read aloud.

'*It involves waiting for the emergency line to ring, drinking coffee and messing about on my phone,*' Dan had messaged. '*I have to be ready to cope with any life or death dramas at the drop of a hamster. I also have to talk to people who think their cat is looking at them funny at 4 a.m. and want me to diagnose depression in goats.*'

Jeannie glanced over the page to Dan's sleeping face. 'That made me laugh out loud,' she told him. 'Something that literally never happened in any dating conversation up to that point, internet or otherwise.'

He didn't respond. Obviously. Had she thought he might? Jeannie ignored the churning in her stomach, and made herself read on.

'*So where are you?*

'*I'm in the flat above the surgery – perks of the job, live-in accommodation with access to as much ketamine as I want. No, wait. As many handwipes as I want. Spot the Dalmatian – not the most original, I know – is here too. She says hi. I'm Dan, by the way. You haven't said what I can call you?*'

Jeannie paused, remembering how the excitement had sparkled through her as Dan's words unfolded on her screen, leading her into this conversation as easily as if they were chatting in a bar. It was strange, speaking them aloud now. She'd never have been this confident if they'd *been* in a bar.

'*You can call me Betty,*' she read, and cringed. And then, for some reason, she'd gone Full Geek. '*Betty, when you call me, you can call me Al.*'

'*Hi, Betty! I didn't get the Al bit?*'

Yeah, she probably shouldn't have led off with eighties' music jokes. ' *"You Can Call Me Al", by Paul Simon? I don't actually know if Paul Simon plays the ukulele. It seems like something he would play. Small hands. My name is Jeannie.*'

'*Ha! Well, hello, Jeannie! Hi!*' She paused and glanced at Dan. 'You put a handwaving emoji there. And then another thumbs up. I didn't send any back, because if I'm being completely truthful with you, Dan, I don't do emojis. I should have said something at the time, but what the hell, I'm telling you now. No emojis, please.'

Did his eyelids just flicker? Jeannie stopped breathing and leaned forward, her heart in her mouth.

'Dan? Dan!' She glanced at the machines: nothing was different; nothing was bleeping or flatlining or anything.

He didn't move again, and she rubbed her tired eyes. *Had* his eyes flickered? As if he was laughing, somewhere out there in the floating twilight space?

It must have been the light. Or maybe the timed sedation had slipped into his vein, working its way silently through his nerves and blood vessels.

'Back to you.' Jeannie turned the page. '*It could be a long night*, you say. *Surely you've got work in the morning? Or are you a full-time ukulele player?* It was about quarter past eleven at this point.' The time stamps of the messages told their own story: seconds between their responses. Like a proper conversation.

'I said, *I don't have to be anywhere until lunchtime. When we're not gigging, I work in a pub, and I teach music. Any age, any ability. Mostly under tens and retired people.*

'*Sounds fun! I can't even play the triangle. Wait! I have a call coming through. Don't go away.*'

Jeannie closed her eyes, and she could feel the faded checked shirt she'd been wearing, the sweet-soap smell of freesias in a glass by her bed, Eliza Carthy playing on her speaker. More than that, she remembered the electricity in the air – the energy of something new starting. The flat 'what now?' blankness of the future she'd felt a few days before, suddenly cracked by a wide road stretching out into mountains and blue skies. Going somewhere.

Words didn't come easily to Jeannie, as they did for Edith. But talking to Dan had felt like the first stirring of a song in her head, when the notes swirled and she had to be quick to catch them.

She reached out and touched his bare arm, wanting to connect with him in the same way she'd longed to hear his voice that night.

Then, within a few exchanges, she'd almost sensed Dan in her head. She'd sat cross-legged on her bed stretching the tiny icon of him to its maximum size on her phone, the air-punching boy with the sunshine-blond hair falling into his eyes, smiling up at her between her fingers. It wasn't a carefully selected photo with flattering filters: it was a snapshot of celebration, of being alive, and she loved that.

Footsteps. People were walking into the ward, heading towards the bed at the end. Jeannie recognised Mr Allcott's voice; he was talking to another doctor, in low and urgent tones. She couldn't hear the words, but the tone – that was familiar, and not in a good way. Her stomach tightened in sympathy for Hannah and Tyler.

She hurried to build a wall of conversation between them. 'Tell me if you get bored, won't you, Dan? So you said, *That was a call from a man wanting me to diagnose his dog over the phone. He said he was bathing the dog and he's found lumps on its belly and he's worried it's cancer.*

'And what did you say?

'I asked him if they were very small lumps, in a line? He said yes. I said, congratulations, your dog has nipples.'

Jeannie paused. 'And you sent me another emoji there.

Really, if I'd known how dependent you were on your emojis, I might have left it. But then you made up for it by sending me a photo of a puppy on a drip that you were checking up on overnight and I was . . . well.'

She was gone. Utterly gone.

Jeannie, smiling at her phone in the darkness, had asked for more puppy pics. Dan sent them, plus a selfie of himself with two feral cats who usually dropped in on the night shift for snacks, and she'd been shocked at how his smile caught her just above her heart. As if she'd known him for ages.

'*Listen, if you want to call it a night, I'll understand,*' he said, at half one.

'*I'm enjoying it!*' Understatement, she thought, as she read her own words. '*I want to know if the man with the depressed dog calls back. Or maybe if the dog calls, wanting you to have his owner put to sleep.*'

And then she reached the words that had turned her inside out, alone in the attic. '*When can we do this again?*'

'*When's your next on-call night?*'

'*Does it have to be an on-call night?*' Jeannie paused. 'And you sent me a raised eyebrow emoji. And I just laughed.'

Her voice stuck in her throat. Reading this again, she could feel the old feelings stirring and crackling – it couldn't have been more perfect, or more romantic. So how had it gone wrong? Jeannie sat very still on the hospital chair, trying to stay in the moment, in that place in her head. With Dan, in the beginning, willing herself back so she could try to start again from that good point, and fix whatever had gone wrong along the way.

'I loved those nights we spent messaging. Didn't you

feel it was more . . . intimate than talking, somehow? I know we asked each other loads of silly questions, but there are so many more I still want to ask.' Her voice cracked. 'Like, who'd play you in a film? Or what's your spirit animal? Do you believe in ghosts?' She swallowed. 'What do you like best about me? How did you meet Owen — and how did you two click? You two seem like very different people, if you don't mind me saying. He's so quiet and you're . . . not. Well, a bit like me and Edith, I suppose. Although I can't see Owen doing an Edith on you . . .'

'Hey,' said Owen behind her. He was quite close behind; the cubicle was small.

Jeannie jumped. 'How long have you been there?'

'I just walked in.' He peered at her. 'Oh, sorry, are you crying?'

Hastily she brushed her hand over her face. 'I'm fine,' she said, waving the paper. 'Just . . . memories. You know.'

Owen put his hand on her shoulder awkwardly. He patted, twice, then removed it. 'I can tell you,' he said. 'If it helps.'

'Tell me what?'

'How he and I met. I was Dan's "school buddy".' He settled into the chair opposite, squeezing himself into the limited space between the monitors and breathing equipment. 'He started halfway through the Easter term, and our form teacher put me in charge of helping him to settle in — I was the last of a long line of Pattersons, so the teacher thought I'd know the ropes. What he hadn't really noticed was that unlike my three big sisters, I was chronically shy and didn't have that many friends.' Owen shrugged, as if she could have guessed that. 'So, in the end, Dan ended up taking *me* under his wing, and doing the friend-making for both of us. He never let me feel like that, though. Not for a second.'

'And you've been best mates ever since.'

Owen gazed at Dan. 'I'm sure people wonder why. He got on with everyone – the popular kids, the sporty kids, even the weirdo drama set? But I got to know a side of Dan that most people don't see. He was so lost when his dad left, worrying about Andrea, how she'd cope on her own. My family lived nearby – we're a big clan, Mum loves a party, and Dad's mad on football – and we just . . .' He mimed pulling Dan into a bear hug. 'Mum loves him like one of us. We all do.'

Jeannie wondered if *she'd* seen that side of Dan: he was always unbreakably positive about everything. But she could easily imagine a younger Owen's emotional bear hug of concern, comforting a friend trying to put on a brave face. 'Do you think he'll build bridges with his dad? Now he's a bit older?'

The answer was quick. 'Nope. I don't think Dan ever wants to see Malcolm again. Reading between the lines, he was financially very generous, but he treated Andrea badly, you know. Really badly. Dan once told me his worst fear was turning out like his dad.'

He glanced towards the bed again, clearly torn between betraying a confidence and wanting to help Jeannie understand. 'I shouldn't . . . You two haven't talked about it?'

She shook her head, but Owen wouldn't be drawn further.

'Well, if he turns out like Andrea, he'll be fine,' she

131

said instead. 'And if I turn out like my mum . . . well, I'd be happy about that.'

Owen visibly relaxed. 'Your mum's *great*.'

She smiled, glad he'd noticed. 'I know. I'm lucky.'

'I think we're both much luckier than we realise,' said Owen and, for a moment, he looked very sad.

Chapter Ten

Rachel knocked on the front door first thing the next morning and Jeannie knew immediately that something was up. And in a good way, for a change.

Rachel's eyes were sparkling and she was bouncing on the balls of her feet as she stood on the step, Gem hovering behind.

'I need your help,' she said, without any preamble. 'I know you're busy, but would you come up to the house for half an hour and tell me honestly what you think about something? It's either a brilliant fundraiser idea or a really, really bad one and I honestly don't know which.'

'Has Natalie already given you *her* opinion?'

Rachel's expression shifted. 'I haven't run this by Nat. I need a completely unbiased opinion. Natalie doesn't do those.'

They strolled up the lane to the Fenwicks' house, with Gem trailing behind like a wisp of mist. Inside, Rachel led Jeannie upstairs past the bathroom with the huge bath, past Fergus's room, past a landing full of ancient black and white photos of dogs, and up a less fancy back staircase.

They emerged into a cavernous attic room running the length of the house. Sunlight falling through the window at the far end cast wide columns of swirling dust motes across the wooden floors. The walls were stacked with boxes, old furniture and, along one wall, a herd of clothes rails shrouded in sheets. The heavy oak beams still had a few unravelling Pony Club rosettes pinned to them, slowly disintegrating among the cobwebs, and a pock-marked dartboard hinted at someone's intensive practising, decades earlier.

'I keep promising Ferg we'll turn this into a den for him and his mates,' said Rachel, seeing Jeannie gazing round, 'but then George reminds me it'd mean having teenagers in the attic like giant squirrels, and we *cannot* afford that much toast. Plus I'm not sure the wi-fi reaches up here, so he'd probably refuse to venture so far into unknown territory.' She was unveiling the rails, flipping through the hangers to reveal flashes of bright marmalade brocade and scarlet satin.

'Are these your clothes?'

Rachel sighed, holding out a sparkling gold maxi dress. 'Some of them. Those are my aunt Dot's – she was a real glamour puss in the sixties. These are my rails. Mostly black, as you can see.'

'Why are they up here? Isn't it a pain coming up to get dressed?'

She laughed. 'No, this is where I keep the clothes I can't wear any more, either because I can't fit into them, or they're too nice to be ruined by the ravages of the countryside and childrearing. My past, in mothballs, in other words . . . Ah, here it is.'

Rachel pulled out an expensive suit carrier, hooked the hook over the rail and unzipped it, leaning over to breathe in the trapped air as she did.

'Aaah. I can still smell the perfume I was wearing. Isn't it lovely?'

Carefully, she pulled out the dress inside the carrier, spreading the ivory silk with a reverential hand. It was a butterfly emerging from a plain cocoon: a beautiful silk knee-length dress. The understated design looked simple, but was clearly anything but simple.

Jeannie recognised it immediately from the wedding photograph on the stairs. 'Wow. Is that your wedding dress?'

'It is.' Rachel couldn't take her eyes off it. 'My last Net-a-Porter hurrah before I resigned myself to spending the rest of my life covered in a dog-hair apron. It's Givenchy. I pretended to myself that I could wear it again, or dye it, but . . . you can't. You just look like some mad Miss Havisham with access to Dylon.'

'I wish I'd worn something like that,' said Jeannie, and it was the truth. It was only when she'd been well into the wedding planning that it dawned on her that she didn't *have* to go for the big white meringue just because the magazines said it would suit her body shape. But by then the big white meringue was chosen, paid for and already being made.

'I always wanted to look like the most beautiful version of myself on my wedding day, not a toilet-roll holder.' Rachel was still stroking the invisibly tailored folds. 'George had some surprisingly specific views on dresses – I had no idea. I think he was more worried I'd turn up at the church in a Lady Gaga meat dress. Or trousers. We compromised on white. I was too old for a princess frock, anyway.'

'How old were you when you got married? If you don't mind me asking?'

'Forty-five,' said Rachel. 'George and I met when I was thirty-nine. It took him six years and Ferg's kinder-garten education to persuade me it'd be a good idea to make it official. He used to insist it was for tax reasons, but he's an old romantic, deep down. He wanted to be my husband, and for me to be his wife.' She paused. 'I only kept saying no because I couldn't bear the thought of messing it up, after he'd waited so long.'

Her eyes drifted away and she smiled, remembering – Jeannie assumed – George's reaction when he turned and saw his wife-to-be at the church door, looking so mag-nificently *herself*. She couldn't imagine Rachel in a flouncy meringue anyway; she was too tall and angular, too much her own person to dress up as someone else on her wedding day.

'How about Dan?' Rachel asked. 'Did he have specific ideas about what you should wear?'

'No, not at all. He just said wear something you like.'

'And did it take you long to find the dream dress?'

'It was the first one I tried on. It fitted, it looked beau-tiful, the lady in the shop cried . . .' Jeannie touched the fabric of Rachel's dress. It was a completely different quality to her dress: proper couture silk. 'It made me look like a bride.'

'Oh, that's lovely! You said yes to the dress!'

'I think the dress said yes to me. It wasn't like any other clothes-shopping experience I've ever had, to be honest. I've always chosen clothes because I liked them, not because it was a sort of . . . uniform I had to wear.' It felt strange to admit that, but the words slipped out and Jeannie felt a looseness in her chest, a bit like when the corset itself had come off. 'I didn't think about how it might feel to sit around in full body armour for more than half an hour. I certainly didn't take into account how easy it would be to get into an air ambulance in it. Or not, as it turned out.'

'Well, air ambulance accessibility isn't the first criterion that springs to mind when you're trying on a wedding dress.' Rachel pulled a sympathetic face. 'Did you have the full crowd of bridesmaids to help you choose? Didn't they make you try on a few more, so their Prosecco would be topped up?'

'No, I went on my own. Whole thing took under an hour.'

Rachel seemed surprised.

'I didn't want a big fuss,' Jeannie explained. It hadn't felt odd until now, going on her own, but . . . suddenly she wondered why she hadn't wanted anyone else there. 'I didn't want to drag my mum down to Bristol – she hates shopping, anyway. And I didn't have any bridesmaids at that point. Edith and I weren't talking – she'd sodded off to London – so my sister-in-law Teri stepped in. But she couldn't get any time off work to choose dresses. She's a teacher. So it was just me in the end,' she finished, rather lamely.

'I suppose it's easier for decision-making?' suggested Rachel, unconvinced.

Jeannie nodded. 'How about you? Did you try on lots?'

'I'm afraid I did, yes. I had an ominous feeling it'd be my last chance to splash a shameful amount of cash on a frock so I went for it. I had trying-on parties, visits to London, everything. It was more than just buying a dress. It felt like . . . saying goodbye to something.' She pulled a face, confidentially. 'I'd never tell George that, of course.'

'I know what you mean,' Jeannie murmured.

Rachel ran a loving fingertip along the tapered sleeve. 'I never wore this out again but I used to sneak up here and try it on when no one was at home. While it fitted. But my sister gave us a breadmaker *and* an ice cream maker as a wedding present, and I'll be honest, we ballooned. Especially me. I stopped trying on the dress because I couldn't get it over my knees. Then one day, I just decided. I didn't tell George I was going on a diet, I just ate less and jogged round the paddock, and then came up here once a week to try to zip up my wedding dress. I felt like I owed it to be able to fit into it still.'

'And you got there, presumably?'

Of course she had. Rachel was lean, almost gangly, the perfect shape for 7/8 jeans and bracelet-length striped shirts and white plimsolls.

'Yes.' She grimaced. 'I imagined it hanging in its bag, lecturing me in a bossy French accent when I was pounding round the field.'

'So it's more than just a dress. It's a personal trainer. Two for the price of one.'

'Yes! When you put it like that, it was a bargain.' Rachel smiled sadly. 'Anyway, I'm going to sell it.'

'What?' Jeannie hadn't expected that.

'I'm going to sell it. I'll never wear it again; it doesn't look right on me now, my body's changed shape. And I'm nearly fifty: there are some things you just have to accept. Trying to get into your wedding dress isn't just undignified, it's borderline crazy.'

'But . . .'

'I know, it's not a wedding dress. That was my reasoning too – *sooooo* many chances to wear it again. But there's not much going on round here where you need to wear a Givenchy cocktail frock.' Rachel turned to Jeannie, and her expression was suddenly less readable. 'Even if I married again – which I hope I won't – it's not like I'd drag this out of the wardrobe, would I? No, it's time. Give someone else the chance to love it. And be bossed around by it.'

'But what will George think?'

Rachel raised her chin. 'George told me to raise some money instead of asking him for it, so I am.'

'But it's your *wedding dress*!'

'It's just a dress at the end of the day,' said Rachel, and they both knew she was lying.

Jeannie didn't know what to say. Why was Rachel doing this? Either she really didn't care about the dress, or she really wanted to make a point to George, or she really, *really* cared about raising money for the dogs.

She made a split-second decision. 'Then you can have mine too.'

Now Rachel looked startled. 'No, come on, Jeannie. You don't have to do that.'

'I don't want to wear mine again either. It's too small for me anyway, if I'm being honest. People keep going on about how I should save it to wear it again when Dan's better, but it's got so many bad memories attached now that I wouldn't wear it even if I *did* want to go through with—'

She froze, horrified at what she'd nearly said aloud for the first time since that awful moment with Dad in the car.

Even if I did want to go through with . . . hung in the dusty attic between them. Jeannie knew she should say something, anything, to blow those words away fast before they stuck, but her mind had gone blank.

Rachel didn't speak. She gazed into Jeannie's face, reading her expression with curiosity but no judgement. Jeannie felt the strange certainty that if she'd confessed everything to Rachel, even the shameful truths she couldn't face herself, Rachel would have understood. But she couldn't risk it.

'Even if I did want to go through the corset torture again.' Jeannie finally recovered herself, and tried to look normal. 'Have it,' she said. 'And you can have the veil and the storage bag too. It cost a thousand pounds; it's from a really lovely boutique.'

'Are you sure? Don't feel guilt-tripped into this, for God's sake. I'm not sure it's even ethical to let you offer, given the circumstances.'

'No, I'm sure. I'd like to help out those poor dogs. And as you say, it's a beautiful dress. It deserves its day in the spotlight.'

'What about Dan?'

'Dan's a vet,' said Jeannie with confidence. 'He'll be pleased I've done something to help out animals in need.'

It was a good answer. She was pleased with how easily it had tripped off her tongue. And it was true. Dan probably would prefer her to raise some money for the dogs than hang on to a dress she'd never wear again. 'It doesn't have happy memories, not like yours,' she went on. 'That's much harder to give up.'

'It only got one trip out, but it's been nice knowing it's here.' Rachel stroked the bodice, brushing away imperceptible dust motes, then carefully slid it back into its cocoon. 'But we've all got to make sacrifices.' Her eyes turned distant. 'Apparently.'

Jeannie sat at Dan's bedside with her own notebook on her lap, and wrote 'TO DO 3 JUNE' in capital letters, underlining it twice. Her pen stopped. There was so much she should be doing that she didn't know where to begin.

Bills. Council tax. Car insurance. Money? Bar shifts? Music lessons?

None of it seemed important in the hospital but Jeannie's new life outside the ICU was carrying on, despite her only dipping in and out of it at the beginning and end of each day. She'd never lived on her own before, and often woke in a panic that she'd forgotten to lock the door or turn off the oven. Making 'to do' lists had become her way of pinning herself into the world away from Dan's bed.

She pressed play on the message Owen had passed on from Dan's friend Nick, and chewed the end of her pen. She'd heard this one before: it was the story of a lads' holiday in Greece in 2015, and, disappointingly, didn't contain any startling insights, other than the fact that Dan was allergic to retsina.

. . . never realised just how much sun cream you have to use in order to tan out a clear outline of ha ha ha a certain picture on someone's back ha ha ha . . .

Jeannie knew she needed to earn some money soon; Rachel and George were being generous about rent for the house, and her parents had put some money in her account 'until we hear about the wedding insurance', but she needed to make plans. I need to get back to playing, she thought, her eyes wandering blankly across the ward. I can't be a music teacher who can't play.

Hannah wasn't in today. Tyler's parents were sitting by his bed, alternately staring into space, crying, and sporadically throwing out weak conversation starters that sank like stones in the hushed ICU. Tyler was heavily sedated, although his eyes were open and he seemed much more 'there' than Dan. Jeannie gleaned that Tyler was able to breathe unassisted but he had complex spinal injuries, and recovery plans would have to include long-term physio and probably lower-body paralysis.

Poor Hannah, she thought, trying not to think about the possible outcomes for Dan, none of which had even been explored yet. Everything was still to come for them. Dan's diagnosis. His reaction. Their reactions. Their new lives, when all these pieces finally landed.

Jeannie bit her lip and started making her list.

The cottage felt stuffy and lifeless when Jeannie let herself in that evening. For the first time she thought it might be nice to have a cat or a dog, slinking or bounding up to welcome her back, a spark of life in a house with no books on shelves yet, no family photos on walls.

Maybe Rachel could lend me a dog from the rescue, she thought, hanging her bag over the carved apple at the end of the banisters. Or maybe I should get a hammer and start hanging pictures up.

It would make her presence there permanent, which made Jeannie feel strange. Funny how it was easier to imagine staying here on her own, visiting Dan every day and then coming back here, than it was to imagine a future in which he was already cooking in the kitchen when she came home, singing as he made his signature spaghetti.

Jeannie pressed the voicemail button on the old-fashioned answering machine before she could think too hard about whether that *was* his signature dish.

'Hello, love, just Mum ringing to see how you're getting on. Call me back when you've got time to chat.'

She deleted, and pressed 'next'.

'Hello, Jeannie, it's DC Lyons from Longhampton Police. Nothing urgent, just an update call. Could you give us a call back on this number, please. Thank you.'

Then another call with no message, no number. Jeannie frowned, and deleted it too. Maybe it was for Megan, the previous tenant? She'd ask Rachel.

After supper, Jeannie went upstairs to the room where she'd stacked her musical instruments. She'd hidden them behind boxes of books and clothes, where she couldn't see them and feel bad about not playing them. She moved a couple of boxes, and hesitated in front of the cases.

Which one?

You don't have to do this, said a voice in her head, but it was immediately followed by another, louder one.

Do it. Do it. *Do* it.

There was her lovely Martin acoustic, nestling like a jewel in its red velvet-lined case, the mahogany-bodied beauty she'd bought second-hand with the money she'd saved up from her bar work. It had been that or an upgrade to the old Corsa she and Angus had both learned to drive in. The choice hadn't been hard.

Behind that there was an electric guitar she didn't play much – the sound wasn't right for the music Jeannie heard in her head, but she was trying to find a way into it – and two ukuleles. One was her own; one was a present she'd given Dan in their early days, after he'd told her he could only play a triangle. It had been a gift of her time, and her skill and patience, as well as the instrument. He'd loved the idea, but hadn't managed to find a spare afternoon to get started yet.

It felt wrong to open the guitar case. Too many memories and expectations to fly out like battling moths.

Instead Jeannie made herself pick up the ukulele's cheery star-spangled case and unzipped it. It was the instrument she took into schools, to teach the children taking their first wobbly musical steps. Something about it was friendly, and Jeannie loved the simple songs she sang with them. She curled her hand around the narrow fretboard, letting her fingers feel automatically for chord shapes. There was a gold star sticker on the side: one of the teachers had presented it to her at her last class before she left. A gold star for effort.

It had been months since Jeannie had picked up any instrument, and the nylon strings hurt her fingers, biting into toughened fingertips that had gone soft. She pressed down, ignoring the pain, but her other hand didn't pluck the strings. Her brain was telling her to play, and there were distant ripples of melody in her head, but something heavy was blocking out the impulses.

I'll just tune it, she thought as the urge to unleash music into the room struggled against the stifling reluctance choking her. I don't have to play. I'll just tune it, that's enough.

Jeannie plucked and listened, and turned the pegs until the strings were in tune with one another. She sat for a while with the instrument in her lap, listening to the music running through her brain, the chords, the movements, the cadences. They were echoes – songs that had come from her heart, but which didn't mean anything to her now in this new world.

Nothing would come. No music here. A damp sadness sat like a cloak round her shoulders.

Jeannie put the ukulele back in its case, zipped it up and rested it behind the box of her books.

Then she went to bed, alone, and fell into a black and dreamless sleep. But at least, for the first time since Dan's accident, she slept through until morning.

Chapter Eleven

Jeannie checked Rachel's eBay listing for her wedding dress in idle moments at the hospital, and was surprised to see that the exquisite cocktail dress still had no bids.

She didn't know why. Rachel was, obviously, the sort of person who had a handy tailor's dummy to display her eBay listings to their best advantage and the description of the dress was concise yet detailed. The photograph of the receipt made Jeannie's eyes water, so there was no doubt whatsoever about its provenance. And Rachel had started the bidding at what Jeannie considered a very reasonable level.

But nobody seemed to want it.

Rachel was equally baffled.

'No bids.' She was staring at the office computer and shaking her head in disbelief. 'I can't believe it. Literally no interest.'

It was the brief quiet period in the kennels' morning routine, between first walks and food. Rachel had called Jeannie before breakfast to see if she'd mind giving her a hand with the early exercise as the kennel maid, Mel, had called in sick. Jeannie had been happy to help out, and now, an hour later, she'd galloped ten dogs of various sizes around the paddocks behind the kennels, and was tucking into a pile of toast, feeling pleasantly knackered.

'Selling wedding dresses is hard.' Natalie looked up from her own laptop on the other desk. She'd taken the morning off from her café to deal with the rescue's quarterly accounts and also 'help socialise the puppies' by hoovering at them while wearing a hat. 'Why did you list it on eBay?'

'Because that's where I've sold loads of stuff. And I didn't just list it on eBay, I listed it on that pre-loved wedding site too.'

'Oh, that's a good idea,' said Jeannie helpfully. 'Has anyone favourited it?'

'No.' Rachel huffed and spun from side to side on her chair. 'I even offered to throw in the dress cover! That's worth fifty quid on its own. What? Why are you looking at me like that, Nat?'

Natalie was staring at her. 'Because I can't believe you didn't ask me first. I would have told you it's a total waste of time trying to sell wedding dresses on eBay.'

'But it's not just a wedding dress! It's a couture cocktail dress!'

Natalie rolled her eyes. 'Would you spend hundreds of pounds on a dress for the most important day of your life based on four photos online?' She opened up a different screen on her laptop and started typing. Her fingernails clicked on the keys; she was a fast and furious typist. 'If you want to sell the dress, you need to sell the whole experience first. We need a proper approach.'

'Here she goes . . .' Rachel gestured towards Natalie. 'Natalie was personally responsible for the success of Cococoa organic chocolate, don't you know?'

Jeannie didn't know. But she knew the chocolate well enough. 'Really? That's amazing!'

'Before I was made redundant and started my own business purely so I could *take my rescue dog that my friend Rachel had persuaded me to adopt* to work.' Natalie was scrolling through sites, chewing her lip. 'OK, so you've got this . . . And this . . . Hmm.'

'What are you looking for?'

'I'm looking to see if anyone else has had the idea I've just had . . .'

'Nat came up with the idea of getting local businesses to sponsor individual kennels – that's why they've got those carved signs above them,' Rachel explained. 'She's so good at wringing cash out of people that sometimes *I* give her a fiver.'

'If we're going to do this properly, we're going to need more than one dress, though. So you might as well have mine.' Natalie didn't look up as she typed percussively. 'I'm never going to wear it, and I've got no kids to pass it on to.'

'Oh, Nat . . .' Rachel mouthed 'Vera Wang' at Jeannie and then held up six fingers and pretended to look appalled, but couldn't help looking impressed at the same time.

'Vera Wang?' Jeannie mouthed back, in shock. She'd looked at Vera Wang. Looking was as far as it had gone. Their budget for the whole day, including food and wine, wouldn't have stretched that far.

'Well, I can't get into it and it's taking up space in our wardrobe. I'd like to give someone else a chance to Wang on their wedding day.'

'And there's my dress too,' said Jeannie. 'I'm donating that.'

That made Natalie look up from her laptop. 'What?

No, Jeannie. Just . . . *no*. I mean, me and Rachel, we're old married women. You still *need* yours. Don't do anything you might regret – you should still be on honeymoon, by rights. This isn't the time.'

Jeannie glanced at Rachel. 'We've been through that. I don't want the reminders of . . . of what happened. I wouldn't want to wear it again anyway.'

Rachel's cool gaze lingered on her, and Jeannie flushed. Was Rachel remembering what she'd said about not getting married again? Guilt was making her so paranoid.

'So what are you planning?' she asked, hurriedly, to move things on.

Natalie swivelled in her chair. 'I think we should launch a wedding website, but with a twist.'

'A twist!' Rachel leaned forward, agog. 'Do we put the dresses on the dogs?'

'No, we don't. So.' Natalie went into presentation mode. 'Most women never do anything with their wedding dress after the big day. They say they're going to dye it, but they never do. Or they say they'll keep it for their daughter, but seriously . . . It's such a lot of money to spend on eight hours for one outfit, and pretty much everyone feels incredibly guilty about it afterwards. I know I do. I had to move my wedding dress to the wardrobe in the *spare* spare room because every time I opened it, I just saw a European minibreak, or laser eye surgery or a new boiler or something.'

'You *are* very romantic, Nat.'

Natalie swept on. 'So we appeal to local people to do something life-changing with the dress that changed *their* lives. They donate their dresses to be sold, to give another woman the chance to have a beautiful day, and to give the dogs the chance of a new life. It's charitable, and it's eco-friendly!'

'It's like rehoming the dresses,' said Jeannie. 'To help us rehome the dogs.'

'Oh, now that's very good,' said Rachel. 'Why didn't I think of that?'

'But we don't stop there.' Natalie lifted a finger. 'We build a story around our wedding dress collection, so that we're not just relying on *selling* the dresses for cash. We could hold a fashion show to let people wear their dresses again – Longhampton's Weddings Through the Ages! We can throw one of those wedding-dress dinner parties with canapés and cake in the Memorial Hall!'

'So where would you sell the dresses?' Jeannie looked round the office: there were two crates of squeaking, squabbling, sleeping, pooing puppies, shredding the bedding for all they were worth, and a basket where Lady Sadie the Staffie was snoring loudly and pretending none of it was anything to do with her. Three sacks of dog food were propped up against a wall, the cleaning equipment for the morning hose-down was set out, and despite Rachel's constant sweeping up 'to get them used to brooms', there were still dog hairs everywhere.

'Not here, obviously,' said Rachel, seeing Jeannie's expression.

'We've got a charity shop in town,' Natalie explained. 'But I need to think about that. I'm not sure we can make the back room luxurious enough. It's got to be . . . special.'

Jeannie thought of the boutique she'd bought her dress from. A soft-focus haven, far away from real life. A place of dreams, where romance and fantasy dissolved any tacky real-life concerns like money, or visible bra straps.

'What about alterations?' she asked. That had been part of the boutique service. 'What if someone loves a dress but needs it to fit? Can you arrange that too?'

Natalie turned to Rachel. 'Is it Freda or Shirley who does your alterations?'

'Hey now!' Rachel pretended to look affronted. 'Don't give away my trade secrets. No, it's both of them. And Pamela Hayes. They're in the Embroiders' Guild. Incredible with a needle. Did you know Freda's daughter has set up her own dressmaking business in Little Larton? She might offer a discount on bridesmaids' dresses to match.'

'They won't mind helping out?'

Rachel shook her head. 'Not if it's for the dogs. People are so generous round here. And we wouldn't push our luck; maybe get them to agree to a couple of dresses each. They love a bit of wedding fuss.'

'I think that's a plan,' said Natalie. 'I'll get on to the *Gazette* and see if someone can come out to do a feature. Get people talking about it.' She tapped a pen against her square white teeth. 'Who's that bossy wedding planner from the Women in Business group? Sara? She'd help, I bet. I'll give her a call and see if we can't pick her brains too.'

'Blimey, what did I put in the coffee this morning?' Rachel murmured.

'And you know what we're going to call it?' Natalie announced with a final flourish.

'Tell us, Nat.'

She made a proud jazz hands gesture. 'Bride's Dress Revisited.'

'Oh, very good. I was thinking Holy Muttrimony,' said Rachel. 'But I'm willing to concede that yours is a lot better.'

Regaling Dan with the entire wedding-dress fundraiser idea gave Jeannie at least half an hour of monologue at his bedside that afternoon.

She waited until Andrea had said her goodbyes and left; she wasn't sure she'd think it was such a great idea. Jeannie certainly didn't want to answer any questions about whether she'd be offering up her own dress. Dan, she told herself, would love the idea of her doing something proactive, and getting involved with their local community.

'. . . but the best thing is,' she finished up, 'that the puppies are already getting adoption applications! They're doing really well, and we're going to be raising awareness for the rescue at the same time. So that's good, isn't it?' Jeannie squeezed Dan's hand and smiled down at him.

Ironically, she felt more comfortable chatting to Dan now than at any point in the past few weeks. Reading that first 'date' aloud seemed to have rewound the clock to an easier time. That was the Dan she was talking to now, not the slightly distant one who'd made it hard to start conversations about anything un-wedding related in the run-up to their wedding.

He had been distant, hadn't he? Jeannie thought suddenly, then pushed on with her news.

'Rachel keeps hinting about me taking one of the puppies,' she told him, 'but I told her it wasn't fair, if I'm leaving it half the day to be here with you – even though she offered to puppysit for me.'

She glanced down the ward. Tyler's curtain was drawn, and she could hear his parents having a loud conversation about someone's brother who hadn't even bothered to pick up the phone to see how Tyler was.

'How'd you feel about a dog?' she asked, as much to avoid overhearing them as anything else.

Dan didn't respond, and Jeannie realised it was a rather belated thing to be asking him.

She'd been thinking about *herself* with a puppy, in that house, right now. A dog waiting for *her*, shadowing her as Gem shadowed Rachel – although she sensed devotion like that didn't come overnight. She wasn't sure she should get a dog with Dan, because . . . well, what was the future going to be when Dan woke up? Was she going to stay? *Should* she?

This isn't going to go on for ever, Jeannie reminded herself, this weirdly bearable interlude where Dan was critically ill but showing no immediate signs of forcing her to face the reality of her wedding-morning actions. It was all very well, settling into cosy fundraising meetings and playing with puppies, but everything could change in the next half hour, if one of the machines started bleeping.

In the next half hour. Tonight. At four thirty in the morning – any moment. Now.

She felt cold.

'I've got another internet date to read out,' she said quickly, reaching into her bag. 'It's the one where I messaged you from that train journey I was on with Edith, when we got stuck outside Reading. And you were on call again. So, I start off: *Hi, Dan!* And you reply, *Hey, Betty!*'

Jeannie threw herself into the pages, doing different voices for Dan and for herself, and tried to keep it down to a level that wouldn't disturb the other patients, but when she got to the part where she and Dan were discussing which breeds of dog would make the worst flatmates, she had to stop: the conversation at the end of the ward was coming to a boil.

'Hannah, this is hardly the time, is it? You pick your moments!'

It was Tyler's dad. He sounded nasty.

'Mike, come on . . .' That was Tyler's mum. 'Everyone's under a lot of pressure.'

'I'm sorry! I just don't know what I'm supposed to do. I don't understand these choices!' That was Hannah.

'Me me me me!' An impatient, mocking tone. 'It's not about any of us any more. It's about Tyler. Can't you understand that?'

Then the sound of a chair being shoved back. It screeched on the floor, ripping the air in the ward. The ICU was never quiet but there was usually a hush of consideration.

Jeannie turned to see Hannah push the curtain back and stumble out of the ward, her hands held up to her face to hide the tears streaming from her eyes. Her distress triggered a burst of tension in Jeannie's own chest. She looked around for one of the nurses, but they were busy monitoring new patients, no time to fuss over relatives.

Tyler's dad snorted dismissively, aware of his audience. 'If she thinks one of us has got time to run around after her, she's got another thing coming. Bloody drama queen.'

Jeannie didn't think Hannah looked like a drama

queen. She thought she looked like a woman struggling with too many things she couldn't understand.

Tyler's dad's gaze fell on Jeannie, and he rolled his eyes, expecting her to agree. It was such a small ward, Jeannie could hardly pretend she hadn't heard what was going on.

She met the older man's gaze but refused to roll her eyes back at him, which surprised her; she was normally so anti-confrontation that she'd agree with almost anything to avoid a scene. She'd found herself nodding along obediently to some very weird stuff about the rights of bacteria while trapped by the window on a bus, for a start.

But now she stared back, refusing to agree, and Tyler's dad looked away huffily, leaning over to his wife and muttering to her while casting side glances in Jeannie's direction.

Jeannie turned back to Dan. He would want her to be kind. So would Owen. She touched his hand, and tucked the printed conversation under the water jug on the bedside table, next to the latest crop of Get Well Soon cards.

'I'm going to get a coffee,' she said. 'I won't be long.'

Hannah was sitting in the corner of the café in a position Jeannie found painfully familiar: palms covering her eyes, hair over her face, shoulders bearing the weight of the world. An untouched cappuccino was deflating on the table by her elbow.

Before she could talk herself out of it, Jeannie went over and slid into the chair opposite.

'I'm sorry for intruding but . . . are you all right?' she asked.

Hannah's head jerked up, and she stared at Jeannie as if she'd just been shaken awake from a dream. Her bloodshot eyes moved around Jeannie's face, trying to work out if she was a nurse, a doctor, one of the tens of strangers who'd passed into her life in the past few days.

'I'm Jeannie,' she said. 'Dan's girlfriend – Dan Hicks . . . in the ward with Tyler. I'm sorry, I didn't mean to disturb you, but I . . . saw you were upset . . .'

What are you doing? roared a voice in her head. You would *hate* someone to do this to you! But something was pushing Jeannie on – a combination of sympathy and a strange compulsion to hear what she'd say to herself if she could step out of her own body.

'Thanks.' Hannah smiled, briefly and wanly, then chewed at a hangnail on her thumb. Every one of her nails was bitten right down: a tidemark of chipped varnish. She was silent for a while and Jeannie was on the point of getting up and leaving when she finally spoke, very quietly. She had a soft Birmingham accent.

'We saw the consultant this morning. He told us that basically Ty's not going to walk again. He'll have to learn how to feed himself, how to go to the toilet on his own, how to do everything. We've got to work out how we're going to look after him when he comes home. If he comes home.'

The despair in Hannah's face sent cold fear across Jeannie's whole body, radiating from the chest as if she'd swallowed ice cubes.

'I'm so sorry.' She struggled for the right words to dress up the next question: how to sound concerned without coming across as ghoulish – or nosy? This is how it feels, Jeannie realised, when people try to ask me how Dan is.

They want to know, but they don't know how to ask without hurting me. And they don't really understand.

'I don't know what I can do!' Hannah burst out. 'Cath's coping fine, but then Ty's always been her baby, hasn't he? She's changed his nappy and washed him when he was little – she loves looking after him. I'm not saying this is a dream come true for her, but she's his mum. I'm his girlfriend and I love him but . . .' She bowed her head, too ashamed to look up. 'I don't know if I can do this. I don't know if I'm strong enough.'

Jeannie's mind went blank. She desperately wanted to offer some reassurance but knowing what they both knew, it wasn't that easy.

'It'll be fine,' she said, and hated herself.

'Will it, though?' Hannah whispered, as if she was frightened of the words. 'I mean, I love Tyler, I love him *so much*, but we had a physio come round this morning to talk about rehab, someone else to talk about counselling, for us as well as him, then the nurses brought us leaflets about grants we can get to make the house right for him. Ty needs someone *strong*, and *capable*. And I just feel . . . I just feel . . .' She struggled for words, then gave up.

'It's natural to feel overwhelmed; it's bloody scary, this.' Jeannie felt as if she was telling herself as much as Hannah. 'It doesn't mean you can't cope, it just means you need to work out *how*.'

'Can I cope, though?' Hannah looked up and her expression was almost angry. 'I'm not a doctor. I'm not a physio. That's what Tyler needs now. Round-the-clock care, they said, worst-case scenario. I've got a job – my first proper job. I'm a primary school teacher in Bromsgrove. I'm already in trouble for taking time off this week.

We were going on holiday this July. Disney World, trip of a lifetime. I think . . . I think Ty was going to propose. That's not going to happen now, is it?'

'You don't know that. It's like the doctors keep saying: you never know what the final outcome will be.'

'But we do.' Hannah stared at Jeannie, as if she hadn't been listening. 'He just told us. Tyler's going to be in a wheelchair. What am I meant to do?'

'You're still you,' she said. 'And Tyler's still Tyler. That hasn't changed. The other stuff . . . well, that's what the support teams are there for.'

Jeannie's stomach was knotting and reknotting, twisting and retwisting. This could be me next week, she thought, jittery with adrenalin. This could be me, as soon as Dan wakes up and they can test his responses to find out how much of his old future is left. Why are you guilt-tripping her into staying? You'd hate someone to do this to you.

Hannah was turning a ring round and round her finger. But it's not the same situation, Jeannie thought. You and Dan – you'd have broken up if he hadn't had his accident. The wedding would have been off. Last-minute and exceptionally awkward, but off. Hannah and Tyler love each other; they're making plans. She's not talking about leaving; she just doubts herself. She *deserves* some support.

'You're stronger than you know,' she said. It was a platitude, but true.

Hannah looked bleakly at her coffee. 'Am I?'

Jeannie nodded, and her mum's words started to pour out of her. 'Don't look too far ahead. Deal with today; then deal with this week. Tyler needs people who love him around him, and you obviously love him. He needs your Disney World plans. It doesn't have to be this year. He needs to know you want to look that far ahead *with* him.'

Hannah's tired eyes were smudged with days' old liner; she seemed grateful for the reassurance, however empty Jeannie feared it was. 'His mum and dad are trying to push me out.'

'They're probably afraid you'll leave,' Jeannie said honestly. 'I bet they're as scared as you are. They maybe don't know if they're up to it either. And they're his *parents*.'

'My mum said that.' Hannah wiped her nose. 'But *I'm* the one Tyler lives with. Not them. *I'm* the one he was riding home to.'

'I know,' said Jeannie.

Hannah sniffed loudly, dragging the energy back inside her. 'Thank you. I feel better saying it out loud.'

Jeannie wasn't sure she deserved it. She'd basically repeated everything her mum had said to her without the faintest idea it was cutting into the sorest point of Jeannie's troubled conscience. But Mum gave good advice, she told herself. It was *her* that was wrong. 'Get to the end of today. Maybe plan something for Friday night.'

Hannah managed a pulled-together, ragged smile. 'Cheers,' she said.

'You're welcome,' said Jeannie, and made a mental note to plan something for Friday herself.

Chapter Twelve

The 'Sorry we missed you' card from the postman had been on Jeannie's sideboard for over a week, and if she hadn't dumped a fresh pile of junk mail on top and made the whole lot slide on to the hall tiles, she'd have forgotten it altogether.

It was tucked in with a couple of official-looking letters she'd been ignoring for several days. The wedding cards had thankfully tailed off, but they'd been replaced with envelopes that set Jeannie's nerves jangling in a different way – bills, and registration documents. Officials chasing her in a new life that hadn't actually started. Some were even addressed to Mr and Mrs DRA Hicks, as if Jeannie McCarthy had vanished.

She skipped past those and looked instead at the notification card. How long had it been there? Dates had ceased to mean anything, which was weird since 26 May had loomed so large in her brain for months. The parcel had arrived 1 June. She couldn't remember what day of the week that was.

Jeannie flipped the card against her hand. The postman had scrawled 'Hicks' and the address, no other details other than a tick to indicate she could collect from the town's main post office. It was a good reason to catch the bus into Longhampton, she decided. It was about time she actually wandered around the town she now lived in instead of just trudging in and out of its Victorian railway station.

The parcel, when the man at the sorting office finally handed it over, was for Dan.

Luckily, the joint bills were still in Jeannie's bag so he agreed, reluctantly, to let her take it. It didn't offer any clues: it was a black package the size of a shoebox, with a typed name and address, and no postmark to suggest where it had come from. When she shook it, Jeannie thought she could hear a faint rattle inside but nothing else to give away the contents.

She shoved it in her bag and left the long queue, wondering what it could be. Something for work? But that would have gone to the surgery. Or a wedding present? But surely that would have been addressed to the two of them, not just Dan? Jeannie hiked the bag up on her shoulder and toyed with the idea of opening it, just in case it was urgent, but something stopped her.

It wasn't hers to open. And, once again, she didn't know Dan well enough to guess what was inside. What if it was a surprise for her?

Jeannie's steps increased in pace as she tried to march off her frustration. Maybe I *should* be opening boxes, she thought to herself. This box, his boxes at home, every bloody box I can find! I *need* to get to know this man as quickly as possible, if I'm going to be looking after him for the rest of my life.

Her inner argument stopped as she came to an abrupt halt in front of a shop window.

Rachel's wedding dress was on a tailor's dummy, the

star display of the charity shop, casting an aura of elegance over the high street. Someone with an impressive grasp of styling had accessorised the dress with a long garland of creamy silk roses and ivy foliage, and pinned a billowing veil like a cumulus cloud on the wall behind. Brass candlesticks formed a shining aisle along the window, and a jade-green tea service danced in mid-air, suspended on fishing wire, porcelain teacups floating at different heights next to silver teaspoons and a tall knitted wedding cake.

And next to the dummy, where the groom should be, was a large toy Staffie.

'Four Oaks Charity Wedding Event, enquire within' read the card in the gold frame. 'A chance to change a life when you start your new one together.'

I wonder how Rachel feels, seeing her dress for sale? Jeannie wondered. Her mind slid sideways to her own dress, and she probed her unpredictable emotions like a loose tooth. How would she feel if she saw it in the next window? Sad? Regretful?

I will be relieved, Jeannie thought, with a sudden shocking clarity. Please let someone see it, fall in love with it, and take it away.

'What do you think?'

She spun round. Rachel was standing behind her, arms folded. 'Sorry, I was over the road – I wanted to see what it looked like from a distance.'

'It's magical!' Jeannie swiftly adjusted her expression. 'Did *you* do all this?'

'I did indeed.' Rachel seemed endearingly pleased with her efforts. 'I used to spend hours on the displays when we first opened the shop. It's reminded me how lazy I've got.'

'Come on, you're so busy – the dogs, and Fergus, and everything . . .'

She shook her head. 'A bit of stress is good for me. I need a challenge. Kick up the bum. Mid-life wake-up call, whatever. George and I are in a bit of a rut and . . . well, I'm the one who wants to get out of the rut. He *likes* his rut. He can't wait to be in his rut full time, bless him. He's already planning the shed he's going to build in it.'

They stared at the dress, in its dramatic, timeless glory. It was not a dress that had any intention of standing still, let alone slumping to a middle-aged halt.

Jeannie shot Rachel a cautious side glance: her strong face was wreathed in a strange, sorrowful determination. But not sadness. She looked almost . . . cross.

Jeannie was only just inside the hospital foyer, deliberating over whether to get some chocolate to take to the ward with her, when she heard someone calling her name.

'Jeannie! Jeannie!'

Hannah was hurrying across the open space, waving to get her attention. There were still dark circles under her eyes, but her hair looked freshly washed, and her face glowed with an energy Jeannie hadn't seen before. Something had changed in the three days since they'd spoken. A light had gone on inside Hannah, and she moved with a new determination.

Wow, thought Jeannie, with a pang. She looks almost *happy*. Had Tyler made an unexpected recovery?

'Jeannie!' she panted, skidding to a halt by her side. 'I wanted to catch you before we left.'

'You're leaving?' Maybe Tyler *had* had some good news.

Hannah nodded. 'They've found a place for Ty in a brain injury unit much nearer home – turns out there's a specialist place literally down the road from his parents. We had no idea that's what it was but . . . there you go. On our doorstep.'

'Well, you wouldn't know, would you?'

'Right? I used to drive past it twice a day. Funny how you never find out these things.'

They shared a bittersweet shrug at the new world they were discovering, worlds that had been there all along while they'd been going about their lives, oblivious to what lay just a tiny slip, a careless step, an oil slick on the road, away.

'Anyway,' Hannah went on, 'I wanted to see you so I could say thank you. A really big thank you.'

'For what?'

'For listening to me the other day. I so needed someone to tell me I could do it, that I was strong enough to be there for Tyler. I mean, everyone's been great, but I really needed to hear it from someone going through the same thing. You *understand* about how hard it is when you love someone, and you have to accept that they're going to be . . . different. And *you're* going to have to be different too.'

Jeannie's conscience prickled. Had she said that? 'Hannah, that's kind but I didn't say anything you didn't already know deep down.'

'You made me realise I won't be alone. There'll be other people like me out there in the same boat, and they're coping. Like I will be. Like you are, right now.' She grabbed Jeannie's hands, and for a surreal moment Jeannie felt as if they were about to do some kind of dance. 'And for you to take time out to notice how bad I was feeling – it meant a lot. I can't even imagine what you've been going through, almost losing your husband on your *wedding day*. Seriously! But you're there for Dan, every day. So calm and caring and . . . positive. That means more than any vows, right?'

Jeannie smiled tightly. Her wedding day had turned into some sort of hospital myth, with her at the centre, the tragic bride. Just as she fitted into Andrea's idea of the stunned but supportive daughter-in-law, and Owen's idea of the brave fiancée. It made everything easier in some respects – she knew what they expected of her, and it was easy enough to make the right noises. Easy enough to be the brave girlfriend other people expected, rather than admit her real part in this.

'You obviously have an amazing bond with your husband,' Hannah went on, with an earnest nod that reminded Jeannie painfully of her mum's earnest nod. 'I've been watching: you sit with him for hours, reading to him, playing him messages – it's given us some great ideas about how we can help Tyler work on his memory gaps.'

Jeannie's conscience couldn't bear much more. 'Hannah, I've got to be honest, it was Owen who came up with that, not me. Now *he's* been incredible . . .'

But Hannah wasn't having it. 'Aw, but at the end of the day, you're the one who loves him. He's got his mum, he's got his best mate, and that's brilliant – but it's *us* who have to be there for them, to remind them they're still the blokes they were before the accident. We're the ones making the future they can believe in. You and me. *Us.*'

The solemn way Hannah said *us*, as if she and Jeannie

were in some kind of honourable club, cut through her heart like a scalpel, straight to the wicked secret at the centre of her: the empty space where love should have been.

Jeannie struggled to hold back her tears of shame. Hannah adores Tyler, and she thinks I love Dan the same way, she thought. If she knew what Dan's going to have to deal with when he comes round, she'd think I was the biggest bitch in the world.

'Hey! Don't cry!' Hannah was crying now, but smiling through her tears. Her smile was gappy-toothed, sweet and childlike. 'We can keep in touch if you want? Give each other some moral support, when the parents get a bit much? Want me to text you my number?'

Jeannie nodded because what else could she do? And when Hannah hugged her, she was glad the other woman couldn't see her face, because it was crumpled in disgust.

She managed to keep herself together until Hannah had darted back down the corridor, following Mike and Cath out of the main doors with Tyler wheeled along by the paramedics between them, a ship in sail with them hanging on to the rails. Out of habit Jeannie set off back towards the ICU – before she realised that was the worst place she could go.

Jeannie leaned back against the nearest wall, too tired to think, too over-familiar with her own emotions to feel them properly any more.

Should *I* tell someone, she thought helplessly; might it help me get some perspective? But whom would she tell? It was bad enough poor Dad knowing, worrying when he was going to crack and tell Mum. What would be the point of opening this can of worms anyway, until Dan turned a corner and they knew what the future held? If she told someone now, they'd only be watching her, to see what she'd do.

Jeannie squeezed her eyes shut, feeling trapped. She had to be there when Dan woke up – she needed to know he was going to be fine, that he was going to survive this horrible moment she'd set in motion. Andrea's face, Owen's face floated in her mind's eye: they were both depending on her. They'd be making plans for the future soon, the second the consultant gave them any hope. She was part of those plans. There was no way she could leave.

If only she had the same unquestioning love that was strengthening Hannah. Jeannie wished so hard she could flick a switch and feel it flowing through her. If only she could look at Dan and think: There is no life for me without you in it . . .

We're the ones making the future they can believe in.

The weight of what she'd done closed in on her and Jeannie felt an overwhelming urge to *run*. Run out of here and never look back. Even now, she couldn't articulate exactly why.

A hand touched her arm. 'Jeannie?'

She jumped. Oh God, it was Owen. He was early. *Really* early.

'What's up?' His voice was gentle; he'd obviously spotted her tears before she could cover her face.

There was no escape. This was the real punishment: sympathy she didn't deserve, everywhere she turned. 'Just . . . I need a moment. I'm fine.'

'You're not fine. Has something happened?'

167

She made herself look up, and when she saw Owen standing there in the corridor, a stranger who'd become familiar, *indispensable* even, in a matter of a few short days, it took all Jeannie's self-control not to lose it completely.

Owen was a sweet man, kind and practical, not boring or average – as he thought – but a real tower of strength, and she'd misled him too. His honest face was furrowed with concern, for her now, as well as Dan: he obviously thought there'd been bad news from the ward, and she needed support.

Jeannie shook her head, clamping her hands over her mouth; she didn't trust herself not to blurt out everything if she opened her mouth.

Owen put his hands gently on her shoulders. Not a hug – definitely not a hug, but a calming grip. Something about the slow pressure of his hands seemed to ground her. She felt small and safe, shielded from the light and white noise in her brain. Inside Jeannie's chest, her heart was beating out of synch like a pinball ricocheting around her ribs.

'Tell me what's happened,' he said. 'Is it Dan?'

She shook her head again.

'Andrea? Has Andrea said something?' Then his expression crumpled. 'Have *I* said something to upset you?'

'No!' She couldn't let him think that. Owen was the only thing holding everything together.

'So what is it? Was it the messages? Something one of the lads said?' He seemed genuinely worried. 'Be honest. Was it the story about the football tour? Because I think Sam was exaggerating. Dan wasn't *that* drunk . . .'

Jeannie wavered, but she couldn't bear to watch him trying to pin the blame somewhere it wasn't warranted, defending Dan even now.

'It's that girl, Hannah.' She made a superhuman effort to keep her voice level.

'Hannah . . . ? Oh, from the ICU? With that bloke in the end bed – Tyler?'

Jeannie nodded.

'What about her? Did she say something?' He glanced back towards the ward.

She swallowed again. Get it out. Confess as much as you can. 'Hannah and I had a chat a few days ago. She was upset about Tyler's diagnosis, and I just . . . talked to her about taking each day as it comes. Nothing special, or wise, just the things people keep saying to me. Things I remember from when Mum was recovering.'

'Sorry, Jeannie, I'm being dim.' Owen shuffled apologetically. 'Do you feel we're not supporting you enough? I know I'm not the best at emotional stuff . . .'

'No!' She wiped her running nose. 'No, you are. I do feel . . . supported. Hannah came over just now because she wanted to say thank you. Tyler's being moved to a different hospital and she felt that I'd . . .' The words vanished in a sob – to her horror.

'She felt you'd what?' He was almost impatient. But not quite.

Jeannie's voice was a broken squeak. 'Dan – he deserves so much more. More than I can give him.' The words tumbled out in a shameful rush. 'I'm just not . . . not enough. He deserves someone better.'

There. She'd said it.

To her surprise, Owen didn't react as she'd expected.

He simply put his arms around her and held her, gently smothering the frantic panic inside. He didn't speak, and within the soft darkness of his shirt, where Jeannie's head was pressed, it felt as if her whole body was melting into Owen's shoulder.

The comfort didn't just come from the feeling of being held, it came from releasing the words that were constantly stinging away at the front of her mind like angry bees in a jar. *I'm not enough. I can't give Dan enough. He deserves more.*

She'd set the words free, and Owen, weirdly, hadn't gone mad.

Does he know I tried to bail out? Jeannie wondered, dazed. Has Owen guessed? The thought scared her, but at the same time, the relief of not having to hide it any more made her light-headed with relief.

Owen squeezed her, then pulled away, keeping her at arm's length. He fixed his eyes on hers: they were solemn. 'Don't say that again, Jeannie.'

'What?'

'Don't say you're not enough. You are enough. You're *more* than enough.'

Jeannie could feel her face falling as the relief drained away. 'What do you mean?'

'I'll be honest.' Owen didn't drop his gaze, and Jeannie had a feeling he was really opening his heart, perhaps against his better instincts. 'When Dan told me about you, I didn't know what to think. Don't take this the wrong way, but you're very different from his . . . from anyone he's dated before. I tried to get together with the two of you quite a few times but there was always some reason we couldn't meet; then suddenly – pow – you're getting married! And, well . . .' He hurried over what he was thinking. 'I wasn't sure what was going on, put it like that. I thought it was a bit of a rush. But I was wrong. You're not what I was expecting.'

Jeannie wondered what he *had* been expecting.

'I don't mean that in a bad way,' he added quickly. 'You're . . . more than I expected.'

She definitely didn't know what to say to that.

'You've been incredible throughout this.' Owen's eyes filled with emotion. 'Not just for Dan, but for Andrea. And me. Strong, and caring, and brave. Now you've been kind to this girl you don't even know – it sounds as if you've really helped her. Dan would be proud of you. No, he *is* proud of you.'

Jeannie knew her lip was wobbling. Not just her lip, her whole face. Owen was the last person she wanted to know her secret, and yet there was something about his sweet loyalty to Dan that seemed to be dragging a full confession out of her like iron filings. She fought to stop it.

'I don't know you very well, Jeannie – yet! – but it strikes me that you're the sort of person who *never* thinks you're enough,' he went on. 'But you're more than enough. If anything,' he added unexpectedly, 'it's Dan that doesn't deserve you.'

'What do you mean?'

This time he faltered. 'I mean that . . .'

Jeannie carried on staring at him. 'What?'

Owen recovered himself. 'I mean that he's partly to blame for why you feel so out of your depth now. He should have made more of an effort to introduce you to his friends instead of keeping you to himself. It wouldn't be so awkward if you'd met us and knew you could trust us.'

She'd never thought of it like that. Why hadn't Dan introduced her? Was he ashamed of her? Didn't he think she'd fit in?

'But we can put that right. I've been speaking to Mark and Adam, and they're keen to visit, if only to say hello to you. They're sorry they didn't get the chance to meet you properly at the wedding.' He paused. 'Is that OK?'

She nodded, dumbly.

'Great!' Owen beamed. 'Now, can I get you anything from the café? I was going to get a coffee for myself . . .'

Jeannie realised the moment had passed. Owen thought she'd said that she loved Dan and was worried she couldn't *help* him enough – not that she didn't *love* him enough to be there in the first place. Her heart sank. She hadn't shared her awful secret. She hadn't got it off her chest. It was still there, festering away, and she was on her own.

She drew a long, shuddering breath. I'm just going to have to take my own advice, thought Jeannie. I'm going to have to take my own wonderful advice. I'm going to have to be the adoring girlfriend everyone thinks I am, at least until Dan wakes up and we can start this over again. At least there's no wedding now. At least that pressure's off.

'A latte would be great,' she said. 'Double shot.'

Chapter Thirteen

Jeannie hadn't slept well. For the third night in a week, she'd found herself in the middle of what had become a recurring dream.

It started the same way every time: she was in the Rolls-Royce, driving to the venue with her dad, only when she turned to tell him she didn't want to go through with it, it was Dan sitting next to her, not Brian. But not Dan as she'd known him, Dan as he was now, unconscious in his green hospital gown, there but not there, the huffing sound of his ventilator eerily loud in the car. Jeannie was paralysed with terror that he'd open his eyes and look at her.

In the dream, she could feel the bones of the corset squeezing her chest, crushing the breath out of her lungs like a giant hand. She knew she had to escape from the car before Dan noticed, but as her fingers scrabbled for the door mechanism, Dan's body turned, slowly, silently, and he opened his glassy eyes. They were beautiful, but angry, and full of blame. When Jeannie tried to scream no sound would come out, and the choking feeling across her chest spread over her entire body until she couldn't breathe.

She woke, clammy with sweat. This was the first time Dan had opened his eyes in her dream, and it gave Jeannie a crawling fear that carried on creeping deep down inside her soul, even as she floated up to wakefulness. Outside the birds were singing, as a watery dawn light broke over the cottage garden. *Dan knew she'd tried to jilt him.* She told herself it was utterly irrational – she had no idea if he'd listened to her messages. And even if he had, there was no guarantee he'd remember anything before the accident – but still the fear crawled on. *Dan knew.*

It was impossible to sleep after that. Jeannie lay in bed with a headache pinching her brain, half-listening to the local radio station's early breakfast show. It surprised her how many of the village names she recognised from staring out of the window on her train journeys back and forth to the hospital, and from the general chat in the kennel office. Natalie and her husband Johnny were house-hunting; there was daily, detailed discussion about whether Little Larton was more up-and-coming than Hartley, and which bits of Longhampton were 'worth the money'.

She'd begun to doze off when she heard Rachel's voice somewhere close by. Jeannie sat up, startled, wondering if she'd let herself in downstairs. But Rachel's voice was coming from the radio: she was halfway through an interview about the Bride's Dress Revisited project.

'. . . if you've got a wedding dress taking up space in your wardrobe, then *please* consider donating it to our sale. Every penny we raise goes towards rehabilitating our three puppy farm families, and finding them the forever homes they deserve.'

'A very worthwhile cause,' agreed the interviewer. 'And Rachel's brought one of the puppies she was telling us about in with her today . . . very sweet! Hello, there! Ow! Ow! For f—'

'Mind your fingers,' said Rachel belatedly.

That'd be one of the collie girls, Jeannie guessed. Molly, Dolly, Holly, Polly, or Lolly – they were easily the sassiest of the puppies, nosing and tumbling their way out of the crate at any opportunity, always up for some socialisation. And a bit nippy, truth be told.

'It's a chance to snap up a stunning wedding dress for a bargain price!' That was Natalie, butting in while the interviewer was busy extracting his fingers from whichever puppy had grabbed him. 'We have some *very* exclusive designers on our racks, some brand new, some only worn for a matter of hours, for a fraction of what they cost originally.'

'It's basic economics,' Rachel agreed. 'If you've already budgeted for an expensive dress, buy one of ours instead, and you can spend the savings on more wine.'

'We absolutely understand how hard it is to give away a dress that means so much,' Natalie went on swiftly, 'but you'll be giving an abandoned dog the chance of a new life, and playing a fairy-godmother part in another woman's big day! Everyone's a winner!'

'So where can people donate their dresses?' asked the interviewer. His voice was muffled, as if he was sucking a small puncture wound.

'They can bring them direct to our rescue centre on the Hartley road outside Longhampton, or to our charity shop on the High Street. We'll be displaying the gowns in shop windows in the town over the summer, and at a gala event to be announced soon.'

'Sounds great. Well, thanks for coming in, ladies, and thank you . . . small dog.'

'Polly is available for rehoming at the end of the month,

along with her sisters. Please call into Four Oaks and fill in an adoption form!' Rachel chipped in, just in time.

'Rachel and Natalie there, from the Four Oaks Dog Rescue in Longhampton. Have you got a wedding dress in your wardrobe, Paula?' The presenter turned back to his co-host with an audible chuckle in his voice.

'Ha ha, you know I do, Terry!'

'Yes, you've got . . . *three* wedding dresses, haven't you? She's got a taste for wedding cake, this one!'

'Ha ha! Whereas you've got a taste for *any* kind of cake, Terry. And speaking of which, here's Meghan Trainor with "All About That Bass" taking us up to the news and travel at eight o'clock . . .'

Jeannie slapped the off button down on her old clock radio and swung her legs out of bed. Time to get up. And for the first time in what felt like ages, she really wanted to get on with her day.

Her task for the morning was to tackle some of the sealed boxes in the sitting room. The nearest one was Dan's, and marked 'BOOKS/LIVING ROOM', so she wasn't anticipating any nasty surprises beyond one too many Jeremy Clarksons and possibly an unwashed mug or stray sock that had got swept up in the chaos.

Jeannie had been in the sitting room of Dan's flat three times, when she'd stayed for the weekend, and it had been nice enough: a striking abstract painting bought from a fundraising auction on one wall, cushions that looked suspiciously like Andrea's choices, now she knew Andrea better, and a massive footstool – for maximum lounging comfort when watching football, apparently.

Now they had a sitting room of their own, with a view of the cottage garden and the hills beyond, Jeannie was hunting for personal items to make it seem a bit less like the furniture section of a charity shop. Dan's sofa and her precious squashy double armchair sat in there alone, with only his hulking great plasma television for company. It desperately needed framed photos, or a vase for flowers, or bookshelf of favourite novels. Dan didn't have many books in his flat, or, Jeannie had noticed at the time, anything to play music on, other than his phone.

The top layer in Dan's box was tea towels (who knew he'd have so many?). Jeannie was marvelling at the multiple sets of *Doctor Who* DVDs, which just kept coming and coming out of the depths like a clown car, when the doorbell rang.

Thinking it might be Rachel and Natalie on their way back from the radio interview, Jeannie hurried to the front door, ready to congratulate them, but there was a woman standing on the step with a huge dress bag containing a wedding dress.

'I'm so sorry to bother you,' she said, flustered, 'but this is for Rachel – can I leave it with you?'

'Oh, you need the house up the lane.' Jeannie pointed up towards the Fenwicks' house. 'That's where Rachel lives.'

'I know, but there's no one in.' The woman hefted the dress on to her other arm. Now Jeannie looked closely, there were two bags, both silvery and monogrammed with soft satin hangers just visible. 'I rang a couple of times, but I didn't want to leave these outside.'

Jeannie glanced up the lane to the house; there were no cars visible. George was probably doing the school run if Rachel was on the radio, and Jeannie had no idea when she'd be back.

'The thing is, there's a story. I need to explain them to you,' the woman went on, fussing over the zips. 'It's not quite what it looks like, and I want whoever buys them to know the whole tale.'

'Come in,' said Jeannie. It would make a change to hear someone else's 'not what it looks like' wedding story.

Unzipped and laid out over Jeannie's scrubbed pine kitchen chairs, the dress bags looked like popped peapods. Two different dresses nestled inside: one full-length fishtail gown with delicate webs of crystals spiralling round the bodice, and one red and white gingham swing dress with jaunty crimson-tipped net underskirts.

'So, Henry and I got engaged on my birthday.' The woman – Rhiannon – wasn't in too much of a rush to pass on Jeannie's offer of a coffee, it turned out. 'He'd bought tickets for the theatre which he normally *never* wants to go to if there's rugby on, and he'd hidden the ring in a box of my favourite chocolates. He'd taken out the ones I didn't like, and replaced them with pralines, which I do like.' She smiled with each little revelation. 'The engagement ring was in the bottom layer. I nearly ate it in the dark! I couldn't work out why he was hustling me to scoff the lot. Then he proposed in the interval with a bottle of champagne.'

Jeannie scribbled the details; she wasn't sure how much Natalie and Rachel would want. She wondered if she ought to prepare a version of her own proposal to go with the dress. The knot in her stomach tightened again. That was where it had started to go wrong for her and Dan. The proposal. How stupidly ironic was that?

'That's lovely,' she said, clearing her mind. 'Champagne!'

'I know!' Rhiannon sighed happily. 'So, anyway, I got going on the wedding planning – I'd been stalking this dress online for ages.' She caressed the pearly satin with a gentle hand; the same gesture Rachel had made when she'd shown Jeannie her dress. 'I tracked it down in a shop in Cardiff. It was *way* out of my budget but once I'd tried it on, I knew there wasn't going to be another. You just know, don't you?'

'Mmm.' Well, sort of.

'So I bought it. I had the alterations done, got shoes dyed to match. And then' – Rhiannon's blue eyes widened – 'I found out I was pregnant.'

Jeannie wasn't sure what the right response was. 'Oh . . . congratulations? No. Oh dear?'

Rhiannon nodded. 'The baby was due around the wedding date. So we had to postpone – that caused so much drama. You would not believe.'

'I would,' said Jeannie. 'Cancelling a wedding is . . . well, some bits of it are easier than others.' Sue and Owen had done an incredible job of erasing her wedding from the landscape. Only a freezer full of party food and some bills remained.

Rhiannon gave her a funny look, then carried on. 'So, anyway, we postponed and told everyone the new date, and then . . .' She looked down at her hands. 'I lost the baby.'

Jeannie's pen halted in mid-air. She glanced up, shocked. 'I'm very sorry.'

'It was quite late on. I knew something was up, I just had this . . . bad feeling. Henry took me to A & E and we had a scan and he'd gone. He'd stopped growing at twenty weeks.' She bit her soft lower lip. 'It was the worst moment of my life, seeing our baby on the ultrasound. Not moving.'

'I bet,' murmured Jeannie.

'I'd failed. I'd failed our little bean, and Henry. We called him Philip, after both our dads.' Rhiannon's voice vanished into a hiccup of sorrow. She flapped her hand around her face, embarrassed. 'I'm sorry. It's been so long since I've talked about this, I thought I'd stopped . . .'

'Don't, please, if you don't want to carry on . . .' Jeannie reached out to touch her hand. There were some tissues on the table – there were tissues wherever she went – and she pushed them over.

'Thanks.' Rhiannon smiled gratefully through her tears.

Neither spoke for a moment or two.

Rhiannon wiped her eyes and coughed. 'Anyway, things were really horrible for a while after that. I couldn't eat or sleep. I lost my job, because I was turning up late, I was drinking too much. I wasn't a nice person to be around. But Henry stuck by me. He was amazing. He didn't blame me, or give me a hard time, even though he was torn up inside himself. I don't know why he stayed but he did. We didn't talk about the wedding any more. He and my mum cancelled everything and I didn't ask. But . . .' She waved a finger at Jeannie, smiling through her tears. 'One day, I woke up early and I saw Henry lying there with his arm round me, his lovely strong arm, and I thought, *This* is what marriage is about. Being there for someone you love even when they don't love themselves. We'd already done for better and for worse, hadn't we?'

Jeannie nodded. Her eyes were filling up too now, at the love in Rhiannon's face.

'So I found a counsellor and, long story short, I put my head back together. For him, and for me, and for our Philip. He wouldn't want his mum and dad to fall apart, I knew that much. And when I felt like myself again, I asked Henry to marry me. Just one night, while we were ordering a curry. Nothing fancy, I just said it: "Will you marry me?" And he said, "Yes, babe." So we did!'

'And did you replan the whole thing?'

'Totally.' Rhiannon nodded. 'Town hall ceremony, beer and pies at our local pub, just a few friends and family. We had a blast. I didn't want to wear that dress, though. It reminded me of . . . too much. But I couldn't bring myself to sell it either! Daft, isn't it? My mum and my sisters took me shopping and bought me this one.' She gave the fun swing dress a playful flick. 'Mum said it was more me. And it is, to be fair. I danced all night in it.'

'It's beautiful.' Jeannie touched the stiff petticoat, made for swirling and dancing. Celebrating, and loving. 'I bet you had the most amazing day.'

'We did. But it was the ceremony that blew me away. I'd been to so many weddings, and I thought I knew what it'd be like, but when I looked at Henry during our vows, and he was promising to protect me from every storm life threw at us, and love me for who I was . . . I knew he meant it. Because he'd already done that. We *knew* how strong our love was. It wasn't just words.'

There was such gratitude in Rhiannon's face, and relief, that the man she loved had waited for her to find herself. They were partners, who knew each other, inside and out, bad and good, weak and strong. How else could you make promises like that, unless you really knew the other person?

Jeannie saw Dan in her mind's eye, in his hospital bed. He wasn't that man, and she knew it. But how could she leave him?

'Oh no, I've set myself off again!' Rhiannon wiped her running mascara with the side of her finger. 'But it's true, isn't it? You've got to be there for the bad bits as well as the good. That's the real test of a human being, as well as a relationship, I reckon. Sticking around. I just wanted people to know that things work out. Not always the way you think, but if you love one another enough, it works out somehow. That's why I needed to explain why the first dress is unworn – I didn't want you to think it was unlucky!'

Jeannie looked at the two different dresses over the chair: one pristine and elegant; the other loose and fun. 'It's the opposite of unlucky. But are you sure you want to give us both dresses? I feel bad taking these from you,' she said. 'They mean so much.'

'Nah, it's time.' Rhiannon tucked her hair behind her ears. 'Soon as I heard Rachel on the radio this morning, talking about those poor puppy farm dogs, I just thought: Right, it's a sign.' She fished a phone out of her handbag. 'We got our Angel from up here; she was Henry's birthday present. Let me show you our girl . . .'

Jeannie let Rhiannon show her a stream of photos of a patient, kind-faced Staffie in a variety of neckerchiefs,

Christmas antlers, woollen jumpers and a tutu. She could see why Rachel's radio appeal had struck a chord with Rhiannon – Angel was exactly like Sadie, the wide-eyed Staffie in the pen down the lane. Stocky, chicken-legged, sweet-natured.

'There but for the grace of God,' said Rhiannon, looking up, suddenly very solemn, and Jeannie had the feeling she was looking straight into her heart.

Chapter Fourteen

The puppies were growing quickly and exploring the expanding boundaries of their new world as if they'd never known anything different. Every morning Jeannie called into the office to find them freshly plumped up again overnight, a bit leggier and a lot bolder. The Staffie pups were chunky, amiable little monsters, tumbling around in their big crate, roaring and playing, trying to swallow one another whole, while the black-and-white collies were into everything, nosing and sniffing and attempting to escape by using their littermates as ladders up the side of the playpen. Grace's curly apricot puppies, Rachel thought, were most likely cockapoos, rather than pure poodle and they were the first to bark a hello to the postman and the vet nurses, and reacted with curiosity to Rachel's diligent checklist of sounds and smells.

'I never want them to be frightened of anything, ever again,' she insisted, even if it meant her, Natalie and Jeannie sitting in the office, typing up descriptions of wedding dresses while listening to CDs of thunderstorms and brass bands and, bizarrely, male voice choirs to start getting the pups ready for the outside world.

Their traumatised mothers, though, were a different story.

Rachel had taken a lot of advice from Debbie, the

woman who'd helped rescue the dogs in the first place from the farm near the border. 'You've got to be very, very patient,' Debbie had warned her. 'These poor girls – they've never walked on leads, they've never lived inside, they've never learned how to play. They don't know anything other than the shed they were kept in. You've got to take it slow, slow, slow.'

And so the rules were posted up. The three mothers – Lady Sadie the Staffie, Constance the collie, and Grace the poodle – were never to be left alone during the day. There always had to be one human being there, supervising the puppies but also keeping their mums company. They weren't to be patted or stroked without plenty of warning, and given space to escape if they wanted. Instead of walks, they were shepherded into the secure paddock that the boarding kennel dogs played in, and Rachel – or one of the volunteers – would let them do their own thing while throwing balls around in the hope they'd join in. Sometimes they did, briefly, and it nearly made Jeannie cry to see their tentative skips.

It was a heartbreakingly slow job but Rachel was determined to teach the dogs they could trust her. Gem was her secret weapon: he shadowed her, observing every interaction, and seemed to be trying to show the puppy farm dogs how pet dogs behaved. Jeannie watched him one morning, pawing the door to make Rachel open it; he slipped outside, then immediately came back in, nudging the door open with his silver nose. Rachel got up to close it, then seconds later, Gem pawed for it to be opened again. Jeannie started to say, 'Oh, Gem, what's up?' but then realised Grace and Constance were watching him: he was showing them how to ask to go out.

'Gem's amazing,' Rachel said, kicking a well-gnawed football towards Jeannie in the paddock. 'I sometimes think he knows what I'm thinking before I do. Did you know collies recognise the same number of words as a three-year-old human being?'

Jeannie stopped the ball with her foot. 'No, I did not. Which words?'

'Bacon. Sandwich. Walk. Worming tablet. The usual.'

Constance the Border collie was watching the football intently, lying in the grass with her head on her white paws. Of the three bitches, she was the closest to learning the ropes of the house but her energy was the tightest coiled. Every movement made her spring to her silent paws, light as a feather floating on the air. Sadie the Staffie had curled up in the sun and was ignoring everyone, enjoying the warmth on her dappled back. Grace was stalking around the edges of the paddock on elegant tiptoes, as if the feeling of the grass under her paws was still confusing. Sometimes the girls shrank close together for support; sometimes they seemed in a bubble of their own anxiety, closed off from everything.

'I did one of those online compatibility tests this morning,' Rachel went on. 'Which dog suits you best?'

'And?'

'Afghan hound.'

'Really?' Jeannie pretended to look surprised, as Rachel clearly wasn't that happy about it, but it wasn't a surprise, really: slinky, stylish, well-groomed, big nose . . .

'I have no idea how. I was trying to get Border collie.'

'Maybe you didn't mention your flock of sheep? I wonder what I'd get?'

Rachel tossed some treats out for the dogs, and said casually, 'You should get Lady Sadie.'

'No. What? As in . . . have her?' Jeannie shook her head. 'I don't think I'm a Staffie person!'

'People *never* think they're a Staffie person, but why not? Look at her. She's spent most of her wretched life in a shed but she's lying there in the sun like a queen. Sadie needs company, and so do you. You're a perfect match.'

Jeannie was tempted. Lady Sadie's bright eyes waiting for her in the kitchen when she came home; her solid, butterball body learning to lean into her side. Of the three, Sadie was the most eager to trust again. Constance needed a job; Grace needed dedicated grooming from someone with a thing about combs. Lady Sadie just needed someone to love.

She shook her head and hoofed the ball back to Rachel. 'Sadie needs company. I'm out of the house half the day. I don't want to let her down.'

Rachel went on as if she hadn't spoken. 'It's funny – my aunt, Dot, she used to match people to the right dog, and she was never wrong. It wasn't always the type of dog people came for, either. Sometimes we can't always see what we need.' She gave Jeannie a funny look. 'I mean, how did you know you were a Dan person?'

'The computer worked it out for me. You can't argue with computers.'

'And how exactly did they do that?'

Jeannie wasn't sure if Rachel was winding her up. Hadn't everyone dipped their toe into online dating at some point? Even just out of curiosity? But then Rachel had been with George a long time . . .

'It asks lots of questions. Are you a cat person, or a dog person, or an iguana person? Do you prefer the films of Hitchcock, Spielberg or Pixar? Would your ideal date be up a mountain, or in seventeenth-century Venice? That type of thing. Saves you falling in love with someone who turns out to have strong views about reincarnation. Or Diet Pepsi.'

Rachel considered this. 'Fair enough. But how come you were online dating? I'd have thought you'd have met lots of people through your music? No?'

'Oh, yeah, plenty. But they were usually too in love with themselves to fall for anyone else. That, or they were off their faces. Or, you know, *Edith* . . . Anyway, online dating means you can meet anyone from anywhere.' Jeannie knew she sounded defensive, but it had worn her down, the constant hunt for someone normal. Someone whom she could just be with, and not have to compete with all the time. Dan's cheerful lack of interest in the music scene had, in some respects, been a relief. To begin with, anyway.

'How did you know George was right for you?' she countered.

Rachel laughed. 'I didn't! There's no way George and I would have ended up being matched by a computer. We've got nothing in common. I still wonder how on earth we ended up together – when we met, he thought I was shallow and totally unsuited to country life, and I found him intensely smug and dismissive. And yet . . . the stars aligned, I got pregnant and here we are.'

Jeannie looked at Rachel. The flippant way she said that didn't square up with the way everyone else spoke about her and George. Ted referred to them as the town's Burton and Taylor, which Jeannie wasn't sure was a positive comment on their marriage, but Freda quickly corrected him to 'Newman and Woodward' with a sharp glance. George putting his foot down about money was one thing, but anyone she spoke to at the rescue talked about George and Rachel as if they were the love story of the decade.

'I do love him,' said Rachel, with a strange ferocity, to the air. She stared at the house. 'I just don't always understand why he's so . . . ngggh. So *George.*'

Gem nosed around their legs.

'Hasn't he always been quite . . . George?' Jeannie asked.

Rachel didn't reply at once. When she did, she seemed to be answering a different question. 'The danger about being married is assuming that's it. That you now know everything about someone,' she said. 'You never do.'

'Isn't that a good thing if you're going to be married for the rest of your life? Having new things to discover about each other?' asked Jeannie, hopefully.

'Not if only one person wants to do any discovering,' said Rachel, and marched off.

An unfamiliar woman's voice was chatting away in the office when they got back to the kennel building, and the dogs froze behind Jeannie and Rachel's legs as soon as they heard it. Constance let out a low warning growl, something Jeannie hadn't heard before. Constance barely made a sound, normally. Now her hackles rose up her back and she quivered with tension.

'She's worried about her pups. I'll take these three into that empty pen at the end of the kennels for now,' said Rachel quietly, bending to comfort the collie's pulled-back ears. 'Mel's in there mucking out – I need to talk to her about this morning's check-ins anyway. You go on in, see if it's someone with a wedding dress for us.'

Jeannie pushed open the door. Natalie was behind the desk in the office talking to a middle-aged woman dressed in head-to-toe black, sitting in the one comfy chair with a cup of tea. Rachel had guessed right: a bulging dress carrier was hanging from the shelving unit well out of the way of the crate of cockapoos next to it.

'. . . there'll be a fabulous dinner with entertainment and a wedding cake, of course,' Natalie was saying. 'Oh, hello! I was just telling Gillian here about our gala evening.'

'Sounds amazing!' Gillian widened her eyes and recrossed her plump legs. She was rocking a pair of shiny jet-black patent DMs, even though summer was ramping up outside. 'I haven't seen my bridesmaids in years – but as Natalie here says, what a great reason to get back together!'

'Discounts if they come in their old dresses, of course!' Natalie beamed, then made a discreet note to herself on a pad: it had obviously just occurred to her. 'Anyway, Gillian, you were telling me about your dress. We love to hear their stories, don't we, Jeannie?'

'Oh, this dress. I'm giving it to you because I need it out of my life!' Gillian threw her hands up in the air in pretend horror. 'Out! Out!'

'Now, why's that?'

Jeannie sat on the floor next to the crate full of woolly cockapoos, the drama queens of the puppy pack. All five of them were scrabbling over a toy beefburger, squealing and chomping one another with gusto on top of a pile of *Longhampton Gazette*s and old vetbed.

'It haunted my dreams, that dress. Never gave me a minute's peace. Do you know what I mean?' She clutched her mug and arched a pierced eyebrow knowingly at Natalie and Jeannie. 'I bought it – and I'm not alone, I bet you'll have other ladies done the same – I bought it thinking it'd motivate me to lose three stone before the wedding.'

'And did it?' It was hard for Natalie to pitch exactly the right tone of query there.

'Nooooooo! I put on weight, worrying about the bloody thing!' Gillian hooted with zero remorse. 'I dunno what I was thinking. I suppose I wanted to be that lovely willowy bride in the photos, but let's face it, I'm not. I wasn't going to grow six inches, any more'n I was going to lose fifteen years. Madness.'

'So you never wore it.'

'Nope. It hung on the back of the door in my spare room for a whole year, making me feel bad every time I saw it, then the week before the wedding, my best friend Mandy took me to one side and said, "Gillian, we need to get you a dress because it's too late for you to get lipo or dysentery now."'

Jeannie choked on a snort and pretended to cough.

'So I got a new dress.' Gillian helped herself to one of the good biscuits, dunking it in her tea. 'Seventy quid in the John Lewis sale. Ghost. I had it dyed purple and wore it to parties until my daft lump of a husband spilled curry sauce on it. Mind you, I've put up with that daft lump for twenty years next month, so I can't complain.'

She looked over at the suit carrier, affectionately. 'It's a lovely dress. It might need a bit of alteration, seeing as it's so old, but we're moving and I'm not taking it with me. Have a look – it's a cracker.'

'Oh, it's . . . lovely, Gillian.' Natalie unzipped it and

pulled the dress out: there was a lot of it, mostly covered in crystals. It glittered spectacularly under the office lights. Gillian's was the kind of wedding gown Mariah Carey might choose for a Las Vegas Matrimony Spectacular.

Jeannie blinked. She hadn't been expecting *that*, going by Gillian's gothic daytime look – but who knew what a woman's secret vision of herself as a bride was? She was hardly one to talk.

Gillian gazed wistfully at it, then set her mouth in a firm line. 'Someone's going to look a million dollars in that. But make sure you tell whoever tries it on this . . .' She wagged a finger at them both. 'You've got to be yourself at your wedding. Fitting into a dress won't make your marriage a day longer or shorter. My sister-in-law went on the Atkins for her big day. Passed out face down in the wedding cake before she could cut it. When she came round, first thing she said was, "For Christ's sake, put me back in the cake, Mum."'

'I'll bear that in mind,' said Natalie brightly. 'If I ever decide to get married again.'

'Right then, I'll be off.' Gillian put the mug down with a smack of her blackberry lips. 'Good luck with the sale, ladies. I'll keep my eye out for that gala night announcement!'

When she'd left, Natalie got up to clear the mugs away, and looked apologetically at Jeannie.

'Are you *sure* you're OK with this?' She nodded over at the dress. 'I did *say* to Rachel, maybe Jeannie was still in shock when she agreed to help out . . . Please tell us if it's upsetting, having to talk about weddings all day long. Rachel can be single-minded once she gets going. Not a criticism: I can be just as bad.'

Jeannie shook her head. 'Honestly, I'm fine. I'd say if I wasn't.'

'Really?'

'Really.' Hearing the donation stories for each dress was making Jeannie think about weddings in a very different way – not the day itself, but the marriage that had come after, and the love that had come before. Maybe hearing enough people talk about how their other halves drove them mad, and weren't perfect, and how love had grown back after strife or started in inauspicious circumstances . . . maybe that would help her work out what to say to Dan? Jeannie clung to anything that might help her sort out feelings she still didn't properly understand.

'Well. Do say. We're used to being frank with each other, me and Rachel.' Natalie smiled, then rinsed out the cups and gathered her things together with a groan. 'Well, I'm off, wish me luck.'

'What for?'

'Johnny's asked me to listen to his ukulele orchestra. They need practice playing in front of people, apparently.'

'Everyone does. It's not easy at first. Where is it?'

Natalie swung her bag over her shoulder. 'At school. Johnny teaches history at the high school – they have a ukulele orchestra one lunchtime a week, and Johnny's in charge, for his sins. They've got concert commitments coming up, hence the practice. I mean, they're a nice bunch – he herds them into the minibus to play to the old people's home, and they go carol singing. And at least you can sing along, not like the violin group.' She rolled her eyes in horror. 'There should be a law against the violin group, if you ask me.'

'Does he teach them?'

'God, no. He's learning himself. Johnny's more . . .' she struggled for the diplomatic word, '. . . enthusiastic than qualified. They did have a teacher but she's on maternity leave and there aren't many round here. I don't suppose you know anyone?'

'Well, me?' Jeannie wondered why Natalie hadn't asked before. 'I wouldn't mind helping, if he's stuck – one lunchtime a week?'

Natalie nodded. 'Yes, every Thursday. You honestly wouldn't mind? I didn't like to mention it when you've so much on your plate. But Johnny'll be over the moon. "Moon River", that is. Or "Somewheeeeeere, over the rainbow" . . . They play that a *lot*.'

'Oh, I love that,' said Jeannie. 'It still makes me cry.'

'Makes me cry too. Johnny's never been able to reach that high note.' Natalie winced. 'Can I give him your mobile number? This is incredibly kind of you.'

'It's my pleasure – it's helpful to have a few other things to think about. Mr Allcott actually told us Dan needs more quiet time without visitors, so I've got a few spare hours now.'

'No news?'

Jeannie shook her head. 'But we never know when something might happen. Dan's under constant observation, and they always say it could happen any moment.' She checked her watch. 'Speaking of which . . .'

Rachel had offered to give her a lift to the station, and once Jeannie had given her contact details to Natalie, she hurried off to find her.

The covered runs where both the boarders and rescue dogs stayed were down a long corridor off the main office area. The Fenwicks had invested in upgrading the kennels, and now they boasted brightly painted pens with underfloor heating, and long windows looking out on to wild flower paddocks where the dogs let off steam three times a day. A radio provided constant music during the day, (non-argumentative) talk radio in the evenings, and classical overnight, for the insomniacs.

It was, as Rachel had explained when she'd first shown her round, as close to a 1960s holiday camp for dogs as she could make it, short of an Olympic-sized swimming pool. And she was working on that.

Jeannie could see Rachel at the far end, chatting to Mel the kennel assistant about a couple of Jack Russells who'd come in that morning. They were discussing who could go out to play with whom later on, using the master list of dog friendship preferences. Playtime was a complex process, and one Rachel took very seriously.

'Yan and Tan can go out with Abbey and Max,' she was saying. 'They're calm. Well, calm for terriers. Just make sure you take one ball for each of them or else it turns into *Game of Thrones*, dog edition.' She looked up when she heard Jeannie's footsteps. 'One second, I'll be right with you . . .'

Jeannie crouched by the run where Grace, Constance and Lady Sadie were waiting. Lady Sadie had commandeered the dog bed and had curled up in one end; Grace had wedged herself in what was left, sitting upright with her long nose high in the air. Constance sat by them, ears pricked, eyeing the fat chocolate Labrador snoring in the run opposite as if she'd like to spring silently on his head, just to see how he'd react. Jeannie was starting to see a lot of Edith in Constance.

'Bye, ladies,' she said softly. Grace carried on staring, but Sadie twitched awake in the basket. To Jeannie's surprise, she unfolded herself, then tentatively tottered straight over to her on legs that still seemed too skinny for her broad body. She hesitated a foot away from Jeannie, and plopped down, maintaining eye contact.

Jeannie poked her fingers through the wire and wiggled them. 'You're a good girl, Sadie,' she said. 'It was nice playing with you. I'll see you soon.'

The Staffie stared at her, her dark eyes liquid-soft in her smooth white head. She didn't move, she didn't come any closer, but Jeannie sensed a connection, the first silvery threads of trust. She felt a tug of a new emotion and smiled at the dog through the kennel door. The dog – was she going mad? – seemed to smile back. It was the sweetest smile.

Chapter Fifteen

Johnny's ukulele orchestra were, as Natalie had said, a fun bunch.

What had started out as a CV-enhancing 'hobby' class for the less career-minded students had unexpectedly turned into the coolest uncool hangout, and spaces were in high demand. When Jeannie dropped into her first Thursday lunchtime session in the high school's music block, all twenty-five of the current orchestra were already there, tuning up and chatting: a mixed bag of teenage girls with silky curtains of honey-streaked hair, a few geeky boys, and a few far-from-geeky boys; a couple of first years swimming in their blazers up to sixth formers in non-uniform. And Johnny, Natalie's husband, in his cords and George Formby T-shirt under his checked shirt, which he revealed with a theatrical flourish to groans from the assembled students.

'It's Uke Club!' he protested, displaying it proudly. 'This is how we know it's Uke Club and not History!'

'Just don't make *us* wear them, sir,' grumbled one of the boys.

'No way. I am the only George Formby in this orchestra,' said Johnny. 'Now, please welcome Jeannie, who will be suffering our renditions for the rest of the term – I hope. Unless you put her off today, which I hope you won't,

Liam,' he added, with a meaningful look that spoke of several bad experiences.

'You'd better not sing then, sir,' retorted Liam from the back of the room.

Jeannie wasn't fazed by the expectant faces turning to her – she never knew whether teaching primary school kids made performing in front of festival audiences easier, or vice versa – and they had an enjoyable forty-five minutes running through their repertoire, with space in the middle for her to teach them her version of 'Wuthering Heights', which Johnny said was educational *and* musical.

It amazed Jeannie how easily she'd walked into her room and picked up the ukulele to play with the kids, when she'd walked in so many times before and walked out again without playing a note. The difference was that this wasn't about her. She didn't feel exposed when her voice was lost in the middle of twenty-six other varyingly tuneful voices. Plus Jeannie had consciously tried not to think too hard about this, beyond the favour she was doing for her new friend Natalie. She'd told herself she didn't have to play or sing, she could just stand there and demonstrate the chords, but when it came down to it, her fingers moved and her voice had joined in and . . . well, there she was.

Obviously she didn't play any songs she and Edith had performed together, much less any of her own music. But it felt good to be singing again. A cloud she hadn't been aware of moved away for the time they were playing, leaving her unexpectedly sunny inside, and when they finished, and the kids spontaneously applauded themselves, Jeannie applauded them right back.

'I don't know what you did but I've never heard them play as well as that,' said Johnny as the end-of-lunch bell rang and the last student trailed out of the music room. 'Usually we have to stop halfway through for a fight about someone singing out of tune or someone getting the words wrong.'

'Isn't it the way with new teachers?' Jeannie zipped her ukulele into its star-spangled case. 'Everyone tries their best?'

'Ah, no,' said Johnny firmly. 'The exact opposite, in my experience. I think they just sensed they were playing with someone who knew what they were doing for once.' He held the door for her, and added, with a grin, 'And that goes for me too, thank you very much.'

There wasn't time to go home before her train left, so Jeannie caught the bus outside the school gates to the station. She was collecting a ticket from the machine when her phone rang in her bag.

It was Andrea.

'Just so you know,' she said, after the usual pleasant-ries, 'I've finally managed to get Danny moved into a room on his own, so don't go to the usual ward – ask at reception for directions.'

'What? Is he all right?' Jeannie juggled her bag, her bottle of water and her ukulele case, trying to retrieve the ticket from the slot without spilling or dropping any.

'Yes, he's fine. I just feel it would be best for him to get some peace and quiet. He's definitely showing signs of trying to wake up, Jeannie. I'm *sure* his eyes were moving while he was listening to today's messages. He seemed *there*, if you know what I mean.'

Dan's *eyes* were moving? That was new. A heaviness spread in Jeannie's chest: fear and relief and something else she didn't want to examine too closely.

'Wow,' she said. 'Did any of the doctors see?'

'No, but Kate's keeping a close watch. I saw his eyelids flutter, as if he was trying to show he could hear me.' Andrea's voice was teary with emotion. 'I just *know* he's trying to come back to us, Jeannie. When will you be here?'

'I'm leaving Longhampton now. So about an hour?'

'I'll hang on until then. I just can't bear the thought of Dan trying to show us he's coming back, and there being no one to see him! It must be such an effort . . .'

'I'm on my way,' said Jeannie, wondering why her toes were wet. When she looked down, she realised she'd gripped her plastic water bottle so tightly it had split.

Andrea stood up as soon as Jeannie put her head round Dan's door; she had her lightweight mac on, handbag on her knee ready to go, but was still holding Dan's hand until the very last second.

'There you are!' she said with her sweet smile. Every improvement in Dan's condition seemed to take years off Andrea: today she looked transformed. 'Now then, Danny, I'm off to my own appointment, but here's Jeannie to keep you company this afternoon.' She pointed at the phone on the bedside table. 'There's a new recording here from Dan's auntie Claire. I've been playing him some of the older messages this morning. I think that's what got his eyelids moving, you know. Such a wonderful idea! You and Owen are so clever!'

'Any more . . . movements?'

Andrea shook her head. 'No. But it must be *so* exhausting for him. We shouldn't expect too much. Please, if you notice *anything*, call me. I've got to go back to Newcastle tonight for my check-up with the heart specialist, but I'll be back as soon as I can. I tried to reschedule but they wouldn't. Appointments with Mr Davies are like gold dust and he did say, what with the strain I'd been under, it was vital to review my medication.'

'You've got to look after yourself,' murmured Jeannie. She hadn't been able to take her eyes off Dan in the bed since she'd walked in. His cheeks were slightly pinker – that could be the lighting in the room? – and one of the nurses had changed his gown and shaved him, ruffling his hair up in the process. It made him look asleep, rather than unconscious. Tiny changes but definitely changes. Was Andrea right? Was Dan slowly rising to the surface?

'I've got lots to talk about, Dan.' She settled herself in the chair by his side, close enough to see the tiny hairs on his sideburns move as the ventilator worked. 'I started a volunteering role up at the high school today.'

'Really?' Andrea hesitated at the door.

'Yes, I'm giving them a hand with their ukulele orchestra!' Jeannie indicated the case. 'I've come straight from there, our first session. It was a lot of fun!'

'That's nice.' Andrea's mouth shifted, trying to frame unwelcome thoughts. 'But it's maybe not a good idea to commit to too much, Jeannie – it would be a shame to have to give them up suddenly. Dan's going to need us round the clock any day now.'

'It's only once a week,' said Jeannie with a smile that she hoped looked supportive and positive. She didn't want to say, Andrea, be realistic, Dan's going to need much more than just you and me for a while, because that wasn't what a supportive daughter-in-law should think.

'Well, you'll know best. I suppose it's good for you to use your music skills!'

'I've missed playing,' said Jeannie, feeling her sore fingertips, and realising that, for the first time since that awful conversation with Edith, she *had* missed making music with other people. She really, really had.

Once Andrea had gone, Jeannie settled into her chair and played the message from Auntie Claire again. Ironically, she learned a lot more about Claire and her son Gene, the British drone-flying champion, and her husband Tom, the big potato of Cheltenham's organic vegetable scene, than she did about Dan. It made her wonder seriously when Claire had last seen her nephew, and if she remembered he was now an adult. Dan had always been a nice boy. Aunt Claire had always known he'd do well. He'd been right about her cat's leg. Fluffy was nearly twenty-three now! That was the size of it.

Dan's eyelids did not move through any of it. Jeannie assumed it was because he'd rolled his eyes right back in his head with boredom.

She scrolled through the older messages Andrea had been playing: school friends, work colleagues, Dan's last boss. If she'd worried about not knowing Dan well enough, then here were precious chances to fix that: the people who knew Dan best were offering memories she could legitimately listen in on – surely it should give her some clue into his personality, his character?

And yet they didn't. She didn't feel as if she was learning anything new at *all* about him.

She touched the screen and played his friend Andy's message.

'So, mate, here's another story. We were in London with Mark, and Owen and Stu. And, wait, was Matty there as well? Yeah! Matty was there, and it was just after Stu had started his medical practice in Cork, at that stud farm? Ha ha! Oh, man, remember the emails he used to send us from the stud farm? Ha ha! "Cucumber sandwiches"! Ha ha! Say no more! Ha ha! Anyway . . .'

Andy rambled on about a Chinese meal, and then finished. If there was a punchline, Jeannie didn't hear one. Dan's role had been mainly to divide up the bill between the six of them using the calculator on his phone.

'I guess you had to be there, eh, Dan?' she said and watched his face to see if Andy's hilarious non-story about hiding prawn crackers in strangers' coat pockets would result in an eyelid flicker.

Nope.

No flicker in her heart either; they just sounded like any other bunch of lads out on the town. Albeit well-brought-up ones who remembered to tip. None of them sounded as nice as Owen.

However: 'Let's try another,' she said, and selected Nick from the list.

Nick's anecdote about Dan's legendary hat-trick for the vets' football team was equally jovial and equally unrevealing. Jeannie sat through every message, hoping for just one nugget of controversy or quirkiness – a secret scar in an embarrassing place, an unexpected talent for bread-making – but there was nothing. Dan was a nice guy, whom everybody liked very much. There was only one thing that stood out like a red flag: not one of his friends mentioned Dan's wedding to her.

She searched to see if Owen had left a recorded message – now, those memories she'd like to hear – but there was nothing, and she felt disappointed.

After an hour, Jeannie gave up on stories of sporting achievements and cat-saving heroics and let silence fill the room. Her breathing synchronised with Dan's, in and out, up and down, and she gazed out of the window at the flat blue-grey sky. No clouds. No sun. No sounds, just the hum and huff of the equipment holding Dan in a web of wires. The noisy music room, echoing with giggles and missed notes and teenage energy, seemed a long way away.

'Tell you what,' said Jeannie, pulling herself together. 'I'm going to play you some of the songs I played with the kids at school. No singing, I'll just strum, and chat over the top. That OK?'

Dan didn't respond.

'Brilliant,' said Jeannie, and started to form the opening chord of 'Hey Jude', which Johnny had specifically told Liam not to sing his usual words to.

'So . . . here's an update from your place of work,' she said as the chords softly filled the space in between her words. 'George and Rachel are locked in a stand-off about kennel funding, according to Mel. She's the kennel assistant, and also your part-time surgery receptionist. She said George is a good boss, firm but fair, and it takes a while to get used to his sense of humour, *whatever that means . . .*'

Feeling the strings bending under her fingers soothed

Jeannie. She hadn't really played much to him at home. Their time together was usually spent out, exploring somewhere new, then rushing home – and rushing straight into bed. Plus, Jeannie had a horror of insufferable muso types who insisted on carrying an instrument around with them and whipping it out at every opportunity. That wasn't her. Her music was private, intensely personal. Anyway, Edith had turned her guitars into symbols of everything she'd lost – and Dan was her escape from that.

She played quietly, conscious that she might be disturbing other patients, and over the rolling ebb and flow of chords told him about the puppies with their tiny paws that smelled of biscuits, and the broken girls learning to play in Rachel's lush paddock of wild flowers. Jeannie told him about the courageous way Lady Sadie had eventually dared to meet her gaze.

'Rachel says I should let Sadie come and live with me,' she said. 'We could keep each other company. What do you think?'

Live with me. Not Dan. Rachel hadn't mentioned Dan either.

Jeannie's fingers stumbled on the frets, and it snapped her out of her half-trance.

'Am I disturbing you?'

She swivelled round: Owen was leaning on the doorframe. How long had he been there?

Jeannie flushed and put the ukulele down hastily. 'No, not at all, come on in.'

'Don't let me interrupt you.' He nodded at the uke, then, seeing her discomfort, self-consciously checked his watch. 'Or I can go away and come back in a bit, if you want? I'm early.'

She'd noticed Owen was often early, overlapping with her afternoon visits, but then it wasn't fair that he always had to give up his evenings just because he lived nearby. He hadn't complained, but he surely had other places to be. Even if it was ballet recitals.

'No, come on in. I was just fiddling around while I talked to Dan.' She moved her chair to make more room for him. 'Did Andrea tell you about Dan's eyelids flickering?'

'She called while I was driving here. Ten-miles-of-the-M6-worth of very detailed detail.' Owen took off his jacket and sat down; she guessed he'd come straight from work, from the lanyard still round his neck. The ID photo wasn't the most flattering, but he'd been modest about his job title: he was actually Operations Director for Patterson Haulage Ltd.

'Have you noticed anything?' Jeannie asked.

He shook his head. 'To be honest, no. But at this stage maybe it's a once-a-day thing.'

They both glanced over at Dan's sleeping face, and Jeannie held her breath in case the eyelid flicker might happen now they were both here. It didn't.

'Don't let me stop you.' He nodded at the ukulele. 'This is the closest I'll get to a front-row seat at a gig. Private audience! I always thought of the ukulele as being, you know . . .' He mimed someone frantically strumming a tiny guitar just under their chin.

'It's not all George Formby, you know.'

Owen laughed, and she fidgeted with the tuning pegs, awkwardly reminded of her first conversation with Dan. 'It sounds stupid, but I'm not used to playing on my own. I sing harmonies. That's my thing, harmonies.'

'Is that . . . different?'

'It's more reactive. You don't lead, you blend in. Apparently, I used to sing harmony naturally as a child. To anything, on the radio. Mum thought I was a child prodigy, but it was really because my gran had a lot of Everly Brothers records and we used to sing together.'

Owen settled in his chair, crossing one long leg over the other, carefully so as not to kick any of the delicate equipment surrounding the bed. 'Are your parents musical?'

'Dad likes country music. He bought a banjo by accident at an auction, but never really played it. When I was about three, they propped me up with it on the sofa for a laugh, and I just started trying to copy what I'd seen him do once or twice. Gran took a photo of my parents' faces instead of me.' She did an impression of the famous family photo of Brian and Sue gawping in shock at their tiny offspring, almost hidden behind the banjo. It was on top of their television, faded to orange. Jeannie had always planned to hide it on the cover artwork – if she and Edith had got a record deal that involved a proper old-school cover.

'Do you play anything?' she asked, flicking that unwelcome thought away.

'God, no.'

'I bet you could.' Jeannie brandished the ukulele at him. 'Go on, have a go. It's just four strings . . .'

He waved it away, blushing. 'No, I was the kid at school who got handed those sticks that don't actually make a noise. Which isn't to say I don't envy people who can hold a note,' he added. 'I think it's an amazingly cool skill to have.'

The more Owen protested, the pinker his cheeks became and it tickled Jeannie; she sensed he was secretly dying to have a go. 'I bet I could teach you,' she said. 'I've wrung music out of kids from the age of four – including, today, one young man who was sent to learn as a punishment for habitual truancy.'

He raised a shaggy eyebrow at her. 'Are you offering to teach me?'

'If you want to learn.'

'That's brave. And what should I teach you in return? How to reverse an articulated lorry?'

'A woman always needs to know how to do that,' she said.

'You could have a deal there.'

Jeannie looked at Owen, shyly eyeing up the ukulele, and thought, I'm so glad you're here. What if she'd had to handle this living nightmare with 'football bants' Nick, or 'cucumber sandwiches' Stu? They sounded pleasant enough but . . . Jeannie wondered if she and Owen would be having this conversation if Dan was up and chatting.

No, she thought. I don't think it would be quite the same.

'Mind if I do some checks?' A new nurse, Kim, popped her head around the door and broke into Jeannie's thoughts. She watched the nurse fiddle with Dan's drips and cannulas. Owen asked about the eyelid flickering, and Kim explained what it could signify and Jeannie wrote everything down in the notebook, so Andrea would see when she came back that it could be positive, but might also just be a reaction to different sedatives.

When the nurse had gone, Owen asked Jeannie if

she'd mind playing again. 'Songs I might know?' he added. 'So nothing too new!'

She closed her eyes to block out any awkwardness, plucking as lightly as she could to stop too much sound drifting from the room, and as the music took over her thoughts, Jeannie heard a voice humming: her own.

She hummed 'Live to Tell' and 'Let It Be', and after a while she heard another voice humming along, rather off key, with her. It was Owen. The feeling of companionship – and trust – warmed her inside. Thank goodness Owen was here, she thought. Thank goodness she didn't have to deal with this on her own.

She was feeling her way to the chords for 'Don't Give Up' when she heard him speak.

'Jeannie,' Owen murmured, and she didn't dare look up straight away. There was a whisper in his voice that sent a disorientating ripple through her bloodstream.

'Jeannie,' he whispered again.

She forced herself to raise her head, but Owen wasn't looking at her. He was staring towards the bed, his gaze fixed on Dan's face.

'Did you see that?' Owen breathed the words.

Something swooped and dropped in Jeannie's stomach. 'See what?'

'Dan's eyelids. They *moved*.'

She gripped the neck of her ukulele. The room felt as if it was tilting.

'He almost opened his eyes.' Owen leaned forward, grabbing Dan's hands. 'Dan. Dan, mate. Can you hear me? Can you do that again? For Jeannie? Seriously, I don't think this is a drug reaction, I really think he's coming round.'

Suddenly, everything changed, as neatly as a departure board rattling into a new formation. Dan was coming back. The pause button was off; life was going to restart where they'd left it. Even when Jeannie had told Natalie things could change at any moment, a part of her hadn't believed it, but now it was happening. Her time to fix things was up.

Owen beckoned her over. 'It was such a tiny movement, you might miss it.'

Jeannie pushed herself off the chair, put her ukulele on the floor and leaned in.

Dan's face. She focused on his nose, the shower of tea-coloured freckles across the golden skin, the eyebrows that thinned out at the end to a tiny scar on the right side that she'd always meant to ask him about, the top lip with the tiny peak like a duck's beak, pointing down to the full lower lip. These days in the hospital had given Jeannie so much time to study Dan's face, to find its secrets and flaws, but she still felt intrusive, gazing at him.

She couldn't shake the horror-movie sensation that his eyes might snap open and look straight at her. *I know what you did.*

'Don't worry, I'm sure he'll try again.' Owen stroked Dan's bare arm. 'Come on, mate, you can't show your mum, and me, and not Jeannie! Or are you saving something special for her?'

No response.

The moment stretched, agonisingly, and finally Owen released a long breath. 'Oh. Sorry, Jeannie. Let's give him a moment. Putting the poor bloke under pressure here.'

He sat back on his chair and tried to look normal. 'Maybe you should play again? He seemed to like that.'

Jeannie forced a smile. Her head was ringing.

But just as she was about to pick up her ukulele again, a second sense stopped her and she stared, her heart thick and high in her throat.

Dan's eyelids flickered, pressed together enough to make the lashes move against his skin. And then they fluttered, revealing an edge of pale white, a tiny half-crescent of blue, his famously blue eyes.

Jeannie dropped her ukulele and it clattered, louder than anything she'd ever heard, on to the white floor of Dan's hospital room.

Chapter Sixteen

When Jeannie phoned her parents to tell them that Dan was showing signs of regaining consciousness, Sue sounded so relieved and delighted that Jeannie sank into a chair at the kitchen table and covered her face: it put her own complicated response to shame.

'Oh, my darling, that's wonderful!' Sue cried. 'Would you like Dad and me to come down to support you? I can phone next door and have Carol look after the horses – she owes me a favour.'

'Mum, there's nothing much to see,' Jeannie warned her. 'Dan's still sleeping most of the time. Mr Allcott says it's going to take a while for the sedatives to work out of his system and when he wakes up there's a strong chance he'll be acting strangely . . .'

'Darling, don't I know that.' Sue's voice was comforting; Jeannie's eyes filled with tears at how much she missed her. 'But it's *you* we want to be there for. There's going to be a lot to take in over the next few days.'

How much more? thought Jeannie, and fear crawled over her skin.

The next day, Brian and Sue came straight to the hospital. The sight of the two of them sanitising their hands as quickly as they could at the entrance to Dan's room made Jeannie want to grab their hands and run away with them, right out of this situation, but she knew she couldn't.

'There she is!' said Brian, pointing with delight. 'There's our girl.'

'And here's Dan,' Sue added quickly. 'Oh, Andrea, love – we were so glad to hear the news.'

Andrea had rushed back from Newcastle and had been holding Dan's hand ever since. She hadn't dropped it when Kate and Kim did his daily readings, or when the doctors arrived to discuss his sedation. She'd sat there, chatting away to him as if he was awake and listening, hope transfusing through her veins.

It took a while to bring the McCarthys up to speed on the new treatment plans for Dan – Jeannie and Andrea were now experts in brain oedema and intercranial pressure sensors – and then, as conversation dried up, Sue pointed at Jeannie, as if she'd just remembered something.

'I've got this for you.' She reached into her bag and retrieved a plastic sandwich bag. 'I popped it in a bag because I wasn't sure about germs.'

Dan's phone.

Jeannie stared at it, frozen. It dangled from Sue's fingers like official police evidence, and the smashed screen brought the shock of the accident scene crashing into her mind: the blue lights flashing round and round, the whispering forest of people, the ominous stillness behind the crackle of activity.

There was the phone. The phone containing her nuclear-bomb secret: that *she* was effectively the one who'd triggered this nightmare.

Jeannie glanced over to her dad; Brian's face was tight

with tension and his eyes seemed to be pleading, *I did my best.*

'It was in your dad's jacket,' Sue went on conversationally, oblivious to the torment she was inflicting. 'I was getting his suit ready to drop off at the cleaner's, and it was with the inside pocket gubbins. Is it Dan's? Your father says he can't remember where he picked it up but I'm assuming it must be. I mean, who else's would it be?'

'Yes, it is. That's Dan's.'

Owen spoke, and Jeannie's head snapped over to the door, where Owen had arrived just in time to see Sue presenting the one thing Jeannie didn't want him to know about. She kicked herself. *Why* had she texted to tell him her parents were coming in?

Because Owen likes them, and they like Owen, she reminded herself. How was she to know Mum was about to drop this on them?

'It's like Piccadilly Circus in here today,' observed Kate. 'I'm going to have to ask you to take it to the relatives' room, I'm afraid, folks.'

Owen was staring at the bag with as much intensity as Jeannie. Was it her guilty imagination or was he struggling not to reach over and snatch it out of Sue's hands?

He knew. Jeannie's heart pounded. Owen *knows* something was wrong before the wedding, she thought, and he's guessed it's something to do with me. The prospect of him getting his hands on the mobile and listening to her messages made Jeannie breathless with panic.

'Oh, I'm glad we haven't just pinched some innocent person's phone.' Sue visibly relaxed. 'We didn't have a charger to fit it, so we weren't able to get it going to find out who it belonged to – you know us, Jeannie. We're still struggling on with our steam-powered Nokias!' She nodded over at Andrea, trying to lighten the tension in the room. 'Is Daniel the same with you, Andrea? Always after you to upgrade and get more pixies?'

'Pixels, Mum,' said Jeannie automatically. 'They're called *pixels*.'

Andrea beamed proudly. 'Danny sorts everything like that out. He's very good – he always gets two of everything and sets one up for me. In fact . . .' She picked up her bag and unzipped the middle compartment. 'I've got my charger whatsit here. I take it everywhere, especially now – I'm petrified of my battery going flat when I'm out and about.'

Brian said nothing but gazed miserably at Jeannie in a way that reminded her of the dogs in the rescue kennel. Foreboding, mixed with craven guilt that whatever was happening was somehow his fault.

'Here!' Andrea brandished the cable over the bed towards Sue. 'Will this fit?'

Jeannie surprised herself by springing into life and intercepting it before her mum could take it. 'Yes, I should think so. Let me have a look.'

'Should we have given it to the police, Jeannie?' Sue turned to her, less sure. 'As evidence? That's partly why I put it in the bag, you know, for fingerprints.'

'I don't think the police are too worried about evidence.' Owen's reassuring voice cut across Jeannie's. 'They've got witness statements from everyone on the bus to say the driver wasn't at fault. He stopped as fast as he could, but Dan was on the phone, not looking where he was going. I've had several conversations with the police about it – they're satisfied that it was an accident. An awful one, but just an accident.'

'That poor driver.' Sue shook her head. 'I bet he's *haunted* by how much worse it could have been . . .'

'Sue.' Brian gave her a subtle nudge. Andrea was biting her lip.

'Has no one come forward to say they were speaking to Dan when it happened?' Sue went on. 'Surely you'd know if you were talking to someone and they walked into a bus? I remember Brian once dropped his phone while he was in the supermarket and I thought he'd gone over a bridge.'

'Jesus, Sue.' Brian gave his wife a more obvious nudge this time but she wasn't about to let it go.

She turned to Owen. 'Well, maybe we can tell from the phone, can we? Who the last call was from?'

It suddenly occurred to Jeannie that now she had the charger, she'd have to plug it in. And once it was plugged in, she'd have to turn it on. And once she'd turned it on, with everyone watching, the message beep would sound and . . .

'He might not have been talking to someone,' said Owen. 'He might have been checking his voicemail. It's maybe no one's fault.'

Jeannie straightened up with such a jerk that she felt a muscle in her back ping, and Andrea almost jumped out of her seat at the sudden movement. She really wasn't looking comfortable, Jeannie thought, and no wonder.

'Mum, this maybe isn't the most sensitive conversation to be having,' she said. 'Considering . . .'

'Want me to see if there's a plug socket back here, Jeannie?' Owen asked, nodding at the phone in her hand.

Kate had finally had enough, and swept in with towels and gel. 'Why don't you catch up outside, folks? It's time for Dan's daily ablutions and I'm sure he won't want an audience. I know I don't.'

Relief surged through Jeannie. 'Never mind, we'll have to do it later,' she said, zipping the phone into her own bag. Safe. For now.

Did Owen look thwarted? Was she imagining it?

'Andrea? Will you come with us to the restaurant and have something to eat?' Sue reached out to touch Andrea's arm, and though Andrea hesitated – she normally liked to help Kate with the bed bath and any other little ways of keeping Dan comfortable – she let herself be shepherded out between Jeannie's parents, towards 'wherever I can get your father a bacon sandwich, he's been driving since five, poor man, he's crying out for something savoury . . .'

Owen lingered at the door, smiling as they passed in a way that suggested he was waiting for Jeannie, but then Sue said, 'Owen, why don't you come with us? Tell us what you've been up to since we last saw you!' and he had no choice but to follow them.

Jeannie's hands were trembling, but she tried to look casual. A chance to be on her own – she couldn't mess this up.

'I'll catch you up, just need to make a call outside,' she told her mother, and set off at a brisk pace in the opposite direction, Dan's phone like an unpinned grenade in her bag.

Jeannie knew exactly where there was a plug socket: next to the café table she'd been regarding as hers for the past four weeks. There was nearly always someone at it, charging their laptop while they worked, but when she hurried down there, Fate was on her side: the table was free.

Hastily, she dumped her bag and coat on the seat to reserve it, grabbed an orange juice from the chiller, paid and sat down. Her heart was racing in her chest, hammering triplets against her ribs.

She plugged the charger into the socket with wobbling hands, waiting for the tiny apple to appear on Dan's shattered screen.

Maybe it wouldn't work. Maybe the cracked screen meant it was completely dead? In which case, she was safe, wasn't she?

Jeannie stared at the metal leg of the chair opposite. How hard would it be to smash it completely? Before Owen came down. She could slip the phone under the chair leg, then one sharp crack and . . .

The apple appeared before she could follow the thought through, as if the phone was tuned into her worst thoughts. Edith would have done it by now. She wouldn't even have got to the end of the thought.

The screen glowed then flicked on.

Immediately, Jeannie ran into a major problem. It required a four-digit passcode.

Would Dan be as obvious as 1234?

She tried it. No.

What about her birthday: 2809?

No. Jeannie felt a slight twinge of disappointment.

Dan's own birthday: 1908?

No.

The seconds were ticking by – Owen could appear any moment. Even if he hadn't thought about checking Dan's phone to see who'd distracted him so much he walked under a bloody bus, he definitely would now. *Thanks, Mum.*

Jeannie leaned her throbbing head in her hands, her fingertips digging hard into her temples, and stared at the spiderwebbed screen. What dates would Dan consider important? Her own passcode was 2002, the date of her favourite album (*Yoshimi Battles the Pink Robots* by the Flaming Lips) but she didn't know what Dan's favourite album was – or even if he had one. He didn't really support any football teams that might have FA Cup-winning years – as far as she knew.

Should you even be doing this? whispered a little voice. What are you going to look at if you get in there? Are you going to nose through Dan's private emails? Are you going to snoop through his Facebook? While he's lying there unconscious, unable to give you permission – or tidy it up before you see? If you feel bad about going through his boxes, surely you shouldn't be breaking into his phone?

I was about to marry the man, Jeannie reasoned. Surely there shouldn't be anything in his phone that he wouldn't want me to see?

Even as she thought that, she knew that she'd never give Dan access to browse through her own emails, or scroll down her messages. Not because there was anything to find, but just because . . . it was her space. Her privacy. Her head. She wasn't ready to share that with him, or anyone.

But what if there were emails Dan wouldn't want her to see? What if *he'd* had doubts too?

Shut up, Jeannie told herself. She stared at the screen.

How many attempts did you get before a phone locked itself permanently? And would that necessarily be such a bad thing? If she locked everyone out then no one would be able to check Dan's messages or call list . . .

Before she could process that any further, she heard footsteps: Owen was striding across the foyer towards her, a determined expression on his face. She lifted a hand in greeting. He might as well come over; there was no point looking any more shifty than she already did.

'Having trouble?' Owen slid into the chair opposite.

Jeannie dropped the mobile back into her bag, still attached to the charger cable. 'Not unless charging phones is illegal out here as well as on the ward!'

He guessed her problem immediately. 'It's locked?'

'Yup.' Jeannie tried to make her voice sound breezy. 'I don't know what Dan's passcode is. Do you?'

'You've tried his birthday?'

'It's not that.'

'Your birthday?'

She shook her head. 'No, apparently not that memorable.'

'Hmm. Have you tried 2010?'

'Is that significant?'

'It's when he graduated.' He paused, then added, 'Dan always said it was the start of his ten-year plan.'

'His *what*?'

'His ten-year plan – he was always making plans.' Owen fidgeted with a discarded straw. 'Things he wanted to achieve by thirty, another list before forty. I'd never say it to him but I guessed that sort of ambition was something Dan got from his dad? But he wasn't about making money or owning flash cars, just . . . projects, and research. He wanted his own specialist surgery; he wanted to cure equine cancers.' An unhappy shadow crossed his face. 'My worst fear is that Dan comes round and he's not . . . not . . .'

He struggled, but couldn't finish the sentence.

Without thinking, Jeannie reached over the table to grab Owen's hand. His shoulders had crumpled, as if he'd suddenly realised that spreadsheets and rotas might not be able to help his friend with what was hurtling towards them now.

'We're thinking positive, remember?' she insisted. 'Mr Allcott and the team are doing more tests this afternoon.'

'Yes, you're right.' He stared down at the table, fighting back tears. 'Sorry, I shouldn't dump this on you . . .'

'You *should*,' said Jeannie impetuously. 'It's hard keeping up a front for Andrea. Don't feel you have to put up a front for me too.'

'I know. I don't.' Owen looked up, his brown eyes wet and vulnerable. He tried to regain his composure, failed, and shook his head. 'Thanks. We're in a pretty rubbish club, you and me, aren't we?'

'The worst.' She squeezed his hand. 'You can go back to being strong and silent when Dan's better.'

He said nothing, but smiled gratefully at her.

The moment was broken by a shrill chime from her bag. The phone had sprung into life: Dan's new messages arriving, and pinging for attention.

'A-ha! So it's not broken?' he said, glad of the distraction.

'Seems like it.' Reluctantly, Jeannie pulled the phone out of her bag, and they both stared at the cracked screen. 'I suppose we'll just have to wait for Dan to come round to tell us what the code is to get into it,' she said casually.

'Oh! Is that Dan's phone? Is it working?'

It was Andrea, back from the restaurant and heading for the shop.

They both looked up guiltily.

'Bit of a problem, Andrea—' Owen started but Jeannie cut across him this time.

'We can't work out what his passcode is, though, so . . . we might have to leave it for now.'

Andrea was focused on Dan's mobile. She slipped into the chair next to Owen. 'Try 1802. Or 180260. That's my birthday,' she added to Jeannie, in case she hadn't worked it out. 'Danny always came home for my birthday; it was our tradition. He liked to take me out for a meal. In fact, he's only missed it once . . .' She glanced reproachfully at Owen, who shuffled in his seat.

'That sounds like a story, Andrea!' said Jeannie, eager to change the subject.

'I should say so! These two were in Paris at a rugby international the day before, and there was an absolute disaster with the flights back! Don't you remember, Owen?' Going by Andrea's expression, clearly it had been a big deal. 'They had to stay overnight in Paris because of some ridiculous air traffic controllers' strike. Danny drove straight from the airport the next morning and took me to Seaham Hall for tea to make up for it. I did say to Danny at the time, that's what you get for booking with a budget airline, particularly in *France*,' she added.

Jeannie glanced between Andrea and Owen. Something was going on here, but she wasn't sure what. Owen seemed flustered – he'd opened his mouth to say something, then shut it again when Andrea started on about the strikes – but he wasn't denying it, either.

Andrea sighed, presumably remembering the lovely birthday tea. Then she composed herself. 'Yes, 1802. I bet that's what the passcode is. Try it.'

What else could she do? Jeannie clicked the phone back into life and took a deep breath: 1802.

The screen shifted, unlocked, and Andrea's face lit up with delight. 'Oh!' Then the full horror of the cracked screen's implications took over from her pleasure that Dan had used her birthday as his passcode, and she covered her mouth with a hand.

Text after text flipped over the top of the screen, starting with *Congratulations, mate!!!* then abruptly shifting to *Are you OK? We just heard, Dan, call us . . .*

The shattered glass made it difficult to read, but there was a red dot on the voicemail symbol, indicating unheard messages. Was her message one of those? Jeannie's stomach turned to lead. Was it still there, waiting to be heard? Had Dan even listened to it? Had he heard one, but not the second?

Dan's other missed calls held no surprises: Owen, a mobile number with no name (the florist? The registrar?), Mum, Mark, Jeannie. Dan's life, frozen in time twenty minutes before their ceremony began.

Jeannie looked up, her pulse pounding in her ears. Owen and Andrea were staring at the phone, obviously trying to make out the names, numbers and times upside down, then both of them raised their eyes to her.

They were all thinking the same thing. Who was Dan talking to when he walked in front of the bus?

Owen moved to take the phone, but Jeannie snatched it, and touched the voicemail symbol. The splinters sliced her fingers but she pressed the phone close to her ear to stop the sound leaking out. His eyes were locked on hers the whole time and she forced herself not to give anything away.

The sound was distorted, hard to make out through the damaged speaker. 'You have . . . messages. Message received two oh . . . on . . . twenty-sixth . . . May . . .'

Then her nervous voice, a voice that didn't even sound like hers, speaking from the past, disconcertingly fresh. Jeannie felt sick.

'Dan, it's me. Please don't go to the town hall. I can't go ahead with the wedding today. I'm so sorry. I'm so *so* sorry. Please call me when you get this.'

She stared in shock out of the café windows. Dan must have listened to her first message. But not the second.

'To listen to this message again, press two . . .'

Before she knew what she was doing, Jeannie pressed three. Hard, so hard it sliced her finger. Deleted. She'd deleted the message. It vanished into the atmosphere, tiny particles of her guilt dissolving as if they'd never been there.

She let out a shaky breath, and thought, *Oh my God, what have I just done?*

'Was there a message?' Owen leaned forward.

She shook her head. 'Nothing important.' It wasn't. It wasn't important now.

But the first message, the one Dan must have listened to – was that still there? Somewhere on the system? She couldn't remember how long they were kept for.

'Can I see?' Andrea reached out for the phone.

'See what?'

'This is going to sound silly but . . .' Her hand was shaking. 'I didn't want to say upstairs in case he could hear us, but *I* phoned Danny just before he left for the church. I wanted to tell him how much I loved him and how happy I was for you both . . .' Andrea covered her mouth but her tear-filled eyes above it threatened to spill over. 'I got his voicemail, so I just babbled on, left him a silly rambling message. I know I'm being ridiculous but I need to know Danny wasn't listening to that when he . . . when he went under the bus. Can you find out? Is there a way of knowing?'

Jeannie's heart broke for Andrea. In the days they'd spent together, she'd started to understand the complicated reasons for Dan's closeness to his mum and she knew how excruciating this must be for Andrea, realising she might have been the cause of the accident. How long had she been thinking that? Poor Andrea . . .

'Oh, Andrea, I'm sure he wasn't. The screen's broken; you can't swipe, look. But I'm sure he . . . oh!'

Jeannie had showed her the smashed face of the phone, but as Andrea's finger touched the sharp shards, she yelped and pulled her sliced finger back. The phone slipped, bounced on the table, and then crashed on to the tiled floor, too fast for Owen's last-minute grab.

There was a crack, then the screen went dead as the glass screen finally shattered into millions of bits.

'Oh, man.' Someone on the next table gave them a sympathetic look and the barista hurried over, dustpan and brush ready.

Andrea stared at it. Her mouth wobbled like a child's, and Jeannie got up and hugged her, just as Owen said, 'He wasn't listening to your message, Andrea. I'm sure he heard it as we left the hotel.'

'Did he? Really? Are you sure? You're not just saying that?'

'I *know* so.' Owen nodded, and Andrea leaned her forehead against Jeannie's chest with wordless gratitude and sobbed.

Owen was a good guy, thought Jeannie as she stroked Andrea's trembling back. A bad liar, but a really good guy.

Chapter Seventeen

'We want to be helpful,' Sue repeated. 'Just tell us what to do and your father and I will get on with it.'

Jeannie gazed uneasily around the sitting room. They'd already been busy. In the hour she'd spent flinging frisbees around the paddock for Rachel's dogs, Mum had unpacked two boxes and arranged the contents on the sofa and shelves, while Dad had put up a bookshelf in the corner of the sitting room and filled it with Dan's collection of travel guides. He was already at work assembling a second, sitting there with his mug of tea and the toolbox he'd brought down in the car 'in case Daniel's is still in storage'.

Jeannie had no idea if Dan even had a toolbox, let alone where it might be.

It was kind of them, but it made her feel uncomfortable. She couldn't put her finger on exactly why: was it seeing her own things dominating the room that was supposed to be shared – or noticing Dan's boxes open, ready to be unpacked without him?

Or was it the reminder that, after everything that had happened, the marriage she'd tried to stop seemed to be carrying on regardless?

Jeannie drew in a breath and it sounded strangled.

'What's up?' Sue paused, a McCarthy family group

photo from Angus's wedding in her hand. 'Have I put the wrong things out?'

'No, it's just . . . I wonder if we should wait until Dan gets back before we do this? I feel bad, going through his stuff when he's not here.'

Her mother laughed. 'Sweetheart, you're *married* – as good as, anyway. What on earth would Dan have in these boxes that he wouldn't want you to see?'

'Nothing. It's just . . .' Jeannie struggled to articulate the clawing sensation inside. 'It feels wrong, me settling in when Dan's still . . . well, we still don't know when he'll be coming home yet. He might not be able to come back for *months*. This house might not even be practical for him, if he's . . .' She struggled to say it. 'If he's . . .'

'Dan's not dead, love,' said Sue firmly. 'And if he *is* disabled in some way, you'll find ways to manage. We did.'

Jeannie couldn't answer that. It was hard to articulate any doubts in front of two people who'd managed to overcome horrendous obstacles, and thought they'd brought her up to be brave.

Sue put the photo down on the mantelpiece and went over to Jeannie, hugging her tight. 'I know your mind's always on Dan, but you need somewhere nice to come home to as well! You've been so busy, back and forth to the hospital every day, but you've barely unpacked your own things. It looks as if you're not planning on staying! And what would Dan think about that?'

Jeannie's head was over her mother's shoulder so Sue didn't see the grimace that passed across her face at that comment – or the matching anguish on Brian's.

'Tell her!' he mouthed, jabbing the screwdriver towards

Sue, but Jeannie shook her head, firmly, and mouthed back, 'No!'

'Tell her!' he mouthed again, with another emphatic jab.

'No!'

Sue squeezed Jeannie, then stepped back and smoothed the copper curls either side of her round face and kissed her forehead. She had to reach up. 'Now you're back, I'll get the kettle on, and you can find some of Dan's photos to even up the mantelpiece – I wasn't sure who was who, but you'll know, won't you? Another tea, Brian?'

'Thanks, love.'

As Sue bustled out, Jeannie avoided her dad's baleful gaze, pulled back the flap and lifted up a stack of framed photos wrapped in newspaper. The first was of Andrea and Dan at his graduation; she looked bright with joy, linking his arm with hers in her lemon-yellow suit. Andrea had exactly the same photo in pride of place on her sideboard, Jeannie remembered. It had stood out in a sea of portraits of her and Dan through the ages.

She sensed her dad sidling up behind her.

'You're going to have to tell your mother soon, love,' he muttered. 'I was speaking to that nurse, Kate – she reckons there's every chance Daniel will come round properly very soon. Then what?'

Then what? Jeannie shivered. 'Good!' she said aloud.

'Have you changed your mind?' Brian didn't sound his normal Dad-like self. 'Are you going to stay with him? I mean, fair play if you are, but . . . don't do anything for the wrong reasons.'

They stared at each other, mute with horror at the implications of what either would say next.

Jeannie forced out the words. 'What are the wrong reasons, Dad?'

'I mean . . .' Brian's eyes darted to the door and back again. 'If you're going to stay with Dan, then make sure it's because you love him, and not because you feel sorry for the poor sod. If you didn't want to marry him four weeks ago, I can't see why you'd feel differently now.'

'Dad!' Now Jeannie's eyes automatically flicked over to the kitchen. 'I can't walk away from a man in intensive care! And I wouldn't walk away from him if he needs me. What sort of person would that make me?'

'It would make you a human being, Jeannie. I *know* what's ahead, and it's a tough road. *Tough.* If people start flapping their lips, I'll just tell them the truth – that you weren't going to go through with it on the day. And that's that.'

Jeannie could hear clinking noises in the kitchen, Sue rearranging unpacked coffee mugs in the cupboard. The relief of being able – finally – to talk about the only thing she thought about, night and day, was almost physical.

'But no one would believe it! They'd think I was leaving him because he was paralysed.' She ran a hand through her hair. Her head was throbbing and that normally didn't even start until she was within half an hour of the hospital. 'It's not just Dan. Andrea needs me. So does Owen.'

'For crying out loud, you can't live your life going on what other people want you to do! You've done enough of that already with that crazy friend of yours.'

'Edith?' Jeannie was surprised by the venom in her dad's voice.

'Who else?' Brian had clearly said more than he wanted to, but he ploughed on. 'I don't pretend to know the ins and outs of that whole record business malarkey but you let that madam call the shots, and look how she treated you. You've always let other people's feelings override yours, Jeannie, because you're a good woman. Like your mother. But you've got to think of yourself for a change.'

'Are you still going without sugar in your coffee, Jeannie, or are you off that nonsense wedding diet now?' Sue called through from the kitchen.

'One sugar for me, Mum!' she called back, then turned to Brian, and hissed, 'I understand what you're saying, Dad, but I can't deal with that now. It's not about me, it's about Dan.'

'It's never about you.' Brian's eyes were strained, trying to make the pain in his heart fit the words in his mouth. 'But this is *your* life. And if you don't tell her soon . . .'

'Here we are!' Sue reappeared in the doorway with a tray Jeannie had brought from home to remind her of her mum's special TV dinners. 'I picked up some biscuits on our way down, since I knew you wouldn't have any.'

'Thanks, love,' said Brian and helped himself to three chocolate digestives.

Jeannie turned back to the box and lifted out the next photo on the pile.

It was of two people she didn't recognise, both wearing sunglasses, sitting on a Land Rover in a desert, surrounded by donkeys. The donkeys looked bored but healthy. They were sporting bandanas. The man had painful sunburn despite his protective cricket hat, and the woman was tanned, with frizzy jet-black curls tumbling down her back, smiling a brilliant smile and wearing khaki shorts. Her arm was slung over the sunburned man's neck, as if she'd just won him in a raffle, and one long bronzed leg extended glamorously over the bonnet of the car.

I have no idea where that is, thought Jeannie with a familiar dull panic. Or who she is. Or if that's even Dan.

'Oh, isn't that Owen?' asked Sue, looking over her shoulder.

Jeannie peered more closely. 'You're right,' she said, surprised. Owen was thinner, and unrecognisable in shorts. He had quite nice legs, rather muscular. Although they were very sunburned. Who sunburned their knees? 'I think it must be.'

'Where are they?'

'Mum, I don't know.'

'I'd say that's his girlfriend, anyway.' Sue smiled. 'See? I knew a nice lad like him would have one.'

They both peered at the photograph now. The laughing woman in the photo wasn't the type of girl Jeannie would have guessed Owen would go for. Even the donkeys seemed to be slightly in awe of her. But she certainly seemed to be on very intimate terms with him, and he had his arm round her.

Why wouldn't Owen have a beautiful girlfriend? Jeannie reminded herself, ignoring the jerk of disbelief. He was a sweet man. Kind, and practical, and a good listener. Not as gorgeous as Dan, obviously, not conventionally, anyway, but looks weren't everything.

'I don't know, Mum. He's never mentioned her if it is.'

'Oh, dear,' said Sue with a raised eyebrow. 'Maybe that tells you something?'

Sue offered to take Jeannie into Longhampton to catch her lunchtime train to the hospital, and they left early so Sue could see Jeannie's new home town.

It was a perfect summer day, and Longhampton unfolded like a cinema backdrop as they drove down the hill from the kennels: from the terraced houses painted Neapolitan pink-vanilla-chocolate on the approach to the tumbling baskets of petunias hanging from the street lamps. They windowshopped along the high street until they reached Natalie's café, which was mid-morning busy. Two Scottish terriers were crunching biscuits under a table while their owners shared a slice of carrot cake above, and a bulldog the colour of a caffè latte had curled up in the basket by the window, snoring in a patch of sunlight as her owner sipped his tea.

Natalie stopped polishing the black coffee machine when they approached the counter. She was delighted to meet Sue, clapped her hands with happiness at Dan's news, and insisted on loading them up with free coffees and a bag of cake to eat on the train.

'It's nice to see you've made friends here already,' Sue said as they left. 'What a welcoming community it must be.'

'Quickest way to introduce yourself to the neighbourhood, leaving your wedding in an air ambulance,' said Jeannie, and then, when her mum looked taken aback, added, 'Oh, everyone knows about the accident – it was in the local paper. Not much happens round here, Mum. Dan and I are about as famous as you can get without appearing on television or doing something weird with a pig.'

'Oh, Jeannie, I know it's good to keep a sense of humour, but, really . . .' Sue paused outside a shop. 'Is Longhampton where everyone comes to buy their wedding dresses?' In the window, a cathedral-length veil was suspended at each corner by clusters of Christmas tree robins, framing a stunning ivory dress on a silver tailor's dummy. 'That's the fourth wedding gown I've seen just along this street. Oh, this one's *lovely*. It's like yours, isn't it? With the corset and the big skirt?'

Jeannie wasn't listening. Her phone was vibrating in her pocket and the familiar mix of dread and hope immediately crawled under her ribs: was it the hospital phoning with good news, or bad?

She checked the message. It was Andrea. *Hi, Jeannie! Can you bring more foot cream when you come this afternoon? Danny seems to like it! Update from nurse – blood pressure is down!*

Jeannie quickly thumbed a reply. 'They're being sold to raise money for the dog rescue,' she said without looking up. 'People have donated dresses and local businesses have agreed to let Rachel showcase them in . . .' Her words stuck in her throat as she took a closer look at the window display her mother was talking about.

The dress was very like hers because it *was* hers.

Spotlit in the window, detached from Jeannie's unhappiness, the ballerina dress was, once again, as pretty and romantic as it had been in the boutique the first time she'd seen it. Rachel had sensitively styled it so it wasn't quite the same: she'd pinned a gold silk sash round the waist, and lifted up the petticoated skirts as if the dress was swirling around by itself, its frothy perfection reflected in the old-fashioned cheval mirror behind. A jolly crowd of toy poodles danced in the foreground, and there was a heartstring-tugging sign in the window about Grace and her curly brood, each one in need of a loving home.

Sue swung round to look at her. 'Jeannie? *Is* that your dress?'

Jeannie swallowed. This wasn't how she wanted her mum to find out. She hadn't expected Rachel to have moved so quickly in getting it out on display, but after the initial shock, the sight of it there in the window made her feel free, knowing she wouldn't have to be laced into it again. There was fleeting pity for the Jeannie who'd bought it in good faith, but that woman felt like a stranger now. The dress deserved a happy ending Jeannie couldn't give it.

'Yes,' she said. 'It is mine.'

'Why?' Sue stared at her, confused. 'Why are you giving it away? It was your dream dress! And you need it – you haven't got married yet!'

'Mum, I don't want to wear it again,' said Jeannie. 'I'd rather someone else had the chance to feel special.'

'But it's your *wedding* dress! I've still got mine in the attic, and you know I'm not exactly a hoarder . . . Is there something you're not telling me, love?'

Sue could see straight into Jeannie's heart, and her face was creased with concern. Jeannie almost cracked. 'Mum, the thing is—'

'Hello! Yoo hoo!'

It had to be Rachel; no one else would say yoo hoo, not like that.

Jeannie looked round and saw Rachel waving from the shop opposite. The moment of weakness passed. 'Come and say hello to Rachel! That's the charity shop for the dog rescue.'

'What? No, Jeannie, we haven't finished talking about this . . . Jeannie! Come here.'

But she'd set off over the road, and Sue had to follow her.

Rachel greeted them both with the same warmth as Natalie had, and Jeannie watched her mum's line of questioning about the dress evaporate in the face of Rachel's friendly charm. '. . . *so* nice to see you again, Sue, although not in these circumstances, obviously. Jeannie's been amazing, helping me out with my puppy invasion – did she tell you? Has she always been so good with dogs? You had Jack Russells? Ah, that would explain it . . .'

As they were chatting in the doorway, a young woman headed towards the shop, struggling with a bulging plastic bag. It wasn't, Jeannie noted, a dress carrier, but one of the bigger John Lewis Clearance carrier bags, the unwieldy ones designed to fit special-buy slow cookers or duvets. It was basically one step up from a binbag.

'Ah, hello!' said Rachel. 'Is that a donation for us?'

The woman glanced over her shoulder, as if checking she wasn't being followed, and said firmly, 'Yes, it is.'

'Well, that is most generous of you . . .' Rachel started but the woman was already pushing it at her.

'Sorry about the bag. There is a dress carrier what-not, but I didn't want to draw attention to it, in case I saw her en route.'

'Who?' asked Jeannie, intrigued.

'My mother,' said the woman and looked as if she was about to cry.

'Do you want to come inside?' asked Rachel, and the woman nodded and hurried in.

At the counter, the woman – Lou, who worked in the estate agent's opposite – pulled the balled-up frock out of the bag: it popped out in a mass of nylon lace and petti-coat, and they all let out an involuntary *Wow*!

'It's my mum's. I mean, it's mine now, but . . . it was my mum's,' she explained. 'She always said she was keep-ing her wedding dress for me but I thought she was joking, or being romantic, or something. But she *meant* it. I got engaged six months ago, and the next night she brought this round! I mean, it's a lovely dress and every-thing but . . . Well. Look.'

Jeannie had unfolded it out over the counter as Lou was speaking, and now they were able to take in its full, strange glory. The dress was satin, high-necked with plenty of floral illusion netting between the lacy choker collar and the sweetheart bodice. Appliqued lace flowers disguised a punchy pair of shoulder pads, and there was a long slit up the back. It was the sort of shiny wedding gown that wouldn't be out of place in a mid-period Guns N' Roses video set in a cathedral full of flickering can-dles and dry ice.

'I'd say your mum got married in . . . the late eighties?' hazarded Sue.

The woman looked up at her in amazement. 'How did you know?'

'We all wanted a dress like this back then,' she said.

'It's adorable,' said Rachel. Jeannie had realised a while back that Rachel said that to everyone who brought a dress in, regardless of what it actually looked like. 'But are you sure you're happy for us to sell a family heirloom? Won't your mum be hurt?'

'Probably. Oh God. I don't know what to do.' Lou shook her head. 'When I heard about your sale on the radio, it was like the answer to my prayers.' She started to fold the plastic bag into nervous squares, smaller and smaller, between her fingers. 'I've run out of excuses – Mum's been planning this for years. She's always on at me, where we can take it to be fitted, will I need shoes dyed to match.' She swept her blunt fringe out of her eyes. 'Lee and I are having a beach wedding in the Maldives in six weeks' time. There's no way I can wear this on a beach! Even if I wanted to, which, I've got to be honest with you, I definitely don't.'

'Why's she so set on you wearing it?' asked Jeannie.

'Because bits of it are *her* mum's dress.' The woman turned it over to show them the inside, a hand-boned corset top. 'Nan got married in 1964, her own mum was a seamstress, and she made it. And then she tailored the skirt in for *my* mum, and added these lace sleeves on – can you see? And this choker, on top of the netting.' As she ran a fingertip over the meticulous sewing along the bodice, Jeannie could see where alterations had been made, each with a lot of love and care.

'What a sweet idea.'

'It is.' The woman chewed her lip. 'It *is* a sweet idea. I don't want to hurt Mum's feelings, but it's not what I want.' Her chin wobbled, and she started to cry. Shoulder-shaking silent sobs at first, but then much bigger, wilder gulps. 'It's not . . . what . . . I want!'

Jeannie and Rachel exchanged 'what now?' glances but Sue reacted first. She set down her coffee cup and went to put her arms round the young woman, soothing her as she unleashed all her pent-up stress.

'There now,' she said. 'Get it off your chest, love. We know how wedding planning gets everyone in a tizz.' She looked over her head at Jeannie. 'Your mum will only be wanting the best for you – just like her mum did for her.'

'But it's everything! Not just the dress! Nan ruined my mum's wedding – she always said so! She took over. That's why Mum's taking over mine. She wants the wedding she didn't get herself! She's taken over the catering, and wants her and dad to do a special choreographed dance – on the beach!'

Even Sue blanched at that.

'I don't think we should sell this dress, Lou,' said Jeannie gently. 'I think . . . it means too much to your family. You don't want to hurt your mum's feelings over a dress.'

'Please?' Lou gulped. 'I've run out of ideas about how I can *not* wear it. Lee said I should just go nuts eating everything in sight so I can't fit into it but she'd only sew a panel in to make it fit.'

'Can she adapt it again?' Sue suggested. 'Maybe change the sleeves?'

They stared at the dress. Changing the sleeves would be a start. Maybe if you cut them off, thought Jeannie, and then cut off the skirt. And added a different top.

'OK, I've had an idea,' said Rachel. 'We're having a gala dinner to show off the dresses and there's going to be a Weddings Through the Ages section – why don't you *loan* us your dress for that, model it for your mum, and we can promise to send it out to you in the Maldives, once it's been cleaned afterwards?'

'Your mum can see you wearing it, and have her own moment in the spotlight with you,' Jeannie added, catching on to Rachel's plan. 'And then we'll do our best to get it couriered in time. But maybe you should buy yourself a beach wedding dress as well. Just in case the courier doesn't get to you.'

'Just in case.' Lou wiped her face and managed a grateful grin.

It was eye-opening, Jeannie thought, how many wedding dresses were still waiting for their happy ever after. It made her feel a tiny bit more hopeful about her own, and a tiny bit less ashamed of letting it down.

'That sounds like a good plan to me,' said Sue, and squeezed Jeannie's hand.

Chapter Eighteen

'Have you got time for a coffee tonight, about five p.m.? I need to talk to you about something.'

Owen's text arrived as Jeannie was leaving for the hospital and it made her jumpy for the rest of the day. Was it to do with the phone? The wedding? Dan's prognosis?

It turned out to be none of those. 'I'd like to adopt one of those puppies you keep talking so much about,' he told her quite shyly. 'Do you think you can put in a good word?'

Rachel was delighted to hear that Owen was from a family of dog owners (all Labradors, all named after England football managers), and dispatched him an application form to fill in that he claimed was only slightly less rigorous than his tax return. She seemed to like his responses, though, and one morning, later in the week, Owen duly turned up on Jeannie's doorstep, prior to his appointment at the kennels to be interviewed by the puppies.

'I suspect the only reason I've been invited over here is so Rachel can send some private eye to check out my house,' he grumbled as Jeannie poured him a coffee. 'She knows everything else about me, from how long I work to my thoughts on grooming. Dogs, I should add, not myself.'

'Ah, no, you don't need to worry about that.' Jeannie offered him a biscuit from her overflowing tin of home-made offerings. Rachel had cross-checked his form with Street View and confirmed Owen lived on the edge of a village on the outskirts of Birmingham, in a thirties semi with circular flower beds and a drive. 'Our sources have established you've got adequate fences. Rachel was very excited about the trampoline. Did you get that just for the puppy?'

Owen choked on his coffee. 'Seriously!' he spluttered. 'What are you? MI5?'

'Just very keen to make sure our puppies will be living where people say they'll be living.'

Natalie had gone into raptures about Owen's house ('It's a very desirable village!') but Jeannie's imagination was snagged by the trampoline. Who jumped on that? She knew Owen didn't have children, but had he got it for his ballet-dancing niece? Or had the woman with him in the donkey photo had a child? She was surprised by her own curiosity.

'If you must know, I got it for my niece and nephews,' he said, brushing crumbs off his jumper. 'My sister's gar-den isn't big enough for the one they wanted, so I volunteered to host it.'

'That's sweet of you.'

'It's my neighbours who've been sweet.' Owen rolled his eyes in pretend horror. 'I think they're deaf. At least the puppy won't hold any fear for them, noise-wise.' He grinned and then paused, spotting something on the dresser.

Jeannie pretended not to know what he'd seen. She'd moved the photograph of Owen and the mystery woman on to the kitchen shelves, next to some photos of her own. It seemed too nosy to ask him about it directly, but Owen had obligingly walked straight into her cunning trap.

'What's . . . ? Oh, I found that in Dan's boxes the other day. Is that you?' She knew she was failing to sound casual.

Owen pushed back his chair, and picked up the photograph so he could look at it properly. 'Yes, it is. I haven't seen that in a long time.'

'Where are you?'

He didn't answer at once. 'I'm trying to think,' he said. 'Somewhere in Kenya. I helped Dan with a charity project he set up out there. Donkey work, not vet stuff.' He laughed, belatedly, at the unintentional joke.

'Who's the girl?'

A longer pause. 'That's . . . Carmen.'

'Girlfriend?' She scrutinised his face; he was definitely hiding something.

'Hmm!' Owen half-laughed, not answering. 'A friend. She was at vet school with Dan. A very talented woman. Very passionate about animal rights. It was in Dan's box?'

'At the top.'

'Well. Happy days.' He put it back on the shelf, next to one of her and Angus in choir vestments. Jeannie noticed he tucked it slightly behind the others. 'Ah, this is you – and is this your brother?'

'Yes, singing at the church. Angus only did it once; he wasn't asked back. In fact Mum was asked *not* to bring him back.'

'Oh no! So musical talent doesn't run in the family? Whereabouts were you living then?'

Ask him more, pushed the voice in Jeannie's head, but though she tried, she couldn't. Owen had gone red, he'd deliberately moved the conversation on, and it felt too awkward to drag it back.

They talked some more about her family dogs, and whether Jeannie should foster Lady Sadie or wait until Dan was better; then Owen said, as if it had just occurred to him, 'While I'm here, I meant to ask . . . Did a package come for Dan?'

'When?'

'Around the time of the wedding?' He cast his eyes around the kitchen, not so subtly checking her shelves and the big Welsh dresser.

Jeannie was about to say no, then remembered the parcel she'd collected from the post office in town. The one that had been addressed to Dan, not jointly to both of them like most of the wedding presents. 'Yes, why? What is it? Something for work?'

'I want to say nothing but . . .' Owen ran a hand through his hair and looked even more embarrassed. 'It's, er, it's from the stag do. Apparently it's been sent here and . . . well, do you mind if I just spirit it away before Dan even sees it?'

'*What* from the stag do?' As far as she knew, anyway, Dan's stag do had been fairly tame: a long weekend in Dublin with some sort of outdoorsy lads' activity. Paint-balling or quad-biking. She'd gone to a spa with her mum and Teri, a last-minute, too-expensive, 'we need to do *something*' plan. Rather than the gal-pal love-in extravaganza featured in the wedding magazines, they'd had an extortionate pedicure each, and talked about *Line of Duty*.

Owen stopped hunting round the room, suddenly aware of her eyes on him. 'It's nothing you'd want to see. Nothing Dan would want to see either. Ha ha.'

'If you're trying to sweep this under the carpet, Owen, it's not working. Tell me what it is.'

He laughed uneasily. 'Ah, no. Once you've seen it, and all that. Better if I just make it disappear. Dan would do the same if he knew it was coming; I know that for a fact.'

Jeannie couldn't even remember where she'd put the parcel. Was it still in the shopping bag she'd had with her that day? Had she put it away in a cupboard? Her days merged into one long round of trains, walks, bags, coffees.

'I honestly don't know where it is,' she said. 'But if I come across it, I'll have a quick look and if whatever it is makes my hair curl, I'll bin it and we'll never tell Dan it was here. OK? Don't stress about it – I've seen a few embarrassing things in my time, believe me.'

A flash of something Jeannie couldn't identify swept across Owen's eyes – frustration? panic? – but he squared his shoulders, as if he'd done his best. 'Fair enough. Shall we head on up to the kennels?' He took a final swig of coffee. 'I've obviously got my work cut out, explaining the state of my garden to Rachel.'

'Absolutely,' said Jeannie. 'Let me go and change into my dog-proof jeans and I'll be right with you.'

Owen and the puppies got on like a house on fire, as Jeannie had known they would. In their new world, they hadn't met a human being they didn't love. What surprised her was how easily he seemed to put their mothers at ease.

Lady Sadie, Constance and Grace were slowly getting better with people, but were still taken into the kennels if strange men visited. When Jeannie and Owen arrived, they'd been lurking in their safe place, a crate set up under a spare desk, from which secure spot they were watching the Fenwicks with anxious eyes. All three were fine with George – 'George gives off this smell dogs can't resist,' Rachel had explained, 'my theory is he's actually ten per cent Labrador' – but something about Owen clearly didn't trigger the usual frantic barking and cowering Jeannie saw every other time strangers approached.

Instead they sat quietly observing from the semi-darkness, protected by Gem lying between them and the humans, their ever-present intermediary. Owen wasn't ten per cent Labrador, thought Jeannie, glancing at the breed chart on the wall. If he was any kind of dog, Owen was something shaggier, like a St Bernard or a Newfoundland. A gentle dog with massive paws that could scare off wolves and then carry a child home on its back.

She led the mothers away into the main kennel area, where Mel the kennel assistant was scrubbing floors with the radio on full blast. By the time Jeannie came back, Owen was already peeling marauding pups off his stripy jumper. No sooner was one carefully removed than another leaped up and grabbed his sleeve. The little collies, cockapoos and terriers were mixed up in different pens to play, but the cockapoos were the naughtiest, bouncing and pawing as if they were working as a tag team. Owen looked helpless but happy in the face of the nippy, yippy onslaught.

'I only put my arm in!' he protested. 'They climb up

you like spiders! Ow!' He sucked his thumb. 'I didn't even see that one coming!'

'They're feisty, the girls. No fear, just as they should be,' said Rachel, unclamping Dolly the collie from Owen's arm. 'Sorry George wasn't around to say hello – he wanted to meet you, but he's working double shifts, until we find another locum. One's already walked out with stress.'

'Well, Dan's a hard man to replace!' said Owen.

'He certainly is. I had a peek at his CV – he seems to have worked with everything from gerbils to lions.'

'Lions?' Jeannie looked up. 'Seriously?'

Owen nodded. 'Dan spent his EMS year in Africa with a volunteer neutering charity, then won a prize for his paper on the incidence of various viral infections in feral cats. He spent some time in a lion sanctuary working with big cats.'

'Oh, was that when he was in Kenya?' she said, realising. 'What were the donkeys about?'

'That was another project. The charity he was working for asked him to go back after graduation to work with local vets, and he spent a few months helping to set up a mobile field surgery – he could be out there now, if he wanted, running the whole project.'

'Why isn't he?' Jeannie knew she should know the answer, but Dan had literally never mentioned working abroad, despite telling her plenty of funny stories about his time in practice in Northumbria. Calving, fruit cakes, cowpats, thermal leggings in high summer. Nothing about African field surgeries. Why was that? Modesty?

'He wanted to practise in the UK.' Owen busied

himself with the smallest of the puppies, a titchy collie called Lolly.

'Really?' Rachel held up the perfectly white Staffie they'd named Marilyn, on account of the single tiny brown freckle on her muzzle, and made a mou-mou squeak towards her pink nose. 'Dan chose fat ponies and rain eleven months a year when he could have been in Africa working with lions and tigers?'

Jeannie tipped her head, adding her own silent question to Rachel's.

Owen tickled Lolly's round pink tummy. 'Well, he had reasons for wanting to work here. His mum, for a start.'

Now that Jeannie could understand. There was a limit to how supportive Andrea would be even of charity work if it was thousands of miles away. 'Andrea made him come home?'

He screwed up his face, as if he'd already said too much. 'No, that's not fair. It was . . . complicated. Anyway, what should I know about these puppies, Rachel? I hear you're the collie expert round here.'

Rachel put Marilyn down and turned her attention back to Owen. She smiled enigmatically. 'Why do you ask about collies when it's clear you've already been chosen by Pierre?'

'Pierre?' Owen looked down, startled.

A chunky apricot cockapoo had scaled his way up Owen's sleeve into the crook of his arm, where he was now butting his curly head into the soft folds of cotton, paddling at the material with his needle-clawed paws.

'Pierre. Our most adventurous, some might say kamikaze boy. Brother of Jean-Paul, Agnès, Yves and Hubert.'

'No Coco?' asked Jeannie, spotting Rachel's French fashion theme.

She shook her head. 'Too obvious.'

'Completely lost on me, I'm afraid.' Owen unhooked Pierre's claws and lifted him up so they could check one another out, nose to nose. He was much more poodle than cocker spaniel, with a long muzzle and fine paws. 'I think you're going to be a big boy, aren't you? Don't let them tell you poodles are fashion accessories. You're a country lad. Called Pete.'

He looked right with the dog; Pierre's lamb curls matched Owen's own shaggy hair, and he nestled into Owen's body, chewing his jumper. They already seemed like a team.

'I think that's a match.' Rachel smiled and lifted a finger into the air as if agreeing with an inaudible voice.

Owen asked for the full tour of the kennels and Rachel was only too keen to oblige.

She proudly showed off the heated runs and the play areas, and they were heading down the tiled corridor towards Lady Sadie, Constance and Grace when Jeannie's attention was dragged away by something else she wasn't expecting.

She didn't notice at first, not until her mind started humming along subconsciously to the song on the radio, even though she'd never heard it before. But the melody was already there, in her head.

Jeannie strained her ears. It wasn't an old song, but a song she knew. A cover? She didn't recognise the singer.

Then it dawned on her. It was *her* song.

She stopped walking. 'Rachel, can you turn up the radio?'

At the top of the runs, Rachel was introducing Owen to Mel. 'Why? Have we had a request from Kennel Three? Don't tell me – "I Want to Break Free"? Or "Keep on Running"?'

'It's . . . I think that's my song. On the radio.'

'You're kidding?' Mel turned to stare at her. Rachel had told her that Jeannie was a musician – Rachel proudly told everyone – but Jeannie wasn't so vain that she couldn't see how hard that was for most people to believe, unless they'd actually seen her on stage. And even then . . .

'Yes.' The song was already halfway through. 'Can you . . . ?'

Rachel reached over to the shelf and turned the radio up as loud as it'd go. As she did, the last trace of doubt left Jeannie's mind. It was a song called 'I Didn't Know' that she and Edith had written about one of Edith's many break-ups with her boyfriend, Django. It wasn't Edith singing, it was a girl group. Not a very good one, either. When the chorus kicked in, Jeannie felt her stomach fall through the floor.

> I didn't know you could make me so cruel;
> I didn't know I was like that, till I met you.
> I didn't know I was already someone else.
> I didn't know what I didn't know . . .

Jeannie realised she was mouthing the words along with the lead singer, her brain automatically rising and falling on the harmony line she'd sung against Edith's lead. It was her favourite harmony ever – her softer voice winding around Edith's sharp, bitter vocals. These girls were singing in unison, no harmonies other than the autotune shackling them together.

Owen was staring at her, visibly impressed, but she barely noticed.

'Wow!' Mel stopped chewing and let her mouth drop open. 'That's your song? You wrote that?'

'Shh!' said Rachel.

Jeannie nodded, too stunned to form words. She felt as if she'd been robbed, something precious swiped out of her back pocket without her noticing. It was her melody. *Her* song. Admittedly, Edith had written the lyrics, and they hadn't officially recorded it, but it was a song they'd played at gigs loads of times. It was so catchy that crowds chanted 'I didn't know' back at them, often the second time they heard the chorus.

Jeannie's hands clenched and unclenched by her side. The four of them listened in silence as the girls sang on, through an instrumental solo almost note-for-note the one Jeannie had played on her guitar, and then a rap – bloody hell, a *rap* – then the final chorus.

Then it was over, and the DJ was talking over the play-out melody, the one that had sprung into Jeannie's head like a spell. And which was now repeated, tackily, on a sampled recorder. A *recorder*.

'. . . and that was the New Fridays featuring Melting Jay with their new single "I Didn't Know", getting a lot of buzz right now . . .'

'Turn it off,' said Jeannie.

Rachel smacked the radio off with the flat of her hand. There was silence for a few moments. 'I take it you didn't know about that. Was that Edith?'

'No, it wasn't her. That was the band the producer was working with.' Her knees felt weak. 'We agreed that she wouldn't take anything with her. She *promised* she wouldn't take anything with her.'

'And you don't have any legal comeback? It's your copyright, surely?' asked Owen.

Jeannie shook her head. 'It wasn't published. We hadn't recorded it yet. But we were going to.' That wasn't the point. Edith knew it was something they'd pulled out of their own hearts, together, and she'd sold it. Sold it to strangers, so she could push ahead with a life that didn't include Jeannie.

Mel looked between them, agog. 'Seriously? That's your actual song?'

'Mel! How many times?' Rachel boggled at her. 'Yes.'

She didn't seem bothered by Rachel's boggling. 'It's really good.'

'I think she knows that.' Rachel turned back to Jeannie. 'But it is. It's amazing. You're so talented, Jeannie.'

Jeannie stared at the kennel wall. I should be raging, she thought. I should be furious and punching the air and ringing Edith up and telling her what a selfish bitch she is. But instead it felt as if the breath had been sucked out of her body. Every last atom of oxygen. There was no shout in her, no voice, nothing. She felt numb.

'Jeannie, are you OK?' Rachel stepped forward and Jeannie nodded, robotically.

'Hospital,' she said. 'I need to get going.'

'I'll take you there.' Owen touched her arm, then glanced at Rachel. 'Thanks so much for letting me meet Pete. Can I give you a ring later today to discuss . . . what happens next?'

'Sure.' Rachel glanced, concerned, at Jeannie, but Jeannie wasn't listening. She was back in the kitchen of their shared flat, having that painful last conversation with Edith: the one where too many unforgettable home truths had been delivered in that impatient, 'this is for your own good' lecture.

She wasn't strong enough, apparently. She wasn't tough enough to make it in an industry where you needed to push and network and innovate and know the right people. She wasn't enough of anything.

'I can't do it for both of us any more,' Edith had wailed, as if Jeannie was the one making an unreasonable demand. 'You're happy playing these local festivals but I'm not. I need *more*.'

For a long time, Jeannie had tried to blank out that final destructive exchange, burying it deep at the back of her mind and throwing piles and piles of wedding preparation on top until she couldn't hear it any more. But hearing the song had blown all of that away, and Edith was there in front of her again, with her big boots, and harsh eyes. Overnight, transformed by the single conversation with someone who finally took her as seriously as she took herself, Edith had regenerated into a different person: a coolly patronising hipster, bag over her shoulder, ready to walk out. The shock of seeing her childhood friend talk to her as if she were a stranger crushed something inside Jeannie: the hardest thing had been realising Edith didn't even rate her as a musician. How long had she thought that? And was it true?

Maybe this path isn't for you, Jeannie. But it is for me.

Edith had put some money for next month's rent on the kitchen counter and left Jeannie and their band and their plans and their history and their friendship, without a second glance.

Jeannie felt Rachel slipping an arm round her, and then sensed Owen steering her out to the car. She wanted to respond, but she had to concentrate hard to stop the pain from swallowing her whole.

Chapter Nineteen

Owen didn't even ask; once the Starbucks drive-through hove into view, he headed straight in and ordered large lattes and muffins for both of them. Chocolate for him, skinny blueberry for Jeannie – her usual choice from the hospital café. When the disembodied voice asked about sugars in the coffee, he glanced over at Jeannie, and said, 'Two sugars in mine and . . . one sugar in the other.'

She nodded. They'd bought each other enough coffees over the past few weeks. Even the ward nurses knew how many sugars Jeannie took.

Meanwhile Edith's words went round and round in her head, carried on her tune. *I didn't know. I didn't know. I didn't know what I didn't know.* How ironic. How brilliantly ironic that Edith had chosen to steal *that*.

As Owen drove up to the collection window, Jeannie tormented herself with the question she'd asked a million times: why couldn't she write her own words? Edith had turned her melody into something angry. The music she'd heard in her head had been soft, the kind of love song she longed to have sung to her by someone else. But the right words wouldn't come, because they never did, and Edith had fitted her own so neatly that now it was impossible to hear it any other way.

Gone, she thought, with a stab of regret. Edith had leaped into her song like someone jumping into a stolen car and driven it clean away.

Owen collected the brown paper bag and parked up facing out towards the busy road. He handed Jeannie the bag with her coffee and muffin, and started scoffing his own, pulling chunks off the cake as if he hadn't eaten for days and washing it down with milky coffee.

He didn't speak, but his sympathetic silence was comforting. After a while Jeannie heard her own voice confessing in the car, small and sad.

'I dreamed that song, you know.' She stared ahead, straight out towards the road. 'I heard it in a dream, and I woke up and I sang it into my phone before I could forget it. I couldn't believe I hadn't heard it on the radio. It came out *perfect*. It's the song I love the most, the one that made me feel like a proper writer. It made me believe I had that . . . that *magic* inside me, like the musicians I'd admired my whole life.' She paused self-consciously. 'Sorry, it's hard to explain without sounding like a bit of a unicorn fairy child.'

'Not if it's how you feel.'

'I've never written anything else as good as that.'

'It's still your tune,' Owen pointed out. 'I don't know much about this sort of thing, but surely if it's being played on the radio then you're due a fairly massive share of—'

'It's not about the money.' Jeannie watched the traffic speeding past, heading towards new opportunities, meetings, futures. 'It's about . . .' She took a deep breath. 'What if I never have a moment of inspiration like that again? What if that was *it*?'

'Oh, you will.' Owen patiently extracted Jeannie's untouched coffee from the bag and handed it to her. 'I don't know much about unicorn creative worlds, but if you can write a song as good as that once, then there's bound to be more inside you somewhere. Or just rewrite that one? Status Quo made do with the one song for years.'

Jeannie didn't reply. Edith had dealt with every event in her life by *spinning the pain into gold*, as she put it – and she had, she'd written some *amazing* lyrics, throwing them down on the table with pride, rubbing her red eyes as a sign of her heartbreak *and* her creativity. Whereas when Edith abandoned her, when Dan was nearly killed, when she was torn between her conscience and her heart, Jeannie's mind had gone blank.

'Come on,' he said. 'Inspiration isn't just a one-off thing. Not if you're creative, which you are.'

'But *am* I?' she protested. 'I haven't felt inspired for *months*. I'm in the middle of all this emotion and fear and . . . what?'

Owen turned to her. 'I'm sorry? What kind of *human being* goes off and writes songs when their boyfriend's in a coma?'

It was the wrong thing to say, but Jeannie couldn't stop herself. 'Morrissey?'

'Girlfriend in a Coma'. The only Smiths song Edith had condescended to like, because it was 'so outrageous'.

Owen paused. 'OK, fair enough, Morrissey. But do you want to be like Morrissey?' The appalled way he said it, as if he couldn't flick the name off his tongue quickly enough, almost made Jeannie smile.

'No,' Jeannie conceded.

'Good. Bloody hell.' He frowned and sipped his coffee. 'I mean, I like the man's music but . . .'

Jeannie picked the desiccated blueberries off her muffin. Tiny purple scabs that left stains on the cake. She didn't even know why she'd said that; at least Owen had got the reference. Dan wouldn't have done. 'I don't think Morrissey's girlfriend was, you know, actually . . . *in* a coma.'

'I *realise* that.' Owen sipped his coffee as if nothing had happened, then added, as if he couldn't let it go, 'But what kind of person imagines a girlfriend just to imagine them in a coma? Why not "Girlfriend on a Tractor" or something . . . fun?'

A half-laugh burst out of Jeannie, but she frowned it away.

Owen looked out of the window. 'But seriously, did you really expect to be *inspired* by Dan's accident?'

'Edith said she—'

'The more I hear about Edith, the worse she sounds. Does she have any idea what you're going through right now? Has she called to see if there's anything . . . ?' He softened his tone, seeing Jeannie flinch. 'Look, I'm sure when the time's right . . . You didn't expect to write *that* song, did you? It just came out of nowhere?'

She nodded. She had no idea where the inspiration had come from: it had been in her head as if she'd always known it.

'Then another one will. That wasn't the only song you've ever written, right?'

'No, we had a few more.' Edith wouldn't dare take those . . . would she? Jeannie felt a sinking despair. She might. She didn't know Edith at all.

'Good. Listen, I don't mind giving you some space for a few minutes if you want to call her,' he went on, unbuckling his seat belt.

'What?'

'Ring Edith up and just . . . go for it. Tell her exactly what you think of this stunt she's pulled on you. Both barrels. She deserves it. And,' Owen added, more pragmatically, 'better to do it now before we get to the hospital. You don't want to see Dan with this simmering away inside.'

Jeannie stared at him. He was halfway out of his seat already.

'Go on. Oh, wait!' Owen pointed in an 'ah ha!' way, then offered her his own phone. 'Why not do it on mine? Element of surprise, in case she's blocked yours?'

Her chest felt tight. 'I can't.'

'What? Why not?'

It sounded pathetic but it was true. 'I don't know what to say.'

'Really? I can literally give you five things *I'd* like to say to Edith and I don't know even know her.'

'It's not as easy as that.' Anxiety surged up Jeannie's throat, blanking off her mind with a familiar panic. But she needed Owen to understand so she forced herself to find words. 'I keep thinking about what I should have said when she told me she was moving away without me and now there's just too much . . .'

Owen turned back in his seat to face her. 'You didn't let rip at her when she told you she'd dumped you?'

Jeannie shook her head unhappily. 'She just talked and talked about how it was best for both of us. She's so eloquent when she gets going, I almost believed her. I . . . I

259

couldn't speak. I thought she'd see how upset I was, but she just *kept* talking and then . . .' She swallowed, remembering how she'd stood at the window and watched Edith walking down the street outside their flat. Tapestry bag over one bare shoulder, charity shop cowboy boots clicking on the pavement, already on the phone to a new friend. A brand-new tattoo on her left shoulder blade: a starburst. 'Then she left.'

'So Edith thinks you're fine with it?'

'I don't . . . I don't know. No. Well. Maybe.'

Owen chose his words carefully. 'I don't want to sound harsh, but you can't just let things like that *happen*, Jeannie. Would you let someone treat your best friend the way Edith treated you?'

'I thought she *was* my best friend.' Jeannie struggled to distil the fog of pain into words – not just so Owen would understand now, but so she would. 'Since *school*, Owen. It never even occurred to me that Edith would want a break that didn't include us both. She knew I was shy, but I wasn't shy once I was on stage. We sang together; we wrote together. We did everything together. Until that.'

He looked at her. 'Do you think Edith was jealous?'

'Jealous of what?'

'Your talent.' He raised an eyebrow. 'Did she play anything?'

'She played guitar too. It wasn't her main thing, but no, she wasn't jealous.'

'Was she jealous of what you had with Dan, maybe? Did she see you leaving with him to come here and think she had to take her chances while she could?'

That would be a nice way of looking at it, if only the

dates fitted. The truth was, it was the other way around. Dan's proposal had come a few weekends after Edith's departure. Dan's proposal and her acceptance.

'I don't think either of them really . . . got the other, if I'm honest.' Jeannie fidgeted with the coffee lid. She certainly wasn't going to tell Owen what Edith had said about Dan. They'd only met once, at an acoustic weekender in Wiltshire. He'd come backstage to get Jeannie after their set, and Dan and Edith had had what Jeannie had thought was a reasonably civil conversation about Blondie. A few days later, Jeannie had asked Edith what she thought of her gorgeous new man, and Edith had rolled her eyes and replied, 'Oh God, he's sweet, but kind of "Various Artists", no?'

Owen crumpled up his paper bag thoughtfully, then looked up at her, through his dark eyelashes. 'Jeannie, it's not really my place to . . .' he started, but was interrupted by her phone ringing in her bag.

'Bet that's her now.' He nodded. 'I bet she's heard your song on the radio too, and she's phoning to apologise.'

'I doubt it.' Apologising wasn't Edith's thing. 'It might be my mum, though . . .'

She was almost right: it was Andrea.

'Where are you? Are you nearby?' Andrea sounded agitated and Jeannie indicated to Owen that they'd better get going.

'We're on our way,' she said. 'I did text to say we'd be late today. Owen came to see the puppies, and—'

But Andrea wasn't listening. 'Come over as fast as you can – something *wonderful* has happened!'

'What?'

'Danny's woken up! And he spoke to me!' Her voice

was messy with tears, and laughter. 'Jeannie, he *spoke* to me! He said, "Mum!" Oh, Jeannie, I'm so relieved. He's going to be *fine*.'

Owen was close enough to have heard all that himself. Their eyes met, and Jeannie would have given anything to have five seconds inside Owen's head, to know what he was thinking for his brown eyes to look so apprehensive.

'Tell Andrea we'll be there in half an hour,' he said.

'We'll be there in half an hour,' she repeated, without breaking Owen's gaze.

He started the car and reversed out of the car park, and neither of them spoke until they reached the hospital.

When they got to Dan's room, a different doctor and a couple of nurses were standing by the door, taking notes and casting the occasional look in Dan's direction while they discussed the availability of several people Jeannie had never heard mentioned before, as well as throwing around the jumble of half-familiar acronyms. The nurses smiled as Jeannie and Owen walked in, and the doctor said, 'Mr Allcott will be with you soon, if that's all right, for an update?'

Andrea was kneeling by the bedside, gazing up at her son with a joyful glow on her face that was almost like a religious painting. Jeannie couldn't make out what she was saying: it was a low, burbling stream of words, full of excitement and love.

Dan lay there, his blue eyes wide open, a warmer colour in his thin face, looking extremely pissed off. He was awake. He was back. Her boyfriend was back, and he looked just like his old self. Relief surged through Jeannie's body.

He doesn't look very happy to be awake, she thought, then wondered why that even surprised her. Dan must have the worst headache of all time, even with the powerful cocktail of analgesics circulating in his system.

He grimaced as she and Owen approached, as if the action of thinking actively hurt his brain, then he focused his attention on Owen.

'Hey, mate.' Owen pulled out one of the chairs next to the bed. 'Good to have you back. How're you feeling?'

Jeannie's stomach pitched. Dan hadn't even looked at her. His whole attention was on Owen. Was that deliberate? Was he angry with her? Was he ignoring her?

''M good.' It was barely a croak, scratched out of a dry throat, but it was Dan's voice, and he managed to lift his mouth into a ghost of his old smile. Owen's answering smile nearly split his face with happiness, and looked as if he was barely containing an urge to grab his mate and hug him. It was lovely.

Goosebumps raced across Jeannie's skin and she smiled at Dan.

He didn't react and her smile slowly faded.

'Amazing! Good lad!' Owen gently bumped his fist into Dan's – Dan managed to make a very, very weak fist in response – and Andrea lunged forward.

'Be careful, Owen!' she said. 'Mind Danny's drips. He's still terribly weak; we've got to be careful . . .'

The concentration creases on Dan's forehead deepened, and he moved his hand vaguely as if swatting away a fly.

'Hello, Dan,' said Jeannie, but he didn't reply. Had he even heard her?

Owen, Andrea and Jeannie stared at Dan, holding their

breath, waiting for him to say something else. Seconds passed, no words came, then he closed his eyes with a heavy sigh, and they all released a loud breath in unison.

It would have been funny, thought Jeannie, if there wasn't so much tension in the room. Andrea was almost vibrating with it. When Dan closed his eyes she leaned forward, as if she was afraid he wouldn't come back this time.

Owen sensed her discomfort. 'Must be taking a lot out of him at this stage,' he said.

'I guess so.' The emotions from hearing her song on the radio were still firing round her system, and now this – the relief of seeing Dan begin to wake up, and the fear of what might happen next – sent another tidal wave running from an opposite direction. She was starting to feel dangerously tearful.

Andrea got up from her knees and perched on the chair nearest Dan's side. She patted the seat next to her for Jeannie to sit down.

'Isn't this wonderful? Isn't it? I was reading him a post-card from my sister, and one of his monitors started bleeping, and I was calling the nurse in when I heard him say, "Mum."' Andrea's blue eyes filled up. 'I've never felt happiness like that in my entire life, Jeannie. Not since the day Danny was born. Everything's going to be fine.'

'It's wonderful, Andrea. Really wonderful.' Andrea was gripping her hands, and a claustrophobic sensation was creeping up Jeannie's chest. She did her best to block out the urge to pull her hands away, but it persisted.

'Mr Allcott's going to run a lot more tests now Danny can actually speak and tell them how he's feeling.' She shook Jeannie's hands again. 'He could be leaving hospital in weeks! And you know what this means, don't you?'

'Um, no? I mean, apart from Dan being on the mend? Which is . . . amazing.'

Andrea leaned forward, eyes shining with optimism. 'We can start replanning that wedding! Danny's always set himself goals. I know it's a long road ahead, you don't need to remind me of that, but if he's got something as wonderful as his own wedding to focus on, I just know it'll give him that extra incentive to get back on his feet!'

Jeannie felt sick. Actually physically nauseous.

Andrea turned her head to bring Owen into the conversation but he looked as stunned as Jeannie did.

'It's a nice thought, but let's get Dan up and about first, eh?'

'We need to think about dates,' Andrea went on, as if Owen hadn't spoken. 'I won't do too much, I promise – but I know how far in advance you have to plan these things. And if we have to make allowances for Dan needing more support for a little while . . .'

Jeannie had a shocking image of Dan in a wheelchair, supported by his physio, wrangled into an uncomfortable suit, waiting for her at the end of another aisle, with everyone's faces turned towards her, rooting for the ultimate happy ending – how could she tell Dan *now* she didn't want to marry him? How could she rip away the bright light at the end of a punishing timetable of therapy, treatment, rehab – rehab they didn't even know would be successful? She would look like a complete bitch. And why was that? Because she'd *be* one.

Andrea smiled at her, oblivious.

I didn't know you could make me so cruel;
I didn't know I was like that, till I met you . . .

You have to say something, persisted a voice in Jeannie's head. But the thought of how she'd even start was impossible. What was there to say? Calling Edith to yell at her for stealing her best song seemed like a cosy chat in comparison with what faced her with Dan when he was well enough to speak.

This wasn't just about her and Dan now, either. It was about Andrea, and the family Andrea wanted so badly. The Christmases, the grandchildren, people to love her and be loved by her. She was already *in* this family. And it was about Owen. Not letting Owen *or* his best friend down.

Frightened tears finally burst through Jeannie's crumbling defences, and she sobbed, ashamed at herself.

'Oh, darling! I know, it's such a relief,' Andrea said. 'You let it out!' She threw her arms around her, and Jeannie was relieved to be able to hide her face in Andrea's shoulder.

Chapter Twenty

Mr Allcott appeared towards the end of the day to update Jeannie and Andrea on the results of the new tests. Andrea was fidgety with excitement, and maybe because of this, he started with a very clear disclaimer: Dan would be tired and disorientated for the first few days, and they shouldn't expect too much too soon. He might be irritable and disinhibited, he warned, he might be uncharacteristically rude or tactless – or just inappropriate. It might be upsetting for them, but it would, hopefully, soon pass as the post-traumatic amnesia receded and his brain reset itself.

'The human brain can't regenerate dead cells, but it *can* create new nerve pathways to replace damaged areas, and though it's not an overnight process, it looks as if Dan's begun that journey,' he concluded at the end of a detailed explanation that had covered seven pages of Jeannie's notebook. 'We'll be keeping a close eye on his pain relief and giving him plenty of recovery time, so don't feel you have to be by Dan's side every moment at this point. He'll be sleeping a lot.'

'Was it the messages that brought him round?' Andrea had been leaning forward in her chair throughout, desperate for confirmation that Dan was going to be back to normal in no time. Confirmation, Jeannie noted, that

Mr Allcott had been careful to avoid giving. 'Us sitting with him, will he have known?'

'Very possibly. There's plenty of anecdotal evidence from coma patients that suggests they're aware of activity going on around them, although they process it in different ways. Dreams, and so on. You'll have to ask him.'

'We can't believe he's finally turned the corner.' Andrea glanced across at Jeannie with a smile that said 'we'. 'And now we can start looking forward to something happier: Danny and Jeannie's wedding, take two. I know, before you say anything!' She held up her slender hands. 'There's a long way to go yet, but I want Danny to know we're thinking ahead. As a family.'

Jeannie forced out a vague nod of agreement. Andrea hadn't taken Owen's hint about dropping the wedding talk. In fact, she'd overheard her confiding to one of the nurses about how she planned to 'make up for everything' with 'a very special day' in the spring. The nurse, of course, had thought this was a wonderful, generous gesture – which it was.

She hoped Mr Allcott wouldn't encourage that line of thinking, and to Jeannie's relief, he just nodded.

'Daniel's certainly got a lot to look forward to,' he said. 'So! We have some more assessments to do. Let's speak again in a few days when we'll have a clearer picture about next steps – rehab units, or home discharge, or whatever the best option is for Daniel's recovery.'

Whatever the best option is. Jeannie stared at her notes. She didn't know what that looked like any more.

Although it was getting late, Andrea announced that she was going to talk to the physiotherapist before he left for the day. There was, she said, so much they needed to find out.

'You need some time alone with Danny,' she said, touching Jeannie's arm. 'This is the day we've been praying for, and I know you two will have a lot to talk about . . .'

The truth was, as Jeannie found out, sitting by Dan's bedside in complete silence, they had absolutely nothing to talk about.

Firstly, because Dan was still asleep most of the time.

Secondly, because when he was awake, he didn't have any idea who she was.

'Hello, sweetie,' she said when his eyes flickered open. She'd been sitting there for nearly half an hour, not wanting to disturb him, and feeling more and more nervous as the minutes passed. It was like waiting outside an exam room, knowing the second hand was sweeping round, and the moment of truth was coming, whether you liked it or not.

Dan grimaced at her. Physically, his face was the same but something had changed. Jeannie had never seen him radiating tetchiness like this; he'd always been a ray of easy-going sunshine, even in traffic jams and security check queues.

'How are you feeling?' A pretty stupid question to ask, but her mind had gone blank, and she had to start somewhere.

'Are you a nurse?' His voice was rough and laboured but definitely his.

'No. It's me, Jeannie.'

'Jeannie?'

She felt uncomfortable as he carried on squinting at

her; now she really didn't know what to say. Was Dan's vision affected? Maybe he didn't recognise her voice the way he instinctively knew his mother's. She leaned closer, so close she could smell his skin, and the E45 lotion Andrea had diligently rubbed into his hands and feet to stop them drying out. It was a hospital smell, not the intimate, warm smell she remembered. 'Dan, can you see me? It's *Jeannie.*'

'I can see you fine. Who are you? Leave me alone.' And Dan raised his hand and pushed her away with a weak but petulant gesture, and collapsed into the pillow, breathing roughly with the effort.

What? Jeannie felt as if she'd been punched much harder, and in the stomach. She slumped back on the plastic chair and blinked back tears of shock.

Dan didn't know who she was. She should feel relieved – what a way out! Not her fault! All over! – but, she didn't. She felt hurt.

He closed his eyes, ignoring her. One of the nurses came in for an early-evening check, probably alerted by the bleeping machines which seemed to be registering the abrupt lurch in atmosphere around the bed as much as Dan's raised heart rate.

'Hello, Jeannie, how's everything in here?' She checked and reset the monitors with comforting efficiency. 'Getting this young man overexcited, are you?'

'He doesn't know who I am.'

The nurse stopped and put a hand on her shoulder. 'Don't take it personally. Most coma patients go through this, the first few days after they come round.' She went to the bed and touched Dan's arm, getting his attention. 'Hon, can you tell me what your full name is?'

Dan didn't open his eyes. There was a pause, then he said, 'Daniel Richard . . . Anthony Hicks.'

The nurse looked over her shoulder at Jeannie, encouragingly. 'Excellent. And can you tell me what day it is?'

Another long pause. 'Thursday?' he said eventually.

It was Wednesday.

'Pretty close,' said the nurse. Jeannie discreetly checked her badge: Lauren. Her own memory was constantly tested by the multi-headed team surrounding Dan day and night. 'Dan, it's *Wednesday* today. Lemon meringue pie in the canteen! Wednesday. I'll ask you again later, OK?'

Dan grunted.

'This is Jeannie,' Lauren went on, without being asked. 'She's your girlfriend. Well, actually – she's a bit more than that, aren't you?' She grinned conspiratorially; Jeannie wondered if she was the nurse Andrea had been talking to about the new wedding plans. *Everyone* was involved. 'Do you want to tell him or shall I?'

Dan's eyelids flickered, and Jeannie felt a tug of protectiveness that overrode her own complicated feelings. He still looked vulnerable lying in the cradle of white machines. She could never leave him looking so helpless, so damaged his brain wasn't functioning properly.

'You tell him,' she said.

Lauren obviously thought Jeannie was too devastated to say the words. But then you would, wouldn't you? If you had to remind the man you were going to marry who you were.

Maybe I'm the one whose brain isn't functioning properly, she thought.

'Dan, Jeannie's your fiancée,' Lauren informed him in

the calm, clear tones that the intensive care nurses all seemed to have. 'You were on your way to get married when you got hit by a bus. Jeannie's been sitting here next to you ever since you were brought in. Jeannie, and your mum, and your mate Owen. They've been here the whole time.'

With a superhuman effort, Dan opened his eyes and fixed them on Jeannie.

They were the same beautiful blue eyes that had melted her heart, but the gaze was so intense and so unfriendly – so completely unlike the Dan she'd fallen for – that Jeannie's skin crawled. He examined her, closely and slowly, and she could almost sense him thinking as he searched his own brain for glimmers of recognition. Jeannie felt as if she was being scanned for secrets; she didn't dare move. What would he remember?

'No,' he said definitely. 'That isn't my girlfriend.' And then he fell asleep.

Jeannie's house felt darker and emptier than usual when she came home from the station. The silence swamped her from the moment she dropped her keys on the hall table and swept up the post: more bills, junk mail, another *Vet Times* with a scabby guinea pig on the front cover.

Jeannie hesitated on the threshold. With one knock on the door of the Fenwicks' noisy, airy, chatter-filled house, she'd be eating toast, stroking Gem and listening to Rachel recounting the story of the latest wedding dress donation. But she couldn't. It was far too late. Plus, Rachel would want to hear about Dan – obviously, since there was good news to share – and much as Jeannie longed to ask Rachel how she could stop Andrea going on about the wedding, she didn't know how to do that without telling her the truth about why she didn't want a second one. The thought of Rachel – and Natalie – finding out she'd jilted Dan moments before his accident made Jeannie feel sick. Their friendship was based on her bravely coping with his accident, and them supporting her with their generous trust. But how long before everyone found out?

She walked into her empty kitchen and sank down at the table. No dogs, no toast, no drying pants.

Something was buzzing in her bag – her phone. Jeannie hunted for it.

Have you called Edith yet? Just heard your song on the radio again and I was so furious I had to pull over and text you. Don't let her get away with this! O.

Jeannie stared at the screen. The entire text summed Owen up in three lines. The practical instruction, the fact that he'd found a safe place to stop before texting – and the loyal indignation on someone else's behalf. He was looking out for her now, the same way he looked out for Dan, his best mate. Probably all his friends. Owen was that kind of bloke.

She wondered where he was, right now. It had been an emotional day for him, too. Where was he driving so late? He'd had to leave before their meeting with Mr Allcott – family reasons, Andrea had said – so she'd texted him a summary. Maybe he'd been supermarket shopping? Seeing his niece? But before Jeannie could start a reply, another message popped up.

I meant to say before, your song has a GREAT key change. All classic songs have a great key change.

Her finger hovered over the screen. *Thanks*, she typed.

She wasn't expecting Owen to respond so quickly, but he did.

Living on a Prayer.

Pause.

Then *If I Could Turn Back Time.*

Another pause.

Then *Total Eclipse of the Heart.*

Jeannie laughed out loud at the last one. Bon Jovi, she might have guessed at. But Bonnie Tyler? Owen had a secret power ballad soft spot?

That's flattering company to be in, thanks.

So? he texted straight back. *Phoned her?*

He made it sound very straightforward, but then Owen hadn't met Edith. Jeannie flung herself on the sofa and sank into the soft cushions. She could feel the weariness draining from her bones. *Not yet. Just back from the hospital.*

Jeannie knew as soon as they started talking about Dan, everything else would seem trivial, including her song, and she felt ashamed of that.

Need to hear everything – sounds positive! But you have to call Edith while you're angry. Otherwise you never will.

That struck home. Jeannie chewed her lip. Owen was right; she had to confront Edith before she had time to think herself out of it. Life was already moving on; if she didn't think Edith's betrayal was important, who would?

I'll phone her. Promise.

Do it now! Just tell her what you told me.

Ten minutes later she wouldn't be able to say how she'd done it, but Jeannie found herself scrolling through for Edith's number in her call list, and pressing the green dial button, replaying in her head the moment when she'd heard her song on the radio. It was only when it was ringing that the reality of what she was doing struck her.

The phone rang, and rang, triggering an unhappy echo in her memory.

Jeannie's heart expanded in her chest, swelling with every ring until the sound felt as if it was coming from inside her head. She had no idea what she was going to say if Edith picked up, but her mind swirled with indignation and pride: bright acid colours, not words.

Then the generic voicemail started. 'This is the mailbox for' – Edith's sardonic interjection: 'Edie Constantine' – 'please leave a message after the tone.'

And then the beep. The beep that set Jeannie's tongue running on autopilot.

'Edith, this is Jeannie. I heard "I Didn't Know" on the radio. You stole my song. You stole it. What kind of friend are you? I mean, what kind of *person* are you?' Her words snapped out, cold and steely; Jeannie barely recognised herself. She had a bad feeling that she was accidentally quoting song lyrics. 'I just want you to know how disgusted I am that you lied to me. I just wanted you to . . . to know that. I'm not putting up with this any more.'

She stopped abruptly – so much had happened since she'd last spoken to Edith that she could hear the changes in her own voice. Her disaster of a wedding, Dan's near-death experience, the abused dogs, weeks of hospital visiting, even the ukulele orchestra. But Edith didn't deserve to know about that. All she needed to know was that she'd gone too far and, finally, quiet little Jeannie McCarthy was mad enough to pick up the phone and call her out on her behaviour. What had happened since their last meeting to change Jeannie so much was *none of her damn business.*

Jeannie felt drunk. She hung up before she could spoil it.

Then, with trembling hands, she texted Owen. *Done it.*

Silence filled the house again. It was *so* quiet out here, so still and soundless. But she didn't feel alone. Jeannie stood in her unlived-in living room, swaying gently with the effort of keeping her breathing steady. It had been a long, weird day and now she was in a house that should have been her sanctuary but instead felt full of secrets. Hers *and* Dan's.

I need a dog, she thought. This house needs a dog in it.

And then her phone buzzed. This time Owen wasn't texting: he was ringing.

Jeannie wasn't sure whether she had enough energy left to drag the pieces of herself back together for a conversation, but then her finger pressed the answer button and she had no choice. 'Hello?'

'Hope I'm not disturbing you.' As soon as she heard Owen's softly spoken voice, she realised how much she needed to hear someone tell her she'd done the right thing. 'Just wanted to check you were OK.'

'I'm fine.' She didn't sound fine; she wondered if he could hear her heart banging away in her chest. 'Edith didn't pick up. I just talked, and then I stopped talking.'

'Doesn't matter. You've got it off your chest. Don't you feel better for doing it?'

'Um, yes.' The weird thing was, Jeannie *did* feel better. She had the same sense of euphoric exhaustion she remembered from cross-country running at school: she hadn't enjoyed *doing* it, and it definitely hadn't been pretty while it had been happening, but the knowledge that she'd done it was . . . satisfying.

'Good for you. It's not easy, saying things people don't want to hear.'

'Thanks. I don't understand how she thought she could get away with it.' Jeannie squeezed her eyes shut. 'Didn't she think I'd notice?'

'She didn't think you'd make a fuss.' Owen's voice in her ear sounded very close. 'She'll get the shock of her life when she sees you've phoned.'

'She won't.' Jeannie pictured Edith's familiar 'surprised' face: the pointy nose wrinkled cutely in shock, the pierced eyebrow hiked high. It was heavily seasoned with sarcasm, because nothing really surprised Edith. She didn't let it.

Owen changed the subject. 'Great to see Dan talking, wasn't it?'

'Um, yes. Did he . . . did he seem all right to you?'

'As well as any bloke who'd just come out of a coma, I guess. Why?'

'He didn't recognise me.' Jeannie struggled to form her next words. *Speak out. Don't bottle it up.* 'He looked me up and down and he said, "*That's* not my girlfriend."'

It was the way Dan had said it, as if she were some sort of imposter. Had she been crushed out of his memory? Or was he making a point about her nervous call before the wedding? If he had listened to her first message, then it must have been one of the last things he did before the bus hit him, so was it even possible that he remembered? But she didn't want to have to ask Owen that.

Lucy Dillon

'He's still on a ton of medication, Jeannie. He's probably lost some short-term memory.'

'Yes, but to wipe out a *year*? A whole year of us?'

'Don't take it personally. It's early days. Let's see what the next weeks bring.'

'I know.' Jeannie hugged the cushion – one of her favourite things from the flat she'd left to move in with Dan. It had a gold embroidered horseshoe on it, a present from her mum for her eighteenth birthday. It fitted perfectly behind her back when she sat cross-legged on the floor, playing her guitar.

'While it's in my head,' Owen went on, 'Sam's a barrister – remember Sam, from the messages? He told that story about the time Dan organised cat races for Rag Week ... He could write you a legal letter to send to Edith about your copyright.'

'Would he?' Jeannie remembered the story very well: she'd listened to it four times. Would Dan remember Sam's cat races, but not her?

'Believe it or not, when Sam's not wearing traffic cones on his head he's actually pretty scary in court. They call him the Decimator. Well, we call him the Decimator. Shall I put you in touch? In the morning, obviously. Sorry, I probably shouldn't have phoned you so late ...'

'It's fine. I'm not doing much.' Jeannie looked around the sitting room. She still hadn't got much further with the unpacking. She'd have to hurry up with that now if Dan was coming home. 'It's been a long day.'

'The longest one I can remember. I'll see you over the weekend, then?'

'Yup.' Now Owen was about to hang up, the emptiness of her house loomed again. 'Owen?'

'What?'

'Thanks for making me call Edith.' Jeannie hugged the cushion. It was easier to say these things on the phone, when she couldn't see his face. Owen blushed whenever she and Andrea thanked him for his spreadsheets, his tea runs, his lifts, his generous support. This time she was thanking him for something else: his friendship.

'I didn't do the hard bit. You did. It's always easy when you're on the outside.' He sounded embarrassed, as she'd guessed. 'Only good things will come from it, I promise.'

'How do you know that?'

'I just do,' he said simply. 'When you're honest with yourself, everything else falls into place. Family motto, more or less. Night, Jeannie.'

'Night.'

She didn't move from the sofa until the sun had sunk behind the cottage garden, and the salmon and lilac stripes in the clear night sky had faded into an inky greyness.

Chapter Twenty-one

Jeannie was in the shower the following morning, washing her hair and mentally rearranging the chores she had to do before setting off for the hospital, when her odd conversation with Owen about that package for Dan popped back into her head, swiftly followed by a flash of where it was.

It was at the back of the kitchen cupboard, the tall one where cereal packets and pasta containers would go, if anyone was there to eat cereal or pasta. The cupboard was where Jeannie had been shoving any post she couldn't face at the end of a long day: congratulations cards, letters, gift vouchers, invoices, all the wedding-related paperwork that she knew she'd have to deal with at some point – but not yet. She'd half-thrown the package up there to get it out of the way, then promptly forgotten about it.

Jeannie rinsed her hair quickly and got dressed. She decided she wasn't going to hand it to Owen. It was typical that he wanted to protect his best mate from embarrassment, but whatever was inside couldn't be that bad. Some dodgy sex toy? Or a 'hilarious' plaster cast of Dan's privates? Knowing Owen, it was probably something completely innocuous, something that might even end up being a bit of light relief in years to come. And even if it wasn't, surely that was for her and Dan to discuss? There was already enough about Dan that she didn't know. She couldn't start adding to that list with *new* uncertainties.

Downstairs, Jeannie flicked on the kettle and put some bread in the toaster. She could hear the first lot of kennel dogs being released like lottery balls into the paddocks up the lane, barking and yapping as their morning energy exploded. If she hurried, she'd still have time to join Rachel and help out. It was a nice way to feel useful, watching the dogs' simple joy in running around, listening to Rachel tell her about their different personalities in the funny voices she made up for them.

While the kettle boiled, Jeannie opened the tall cupboard and reached inside for the package. There was more post in there than she remembered; she pushed it to one side and patted along the back of the shelf. Then, when her hand didn't hit a package, she patted the other way. Nothing. Just letters.

Had it got shoved to the back? She pulled a chair over and stood on it for a better view, but the back of the cupboard was empty.

It didn't make sense. Had she got the wrong cupboard? Deep down, Jeannie knew she hadn't, but she went through the motions of opening each one in turn.

Mugs and plates. Tins and jams. Saucepans. No package.

She stood back, confusion slowly hardening into something different. She'd definitely put it in that cupboard, and it had gone. Which meant someone had taken it.

The only people who'd been in the house since then were Rachel, Natalie, her parents . . . and Owen.

Jeannie's heart sank.

*

The house seemed to push her out after that depressing revelation. Jeannie packed her bag, including her ukulele for the lunchtime orchestra practice, and caught the bus down into town. It was barely eleven, and once she'd windowshopped listlessly along the main street for half an hour, she found herself walking past the shop window where her wedding dress was still on display.

Jeannie gazed unhappily at its swirling petticoats.

'Are you looking for Rachel, love?'

She jumped. It was Freda from the kennels, on her way back to the shop from an elevenses run to Natalie's café, going by the paper bags of cake.

'She's in the back, with Natalie,' Freda went on. 'Shall I say you're here?'

'It's OK,' said Jeannie. She could hear Rachel's laugh somewhere inside. 'I'll find her.'

The Four Oaks Charity Shop had a back office, located behind the main room stocked with books and clothes. It was small even when it wasn't full of donations, and when Jeannie poked her head round the door there was barely space to move.

Rachel was on the floor next to a crate of mixed puppies, her long legs folded up underneath her; Natalie was behind the main desk on the old candy-coloured iMac, and a tall bald man was sitting in the only spare chair. Seven wedding dresses in plastic shrouds hovered like ghosts on the shelf units. A lively conversation was well under way, which stopped as she appeared.

Rachel was the first to spot her, and she waved from the floor. 'Jeannie! Come on in, if you can find room? This is Howard Ridley from the *Gazette*!'

The man spun on the office chair and held out his

hand to shake hers with a smile. Unlike most men Jeannie had seen around town, Howard Ridley didn't wear a checked shirt and mud-spattered fleece gilet; he wore a tweed jacket with a jaunty red bow tie, topped off with a moustache that pre-dated current fashionable facial hair by about thirty years. The puppies were staring at him, jamming their noses through the crate bars in a fascinated scrum.

'Howard dropped in to see how we're getting on with the dress sales,' Natalie explained. 'We were discussing publicity for the gala night.'

Howard chuckled. 'If we have any more about this sale in the paper, we're going to have to change our name to the *Longhampton Gazette and Matrimonial Times*.'

Bride's Dress Revisited had done pretty well for exposure in the *Gazette*: so far, Diane the fashion editor was running a summer bridal beauty feature, and Gary the motoring editor had even been persuaded to do an 'alternative wedding transport' feature. (Quadbikes.) And every feature had been tagged with a donated dress and one of the rescued puppies, to remind readers why the money was being raised.

'You know us, Howard,' said Rachel. 'You give us a space and we'll give you four ideas and a photo opportunity.'

'If only I had you two on my features staff.' He twinkled at them, then sighed. 'If only I had the budget for a features staff. Anyhoo . . .' He slapped his thighs, checked his watch, and levered himself to his feet with a groan. 'I'll leave that other idea with you, ladies. Give me a ring later, and let me know what you reckon.'

'Will do,' said Natalie.

'Lovely to meet you, Jeannie,' he said, touching her

shoulder as he passed. 'Glad to hear your young man's on the mend.'

'Thanks.' Jeannie shot a quizzical look at Rachel, who pretended to be sorting through a box of crystal tiaras.

'Howard's wife's one of the hospital volunteer drivers,' Natalie explained, once Howard was safely out of the shop and back on the high street. 'They know everything. And I mean everything.'

'*How?*'

'I don't ask. Anyway, people know who you are because Dan left in the air ambulance. That makes you both minor celebrities. The last time we saw the air ambulance in Longhampton was when it was officially blessed by the town morris.'

'She's not joking,' Rachel confirmed. 'They did a special ambulance blessing dance, then threw apples at it. Very carefully, obviously. Rotor blades, you know.' She made an explanatory circular gesture with her finger.

'That's . . .' Natalie glanced at Rachel. 'That's sort of what Howard wanted to talk to us about.'

Jeannie looked between the two of them, and put down the cockapoo puppy she'd been playing with. 'In what way?'

There was a moment's 'You! No, you!' between Natalie and Rachel, and then Natalie rolled her eyes.

'Howard's going to run a story about the gala night, now it's only two weeks away, and I mentioned that you were working with Johnny and the ukulele orchestra. He already knew who you were – like I say, it was front-page news – and he asked if you'd mind talking to the newspaper about the air ambulance, and how great the paramedics were at the scene? Now Dan's on the mend.

The air ambulance is running a fundraising appeal later in the year, so it helps to get the message across about what a lifesaver it is round here. I mean *literally* a lifesaver. Howard felt it would be a positive local news story with a happy ending. God knows we need some of those!'

Jeannie looked between Rachel and Natalie. Yves the cockapoo was nipping her fingers, trying to chew her into retaliation, but a too-familiar numbness was spreading through her, starting with her throat.

'And of course,' Natalie went on, more confident now Jeannie hadn't said no immediately, 'the fact that you're rearranging your wedding is such a good link with *our* gala night. It all fits together so well!'

What? Jeannie had to force out the words. 'How did you know we're rearranging the wedding?'

Rachel looked up from the box. She'd stacked three diamanté tiaras in her hair, and they sparkled in the sunlight. She looked like a fashion editorial, not a crazy toddler. 'Oh, sorry! Was it meant to be a secret? Dan's mum phoned George last night. She wanted to bring us up to speed about Dan's recovery, and she mentioned that she was looking at booking a special venue for you, to make up for your nightmare day, and did we know anywhere fabulous locally? I said: "Well, you can't beat Ferrari's' . . ."' She trailed off, seeing Jeannie's expression. 'Was that the wrong thing to do?'

'Well, there might be a bit of a snag.' She tried to keep her tone light. 'I'm pretty sure the groom has to recognise the bride for it to be legally binding.'

'What?' Rachel hastily pulled the tiaras out of her hair.

'Dan doesn't remember me. He doesn't know who I am.'

'Oh my God, Jeannie. I'm sorry to hear that.'

'He is on the mend, though?' Natalie asked, as if worried she'd got the wrong end of the stick.

'Yes, but . . .'

There was a knock at the door, and Benita, one of the volunteers, put her head around. 'Quick, I need help!' she hissed. 'Customer trying to negotiate on a box set. Only wants the first two seasons of *Mad Men*. Says it went off the boil after JFK got shot.'

'Your department, Nat,' said Rachel. 'I have to agree with the customer on that one.'

'Oh . . . fine.' Natalie squeezed her way around the desk. 'I won't be long,' she said, wagging a warning finger at them both. 'Hold the thought.'

When the door was safely shut behind Natalie, Rachel lifted Marilyn the Staffie pup out of the playpen, and said, casually, 'Just say if you'd rather not do this interview.'

'It's not that I don't want to do it.' Jeannie hated lying to Rachel; Rachel had put so much trust in her, it seemed weaselly to hide something so massive. 'I just . . . it feels like tempting fate. Dan's only just come round.'

Good. That was a good reason. And true.

'But I thought he was almost ready to leave – if Andrea's talking about booking venues?'

'No, he's not almost ready to leave at all. There's a long way to go yet. And I wish she would stop making all these wedding plans.'

'Why? Is it too much too soon?' Rachel was watching her closely. 'Or is there something else?'

Jeannie squeezed the bridge of her nose. She needed to tell someone. It felt as if her head was full of hysterical birds. 'The thing is . . . I don't know if we're going to get married.'

There. She'd said it. Jeannie heard Owen's voice – *When you're honest with yourself, everything else falls into place* – and clenched her fists.

Rachel began to lower Marilyn carefully back into the crate. 'Why?'

She took a deep breath. 'Because I called it off before the accident.'

'What?' Rachel nearly dropped the puppy. '*What?*'

'I wasn't going to go through with it. I changed my mind.'

'*When?*'

'On the way to the church. Dad asked me if I was absolutely sure, and I realised I wasn't. So I phoned Dan to tell him we needed to talk but . . .' *Come on, Jeannie, push the words out.* 'I couldn't get through. I left a message basically telling him I couldn't marry him. Dad and I were waiting for him to call us back when Owen phoned to say there'd been an accident.'

'So did he hear it? When did he get hit by the bus?'

Jeannie's heart was racing, throbbing in her temples. 'I don't know. I don't *know* whether he was listening to the message and got distracted and walked into the road, or if he'd heard it, or what . . .'

'Oh my God!' Rachel covered her mouth, then uncovered it. 'Sorry, that's not helpful. Go on.'

'And now Dan can't remember me, let alone the wedding! He's not himself – he's angry, and aggressive. His whole personality seems different – but just towards me. The irony is, it would be kinder to walk away while he can't remember who I am, but I know Andrea and Owen will do everything they can to jog his memory. For me!' Jeannie put her hand on her chest, hating herself. 'And I can't tell them to stop, because they're both decent people and they *love* Dan and if they knew I'd jilted him half an hour before the wedding, then . . .' Her voice had been getting higher and higher with tension, but now it failed her. She couldn't say it.

'So what are you going to do?'

Jeannie hadn't even tried to put the next thoughts into words. Would Rachel understand? She was kind, and her own marriage to George clearly hadn't followed the most conventional course. But deliberately breaking the heart of a man who could be facing the end of his world as he knew it . . . Jeannie couldn't bear to think of Dan, unable to operate, unable to chase his dreams.

'I don't know. I don't know how to tell him how I feel, especially now everything's changed! But I wasn't going to marry him before the accident. So what am I supposed to do now? He needs me.'

There. It was out.

Rachel said nothing. The puppies rumbled and squeaked in the crate. Traffic passed outside on the high street as the rest of the world went on. Someone, somewhere, Jeannie told herself, was making a harder decision than this. Someone, somewhere, was doing something worse than she was. And the world was still turning.

It didn't make her feel any better.

'Blimey,' said Rachel, eventually. 'That is some pickle.'

'Pickle? I'd say it's a bit more than a *pickle*.'

The voice came from the doorway and Rachel and Jeannie both spun round guiltily.

Natalie was standing by the half-open door, arms crossed.

'Nat.' Rachel indicated the empty chair. 'Come in and hear the whole story. Sit down.'

Natalie ignored her. 'Why?'

'Why what?' Butterflies raced around Jeannie's stomach.

'*Why* did you wait until the morning of the wedding to tell Dan you'd changed your mind?' Her expression was strained, as if she was struggling to keep her voice calm. 'Was there literally no other point in the entire run-up when you could have sat down and discussed this with him?'

Jeannie wanted to ask Natalie why she'd been eavesdropping, but she didn't have much moral high ground to stand on. She swallowed, trying to speak slowly in the hope that the right words would come. 'There wasn't much "run-up",' she began. 'Dan proposed in October and we started planning the wedding straight away. Every weekend after Christmas we were doing some wedding thing – cakes, venues, dresses. It was fun! We were . . . swept up in it. I had a few wobbles, but I thought it was only nerves. And I couldn't put my finger on what it was, anyway. I still can't. Then when I was finally in the car, with no turning back, I suddenly knew . . . I couldn't go ahead with it.'

Rachel looked more sympathetic than Natalie. 'Wasn't there anyone you could have discussed this with? Your mum? Or a friend – Edith?'

'Not really, no.' Edith had left for London, and Edith had never liked Dan anyway, right from the moment he'd demanded to know why their signature cover of 'The Tide Is High' was so 'sinister'. Mum might have understood, but Mum was so excited, so relieved that Jeannie had something happy in her life after Edith had stamped on her dreams. Jeannie had never realised how few real friends she had until she desperately needed one. There were meet-for-coffee friends – Sophie the other music teacher, a few uni mates – but no one Jeannie could trust with such a friendship-changing secret. No one.

'Dan?' Natalie's voice was heavy with reproach. 'You were supposed to talk to *Dan*.'

Miserably, Jeannie met her gaze, wishing she had words to explain how disgusted she felt with herself. How utterly horrified she'd been by what she'd done, how frightened she'd been by that overwhelming urge to escape, but she had no answers. She deserved the silent disapproval radiating from Natalie's kind blue eyes.

'Nat, Jeannie feels bad enough already,' said Rachel. 'I think you should explain why this is such a hard thing for you. It might help her work out what to do.'

Natalie frowned, and tucked her hair behind her ears. 'What you did – it happened to my cousin Beth. I was her bridesmaid. The week before the wedding, her fiancé didn't come home one night. While she was phoning round the hospitals, thinking the worst, the best man turned up with a letter, "explaining"' – Natalie put air hooks round the word – 'Chris couldn't go through with it. They'd been engaged for three years. They had a cat, and a mortgage.'

Jeannie heard the pain between the words. 'That sounds awful. I'm sorry.'

'That was five years ago. Beth hasn't had a relationship since then,' Natalie went on. 'She doesn't trust anyone. And she had to move house to get away from the memories, thinking people still talked about it. It was humiliating for her, on top of being dumped by the man she loved.'

'But no one actually knows . . .'

'I guess that's the silver lining for Dan, eh?' Natalie looked bleak. 'At least being airlifted to hospital meant he didn't have to face everyone at the town hall when you didn't turn up.' She paused. 'I'm sorry if I sound harsh. But if you love someone enough to accept a proposal you owe them a proper explanation. It's so cruel, leaving it so late. It's something Dan will have to live with for ever.'

'And I will too,' said Jeannie weakly, but she knew it wasn't the same.

Uncomfortable moments passed as the three of them digested Jeannie's confession. The puppies in the play-pens carried on tumbling as if nothing had happened at all, and Jeannie felt her heart crack in a brand-new, painful place.

Rachel and Natalie had made Longhampton feel like home. They'd been generous, and thoughtful, and welcomed her into the hilarious, good-natured world of the dog rescue, trying to make her feel less alone in her waking nightmare of hospital runs and worst case scenarios. And now Natalie knew she was a cowardly bitch and Rachel was trying to be nice but George would side with Dan, his colleague, and that would be the end of that.

'I honestly never meant to hurt Dan,' she insisted, trying not to cry. 'I wish I could turn back the clock and do everything differently, but I can't.'

'Well, who else knows?' asked Natalie. 'Apart from me and Rachel. You can't keep something like this quiet. He deserves to hear it from you.'

'But does he *need* to know?' It burst out of Jeannie. 'I mean, that moment's gone . . .'

'Yes!' exploded Natalie, as Rachel said, 'You have to tell him if Andrea's dead set on rearranging the wedding. Look, you can't change what's happened – what's done is done – but you can't hurt him a second time . . .'

They were both waiting for Jeannie to say the Right Thing but Jeannie's throat had closed up. What was the right thing to do? Every option seemed like the wrong one. Before, 'saying nothing' meant no one was hurt. It was the exact opposite now.

After a few moments, Natalie broke the silence.

'Sorry, guys, but I'm out. I'm going back to the café.' She grabbed her coat from the hatstand, which was covered in donated veils like a gothic spiderweb. 'This whole conversation's bringing back some bad memories, and I don't want to make you feel worse, Jeannie.'

'I'm sorry,' Jeannie began, then wasn't sure what she was apologising for.

I'm just sorry, she thought. So sorry.

'Stop saying sorry, it means nothing.' Natalie turned and gave her a funny look. 'Make sure you do the right thing, is all I ask. Because this will affect the rest of Dan's life as much as whatever's going on in that hospital.'

Dan was dozing, recovering from Andrea's visit, when Jeannie arrived later that afternoon, fresh from a somewhat distracted lunchtime session with the ukulele orchestra, and she noticed at once that a couple of the monitors had been removed from the room: a positive sign.

He still had no idea who she was, though. When he woke up and saw her there, after she'd spent a long hour sitting by his bedside reading Get Well cards, Jeannie saw hope, then irritation cross his face.

'Why are you here?' he demanded. 'Who are you?'

'Her name is Jeannie.' Nurse Lauren had come in to check his pupil reactions. 'And she's here because she's your fiancée.' She flicked her tiny torch off and made a note on his chart. 'What day is it today?'

'Thursday.' He eyed Jeannie with suspicion. 'Are you an undercover doctor?'

'No, she's your fiancée,' Lauren repeated.

'I don't *have* a fiancée.' Dan sulked, like a teenager, then closed his eyes. Conversation over.

'Give it time,' Lauren reassured her. 'We'll keep reminding him when you're not here. Your friend brought in some photos – keep showing him yours too. We'll get there!'

Jeannie flipped through the images Owen thought would spark happy memories. Dan was active in every single one: skiing, smiling, drinking, hugging, laughing. She searched for Owen in the crowds of beaming strangers, noting how his shaggy hairstyle and thick glasses never changed, unlike Dan's frequent fashion cuts. He was there, watching, supporting, standing in the shadow of Dan's energy.

When Dan didn't offer any response to her tentative conversation, Jeannie scrolled through her phone, looking at selfies of them cosied up on bridges, in bars, in parks. Is that *really* me? she wondered. It was bizarre how detached she felt not just from Dan but from herself: two people living a weekend life that had seemed so colourful, compared with her round of students who never practised and bar shifts. That's what it had felt like, she realised. A holiday.

Dan fell asleep and as Jeannie watched him, a sharp thought slid into her head: maybe he didn't *want* to remember her. She couldn't turn back time, but in a funny way, *he* could. Wouldn't it be kinder to leave and let Dan have the last year back, to find someone who did want to marry him? The sudden sadness of that took her by surprise but it still felt like leaving something precious behind.

She slid on to her knees by the side of the bed and took his hand in hers. It was warmer now, more like the hand she remembered holding on buses, over white-clothed dining tables.

'I'm sorry,' she heard herself whisper. 'I'm *so* sorry, Dan.'

She'd said it over and over since the accident, meaning it in different ways, but now Jeannie felt she was apologising in advance, for pain she couldn't avoid inflicting whether she slipped away, or stayed.

To her surprise, Dan turned his head towards her on the pillow. His eyelids flickered, and his dry lips moved in response. Jeannie had to lean forward to catch the words.

'Sorry, darling,' he whispered. 'Sorry, darling.'

Hot tears filled Jeannie's eyes as she laid her forehead against the cool sheets. He'd recognised her somewhere in his subconscious, even if he'd never called her darling before.

Chapter Twenty-two

What have you done with Dan's parcel?

Too accusatory.

Where have you put that parcel you took from my kitchen?

Too wordy.

Why didn't you tell me you'd taken the parcel?

Too whiney.

So tell me – what was in that box you nicked?

Way too accusatory.

Jeannie deleted the last message and stared at the screen, defeated by the English language for the millionth time in her life.

How could you accuse someone of stealing from you – when you had no proof other than a strong gut instinct – without kicking off a huge row? And if he had sneaked through her cupboards and taken that box, what on earth was in it that Owen would do something so un-Owen-like to stop her seeing it? It was so disappointing. She'd trusted him. Why didn't he trust *her*?

Three cups of coffee had been no help with the message. Jeannie was still staring at her phone when the screen changed, and a landline number she didn't recognise flashed up.

She hesitated a moment, then – since it could be any

one of any number of people calling about Dan – she picked up.

'Hey, Jean Jeannie,' said a familiar voice. 'How's things?'

It was the one and only Edith Constantine.

Edith's voice had changed in the months she'd been in London. She sounded less Scottish, more confident (something Jeannie would have previously sworn was impossible) and her quirky stream of consciousness babble had vanished. Instead she spoke with a deliberate upward swoop in every sentence, as if she was live-tweeting her own conversation.

Jeannie gripped her phone with one hand and the back of a chair with the other for balance.

'So, yeah, I got your message,' said Edith, and paused.

'And?' It sounded cool; the truth was Jeannie's mind had gone blank and she couldn't think of anything else.

'And . . . I'm sorry? I guess I should have let you know we had an airplay date.' She said it as if she'd forgotten to tell Jeannie about leaving an iron on. 'Were you blown away? Did you think: Oh my God! Is this for real?'

Jeannie stared at the table. 'That's exactly what I thought.'

'You've got to admit, it's a moment, hearing your song on the radio.' There was a giddy gurgle in Edith's voice and Jeannie wondered if she was a bit pissed, even though it was only breakfast time. She certainly didn't sound anywhere near repentant enough. 'I was like, wooooooooo, *we did it*! For the first, like, twenty times. Ha ha! Weren't you?'

Edith's real-life energy burned away Jeannie's outrage, until her head felt empty and sore. Even on the end of a phone, Edith filled the room, pushing her out to the edges.

'Well? Didn't you?' she prodded.

'Not exactly.'

Edith laughed. 'Oh, come on, Jeannie, don't pretend to be too cool for school. It's getting *so much* airplay! The downloads are crazy! Aren't you excited?'

We did it. Jeannie bit her lip. The *we* didn't mean her and Edith, the two people who'd written the song. There were other 'we's now. Strangers. A flicker of fighting spirit stirred inside her. 'When you say "we" does that mean me as the co-writer? Or the wes who recorded it?'

'Oh God, Jeannie . . . Don't be like this. It's out there, being heard, and that's more than we'd ever have managed on our own, going round the festival circuit, maybe releasing one tiny album on some tiny indie label that seven people downloaded and no one ever talked about.'

What? 'So I should be grateful you stole it?'

'Yes! I mean, no . . .' Edith laughed again, that dismissive conversation-ending laugh.

'Why didn't you tell me they'd recorded it?' *They.* She couldn't bring herself to say the New Fridays. Stupid cheesy name for a band. 'You knew I'd hear it on the radio.'

'Because I didn't know until . . . quite recently.' Edith had the grace to sound faintly sheepish. 'It happened, like, almost overnight? Amir heard me singing it in the studio and asked what it was, so I played him it on the piano, and, well, things snowballed.' Jeannie could picture the shrug. It had always covered any explanation Edith didn't feel like making; it came with a winning half-smirk and a wink that Edith thought made her look like Madonna, circa *Desperately Seeking Susan*.

'Did you even *tell* them I wrote the music? Did you just pass it off as yours?'

'No! I told Amir it was one of our old songs. For your information, it's very different to what I've been writing here. I don't normally play our old stuff – we're going in a different direction. More commercial, more EDM.'

'So does that mean I'm on the credits?' Jeannie got up and started unloading the dishwasher. She needed to keep connected to normality because this conversation had already tipped into surreal.

'Sooooooo, about that, yeah,' cooed Edith, shooting off at a convenient tangent, 'the reason I'm phoning is I've got amazing news! I've been talking to people here, and telling them about you, and your songs. If you can demo a couple, Amir will listen to them, and if there's something we can use, then you can come down here and work with us!'

She paused, expecting Jeannie to react with delight and gratitude. 'In the writing room! With everyone!'

'Uh huh.' Jeannie refused to give Edith the reaction she wanted: not entirely on purpose – she still couldn't think of anything cutting enough. Very occasionally her inability to find the right words came good. Like a stopped clock twice a day.

'Well?'

Jeannie leaned against the Aga and closed her eyes. She didn't want to admit she hadn't written anything else since Edith had left. She'd only played with the ukulele orchestra – which had been a lot more fun than playing with Edith, of late. She definitely hadn't had any lyrical inspiration. Not even rage-filled revenge songs.

'Jeannie? Are you still there?'

'Yes.'

'Look, I shouldn't even be telling you this, but Amir's talking to another producer who's pencilled in on a project we're not supposed to know about. It's going to be *massive*. It's someone famous, who you wouldn't expect to be any good but they are, and she wants . . . I mean, *they* want an authentic singer-songwriter sound.'

'Our old sound, you mean.'

'Yes, our old sound. You're not being very enthusiastic.' The pretty lower lip would be jutting, twinkling the silver hoop. 'I went out on a limb for you here, Jeannie.'

'Because you ripped me off.'

'Well, I'm trying to make it up to you now, all right?' Another pause, then a crack of vulnerability. 'I miss you. I want my writing buddy back.'

Jeannie still couldn't find the words, but her silence seemed to be pushing Edith's buttons, without even trying.

'It's a great song, Jeannie, "I Didn't Know". You know I loved it. We can still do our own version. Without the rap. Unless you want to do one? MC Jeannie M? On the mike? I wish you'd seen my face when Melting Jay came in to do that. I had to hide. His real name's Tom.'

Despite everything, Jeannie could feel herself being pulled back into Edith's magnetic force field, and somehow Edith detected her weakening resistance.

'It's such a cool team to work with, you'd love it here,' she chattered on. 'We hang out in the studio and just riff and bounce ideas off each other. Josh, one of the session guys, is teaching me the bass! And I'm sharing a house in Highbury with two of the other girls, and there's a spare room so if you wanted to move down for a bit, you could . . .'

She stopped, evidently remembering why Jeannie might not be able to do that.

Jeannie said nothing, on purpose, and was gratified by the embarrassed silence that ensued, albeit only for a few seconds.

'How are things with Supervet?' Edith wasn't being complimentary; she'd probably forgotten Dan's name. 'Did you have a nice wedding?'

'I'm not married. There was an accident,' said Jeannie flatly. It gave her an unworthy kick to be pulling the rug from under Edith's feet for once. 'Dan's been in a coma since our wedding day. We're waiting to find out if he's been permanently injured.'

'*What?*' The shock was genuine. 'God, Jeannie. A *coma*? I'm so sorry to hear that. Are you OK? What *happened*?'

The abrupt reversion to Edith's normal voice only made Jeannie more aware of how much of an act she'd been putting on before. It made her soften a little towards the crazy selfish bitch.

'He walked into a bus. Didn't see it coming. It's a bit . . . surreal,' she admitted. 'I'm spending a lot of time in the hospital. I know everything about neural pathways. And catheters, and Glasgow Coma Scales.'

'Oh my God . . . Have you written anything about it?'

Owen's outraged face floated in front of Jeannie's eyes, and the sympathy door slammed shut. No query about Dan's future, or about her feelings. 'Funnily enough, I'm too busy researching rehab units.'

'No need to bite my head off. But wow, you must have gone through so much. Dig into your heart. No shame – Dan would love it if you wrote something about him. Take that as your starting point for this demo, yeah?'

In Jeannie's head, imaginary Owen walked off, muttering darkly.

She pulled her shoulders back. 'I'll think about it. But I'm not writing about Dan.'

'Fair enough. You've got a fortnight – no, three weeks, I'm going away end of next – to send me something to change your whole life.'

And Edith hung up before Jeannie could answer, neatly getting the last word. Typical.

Jeannie had barely had time to process Edith's call when there was a knock at the back door. It opened, and Rachel popped her head round.

'Hey!' She nodded up towards the kennels. 'It's tennis ball o'clock up there and we need you and that incredible throwing arm.'

'Maybe not this morning . . .' The excruciating scene in the charity shop was still causing Jeannie to make involuntary 'ngggh' noises whenever she thought about it. Which was at least twice an hour.

'Now if this is about yesterday, you need to understand that that was by no means the most embarrassing conversation I've had,' Rachel looked at her frankly. 'I've had exchanges that make me want to claw my tongue out. Like when I moaned to my best friend that I was pregnant with Fergus without realising she was going through hell with fertility problems?' She pulled an 'I want to die' face. 'Or the time my ex and George had a fight in the office – and, yes, that's a whole other hideous embarrassment – during which I referred to George as "my vet" instead of "my boyfriend" in front of him?'

Jeannie shook her head. Both those sounded *fairly*

301

cringeworthy, but not on a par with jilting a man now in a coma.

'All I mean is . . . I'm not judging you. I know sometimes life forces you to behave in ways that make you feel like a stranger to yourself.' Rachel reached out and rubbed Jeannie's arm. 'You don't owe *us* any explanations.'

Jeannie managed a weak smile. 'Nat's judging me.'

'It's personal for Nat. Beth was devastated. But give her time. Nat's forgiven me some pretty shoddy behaviour over the years, and you're a much nicer person than I am. So, have you got time to play with some dogs before you head to the hospital?'

It was done with a complete lack of fuss, and such breezy grace, that Jeannie felt a watery rainbow arch over her embarrassment.

'Yes,' she said. 'I have.'

The morning sky over the orchards was a perfect blue, with herringbone clouds drifting across it like a lacy shawl. Constance and Grace were trotting around after the tennis balls, daring a little chase now and again. It was almost impossible to believe they were the same terrified, matted creatures that had arrived in the back of the van, only weeks ago. Now they were tentatively exploring a new and fascinating world that held more light and air than they could ever have imagined.

Rachel didn't push for details, but as they sent dogs hurtling round the paddock after tennis balls, Jeannie found herself explaining everything she hadn't been able to express before: how she thought she'd finally found the romance she'd always longed for; Dan's proposal in the middle of the bridge; their families' excitement making her own growing doubt seem silly; the impossibility of finding the right moment to stop and talk.

Rachel listened without comment, then hurled a ball and said, 'What was it that finally made you realise you couldn't marry Dan?'

'I don't know.' If only there'd been something specific, one concrete example she could point at and say, That's why I can't marry you. *That*. 'I was in the car with Dad, and I suddenly felt if I could pop myself out of this picture everything would carry on without me – the dress, the service, the food, the party. And it would be better for everyone.'

'Do you love him?' It was the same question her dad had asked in the car, and Jeannie still didn't know how to answer it.

She cared about Dan, yes, but was that enough? She didn't feel him open up to her when they talked; in return, she sensed herself pulling a veil over her deeper feelings, in case he didn't understand or care. That wasn't right, was it?

'I care about him a lot. He's a great boyfriend.' And Dan was. He was a great boyfriend.

'What do your parents think?'

'I haven't discussed it with them.' She paused, unsure how much Sue had talked to Rachel. 'I don't know if she told you, but my mum had a serious accident when I was small. Dad looked after her, day and night – he was amazing. I didn't think about it at the time, but the older I get the more I realise how much it must have tested their marriage. Angus and I grew up during Mum's recovery and she was always honest with us about it, so if Dan *is* paralysed – I'm not scared of that. When you love someone, you look after them. But if I walk away from Dan now, when he *really* needs me just like Mum needed Dad . . . what are they going to think?'

'But they knew you were going to call it off.'

'Mum doesn't. I made Dad promise not to tell her until we knew what was happening. And I have this awful feeling that . . .' She made herself say it. 'That Dan was listening to my message when he stepped in front of the bus. So it's my fault.'

Jeannie gripped the ball thrower. The plastic cut into her palm, hard and sharp like the unavoidable truth.

Rachel offered her a ball to throw for Lady Sadie. Sadie hadn't found the new confidence her two sisters had. She shrank from male voices, and hadn't properly grasped the concept of play; she preferred to hang low by Rachel and Jeannie's feet, watching Grace and Constance leap and catch.

'It was an accident, Jeannie,' said Rachel, reasonably, as Jeannie hurled the ball hard. 'You didn't push Dan into the road; he wasn't looking.'

'I'll never know that for sure.'

'It was an *accident*.'

Rachel offered another ball to Gem, who was lying a few feet away. He hadn't even tried to join in, which was unusual. He was the one who'd taught them how to play, patiently dropping and fetching balls till they got the message. 'Want a go, Gem? Or are you keeping your girl company?'

'He's watching out for Sadie,' observed Jeannie.

'That's my Gem. Watching out for all of us.' Rachel flung the ball across the field, and something about the spontaneous delight in the dogs' barks as they chased

after it opened a crack in Jeannie's aching heart, enough
to let Rachel's quiet words slip inside.

The radio was on in the kennel runs and they could hear
Mel hard at work, sweeping and singing loudly. 'I Didn't
Know', obviously.

She was launching into MC Tom's horrible rap, word
perfect including the fake Jamaican accent, when Rachel
tactfully closed the office door to muffle the sound.

'It's so catchy – even Fergus was singing it in the car,
and he *hates* pop music.' She frowned at herself. 'Sorry.
Has Edith deigned to call you yet?'

'I've called her.' It felt good to say that. Jeannie thought
it made her sound proactive. 'She's offered me the chance
of a lifetime – if I write her two new songs, she'll play
them to the producer she's working with. If he likes
them, I'm in.'

'Big of her! And do you want to be *in*?' Rachel looked
dubious but intrigued.

'Well . . . yes. It's what I've always wanted to do, make
a living from music.'

It had occurred to Jeannie in the middle of another
restless night that if she left Dan, she'd have to move out
of Rachel's cottage. And to rent somewhere else, she'd
need a job. The understanding had been that Jeannie
could pick up some part-time shifts on the surgery reception around any teaching work she arranged, if she
wanted but would that still be on offer if she left Dan?
Probably not.

In which case, what was keeping her in Longhampton?
It was a small place. If she abandoned Dan in his hour of
need, local outrage at her selfishness would make it an

uncomfortable place to live. Jeannie shivered inwardly, imagining everyone's face like Natalie's. And having to walk past reminders of Dan's accident every day . . .

'Can we talk about something else?' she asked.

'Sure!' said Rachel. 'Can you help me sort out these bridesmaids' dresses? We've had five dropped off this morning by someone whose friends really don't like her much, if you ask me.'

Donations were filling the clothes rail in the back room: not only wedding dresses but every kind of wedding paraphernalia, including three ring cushions and a candy cart. They were packing dresses to take up to the new 'bridal display area' in the shop when George appeared. He filled the doorway with fresh air and an aroma of cows.

'Sorry to interrupt.' He waved something at Jeannie. 'This came for Dan. Postcard. Been meaning to pass it on to you for a while but I never seem to catch you.'

'Or you could give it to me,' said Rachel. She held out a hand for it. 'Your secretary.'

George gave her a look. 'I could. But I don't want to open myself up to accusations of treating you like a secretary, so I've just left it in my bag and carried it round the hundreds of appointments I've been on this week to keep our family business afloat in this catastrophic economic climate.'

'Thanks, I'll take it in this afternoon,' Jeannie interrupted before they could escalate the bicker into a full-on squabble.

George passed her the postcard, and she turned it over to see the picture on the front. It was a lion and a lioness, reclining in the sun.

It was addressed to Dan at the surgery, and the message read: 'The sun's hot, the future's bright, I'm great – how are you?' There was no signature but the writing was distinctive: bold and black.

Jeannie looked up at George. 'Who's it from?'

'I don't know. I didn't read it.'

'How can you not read it?' Rachel looked incredulous. 'It's on the same space as the bit you read to see it was addressed to him.'

'Right. I can see what sort of mood you're in,' said George. 'I'll see you later.'

Jeannie willed Rachel to say something kinder as he left but she didn't, and the door closed with a harder slam than necessary.

'There you go,' said Rachel, as if nothing had happened. 'Start with that. Postcards are great for inspiration. "The sun's hot, the future's bright, I'm great – how are you?" Excellent first line.'

Jeannie looked at it again, and frowned. Whoever had sent it had either forgotten to sign it, or didn't think Dan needed a signature to know who they were. Yet another friend of Dan's who was a stranger to her.

She didn't get a chance to tell Dan about the postcard that afternoon: he was away from the ward for most of her visit, undergoing more scans and tests to explore the numbness in his left hand and shoulder.

There wasn't much else for Jeannie to do until Dan was wheeled back. She read his cards and his daily notebook, already the early pages felt like history, her stumbled spelling, Owen's over-detailed observations. Nurses changed linen and checked equipment, a doctor appeared, apologised and left, and eventually she tucked the card behind his water jug, and went home.

Rachel was waiting for her at the station in her Land Rover, with a takeaway coffee ready for her – a sign Jeannie had come to recognise as the precursor to a favour.

'I promise I'm not stalking you! But I was thinking after you'd gone,' she said, turning out of the car park and heading up the hill. 'What you need at the end of a long day is some company. And I have a girl here who really needs some company too.'

Jeannie paused, mid-muffin, and turned round. Lady Sadie was in the boot basket, next to the ever-present Gem. The Staffie's brown eyes darted over to every dog being walked or car that passed, and her fine coat showed shivers of trepidation as the sights ran across her anxious doggie mind. The world outside Sadie's shed was sometimes too big.

'We've talked about this before but I think it's time we took some definite action,' Rachel went on. 'Sadie needs to get used to being in a house on her own – she's very dependent on Grace and Constance. And she'd give you a good reason to get some fresh air of an evening.'

'Have you already decided this?' Jeannie angled her head. 'Is that a bowl and a dog bed I see in there? Rachel?'

Rachel's eyes remained firmly on the road ahead. 'I've seen how Sadie trusts you, and how you trust her. I think you're meant to be together. How about it? Trial period first, of course. No pressure. You can drop her off on your way into the hospital, and pick her up in the evenings on your way back.'

It was like Owen and Pete the cockapoo puppy: Rachel

had a way of pronouncing these things that made it feel as if the decision had been made by a higher force.

Jeannie sat back in her seat. 'Trial period,' she said. 'Till Dan's discharged.'

Rachel smiled into the rear-view mirror, and Jeannie realised she was smiling at Sadie and Gem.

She swivelled round and was disconcerted to see what looked – to her non-dog-owning eyes – Sadie the Staffie smiling back.

Chapter Twenty-three

Jeannie wasn't expecting her first song in nearly a year to be about a Staffordshire bull terrier, but then she wasn't really expecting to write a song at all. Yet somehow it slipped into her head and settled as if it had always been there.

Lady Sadie and Jeannie fell into a routine after only a few days. On their tenth evening together, they were sitting under the oak tree in the back garden after supper, enjoying the last peach-and-gold streaks of the sunset over the lilac sky. Sadie was snoozing on her blanket, and Jeannie was strumming through the songs Johnny had chosen for the ukulele band's performance at the wedding gala. They were now called Johnny History and the Uke-lear Power Station: a name chosen by the students from an eye-wateringly puntastic selection. It just fitted on to the group T-shirt Johnny was having printed for the occasion. The plan was for them to play between the parade of the dresses for sale and the Long-hampton's Weddings Through the Ages catwalk show; requests could be bought with pledges at the silent auction table, and Jeannie would play a couple of solo songs.

Jeannie's fingers framed chords while she watched her lodger dozing. Sadie snored like a walrus, and her drumstick legs twitched in her dreams, chasing imaginary rabbits that she was too timid to go after when she was awake. Compared to her broad creamy body and heart-shaped head that seemed a little too big for the rest of her, Sadie's legs were still skinny. She had a way to go yet to put the scared years in a dark shed behind her, years when she'd barely seen the sun, let alone had a field to run around in. When Jeannie rested her hand on Sadie's back, she jerked, then detected Jeannie's scent and resumed her deep breathing.

'We're friends, aren't we, Sadie?' Jeannie stroked the dog's ear, the colour of demerara sugar. 'Good friends.'

Lady Sadie rolled in her sleep, leaning her solid weight into Jeannie's leg without opening her eyes: exposing her belly in a gesture of complete trust.

What faith she's put in me, thought Jeannie, humbled. She hadn't done anything to make the neglected Staffie trust her, other than be gentle. It broke her heart how grateful Sadie was for crumbs of human affection.

'I won't let you down,' she whispered. 'You can sleep tight, Sadie.'

Sadie snored in response, twitching her delicate rabbit-chasing paws. The words found their own rhythm in Jeannie's mind, and she reached for her ukulele. And then, as her fingers moved, she reached again for her phone to capture the music rising through the clouds inside her head like the rays of setting sun.

Jeannie didn't tell Johnny History and the Uke-lear Power Station that the new song was hers when they had their rehearsal at the gala venue, the town's Edwardian Memorial Hall behind the unlovely precinct. She taught them the simple chord progression so they could join in at the end, but she didn't sing it through, just in case she chickened out on the night. Jeannie knew she should test it out in front of an audience before she sent it to Edith, but something about the song's effortlessness made her nervous. The melody seemed familiar, as if she'd heard it somewhere before, but whenever she sang it, a bubbling sensation started in the pit of her stomach: the thrill of perfect music rushing through her like a river, flowing so fast out of nowhere that Jeannie barely felt involved.

Jeannie toyed with the idea of playing her new song to Owen, but it had been a few days since she'd seen him. He'd taken some time off work to settle Pete/Pierre in, visiting Dan for an hour or two in the evenings. It was out of character for Owen not to be in touch with daily updates, and Jeannie wasn't sure what to think. Was he avoiding her? Or had he only feigned interest in visiting so he could get that package back? That made her sad. She hadn't challenged him yet about whether he'd taken it, though he must have worked out by now that she knew.

But it felt trivial to care about things like that when Dan was still paralysed down one side, and unable to recognise her; when Andrea was ricocheting between extreme relief and private tears in the relatives' room; and when a new specialist seemed to arrive in Dan's room every morning to prod and probe him. Songs, and packages, and guilt seemed a bit self-indulgent when the reality of what lay ahead for them all was becoming clearer by the day.

Every seat at every table in the Memorial Hall had been taken when the event opened on Friday night, and with a display of spotlit dresses for sale down one side of the hall, and the other side draped in shimmering white fabric, the general effect was like stepping into a luxurious marquee.

The guests brought the celebratory atmosphere with them, even before the glass of Prosecco offered at the door. Several bridal parties had re-formed for the occasion and taken tables decked out in their original outfits; others had dug out their worst bridesmaids' dresses and sat in clashing splendour. Local suppliers of flowers, cakes, bunting and other wedding essentials had offered generous support, and the Memorial Hall was bedecked with tumbling garlands of silk roses and twinkling fairy lights. It was almost impossible to imagine that only twenty-four hours earlier Longhampton Zumba Club had been stomping where the chocolate fountain now stood.

Despite the glamour, Rachel had insisted that dogs stayed at the heart of the event: each of the team of volunteers modelling the dresses selected for the fashion show would be accompanied down the catwalk aisle by a dog.

'Either their own dog, or one of ours currently looking for a home – that's the reason we're here tonight!' Rachel explained to the audience in her introduction. 'Every dress we sell will pay for our rescued puppies to start a new life with a family who will give them the love and commitment every dog deserves. For better, for worse, for richer, for fox poo-rer. And now, I'm going to hand you over to Natalie Hodge, our fashion expert for this evening. Natalie!'

Natalie had clearly been swotting up on her bridal magazine-ese, and from the reactions in the audience to her descriptions, they'd picked the right ones to show off. Her own Vera Wang, an elegant Amanda Wakeley column, a romantic fifties Phillipa Lepley: all drew sighs.

Jeannie's favourite was the bespoke brocade trouser suit and detachable skirt donated by a local horsewoman who'd ridden her hunter to the church. The package, Natalie assured the audience, included the matching brocade decorations for any other wedding horses. 'It is, if you will,' she added, with an innocent expression, 'the complete bridle package . . .'

It was followed by the star of the show: Rachel's dress. It shimmied down the catwalk on the confident frame of one Chloe McQueen, daughter of the town's bookshop owner, Anna. Chloe wasn't as tall as Rachel so she wore vertiginous high heels to show off the hemline properly; her platinum-blonde hair was backcombed into a graceful beehive where Rachel's bob had gleamed like a dark helmet. She posed at the end of the catwalk with the elderly family Dalmatian on a silver lead, tilting her head so the chic birdcage veil on the tiny hat tipped over her thick lashes. Pongo sat down with a very unsupermodelish grunt as Chloe jutted out a hip to show the tailoring, and pouted with a faraway gaze that spoke of many hours' practice in the reverse phone lens.

'Chloe is modelling a Givenchy dress with bespoke cocktail hat by royal milliner Jane Taylor. A stunning outfit for a civil ceremony or a town hall event. Or just anywhere.' Natalie's professional neutrality deserted her. 'I mean, it's just . . . wow! Look at those sleeves. And the material. You could wear this to so many events, it's enough to make me want to go on a diet, seriously . . .'

As Natalie was gushing, Jeannie watched Rachel to see

how she'd react. She'd smiled and applauded through the other dresses, but when her own dress appeared, an unmistakeable shadow crossed her face. Her dark eyes followed Chloe down the catwalk with emotion she didn't try to disguise. Was Rachel remembering her own day, Jeannie wondered, recalling how fabulous she'd felt with all eyes on her? Was she remembering the post-wedding afternoons afterwards when she'd squeezed into it in her cobwebby attic, willing herself to fit back in it? Was she regretting letting someone else take the dress – and her memories?

Then Chloe moved, and Rachel's gaze didn't, and Jeannie saw what Rachel was actually looking at. On the other side of the catwalk, towards the back behind the seats, George was standing in his work clothes, hands in pockets. He must have slipped in after the event started. Rachel wasn't looking at the dress any more; she was gazing at her silver-haired husband with a world of emotion in her face. And he was gazing back at her.

The intensity of George and Rachel's locked eyes made Jeannie shiver, even from a distance. There was so much vibrating between them: a challenge, yes, but not an aggressive one – it was as if they were seeing each other for the first time, five years on from the moment Rachel walked down the aisle in that spectacular dress, her goodbye to her old life. Were they the same people? Had life changed?

'And since no dress can possibly follow that, that's it for our first half!' Natalie announced to more applause. 'I'd like to thank our beautiful models and their companions, and if you think one of these beautiful gowns might be perfect for your big day, please grab anyone wearing a silver sash and we can arrange an appointment to view . . .'

Jeannie looked back to check where George was, but he'd gone. Where? She hunted around until she spotted him – he was in the foyer taking a phone call. From the strained expression on his face, and the quick way he shrugged his jacket back on and patted the pockets impatiently for his car keys, it was an emergency from the surgery.

She saw Rachel moving through the crowds to speak to him, but she didn't reach him before he'd marched out of the hall, his forehead furrowed and his expression very dark. Rachel's shoulders slumped, and she threw her handbag back down on to a nearby chair, switching on the networking smile to talk to an eager bride-to-be and her mum. Her smile was too bright.

Oh, George, thought Jeannie. Oh, Rachel.

But she couldn't think too long about what she could do to help, because Johnny History and the Uke-lear Power Station were waiting for her.

The five songs and two encores Jeannie played with the ukulele orchestra took her by surprise: it was more energetic, more raucous and somehow much more fun than any gig she'd ever played with Edith and Edie's Birdhouse. The crowd were cheering right from the first note – mainly because the crowd included at least fifty parents and extended family – and the sunshine sound the massed ukuleles made, jangling away together, lifted the mood in the room until Jeannie felt as if she was crowd-surfing across their goodwill. She'd taught the students more challenging harmony arrangements than anything they'd attempted before, and watching the smiles spread across the orchestra as they hit every note made her feel luminous with pride.

Jeannie didn't want to pull focus, so she sat at the side next to the beginners, while Johnny perched on a high stool at the front, introducing the songs and bantering dad-style with the crowd, all of whom seemed to know him – and, after a while, bantering with the chattier members of the Uke-lear Power Station too – until their final song.

'That's our set! I know, I know, you could listen to us all night . . .' He held up his hands modestly. '. . . but before we get back to fashion, *daaahling*, we've a special treat – a few songs from our own local singer-songwriter-superstar, Jeannie McCarthy!'

That wasn't how she'd asked him to introduce her . . . but she was on.

It was the first time Jeannie had ever stood on a stage on her own. Her heart hammered in her chest as she slipped on to the high stool Johnny had vacated, and she adjusted the microphone as the applause died down, eke-ing out the time to settle herself.

'Thank you, Johnny History.' She looked out at the rows of expectant faces. 'For those who don't know me, my name is Jeannie Music-and-some-Craft-Activities.'

The funny thing was that Jeannie never felt quite as shy on a stage as she did in real life. She was happy to let Edith take the spotlight, flirting with the front row, throwing her distinctive voice high into the atmosphere while Jeannie curled her harmonies above and below, until their voices blended into one – but music was Jeannie's featherweight, invisible armour. She felt no fear on stage, where her music spoke for her.

Tonight, she felt some nerves, but they weren't about performing – she was nervous for her song. She was proud of it, and scared for it.

Should I do it? Should I save it? Is it ready?

The faces turned towards her were friendly, some already familiar from the dog rescue. Jeannie took a leap of faith, opened her mouth and heard herself say, 'I'm going to play something new for you, as a thank you to some special people.'

She checked the tuning of her strings. *Stop playing for time.* 'It's a song about trust, and I want to dedicate it to Rachel and Natalie, two inspirational women at Four Oaks. Not only have they arranged this incredible fund-raiser tonight, they've helped a stranger in the darkest days I've ever known. I'm so grateful. Thank you.'

Rachel was standing at the back of the hall next to Natalie; as Jeannie spoke, Natalie reacted in surprise, and her face flushed with pleasure when she realised what Jeannie was saying.

Then Jeannie closed her eyes and began.

The melody was simple, and her voice lifted over the delicate picking as she found her way into the song. The words weren't great, she knew that, but they said what she felt. Edith would have sung it louder, but that wasn't how Jeannie heard the music in her head. It was a song about being scared of love, but opening your heart anyway.

> I know those nights were long and lonely;
> Wishing for love you couldn't see
> So far away, but right here with me;
> Still scared to close your eyes and dream.

As she played the chords to the bridge, Jeannie saw Sadie drowsily turning her speckled belly to the air, secure and warm for the first time in her short life, and her heart clenched.

Then she saw Owen, sitting on the chair by Dan's bed after a long day's work, his shaggy head bowed as he snatched a few minutes' sleep; she saw Andrea, never taking her eyes off the boy who'd looked after her, as though she could heal him by her fierce gaze alone. She saw women who'd donated dresses, still talking with a twinkle in their eye about the boyfriend who'd asked them out thirty years ago; she saw her mum and dad, gripping each other's hands in the hospital when they thought Jeannie couldn't see.

She'd seen so much love over the past weeks: practical, real love; love that cushioned pain and disappointment, and stretched to carry the loved one over obstacles, reaching as far as the horizon, never in doubt. Patient, long-suffering, deep, comforting, and always growing.

Jeannie cared about Dan, and their romance had been colourful, exciting, fun, but it had grown as far as it could. Without warning, tears filled her eyes.

> But when you wake up, I'll be with you,
> I'll hold you while you dream your dreams.
> We'll watch the sunrise and the sunsets,
> I'm learning now what true love means.

The circle of ukuleles softly joined in behind her – just four simple chords they'd practised at the rehearsal – and the audience drew in a whispery collective breath as some of the students, without even being told, started humming in the background. A wash of emotion swept Jeannie's whole body, and she let her exhausted heart flow out into her voice as she sang the final chorus again, reaching notes she hadn't expected to hit.

> Close your tired eyes and trust me,
> And I'll trust you with my dreams tonight.

She opened her eyes; two women in the front row had tears running down their faces.

> I'll trust you with my dreams tonight.

There was a moment's hushed silence, and then the applause started, so loud it made her jump. Rachel was clapping furiously at the back, then whistling – obviously she could deliver a deafening finger-whistle – and next to her Natalie wiped her eyes. Jeannie smiled shyly around the room, acknowledging the audience's generous response.

'Pssst! Psst!' Johnny was trying to get her attention. 'Requests?' He flapped a piece of paper.

Jeannie took it and leaned into the microphone. Her voice was wobbly. 'Thank you! Thank you so much. Um, I've got our auctioned requests . . .' She turned to the list. 'Wow! A *very* generous winning bid – Beverley Morton, you must really want to hear "I Will Always Love You".'

'It's our wedding song!' Beverley Morton shouted from the middle of the hall.

'Well, feel free to join in.' Jeannie's heart was pounding in her chest; she'd never felt so light and powerful, as if she could float to the ceiling, glittering like the angel on a Christmas tree.

*

The musical interlude provided an excellent opportunity for the handful of men in the audience to hit the bar for a restorative pint, and it also sent the models hurrying backstage to change into the second fashion show of the night: Longhampton's Weddings Through the Ages.

Lou wasn't the only bride-to-be whose mother had carefully mothballed her own wedding gown for her daughter to wear – or not wear. Wardrobes and attics all over town had yielded a fascinating selection of vintage elegance. Well, mostly elegance.

Natalie was back at the microphone, with someone's teenage son in charge of a soundtrack that began with light jazz. 'We start our wedding march of love in nineteen thirty-six, when Phyllis Taylor married Stanley Nightingale in the town hall . . .'

The audience applauded Phyllis Nightingale's drop-waisted oyster satin gown, its handkerchief hem floating around the pale ankles of her own great-granddaughter, Lily; she was followed by Jocelyn Harris's wasp-waisted wartime suit, modelled by her great-granddaughter Rosie, who'd been squeezed into the necessary roll-on corselette by three people backstage.

The fifties arrived in a home-made Liz Taylor ballgown held aloft with layers of petticoat, complete with a fleet of daffodil-yellow bridesmaids' frocks – the pride and joy of a farmer's wife with a sewing machine, four sisters and a lot of storage space. A demure bell-shaped sixties frock was followed – to a Motown soundtrack – by a teenager dancing down the catwalk in her grandma's mini-skirt, white go-go boots and huge floppy hat.

Lou was up next, modelling the dress her mother and grandmother had both been married in. The volunteer hair and make-up team had gone to town: Lou's curly bob was MTV huge, and her glossy scarlet lips were going to an entirely different party. Her appearance elicited a big *ooh* from the audience, and Natalie's explanation of the family history of her dress won an even bigger *aaaah*. Jeannie, watching from the side of the room with Rachel, saw Lou seeking out her mum in the front row as she twirled, and her heart melted at the look that passed between them: memories, and love – and a tiny proud nod from Lou's mum that spoke volumes.

Bet Lou gets to wear her beach dress now, thought Jeannie, and felt happy they'd made that happen, at least.

The parade finished with a sculptural Vivienne Westwood corseted dress worn by a lady carrying an apricot-coloured pug under each arm like a Gainsborough painting. 'Eva married only this Christmas, so we're right up to date with this eighteenth-century-inspired neckline,' Natalie announced. And with that, the evening closed.

More than a few people wanted to congratulate Jeannie on her performance, and she bashfully accepted their compliments until the crowd thinned to reveal one person, waiting his turn.

Her gaze stopped as it fell on a face she hadn't expected to see, by the door.

Owen, standing there in his straight-from-work suit. She'd had no idea he was coming tonight; she hadn't heard from him in days. The hall suddenly felt hot and too loud in Jeannie's ears: why had Owen come? Had something happened to Dan?

Oh God. It would be like divine punishment if something had happened to Dan.

'I didn't know you were coming,' said Jeannie. 'Don't tell me you left Pete watching telly at home?'

'I bribed my niece to do some Pete-sitting. Your song was . . . beautiful.' Owen fumbled for words, as if she'd turned into someone he hadn't met before. 'I don't know if that's the right way to describe it.'

'Beautiful's good.' She tried to sound nonchalant, but she wasn't, not inside. She was tingling with electricity.

'I thought you said you couldn't write lyrics?'

'I can't,' Jeannie started to say, but Owen wouldn't let her finish.

'You can. They were the best bit. So simple but so . . . moving. Do you still think you'll never write another good song?' he asked, half joking.

'You're not going to believe this but . . . !' Jeannie told him about Edith's call, and her offer of an 'in' with the producers, a chance to work with the team. As she spoke, Owen's expression registered surprise, then approval, and then . . . was that a shadow of doubt?

'I'm going to send that song to Edith. To let the producer listen to it, see what he thinks,' she concluded.

Owen chewed his lip. 'Are you sure Edith—? No. Sorry.'

'What?'

'Don't take this the wrong way.' He held up his broad hands. 'I'm only looking out for you the way Dan would, if he was here.'

Would he, though? Jeannie had a sneaking suspicion that Dan didn't actually think her music career was particularly serious, not compared with what he did for a living. He'd been the one to suggest doing a teaching qualification so she could get a 'proper' job at Longhampton School. He'd tried to gloss over the word 'proper' as soon as he'd said it, but Jeannie had caught it, and he knew that. They hadn't discussed it again.

She crossed her arms and looked up at him. 'Well?'

'Are you absolutely sure Edith's not going to try to pass off anything you send her as her own?' Owen sounded reluctant but unable to stop himself. 'Sounds like the only song of hers they've used so far is the one you wrote together.'

'No! Edith wouldn't do that. She genuinely sounded like she was trying to make it up to me.'

'Well, you know her.' His face said otherwise. 'But it's such a beautiful song. The way you sing it . . .' Owen shook his head. 'The hairs on the back of my arms stood up. Don't waste it on someone who won't appreciate it, Jeannie. And I don't just mean by putting a horrible rap in the middle and letting a bunch of autotuned *Love Island* extras quack all over it.'

'I won't.'

She looked into his eyes. Something about Owen was different, away from the hospital, here in her Longhampton world. Now Jeannie was lost for words; she wanted to tell him how much his advice might have changed her life, but suddenly didn't know how to.

'I felt proud of you tonight,' he blurted out. 'I knew you could play – I mean, I've heard you, obviously – but you had the whole room in the palm of your hand. Magic. There's no other word for it.'

'Thank you. Thank you for coming.'

Neither of them knew what to say next. They stood, staring at each other, wanting to smile more than they were allowing themselves to, when Jeannie felt a hand on her arm. It was George.

'Have you seen Rachel?' He didn't stop searching the

room for her, peering over the heads of the brides and the models and the parents as he spoke.

Jeannie wondered why he'd come back. 'Last I saw her she was talking to Howard from the paper about the fund-raising target.'

George wiped his hand over his face. 'I need to talk to her.'

'Why?'

'Fergus called me about an hour ago in a real state – that's why I had to leave.'

'What's happened?' Jeannie's stomach tensed.

'Gem's not very well.' George's eyes slid sideways to Owen, and Jeannie saw an understanding spread over Owen's face that made her cold inside.

'I'll find her,' she said.

Chapter Twenty-four

Gem had come in from his nightly patrol around the garden, staggered in a circle, and then collapsed at Fergus's feet. When neither Fergus nor the babysitter could rouse him, Fergus phoned George while Becca drove the limp dog to the surgery where Gem was put on a drip and tested for everything under the sun. The simple truth was, though, Gem was nearly eighteen. Almost a hundred, in human years.

'We always knew this day would come,' George told Jeannie when she called for an update. Then he paused, and corrected himself. 'No, actually that's bollocks. I'm fairly sure Rachel thought Gem would live for ever.'

'How is she?' Jeannie had asked pointlessly.

George sighed. Even though she'd only known Rachel and her devoted shadow for a matter of weeks, Jeannie had felt the bond between them, a wordless love born out of mutual care and some long shared nights. George's broken sigh was the only real way to express what Rachel was feeling.

Gem rallied enough by the next afternoon to be brought home to the kennel office, where he lay on Rachel's best human blankets. He had a stretchy bandage round his front leg where the drips had been and was watching the activity going on around him with his eerie white-blue eyes, but his head was barely raised off the edge of the bed, and he managed only a feeble wag of the tail when Jeannie came in.

Gem looked significantly more chipper than Rachel, who sat slumped by him on the floor, while the puppies in the playpens were more subdued than usual. Most of the puppies had been leaving for their new homes over the previous week, and now there were only two left: Dolly the collie and Marilyn the Staffie. Lady Sadie waddled in behind Jeannie, ignored her yapping daughter, and went straight over to Gem, flopping down next to his basket with her broad head on her paws. They breathed heavily, in unison.

Jeannie sat down by Rachel, and put an arm round her shoulders. 'I'm so sorry, Rachel.'

'Thanks.' Rachel laid her hand on Gem's head. 'He's mortified about this fuss, I can tell. Not your style, is it, old man? Being the centre of attention. If he could speak, he'd be telling me to get on with packing up the dresses.' She smiled; it was an effort. 'Can you guess how much money we made last night?'

'No, surprise me.'

'Nearly four thousand pounds, just in ticket sales, bar, raffle and the auction. That's our target in one go.'

'Wow!'

'The ukulele orchestra was a masterstroke – those parents and family turning up in support, as well as the brides, tipped the balance. They drank a *lot*. Everyone said the music gave the night something magical. I wouldn't be surprised if Johnny's orchestra gets some wedding bookings off the back of it.'

A glow spread through Jeannie; she'd made a tangible difference. To the dogs, to the rescue centre, to Liam in the back row who now sang the correct words to everything – and in tune too.

'And your song! Oh!' Rachel clapped a hand to her chest. 'I had goosebumps. Everyone did. Don't forget us when you're on your world tour, will you?'

Jeannie made a non-committal noise. 'You'll get the pick of the merch.'

'Thank you. I'll hold you to that.' Rachel heaved herself up off the floor. 'We've got a lot to do this morning. Please keep me as busy as you can, or else I'm liable to go to pieces and Gem would *not* approve.'

Natalie had left a list of contact details for Rachel and Jeannie to work through: brides who'd expressed an interest in trying on the gowns from the catwalk show, or bringing bridesmaids in to look at the other dresses. The plan was to offer a proper bridal-shop service in a pop-up location in town: two of the volunteers were there, transforming an empty shoe shop into a luxurious boudoir of a boutique, recycling the flowers, drapes and bunting donated to the gala night.

'Nat says if we can negotiate the lease for a reasonable amount, the pop-up could be a fresh revenue stream.' Rachel looked up from the computer. 'Fancy a job running a wedding shop?'

Jeannie assumed Rachel was joking, and answered with her eyebrows.

'No, genuine question,' she insisted. 'There isn't a bridal shop in Longhampton. And we could do with a year-round source of income, especially if George is going to cut his annual donation, as has been threatened. You could do it in lieu of rent for the cottage, if you want?'

Jeannie ignored the mention of the cottage for the time being. 'George won't cut you off.' She paused. 'Will he?'

Rachel's gaze drifted over to Gem, who was sleeping again. 'We can't talk about it without fighting. I think he might, on principle. George has been planning his early retirement for as long as I've known him, and now it's within touching distance. Me needing more money for this place isn't going down well. And neither is me taking on more work to make up the difference.'

'But he knows it's important to you.'

Rachel didn't answer at once. She ran a hand through her hair, ruffling the silver strands. 'I don't even know if it's about the money any more. I think we're at a bit of a crossroads in general.'

'So talk about it.'

'Some conversations are too important to start off wrong. So you don't start them at all.'

'You don't need to tell me that,' said Jeannie, and Rachel smiled sadly.

Rachel wanted to stay close to Gem in the office, and so Jeannie volunteered to take the dogs out for the mid-morning paddock sessions. She hurled balls and frisbees and rehearsed the confident things she fully intended to say to Edith about her song, but without Edith there to talk over her and throw her off balance with unpredictable responses, it felt a bit too easy.

When Jeannie came back in an hour later, arms

aching and ready for a cup of tea, she leaned round the office door to ask Rachel if she fancied a brew too, but the sight that greeted her stopped the words in her mouth.

Rachel was hunched over the desk, weeping and writing at the same time.

Jeannie's gaze swept automatically to the basket, but Gem's milky eyes were wide open, watching his mistress.

'Rachel? What's up? Is it Gem?'

Rachel's head jerked up. Even without the smudged mascara and wild hair, her expression was pure heartbreak. 'Oh! Jeannie.' She rubbed her face. 'Sorry, I'm being ridiculous . . .'

'What's happened?'

'Someone's bought my dress.' She took a shuddering sniff. 'A man phoned up while you were out, and he's just paid for it. Full amount. His fiancée saw it on our website this week and fell in love, so he's bought it for her as a surprise.'

'Oh.' Jeannie didn't know what to say – neither 'That's great!' nor 'That's terrible!' were right.

'He's even bought the hat.' She looked down at the credit card receipt in front of her. 'It's a lot of money. I mean, *wonderful* news. Thank you, Adam Marsden. You generous man. You've paid for Grace's liver scan and all the puppies' inoculations, with enough left to pay some of George's IOUs.'

'No, Rachel, *you* have.' Jeannie hesitated. Poor Rachel: she had enough to deal with, with Gem. The timing was unfair. If only she'd been in to take the call instead. 'Look, if you're having second thoughts about selling it, then don't!'

'No!' She forced a watery smile. 'I said I'd sell it, and George saw me sell it, and . . . I've sold it. I'm just more upset than I thought I'd be now it's happened. Stupid, I know.'

Jeannie remembered George's face at the catwalk show. He'd seemed crushed to her: crushed and angry – and a bit disappointed.

'I'm writing a note to send with it.' She brandished her pen. 'I just want the lucky Tilly to know she's not simply getting a dress. She's getting a dress full of glamour and style and everything else I felt in my heart when I walked down the aisle wearing it. It's a work of art, and it made awkward, flawed me into a work of art too, just for a day. I hope she'll feel the same.' Rachel paused, and rolled her eyes at herself. 'I know, I'm writing a goodbye note to my dress. I've lost my mind.'

Jeannie couldn't imagine what would be in that letter, but she knew there was absolutely no chance of the future Mrs Adam Marsden not hearing Rachel's heart when it fell out of the tissue-wrapped cocoon of love she'd pack for her wedding dress.

The new week brought a fresh crop of specialists and nurses, all focused on moving Dan out of the hospital and back into the outside world. Since his breathing tube and other feeding tubes had been removed, the team calling into his room throughout the day had mutated again to the point where Jeannie was glad she could covertly refer to his now dog-eared notebook to remember who was who.

The newest addition to Dan's care team was Rhys the neurophysiotherapist. Jeannie never had any trouble remembering Rhys: he was six foot five and used to working with rugby players and boxers who'd hit their heads once too often, as well as stroke patients. He had hands like shovels, a rugby-flattened nose and a touch like a butterfly landing on silk.

Although Dan was recovering strongly in some areas, he still had what Rhys described as 'extensive hemiparesis' down his left side.

'It's the same as if he'd had a stroke,' he told them with the same matter-of-fact approach he applied to Dan's daily stretching and pulling and gripping exercises. Jeannie had only seen one of these sessions; Andrea found the floppy uselessness of Dan's previously strong arm so upsetting she couldn't even watch Rhys at work, let alone help in the way she'd eagerly assisted with his bed baths and his shaves.

'His brain's not sending messages to the left side of his body yet, so we need to encourage it to reset itself,' Rhys explained. 'You've heard the doctors talking about plasticity, right? Dan's got tons of brain cells – we just need to get them reorganising.'

'But will it come back? The motor control?' Jeannie cast a nervous look over her shoulder; the three of them were talking outside Dan's room and his eyes were closed, but Jeannie was never quite sure whether Dan was really asleep or whether he was just faking it to make Andrea stop bombarding him with 'helpful' memory-jogging facts.

'We'll do everything we can,' Rhys reassured her. 'There'll be a team in rehab to focus on every aspect of the recovery process, but the main thing is Dan. He needs to be patient and work with us.'

Andrea's face had drained of colour at the first

mention of the word *hemiparesis* and hadn't recovered. 'Rhys, please be honest. Danny's a vet, a *surgeon*. It's what he's wanted to do since he was a boy. Are you saying he might not . . .' She blanched but forced the words out, screwing up her face as if they tasted bitter in the mouth. 'He might not recover enough control to operate again?'

Jeannie thought unhappily of what Owen had told her about Dan's career dreams when he graduated. She'd known before that he was ambitious, but she hadn't really understood how much work had driven his life until Owen explained.

I wasn't listening, she thought. Or did Dan not tell me?

She tried to imagine how she'd feel if she lost control of her left arm, her fingertips. What if the lightness of touch never came back? What if she could hear music inside her and had no way of getting it out? It made her body ripple with panic and frustration.

'I'm only the physio; I can't predict what's going to happen with Dan's brain. And let's not think in those terms just yet.' Rhys had put a hand on Andrea's arm. It looked huge, a friendly giant's hand. 'Let's focus on getting him up and walking, eh? These are questions you can raise with Mr Allcott at the meeting.'

The Meeting on Friday. Jeannie and Andrea exchanged a look. They'd known about Dan's discharge meeting for under an hour and already it had taken on ominous capital letters.

Mr Allcott had called a multi-disciplinary meeting of the various health professionals overseeing Dan's care: himself, Rhys, an occupational therapist, a psychologist, a dietician and various nurses. Even though Jeannie couldn't believe Dan was anywhere near ready to come home, going by the number of sensors connecting him to the monitors, his discharge seemed to be a reality. Referrals to the rehab unit were being processed, and the OT had left Jeannie a message to arrange a convenient time for a home visit, to assess any adjustments necessary for Dan to return.

Jeannie had stared at the message and hadn't known what she was supposed to say. Andrea had – she'd been *thrilled*.

'Oh, wonderful! Maybe I should come over too? See what we're going to need in the way of spare beds and whatnot, for when I'm staying over.' When Jeannie had protested weakly that she needn't worry, Andrea had batted away her words with an affectionate swat: 'Don't be silly – it'd be my pleasure. It'd give you some time off to carry on helping out with your friends up the road, wouldn't it? The dogs?'

Jeannie had nodded. There hadn't been much else she could do. After all, technically it was Dan's house, not hers. Everything that had seemed so comforting and stable just days ago was suddenly shifting under her feet.

'Just think!' Rhys went on with a cheerful wink. 'Danny boy could be out of here by next week! Pretty incredible when you think about it, eh?'

'My Danny boy's always been incredible,' Andrea agreed. She linked arms with Jeannie. 'And so is my Jeannie.'

'It's down to you now,' said Rhys. 'And he's in great hands with you two, I can tell.'

As soon as they went back into Dan's room, Andrea was straight on to a topic Jeannie thought might finally have been parked for a while.

'Now, who do you think I had a call from this morning?' She glanced between Dan in the bed and Jeannie on the other side.

'The Pope?' asked Dan wearily. He'd regained some of his old good humour, albeit slightly darker than it had been. 'Does he do phone consultations now?'

'No, darling! Your wedding photographer, Charlotte. She called me to see how you were getting on. She was very pleased to hear what a good recovery you're making, and she made me a *very* kind offer.' Andrea raised an eyebrow, encouraging them to guess what that might be.

Jeannie smiled but had to bite the inside of her cheek to stop herself shouting, 'Not now!'

'She does hospital photo shoots?' asked Dan. 'Bit grim, Mum.'

'Danny! No! She offered to let the deposit stand if you want to book a new date for the wedding.' Andrea looked at Jeannie. 'You know how popular Charlotte is, so I said we'd get back to her with a new date as soon as.'

Jeannie was struggling to formulate an appropriate response when Dan did it for her.

'Tell her no,' he said.

'What?' Andrea had started to fish in her bag for her diary. Her head snapped up.

Dan's voice was brusque and tired. 'Mum, I appreciate you want to think about happier things than my rehab, but don't you think talking about wedding photographers is a bit inappropriate?'

'But, darling . . . let's just pick a date and then forget it.'

'Mum! For God's sake! Do you honestly think that's

what I'm thinking about right now? Wedding photographers?'

Andrea appealed to Jeannie for back-up, but Jeannie seized the chance to stop the madness.

'There's no rush,' she agreed. 'Let's put our energy into finding Dan the best rehab facilities, getting him back on the road to recovery.' She knew she was using the worst cheery clichés, but Andrea's face had crumpled in crestfallen surprise.

Jeannie glanced over at Dan, and the exasperated but loving way he was gazing at his mother reminded her poignantly of their first dinner; how relieved he'd seemed when she and Andrea had laughed and got on so well.

'She's going to love being a mum-in-law,' he'd confided happily on the drive home, and Jeannie had felt a bit sad that such a standard family night out had been a special occasion for the two Hickses.

'Well. I'm sorry if I've overstepped the mark.' Andrea struggled to compose her face and stood up. 'I'm going to get a cup of tea.'

'Andrea, no . . .' Jeannie started, but she waved away her concern and clicked out of the room.

She and Dan sat in silence for a moment or two.

'Oh dear,' said Jeannie at the same time as Dan said, 'Do you think I went a bit far?'

'The doctors did say you might be ruder than normal.'

'Bit of a free pass, eh?'

They managed a rueful smile. She wondered if Dan was getting any flashes of memory; if that exchange had reminded him of *her*, jiggling a connection loose, deep down.

'So why is my mother so desperate to get us married off? Something I should know?'

He said it lightly, but there was a focus in Dan's blue eyes that Jeannie hadn't seen since he came round: he looked more determined to find his way back to the woman sitting by his bedside.

'Not if you can't remember me,' she said. 'Still nothing?'

He shook his head. 'Some . . . feelings, rather than facts? Like dreams you try to remember, then they slide away before you can . . .' He mimed jabbing them down.

'Have you worked out what your last memory was?' If Dan couldn't remember her at all, he'd lost a whole year.

Dan shook his head. 'I remember going to an international with Owen – that's maybe the last big thing? I'm sorry. Our meeting should be seared on to my brain for ever. It's not very romantic of me.'

'But what about your short-term memory? Are things sticking in your head overnight?' Jeannie paused. 'Hey. This is the first morning you've remembered me.'

'Oh yeah. So it is.' Dan smiled, pleased. 'It's getting harder to separate what I'm remembering from what I've read in that notebook you've been filling in, and what the nurses say, what Owen says. I know from that that you've been kind, and you've spent a lot of time here. I know you're a singer, that you've been playing songs to me. The nurses tell me every day that you're a total sweetheart.' The aggression had gone, as if it had never been there. Dan's brain was resetting, she thought, constantly shifting, renewing, repairing. Inching forward towards the day of the wedding.

'Can you remember taking the job in Longhampton?' she asked. 'The vet's?'

Dan frowned. 'I know I *am* a vet. Ask me about Cushing's disease, hip dyplasia, I'm fine on that. It's just . . .' His expression was apologetic. 'I'm sorry. I'm really sorry. This must be terrible for you. Feeling you've been forgotten.'

'It's hard for everyone,' said Jeannie.

'I've been reading the daily notes . . .' He shook his head with disbelief. 'That all happened?'

'That all happened. It's been quite a few weeks.' She paused, her voice catching. 'We're so glad you're back, Dan.'

'Me too. Thanks for helping me get here.'

'It's been a team effort. Me, Owen, your mum, your friends and family . . . You remember the messages we played? The cards we read out?'

'Should I say yes?'

They sat looking at each other, and Jeannie felt an honest connection between them. It was almost a conversation they could have had before the accident. It felt strangely like the conversations they'd had when they first met, she thought with a pang of nostalgia.

Mention of the vet's pushed a thought into her head. 'That postcard I left the other day – who was it from?'

'Which postcard?'

'The one with the lions. Has it fallen down the side of the table?' Jeannie got up and moved the bedside table, but there was nothing behind it: Dan's room was spotlessly clean. 'It came to the surgery – George gave it to me to give to you. No signature. Two lions on the front, something about having a great time.'

'Nope, don't remember seeing that.' He pulled a face. 'Although, would I have remembered forgetting? Hard to say.'

'I wonder where it's gone.' Jeannie moved the bedside table back and realised she was very close to Dan now. If she'd wanted to, she could have leaned down and kissed him. If he'd wanted to, he could have touched her leg.

She paused, and maybe the thought crossed Dan's mind too. He moved his hand, and drew in a breath as if he was going to say something, to touch her, and instinctively Jeannie pulled away, bumping against the table as she did.

The cards fell over and the water spilled, drawing attention to her sudden movement, and their eyes met. Dan's expression was questioning but vulnerable, as if he was trying to look inside her heart for clues, and Jeannie felt an unexpected tenderness towards him.

Is it too late? Jeannie wondered. Is it too late to fall back in love with him?

'Oh! Am I interrupting?' Nurse Lauren had returned to run a set of tests. She smiled at the pair of them, and Jeannie realised she probably thought they'd been kissing.

She blushed and asked, quickly, 'That postcard, with the lions? Have you seen it?'

'No, I don't think I have. I'll ask the cleaners if they've seen it.' Lauren clicked on her tiny torch for the pupil test. 'But I hear you've got your multi-disciplinary meeting on Friday, Dan? Yay! Your escape from us is in sight!'

Friday, thought Jeannie, as Dan settled back into the pillows and submitted to Lauren's torch. That's how long I've got to work out what I'm going to do next.

Chapter Twenty-five

The postman must have been in a rush on Wednesday morning because half of the Fenwicks' post was bundled up with Jeannie and Dan's meagre selection of fliers and copies of *Vet Times*.

Jeannie didn't mind taking it up. She was glad of a reason to call in at the big house: no news had arrived overnight about Gem's condition, which she hoped was a good sign, but she knew herself that when news was bad, texting other people wasn't exactly a priority.

As it was, the house seemed quiet when she wandered up the gravel path – no music, no familiar smell of toast, no voices chattering, no barking – and as she went to knock on the front door, it swung open.

'Hello?' she called into the hallway. The wellies were in their usual places, the leads and coats dangling from the hooks by the door. The house was holding its breath, the invisible residents gathering sadly in the dark corners.

To her surprise, it was George's voice that answered. 'We're in the kitchen.'

We. Jeannie's heart sank, picturing the whole family gathered around Gem's bed. She hesitated, not wanting to intrude, but she was here now, so she steeled herself and headed down the hall.

George was sitting on the floor by the Aga, next to the

dog basket. Inside, under a blanket, Gem lay in a soft white loop, his long nose laid down along his paws, his eyes a barely visible grey flick on his silver muzzle.

Jeannie's heart caught in her throat. The change in Gem since the previous day was visible. He'd faded. She'd never seen Gem so motionless; even when he was standing by Rachel's side, his inner energy flickered around him like static electricity. Now he seemed so still and slight.

George looked up and gave her a quick smile, a pretend 'you caught me being soppy' grimace. He was in his work clothes, but had rolled up his shirtsleeves and kicked off his boots, revealing a thick pair of red socks with a hole on one heel. His hand rested along the edge of the basket, his weather-beaten fingers on Gem's head tenderly connecting the dog with his human as he drifted further and further away.

'Sorry, we got some of your post by mistake.' Jeannie waved the letters. She wasn't sure whether to sit down with George; it was such an intimate scene. 'Didn't expect to find you here.'

'I've taken the morning off work. Called in some favours with a friend to cover for me.' He made a dismissive gesture. 'Some things are more important.'

'How's Gem?'

'He's sleeping. Not in any pain.' George scratched his silvery stubble with his free hand. 'Not long now. I'd take him into the surgery but, to be honest, there's no point putting him through the stress – I've got everything I need in my bag to let him go peacefully if need be.'

Oh, Gem, thought Jeannie, gripped with a sudden, clenching sorrow. 'Where's Rachel?'

'Fergus had a dental appointment in town. They left about nine – I literally had to kick Rachel out of the house, but she was going stir crazy and Fergus needs to be bribed into that place at the best of times. I promised I wouldn't let Gem go anywhere till she got back.'

'I don't think he'd go anywhere without her.'

'I know. He's waiting for her. He's always waited for her, more patiently than me sometimes.' George ran a light hand over Gem's narrow head. The gesture was so different from the hearty pats and firm flank-slaps he administered to the bigger dogs, so gentle and respectful, that Jeannie had to blink away tears. Don't cry, she told herself. Don't cry.

'Come on, join us.' George patted the floor tiles next to the basket. 'Gem'll know you're here.'

Jeannie sat down on the other side of the basket. There was something comforting about the stone flags under her bare feet, and the heat of the stove, and the gentle doggy smell of the sleeping collie between them. Jeannie didn't know when, much less *how*, but the smell of dogs, their soft fur and nubbly pawpads and warm bodies, had become a real comfort – so different from the clinical, clean smell of the hospital that set her blood pressure rising from her first step through the revolving doors.

'This has always been your spot, hasn't it, Gem? By the Aga.' George stroked Gem's ear with a thick finger. 'From the moment Dot carried you in her jacket pocket into this kitchen to give you a second chance at life. And in return, you gave your little life to her. And then when you lost Dot, you gave it to Rachel. Now you're back here, in front of your Aga. Ready to be with Dot again.'

Tears filled Jeannie's eyes. That didn't take long, she thought.

'You know, I'm biased, but I've often wished human relationships could be as simple as the ones we have with our dogs,' George went on. 'No words to get in the way of what we mean. Human stupidity is the cause of most heartbreak in this world. What a mess we make of our relationships, compared with how we manage to communicate with *them*. What a bloody mess.'

Jeannie didn't know what to say. She knew he was talking about Rachel; she sensed that sitting with Gem, facing the end with him, was opening George's sore heart and letting more out than he'd normally allow.

'He's one of the family,' she said.

'Gem's been here longer than either of us.' George looked down at the dog's narrow ribcage, rising and falling unevenly. 'Rachel will tell you that Gem brought us together – I used to tell her she was bonkers for thinking that, but I'm not sure now. He herds us like sheep, in his own way.'

'Rachel says he told her to make me foster Lady Sadie,' she said. 'And it was the right choice.'

'So I hear. It's doing that dog a power of good, being in a home.'

'And me. It's nice to have someone to walk with, and think about, and talk to.' Jeannie hadn't let herself think about what would happen to her and Sadie after Friday: would there be room for Sadie in their house once Dan was back? Would it be fair? A chilly pebble fell in her stomach at the thought of someone else adopting her sweet-faced girl, basking in Sadie's big-hearted devotion. Don't be selfish, she thought.

'They're good for the soul, dogs,' said George. 'I'm not just saying that because it's my job, either. Dogs keep you straight.'

'In what way?'

'They make you face up to yourself. You need to commit – to feeding them, walking them, teaching them how to fit into your world. If you don't do those things . . . it shows. In the dog, I mean. Your dog's basically a walking reflection of how much you can be bothered to be a decent person. You've got to do your best.'

'It makes me realise how much I enjoy simple things when I do them with her,' said Jeannie. 'I've only had Sadie a couple of weeks but walks are way better with a dog. I notice the sunsets more. The bees. The light. Even just sitting on the sofa's better with her on my knee.'

'Well, that's love, in my book. Even in bad times, you're better together. It's how I felt the moment I met Rachel. I knew that things would still go wrong, and life would carry on being the same unpredictable conveyor belt of great stuff and total cock-ups, but it would just be *better* if I had this particular woman by my side.'

Jeannie laid her hand on Gem's back, feeling the sharp knobs of his spine. She didn't expect to hear something so romantic coming from pragmatic George. It was – word for word – what she'd always dreamed of, that instant 'you and me' certainty of two hearts fitting together like a key in a lock, but she'd never found it. Too many people said it was a myth, and she'd started to think they were right. No such thing as love at first sight; no such thing as soul mates. Romcom nonsense that only set you up for disillusionment. And yet here was George, a logical, serious man nearly twice her age, telling her that soppy meme about 'just knowing' was real.

'You knew that from the *first* moment you met her?' she asked.

George smiled ruefully. 'Pretty much. I didn't know Rachel very well when I first realised that, so it was a bit of a shock. I thought she was self-obsessed and had her priorities completely wrong. She persisted in wearing silly black skirts to walk the dogs, purely because everyone told her she needed to get a pair of sensible trousers. And she kept saying, *I don't like dogs, I'm not a dog person, I will never do an impression of a dog's voice,* over and over, even though no one ever said she would. But there was something about her . . . a sort of bloody-minded determination to do the right thing by this crazy aunt she hardly knew, even though she'd decided she'd hate every minute of being here. It made me think . . . Good for you, you daft cow. I'm happy to join you for the ride.'

The gruff tenderness in his voice cut into Jeannie's heart, and the warmth of the Aga behind her and the warmth of George's love for his wife seemed to merge into one in the kitchen.

'And you fell in love.' Jeannie's voice cracked; it was all she'd ever wanted. It made her ache even harder now, knowing that special certainty was still out there, but she hadn't found it.

George smiled down into the basket, a conceding, inward smile. 'Yes, I did. And life has been madder, and richer, and more infuriating, and better ever since.' His smile faded. 'I can't speak for Rachel, of course . . .'

I have to tell him about the dress, Jeannie thought, suddenly. It *matters* that these two don't lose something so precious. It *matters* to me, because I want to believe in a love like this surviving human stupidity and mistakes.

'Rachel was crying when she sent her wedding dress off,' she said.

'Really?' George didn't look at her.

'She wrote a goodbye note to it.' Jeannie swallowed, not sure how far she should go. Then she thought of Rachel's tear-stained face and threw caution to the winds. 'It broke her heart to sell it, you know. Do you want me to try to find the person who bought it and get it back? She might have written the address down somewhere in the office.'

George said nothing. He checked Gem's pulse, then stroked his ear.

Jeannie felt uncomfortable. I've gone too far, she thought. I barely know this man, and he's Dan's boss. Still, there was a confessional tension in the room, as if George wanted to talk to someone. Might as well be hung for a sheep as a lamb.

'If something's wrong, then you should talk to her about it.'

George stared ahead of him, at the dresser covered in hand-decorated mugs, and Fergus's splodgy kindergarten paintings, postcards and thank you cards, dog show rosettes and village show First Prize cards: the loving, untidy flotsam and jetsam of the Fenwicks' family life.

'We've both done some daft things recently,' he said, after a long pause. 'I lent some money to my godchild and forgot to tell Rachel. Not the smartest thing to do, given our current discussions about the rescue's accounts, but I was busy, I wasn't thinking. I should have just told her, but she jumped to her own conclusions. And she's been on her high horse about those puppy farms – that rescue is a money pit, as you know, but it's not just a business to Rachel, it was her aunt's way of dealing with her own issues, and she . . . *identifies* with Dot in ways that aren't completely . . .' He raised a hand, stopping himself. 'Maybe I've been banging on about retiring too much. Maybe it's making her feel old. I don't want to retire and do nothing: I want us to travel, enjoy our life together. But Rachel's been in a strange mood for a while and I have tried to talk but we seem to end up arguing at cross purposes. Maybe we're just scared of what the other might say, if we *really* get into it.'

Silence fell. Jeannie stroked Gem's head, letting the kindness in the air spread between the three of them.

'I don't understand women,' George concluded glumly. 'Cows are a lot more straightforward.'

'I think if you start with what you've just told me about love—' Jeannie began, but stopped as Gem raised his head off the basket with an effortful grunt, pricking up his feathery ears at a sound neither of them could hear.

Jeannie held her breath. Was he hearing Dot coming for him? Was this the end?

Ten seconds later, the front door opened, and closed, swiftly followed by a conversation in full flow.

'. . . another one wouldn't make any difference, would it? Come on, Mum, it'll be good for Gem! He'd like another brother.'

'Gem's not well, Ferg. You wouldn't want a baby brother jumping on your head if you weren't well.'

'I wouldn't mind.' There was the sound of a bag dropping on the hall tiles.

'Mind that paintwork! Seriously, how many times?'

'I wish I *did* have a brother! You know I've always

347

wanted a brother. Or even a sister. In fact, if I can't have a brother, then I'm entitled to a dog.'

Rachel's voice had a note of pain in it. 'Fergus, we've talked about this . . .'

Fergus burst into the kitchen. 'Dad, can I make myself some toast? Mum says . . .' He trailed off when he saw Jeannie, and then Gem, struggling to wag his tail in the basket, and his freckled face dropped. In a split second, the beanpole pre-teen fell away, leaving only a boy, heart-broken at the sight of his childhood friend fading before his eyes.

'Hey, mate,' said George. 'Gem's tired. Come and give him a stroke.'

Rachel came up behind Fergus and hugged him, pull-ing him into her so he would feel her comforting arms but not see the tears spilling down her cheeks. Her face was drawn with the effort of containing her own grief to protect him.

'Want me to look after the kennels this afternoon, Rachel?' Jeannie asked, and she nodded gratefully, and sank down by the basket, next to her son.

Jeannie called Andrea to let her know she wouldn't be visiting Dan that afternoon, and spent the rest of the day helping Mel with the kennel routine.

Even though George hadn't exactly encouraged her, Jeannie searched high and low for any clue as to where Rachel's wedding dress had gone, in case there was a chance she could get it back, but she couldn't find any-thing. It made her sadder than she'd expected.

Maybe it was for the best, she told herself; it was just a dress, not the marriage itself. But she couldn't believe it.

No one had even tried on Jeannie's wedding dress yet, probably because word had got round about its one unhappy half-trip to the church.

At the end of the day, aching but in a good way from throwing balls and lugging feed sacks around, Jeannie collected Lady Sadie from the run she shared with Constance and Grace and walked her down the path to their cottage. It was a soft summer's evening: the hedgerows were blowzily overgrown with ferns and meadowsweet and, as Lady Sadie brushed past, clouds of wild honeysuckle fragrance drifted across the lane.

It was so peaceful that Jeannie kept walking, past the cottage and back on to the footpath that led down into the town; they strolled alongside the fields of high corn stalks and whispering barley, over a stile or two, and down to the small woodland park that eventually thinned out into the flower beds and lawns of the municipal gardens.

Sadie stopped and sniffed each new scent with interest; she hadn't been this far out of the kennels before, or had the trails of foxes, rabbits, moles or hares teased across her nose. Jeannie kept an eye out for anything that might spook her, and had a bag of treats ready to distract her if it did. She let her gaze wander across the fields and orchards; it was new for her too, something different to think about.

There was a memorial bench at the entrance to the woods, positioned at the perfect angle for passers-by to enjoy the panoramic view down into the town. Jeannie sank down on it and took out her phone.

She dropped a chew for Lady Sadie, and dialled the familiar number.

Her mum picked up immediately. 'Hello? Is that you, Jeannie? Is everything OK?'

'Hello, Mum.' Jeannie hadn't spoken to her parents in a few days. 'I'm fine.'

'How's our boy coming along?'

She bit her lip, needing the pain to focus her mind on the here and now. 'He's grand, thanks. We've a big meeting on Friday to discuss him leaving hospital next week.'

'Next week! Great news! Did you hear that, Brian? Dan's out of hospital next week. Oh, your dad's very pleased. Will he be coming home to your new house, do you know?'

'Probably into a rehab centre first. He's still paralysed down his left side but the physio's very positive about recovering control.'

'And how's Dan . . . in himself?' Sue knew – as did Jeannie – that it wasn't just about the physical injuries. There were deeper scars than the ones on his skin, mental fractures that maybe Dan didn't even realise he had yet. If Jeannie was honest with herself, that worried her far more than the hemiparesis. Those were the scars that needed love, and took time to heal.

'Getting better,' she said shortly. 'A way to go.'

'Andrea will be over the moon. She's been on the phone to us twice this week already, checking our availability for wedding weekends. I tried to tell her to take it easy with Dan, but she says she just wants to arrange dates so you don't have to worry about it. She's asked us if we have plans in June next year. Why didn't you tell us you're setting another date?'

'We haven't, Mum. And we don't want to.' Jeannie squeezed her nose. This really had to stop. First the

Fenwicks; now her parents. She *had* to talk to Andrea. 'We've both asked Andrea to cool it, but it's obviously very important to her.'

'Oh, love.' There was a long pause, filled with concern. Jeannie could hear it flickering on the line. 'Do you want us to be there for this meeting on Friday?'

'No. I'll be fine.'

'Is Owen going to be there?'

'I don't know if he is, actually. He's been away a lot recently. He's adopted one of the puppies, did I tell you?'

Sue refused to be distracted. 'Someone should be there with you, asking questions. These are big decisions, Jeannie. Decisions that could have an impact on the rest of your life. You need some support.'

Jeannie closed her eyes. She did, but she had to do this herself. 'I'll be fine, Mum. I'll let you know how it goes.'

She walked home as dusk fell. She and Sadie saw no one on their way, and when Jeannie paused at the cottage door, she glanced up at the big house to see if the lights were on. Only the kitchen window glowed yellow in the charcoal sky. One light, three grieving humans keeping watch around a basket. Four hearts.

'Be safe, Gem,' whispered Jeannie, and pictured the collie in his prime, running soundless and swift as a breeze across the barley. Something moved in the garden and she jumped: was that a cat? Or a squirrel? It was too dark to make out. Something quick and silent in the shadows, following an invisible scent of a long-gone human perhaps, running home. Running towards a never-forgotten hand, waiting by the lane.

Jeannie shivered and let herself in.

It had been an emotional day and she had one more thing to do before bed. Time was running out for her to record her song and send it to Edith. She'd made a couple of versions but not one that captured the emotion of the performance at the gala night. She wondered if she'd ever sing it quite like that again. After what Owen had said about Edith's trustworthiness, Jeannie had decided to meet her halfway for a change, and send her only one song, instead of the two she'd asked for. Let her ask for the other, once she'd proved she wasn't going to rip Jeannie off.

Jeannie brought her laptop and portable amp and microphone downstairs to the kitchen, and set up next to Sadie's basket. She drew the curtains and made herself a cup of tea as Sadie tramped round and round and then settled in her basket, the classic Staffie smile of contentment curling her muzzle. Jeannie thought of Gem and Rachel as she tuned her guitar; she thought about what George had said about dogs making you decent. Did she deserve Sadie's trust, after the way she'd let Dan down? Probably not. But the small acts of kindness and patience she offered Sadie every day certainly made her feel less worthless.

Jeannie touched Sadie's velvety head, and her heart filled up with a different kind of emotion: a wordless, timeless warmth that made her want to be better than she was.

Jeannie sang her song about trust and love to her dog, with tears in her eyes. It was perfect. Not quite as complicated or flawed or multi-layered as the human love she yearned for, but simple and enough for her right now. Most of all, it was honest.

She sat for a moment when she'd finished, holding the music inside her like a rainbow, then slowly exhaled. She was happy with it, and Sadie snored on.

Jeannie uploaded the file to the Dropbox account she and Edith had always used for sharing demos and ideas, and thought, as her hand hesitated on the touchpad, about calling Owen just to check she was doing the right thing.

She caught herself. How quickly had she started to depend on Owen? Not just for support at the hospital but now for advice about Edith – a woman he'd never even met but somehow had the measure of. You couldn't keep asking your fiancé's best mate for advice. And after Friday, she probably wouldn't be seeing Owen so often anyway. The thought made her feel oddly vulnerable.

Jeannie's brain acted for her. She clicked send and the file started uploading. No time to think about it – it was done. Edith had challenged her and, for once, she'd met it, on her own terms.

She stared at the screen as the icon appeared. *There.* A shimmer of anticipation danced across her skin and she wasn't sure if she was scared or glad.

Chapter Twenty-six

Gem's sleep grew deeper and deeper, and finally he slipped away that night, his paws twitching in pursuit of lost dream-lambs. He was buried in the back garden of the Fenwicks' house on Thursday, alongside Dot's other family dogs, whose resting places were marked with carved stones under the willow tree.

Jeannie stood next to Natalie and Mel as Fergus read a poem, and George gave a brief eulogy to the friend who'd shadowed their movements for more than a decade.

'Gem knew Four Oaks better than we did,' he said. 'It was his home before it was ours. He knew every draught, every creaky stair, every cold spot and warm pipe. Gem was generous enough to share his home, and he took good care of us from that moment on. We were his flock of pet humans, and he looked after us all.'

He glanced up from his notes to Rachel, who was standing on the other side of the small grave, pale with sorrow. Steve the locum had slipped down to dig it before breakfast, before George had to ask or Rachel had to see. It didn't look as if she'd slept. Her face was ashen, and she was gripping a bunch of rosemary with white knuckles.

Jeannie knew she was trying to keep things together for Fergus. Ferg was next to her, holding on to a squirming

354

white ball of fluff and pink paws – Dolly, the last remaining collie pup. He seemed sad but, at the same time, usefully distracted by his attempts to contain the wriggly dog in his arms.

So he got his little brother, she thought. That's good.

'Thank you, Gem, for your love and your patience with the thickos you tried so hard to train,' George went on. 'Whenever we drink gin in the garden on summer evenings, or walk the dogs round the park on winter mornings, we'll know you're padding just behind us, making sure we're not straying off the paths. We often didn't notice you when you were here, you were so stealthy and clever, but we felt your presence. And we'll still feel you at our heels, even now you're padding around a different field. You're always with us, and we're always with you. Goodbye, my dear old friend.'

'Amen,' said Fergus, and Natalie, Mel and Jeannie found themselves saying 'Amen' too.

Steve and George then lowered a wooden box into the ground, and Rachel stepped forward to place her bunch of rosemary on the lid.

'And this,' she added, reaching into her bag for a battered tweed hat. 'It was Dot's. She used to wear it on rainy-day walks. Gem slept on it in his basket for years after she died.' She couldn't say any more, but placed it carefully on top of Gem's coffin.

Natalie and Mel threw wild flowers from the paddock into the grave, then Rachel steered Fergus away so George could start filling in the earth.

After a cup of tea and cake for everyone, Jeannie and Rachel went back to the kennels. The dogs wouldn't walk, feed or hose down their runs themselves, as Rachel pointed out. 'And anyway, it's what Gem would have wanted.'

Dan had a full day of assessments, and Mr Allcott insisted that he rest afterwards, so Jeannie stayed to help Rachel muddle through the routine. She worried about how Dan was feeling, what the tests were finding: what future was falling into place for them. At three o'clock, Mel came into the office and announced that a team of volunteers would finish the day's duties.

'Go home and have a cup of tea,' she said kindly. 'Or wine. Whatever you need. We'll take over here.'

So Rachel and Jeannie went back to the Fenwicks' big kitchen where Fergus was on the floor playing with Dolly the collie, training her to give her soft paw in return for cocktail sausages. When he saw his mum and her friend, both looking gloomy and wearing 'we're about to have an adult chat' expressions, he grabbed three bags of crisps and his puppy, and headed upstairs to his den.

Jeannie cleared some of the post, notes, catalogues and newspapers off the kitchen table and slid into a chair. She flipped idly through the *Longhampton Gazette*, and noticed an article circled in triumphant red biro: the puppy farmer responsible for Sadie and her sisters' miserable existence had been fined £15,000 with a lifetime ban on keeping livestock and a community service order. It was a small good thing on a sad day.

Rachel sloshed out two glasses of wine and put one in front of Jeannie and drank a quarter of hers while she was still standing. Then she sat down with a groan. She didn't need to elaborate.

Jeannie sipped her wine and decided not to ask Rachel

about the puppy farmer. 'George did a beautiful job this morning,' she said. 'I was in tears. Mind you, I was in tears listening to him yesterday, telling me how Gem came here in the first place.'

'Yes, well, he can be very eloquent when it comes to talking about dogs. Just not . . . about human beings. Oh!' Rachel swept a hand through her hair. 'I'm sorry. I have no right to be whingeing about my life, not to you. Big day, tomorrow, isn't it?'

'It is, but Rachel – I don't have the monopoly on difficult situations. It's not Crap Times Top Trumps. And you've just lost your dog.'

'Not my dog, really, Dot's. And if Dot was here, she'd tell me to bloody well pull myself together.' Rachel stared glumly into her wine glass. 'She'd have *loved* to have my life. Husband, lovely son. Unlimited hot water.'

'I'm sure she'd be kinder than that.'

'No, she was pretty straight-talking. What I most admired about Dot,' Rachel went on, half to herself, 'is that she refused to be scared about *all* the things that freak my mother out. She left a good job; she set up her business alone, she never married. She didn't care about getting old, or what people thought. She just got on with life.'

'Like you've done.' Rachel had always struck Jeannie as someone who definitely wasn't scared of very much. 'What are you scared of?'

'Myself!' The answer burst out of Rachel with surprising force. 'I don't know what's going on with me. I'm fifty next month. I don't want to be fifty. Fifty is . . . well . . .' She mouthed the word 'old' and cast a guilty look over towards the door, in case Fergus was eavesdropping.

'You're not . . .' Jeannie mouthed the word 'old' back at her. 'You're just getting started.'

'Nature has a way of reminding you that time's marching on, even if your hairdresser can pretend it's not.' She ran her fingers through her silver-streaked fringe, and corrected herself. 'It's not so much getting old, I can deal with that, it's feeling . . . between chapters? George keeps going on and on about retirement, but Ferg's not even at big school yet. In my head I'm about thirty, but either I'm getting hot flushes or we need to sort out the boiler. And I still need to *do* things. I'm not ready to settle down into middle age and going on runs-out to the garden centre like my parents.'

'*Will* George retire early, though?' Jeannie thought of George's current workload, doubled without Dan. 'Isn't that just something workaholics tell themselves to stop everyone giving them lectures about stress-related heart conditions?'

'Two years ago I'd have said no. Now, I don't know. George has changed. But so have I.' Rachel lifted her head and gazed out of the window, then turned back to Jeannie with a sorrowful smile. 'Have you noticed that's usually the first thing people say when they give us their wedding dresses? "Oh, it's awful, I can't get into it any more!" As if they've somehow let themselves down. But who can? Who *is* the same person fifteen years later?'

'No one?' Jeannie wondered where Rachel was going with this, given that she'd used her own dress as a particularly vicious personal trainer.

'Exactly. Life changes us. And that's fine, it *should*.' She turned her glass round by the stem. 'Weddings are about one single day of perfection, but marriage is about a whole series of tiny changes and adjustments. Because you both change with every bump in the road, and not always at the same time. For as long as you're together. And that one perfect dress you'll maybe never get into again – I'm starting to think women are insane for setting themselves up to fail like that.'

'While paying a fortune for the privilege.'

Rachel sighed. 'Maybe it was better in the old days, when people just got married in their Sunday best – you knew what you were getting then. The same bloke you'd been stepping out with for three years. And you got a nice new hat you could wear afterwards.'

There was a long pause. Jeannie thought about Owen, and the kilt that could be discreetly adjusted for the ups and downs in a man's appetite over the years. So much easier for men.

She stretched her hand across the table. 'I'm sorry if Dan and I have made life even more complicated here for you.'

'Oh, you haven't. If anything, what's happened to poor Dan has made me realise how important it is to talk to each other while we can. George loathes *talking*, especially about what he calls Women's Issues, but I'm going to try to explain why I've been sobbing at horses, and why I've been punishing myself by punishing him. And hope that he'll be man enough to tell me what an idiot he's been too.' Rachel paused, as if bracing herself for the worst. 'He's a stubborn bugger, but we did promise the vicar we'd try . . .'

Jeannie couldn't see George being stubborn in the face of Rachel's apology. She sensed he was only waiting for someone else to start that conversation. She held out her glass for the proffered refill. 'I'm glad.'

'And do you know *why* I'm going to do that?' Rachel went on.

'Because you love one another?'

'Well, yes. I think we've got a few more miles in us yet. But also to try to persuade you to do the same. Funerals focus the mind. Dog ones, particularly – they leave us too soon.' She put the bottle down and looked at Jeannie. 'You need to work out what you want.'

'I have.' She looked back at Rachel, straight in the eye. 'Dan needs my support.'

'You can give it to him. But be brave and think of where you really want your life to go. It's scary how quickly a year turns into five, then into ten. I wish I'd met George *twenty* years ago, instead of letting life float me down its river. We could have had more Fergs, more adventures. You have dreams, Jeannie.'

Was Rachel telling her to leave Dan? 'I don't think I could live with myself if I didn't help Dan get through this.'

Rachel eyed her, as if weighing up whether to say something, a tentative smile playing on her lips.

'What?'

'You know, sometimes, the best things can come from the worst beginnings. It's not a secret – our friends know – but I got pregnant with Fergus on my first date with George. Our *first date*. Can you imagine?' She feigned mortification. 'The shame! We barely knew each other. We were responsible adults. George was on the parish council! And yet . . . here we are. It's as if the universe knew something we didn't.'

'Well, maybe that's how it is with me and Dan,' said Jeannie. 'Not the best start either, but maybe the universe is testing us . . .'

Rachel pushed her chair away from the table and got up. 'I wasn't talking about you and Dan,' she threw over her shoulder.

Jeannie frowned. Before she could ask Rachel what she meant, Rachel smiled brightly and went on, 'So, I had an email yesterday from one of our volunteers asking if she could get in touch with you about some private guitar lessons for her son . . . ?'

It always took Sadie a while to potter down the lane to the cottage, on account of the doggy pee-mails left in the hedgerows by other walkers, and they'd only got halfway down the path when Jeannie heard a car pulling on to the gravel drive.

George, home from the surgery.

Jeannie hurried up towards the house. She wanted to tell him how moving his eulogy to Gem had been, but as she got closer, she saw he was messing around with something in the rear seat.

There was a dress bag hanging in the back. George unhooked it carefully and draped it over one arm with care.

Had he bought Rachel a replacement wedding dress? she wondered. Wait, no – that was a *very* familiar dress bag . . .

Jeannie couldn't stop herself: she ran up the path, straight over to the Land Rover.

'George!' she panted. 'Is that Rachel's?'

George rolled his eyes. 'Of course it is. You don't think

I'd let that ridiculous woman get the last word by selling her precious Givenchy for me, do you? I'd never hear the end of it. I'd pay twice as much to avoid that moral disadvantage.'

He reached into the inside pocket of his jacket and handed her an envelope. 'This was inside. Read it.'

The goodbye note Rachel had written to her own wedding dress. Jeannie wasn't sure it was really for her eyes. She looked up. 'Are you sure?'

'Go on,' he said. 'It contains a pearl of wisdom from my wife which I think deserves to be shared with anyone contemplating holy matrimony.'

'Dear Tilly,' Rachel had scrawled in her distinctive handwriting:

> This dress made me the happiest, luckiest, most beautiful woman in the whole world. And the truly magical thing is that when I took it off, I still felt like the happiest, luckiest, most beautiful woman in the whole world.
>
> I hope your love will be as bespoke as the love I've found. Don't forget that, like couture, if the design's right, a good marriage can be taken in and let out to fit you both for ever.
>
> Never be afraid of adjustments.
>
> With every best wish for your new life together,
> Rachel Fenwick

Jeannie looked up, suddenly emotional. 'That is so romantic. But how did you find the dress?'

'As you probably know by now, I'm a straightforward bloke, Jeannie, but my wife makes me think like a fox. I *knew* she'd never let me buy it outright. Adam Marsden is Sharon our nurse's . . . brother-in-law?' George shook his head at the complication, but there was a proud amusement in his eyes. 'The amount this tomfoolery has cost me in couriers alone is mind-boggling.'

'Worth it.' Jeannie handed back the envelope. They were a good match, Rachel and George. Flawed and obstinate, but smart and loving and – hopefully – forgiving. And they could see it.

'She is more precious than rubies, as the big man upstairs would have it.' He tucked the note back in his jacket. 'Now, if you'll excuse me, I have a wedding dress to hide in my own damn attic.'

Jeannie had told herself she wouldn't check whether Edith had opened her demo on Dropbox but after the two glasses of wine up at Rachel's, she couldn't stop herself.

It was like picking a scab: she knew she shouldn't look but since she'd placed her precious song into the lap of the gods, she couldn't help starting to tingle with excitement at what might happen next. Had Edith played it to Amir? Had Edith played it to her writing team? Did she love it? What if the mystery celebrity liked it and recorded it? How much money could that make? But then the bad thoughts: Or did Edith hate it? Was she embarrassed by it? Was she laughing at her, down there in London with the cool people?

Jeannie's mouse hovered over the icon and she held her breath and clicked.

Oh. Edith hadn't opened it yet.

She sank back on to her heels on the kitchen floor. 'Oh,' she said again, aloud. 'Right.'

Should she email Edith to tell her it was there? She half wanted to, but at the same time, she wanted Edith to be as excited about this as she was. I want her to be *checking* Dropbox, she thought. I want her to care about what I've written.

Lady Sadie lifted her head in the basket enquiringly.

The phone buzzed on the floor. It was Owen. *Can you speak?*

Jeannie stared at the message, still in two minds about whether to alert Edith to her song or not. Owen appearing, even in text message form, only confused matters. He'd say no. He'd say: Don't even give it to her in the first place.

She wavered. He had a point. But then what did Owen know about the music industry? Or Edith? If she replied, he'd ask her what she'd done.

But maybe Owen wanted to discuss tomorrow's meeting. He'd already told her and Andrea that he couldn't be there, thanks to a meeting at work. Jeannie tried not to think about how much better she'd feel if Owen were there to process the information, ask the questions, keep Andrea's emotional energy in check.

Her hands moved before her brain could stop them. *Hey. Everything OK?*

He replied immediately. *There's something I need to talk to you about.*

Jeannie's pulse quickened. She really wanted to talk to Owen, and in a moment of clarity, she realised that wasn't a good thing. Owen understood her in a way Dan didn't – he'd seen her at her worst and best. They'd experienced something devastating, and shared more honest, awkward conversations in a few weeks than she and Dan had in a whole year. And she liked him, a lot. Jeannie could understand why Dan trusted Owen.

But Dan and Owen had been friends for ever. She couldn't encourage anything that might jeopardise that friendship, starting with late-night 'can you speak?' texts.

Sorry, having supper with friends, she texted back. *What's it about?*

There was a longer pause this time. Jeannie wondered if he knew she was lying. The cottage seemed to be breathing with her as she sat on the floor, waiting for the screen to flash again.

I need to talk to you about tomorrow's meeting.

Jeannie closed her eyes, suddenly too tired to deal with hints. Was it the phone messages he wanted to confront her about? Or the package? She didn't care about that any more. There was nothing factual Owen could tell her about the meeting that she didn't already know, nothing she hadn't already worried about. He probably just wanted to let her know he was there, backing her up.

How would Owen react if he knew what she'd done? Probably just like Natalie had when Beth was humiliated. And he'd be right to be disgusted by her. The thought of Owen's face when he realised she wasn't the kind, honest person he'd believed she was . . . Jeannie couldn't bear it.

Fingers crossed good news tomorrow, with Dan into a great clinic and home soon xx, she typed, and pressed send.

Sadie hauled herself out of her basket and waddled across to Jeannie's lap, where she settled herself with a huff. The weight of her square head was comforting, and Sadie's heartbeat fluttering against her leg soothed

Jeannie. They sat together, synchronising their breathing, waiting for the phone to beep with a reply.

The sun set outside, and nothing came. Jeannie was disappointed, then relieved. Then, just as she was about to get up and make some tea, the screen lit up in the dusky room.

Did you send your song to Edith?

She held the phone for several minutes, trying to winnow out what she wanted to say from the contradictory jumble of voices in her head. But Owen texted again before she could decide on the right words.

Don't rush into a decision. Your own voice is too precious to give away.

'Oh, for God's sake,' said Jeannie aloud. 'Even I wouldn't write something as cheesy as that.'

She fumbled with the phone. *I sent it last night.*

There was no reply, and after five minutes Jeannie decided she didn't want to wait any longer. It was getting late.

'Come on, Sadie,' she said. 'Last visit outside, then it's bed.'

She dropped the phone in her bag so she wouldn't be tempted to see what Owen replied.

A full moon had risen over the hillside like a fat pearl. Jeannie let Sadie potter around the rustling border plants, releasing musky wallflower fragrance into the air, and she gazed up at the big house, wondering whether Rachel had found her returned dress yet.

The lights were on downstairs, and the French windows were flung open from the sitting room, letting a thick pool of light fall on to the lawn outside. Two tall figures stood in the middle of the lawn, their arms wrapped round one another, leaning into each other's shoulders as if their perfectly balanced weight was keeping them upright.

Rachel's pale face was just visible, buried in George's shoulder. George's silvery-blond head was bent protectively over his wife's. She was wearing a draped ivory cocktail dress that gleamed in the mingled moonlight and electric light. He wore a checked shirt, rolled up at the sleeves. They looked like statues, strong and sensual. Supporting one another.

Is this a sign? thought Jeannie, desperate for some divine guidance. Rachel and George didn't start well, they barely knew each other, and now look at them. A strong marriage, adjusting and adapting. Should I try to rebuild that for me and Dan? Could we be like that?

As she was struggling to interpret the scene, George started to steer Rachel in a slow waltz. She turned, and the moonlight caught her pale back where the zip of the dress had stuck, only halfway done up. It didn't fit. She didn't care. It could be adjusted. George murmured something into her neck, and Rachel laughed.

And then they kissed, long and slow, as if it was their wedding day.

Chapter Twenty-seven

Jeannie woke an hour before her alarm clock on Friday morning, and lay in bed watching the sky outside fade from deep navy to a pale turquoise. She wanted to savour every moment of this morning, before everything changed.

Lady Sadie was sleeping on a cardigan by the door, next to the ukulele Jeannie had been playing before bed. Outside the dawn chorus was twinkling fragments of song in the darkness, and she let the music flow over her. It had been the strangest, most eventful, happiest and saddest two months of her life, but now it was over. She'd gone back and forwards over the situation until the small hours, and made up her mind: she would never tell Dan she'd tried to call off the wedding.

What was the point? It would only hurt him, and for what? As long as she could put Andrea off from rearranging the ceremony, Jeannie knew she could be there for Dan until he was strong again. She wanted to do that. If the last months had taught her anything, it was that love was helping those you loved through their problems, not walking away. Adjusting your love to accommodate the random lurches of life. After that . . . she'd cross that bridge later.

Jeannie lay listening to the birds singing and her dog snoring, and told herself that she was doing the right thing. If it felt as though a weight had descended on her shoulders, it would be nothing to what Dan was feeling. Absolutely nothing.

Jeannie kept her phone in front of her as she sat on the train to the hospital, watching the sheep-dotted fields outside the window slowly recede as the houses thickened up and a greyer urban sprawl took over.

She was half-expecting Owen to text again, or even ring, but whatever he'd needed to tell her so urgently last night clearly wasn't as important this morning. She flipped away from the blank screen and filled her head with Dan instead, scanning their early chatty WhatsApps and scrolling through their smiling photos, until she felt warm and strong with the conviction that things would be all right.

Halfway to Birmingham, Jeannie checked her Dropbox file, and saw, to her irritation, that Edith still hadn't opened it. Edith had definitely seen it, because there were other files in there she'd looked at. She was playing games.

Sod that, thought Jeannie, suddenly. I don't have time for games any more. If this big break is going to happen, it can't happen while I'm trying to help Dan. Maybe it's already too late.

She dialled Edith's number, the new number she'd got since she moved south.

It went to voicemail first time, but Jeannie left no message and called straight back. Twice.

Third time Edith picked up after five rings. 'Heyyy!' she said, very cool. 'How are you?'

'Great, thanks.' Jeannie didn't feel like telling Edith

where she was going. 'Listen, have you downloaded my demo yet? It's been up for two days.' She knew Edith hadn't; she just wanted to hear why.

'Two days? Wow, sorry, we've just been so busy in the studio since I got back.' Edith yawned like a cat. 'Haven't been to bed yet.'

'So . . . are you going to listen to it?'

'Absolutely. Soon as I get some time to really focus on it.'

Jeannie stared out of the window and wished she had talked to Owen last night.

In the space of a few weeks, Owen had given her advice that had changed the way she thought about herself. He reckoned Edith couldn't be trusted – and he was right. He somehow understood that finding her own voice mattered more than money, and how hard she found it to speak up for herself. And how her music came from somewhere she couldn't explain. Owen's reaction to her song at the gala had told her it was special – and not just because everyone had applauded.

I never got round to teaching him the ukulele, Jeannie thought sadly, as a voice in her head pointed out that Dan also thought Edith was untrustworthy, as did her parents. *And* Rachel. It wasn't exactly an exclusive opinion.

She could always send Owen a ukulele in the post, with a book.

'So what's it about?' Edith asked.

'Sorry?' Jeannie snapped back to attention.

'Your song? Did you write it about Dan's accident in the end?' A cheeky pause. 'Is it about me? Ha! Just joking, is it about Dan?'

Everyone seemed to think that. 'It's about love.'

'Cool! Well, I'm in the middle of something right now so I'll call you back when I've listened, OK?'

'OK,' said Jeannie and hung up.

She watched the terraced houses for a mile or two, feeling the air going in and out of her lungs, in and out, in and out, and then, on one breath that marked a change for ever in their relationship, Jeannie calmly deleted the file from Edith's Dropbox.

It was *her* song, about this strange moment in *her* life, and if no one ever heard it again, that was fine. Jeannie was keeping it for herself. No one else was going to sing this one.

The short walk from the station to the hospital foyer seemed quicker than ever that morning. Jeannie took a moment to focus her thoughts about Dan, and helping him recover his old self.

Deep breath.

Long road, patience and support.

Deep breath.

They'd get to know each other properly. The love might come back – and be stronger as a result. They'd just smothered the flame by rushing too fast. Now they had time. All the time in the world. Who knew what might happen.

Jeannie's stomach lurched.

Deep breath.

Long road, she started again, patience and support – and suddenly she jumped as someone grabbed her arm, hard.

She spun round and was shocked to see her own mother standing there, hanging off her arm as if it were a rail.

'Mum?'

'Jeannie! Oh, thank the Lord, I caught you in time.' Sue's round face was flushed with the effort of fast walking. 'I need to talk to you, missus.'

'What are *you* doing here? Where's Dad?'

'Parking the car. What time's this meeting?'

Jeannie struggled to process this unexpected development. 'In about fifteen minutes. You drove down this morning? From Dumfries?'

'Fifteen minutes!' Sue rolled her eyes. 'Nick of time, then.'

'I'm not being rude, but I can deal with this, you know.' Obviously Mum had decided she needed some support in the meeting, someone to explain to Mr Allcott that Jeannie understood about rehab, and would be able to help Dan when he was discharged home. 'I'm a big girl and—'

Sue didn't let her finish. 'Your father told me what happened. You weren't going to marry Daniel! But now you're going to pretend that never happened, and marry him because he's in a wheelchair and you feel sorry for him.'

'What? Who said anything about marrying?' What had Dad said? Jeannie looked around for his familiar summer jacket. 'Is this about Andrea booking wedding venues? Because—'

'But you're going to stay with him?'

'Yes! Of course I am. He needs me.' She stepped back to avoid a passing wheelchair. Trolleys and visitors were steering a wide berth around them. 'Can you keep your voice down, please?'

Her mother grabbed her arms, forcing her to focus. 'I know what you're like, Jeannie. Always worrying about what people think of you. But I am telling you now, as your mother, that you cannot marry someone you don't love. It's absolutely against everything marriage is about. Everything!'

'But, Mum, Dad must have told you that I *caused* that accident? With my phone call?'

'Love isn't something you *owe* someone. It would break my heart to see you pretend to feel something you don't, and believe me, it would break Daniel's too.'

'More than seeing me walk away from my responsibilities? Wouldn't that break your heart more? After everything you taught me and Angus?'

'If it means giving up your own life, then yes, Jeannie! Yes, it would break my heart!' Sue's eyes were bright with fervour. 'Your father and I *love* each other. It was never a question of would he stay. Married or not married, it'd have made no difference. We couldn't live without each other. You and Daniel, be honest with me now, it's not the same, is it?'

'Mum . . .'

'Jeannie, I can see it in your face.' Sue shook her hands. 'I like Daniel, very much, but if you don't love him, you're doing him no favours by pretending you do. Because one day someone will come along who *will* turn your head and there'll be nothing to stop you being swept away. Just some empty vows you know you never meant. And in the meantime, what about him? He deserves someone who loves him as much as he loves them.'

Jeannie struggled to free herself. 'Mum . . .'

'Jeezo, Susan, the parking is insane . . .' Brian staggered up and realised who his wife was talking to. 'Did she . . . ?' He looked between them both, gasping for breath.

'She did.' Jeannie's heart hammered painfully. None of this was helping. 'Made her point loud and clear.'

Sue turned and patted his arm. 'Thanks for getting us here in time, love.'

'No problem.' Brian panted, his face bright red. 'My fault for leaving it so late to tell you.'

'Well, if I'd *known*, Brian . . .'

'Why don't you have a coffee and argue between yourselves about whose fault this is,' said Jeannie, ushering them into Costa Coffee, 'while I go to this meeting?'

Jeannie couldn't let her focus slip now.

Dan, she thought. This is about Dan. Not me.

Andrea was already in Dan's room, fussing over his dressing gown and checking with the nurse exactly how to operate the wheelchair he was sitting in, ready for the meeting.

The wheelchair was a major milestone in Dan's recovery. His strained face betrayed what an effort it was for his weakened muscles, but he was determined to hide any strain under a veneer of positivity.

'Morning, Jeannie!' he said when she walked in.

It gave her a moment's shock. He sounded exactly like his old self. But as Jeannie returned the cheery greeting, she guiltily reminded herself she was her 'new' self to Dan – the faithful fiancée who'd visited every morning. The woman he'd known for less than seven days.

'Good morning, my darling,' Andrea added, giving her a big hug and a kiss. She was wearing a daffodil-yellow blouse and a white skirt.

They were joining the rest of the team in a part of the hospital Jeannie had never visited before. She managed to keep up a reasonably animated stream of conversation with Dan and Andrea as the nurse wheeled Dan down the corridors into the meeting room where Rhys, Heather the occupational therapist, Ulla the dietician, Bradley the psychologist and two new nurses were already sitting in readiness.

'We're just waiting for Mr Allcott,' explained Rhys. 'He's had an emergency. RTI.'

'Any idea how long he'll be?' asked Ulla.

Rhys shook his head. 'His secretary's updating me when she has news.'

There was a moment's polite silence, and then Ulla leaned over and asked Heather something about her holiday in Greece, and muttered conversations broke out round the table.

Jeannie fiddled with her glass of water, and turned her head to smile nervously at Dan. He smiled back, but his expression seemed off. She blinked, then chided herself. He must be dreading what's coming next, she thought. Even if the doctor's plans are good, it's a long road to get back to his old life. Her stomach lurched. *Our* old life.

She felt Andrea pat her knee to get her attention.

'I was going to tell you two later, but I've got a surprise,' Andrea announced to Dan and Jeannie. 'I know you said not to, but I've booked a venue for June the first next year. Cadogan Hall. I've paid the deposit so you don't need to worry about a thing.' She looked so pleased with herself, Jeannie could hardly bear it. 'I spoke to your parents last night, Jeannie, and they're saving the date. Now all we have to focus on is getting Dan there!'

Bleak panic swept through Jeannie's chest. So that was

what had finally prompted Dad to spill the beans. How much money had Andrea just wasted on a non-refundable deposit?

'Oh, Mum . . .' Dan tipped his head back and stared at the ceiling. '*No.* How many times?'

'Don't be like that, Danny, I just want you two to have your happy ending,' Andrea insisted. 'Is that so bad?'

That was it. Jeannie knew what she had to do. If Andrea kept pushing for a wedding, her tactic of staying but without commitment wouldn't work. Sooner or later, she'd have to give a reason, and it was better to do it now, before Dan's memory came back. Before the anaesthetic of his amnesia wore off and this hurt more than it had to.

'Dan.' Jeannie's voice was dry in her throat. 'I need to talk to you.'

'So?' Dan said. 'What's this about? Or are you just as bored of meetings with doctors as I am?'

They were sitting in a quiet corner down the corridor, near a large window, where they could talk without being disturbed. Dan looked straight at her and Jeannie's confidence wavered. He was almost the golden boy she'd kissed on Brooklyn Bridge nine months ago. It was almost impossible to carry on.

Andrea has put a deposit down on our wedding and she's not going to give up.

Jeannie leaned forward and took his hands.

'Oh God,' he said, deadpan, 'there *is* bad news.'

'I know you don't have any memory of the accident,' she started. 'Or the wedding day.'

'I've heard a lot about it from Mum,' he said. 'I almost feel like I was there.'

It was a brave stab at humour, which Jeannie appreciated under the circumstances.

'Why? Do you have some details you'd like to add?' he asked.

'Well, yes, actually . . .' She swallowed. 'I called you on the way to the church because I'd realised we were making a mistake.'

The words hung in the air.

'What?' Dan's forehead creased, as if he'd heard wrong.

Jeannie tried to tell herself that this couldn't hurt him if he didn't remember her. 'I couldn't get through, so I left you a message, asking you to call me. Then I rang again, but you were still on the phone, so I left another message telling you we shouldn't get married. And at some point, I don't know when, you stepped into the road . . . and here we are.'

Dan stared at her. '*Why* were we making a mistake?'

'It was too fast.' Jeannie hated hearing herself speaking words that made her sound so shallow. 'I wasn't expecting you to propose so soon, but you did, and I said yes because . . . what else could I say? It was a *dream* proposal. You've seen the photos – it was beautiful. We were so happy. But from that moment, it was like being on a motorway with no exits. All we talked about was the wedding. We never had time to talk about what would happen afterwards.'

Dan didn't speak. At least we're being honest *now*, Jeannie told herself as she filled the unbearable silence with apologies and guilt.

'I only saw you at weekends, and we spent those going away and exploring new places, but we should probably have been doing nothing, just watching films and learning how to *be* together. We were making this huge commitment to each other, and I barely knew you.' She struggled for an example. 'Like when I had to ask about your family to send Christmas cards, and I had no idea how many cousins you had but we were getting married a few months after that. I mean, we discussed things like moving here. But not who we wanted to be. Or what we were scared of. You only ever saw the date night me. Not who I am inside.'

Her voice caught as she realised something she'd been trying to ignore: Dan had never cared enough about the things that mattered to her. Jeannie had tried over and over to articulate what it felt like to feel music rushing through her like a river of sound; what her friendship with Edith had meant to her own self-esteem; how she worried that she wasn't living the life she was supposed to lead; but she'd never been able to make him understand. She'd thought it was because she wasn't good with words, like Edith, but actually he'd never heard what she was trying to say. Dan was curious about the minutiae of her life, but not, she realised, about her soul.

There was a long pause. 'Did you try to bring this up before the wedding?' he asked. 'Did I miss it?'

She shook her head, ashamed. 'I thought it was nerves. And on the face of it, I was the luckiest girl in the world, marrying a man like you. You're way out of my league, Dan.'

'Ha.' Dan managed a grim laugh at her apologetic expression. 'Thanks.'

'But then, on the way to the church, my dad was talking about what his marriage had meant to him, and . . .'

It was as simple as her mum had just said: they couldn't live without each other. 'I knew I couldn't make those promises to you.'

Suddenly Dan didn't look like a man who had no memory of her. His shoulders slumped. 'Are you sure that really happened, Jeannie?' he asked. 'You're not just trying to bail out now I'm in a wheelchair?'

'No!' Jeannie bent down and grabbed his hands, but he shook them off. 'I promise you, Dan, I'm not going anywhere. I *want* to help you get through this. I care about you. We had some great times – well, you've seen the photos. We had so much fun. But marriage is different. It needs something special. A sort of . . . click.'

She held her breath, waiting for Dan to say something.

He turned his head away. When he looked back at her, his eyes weren't full of tears, as she'd dreaded. But they were hurt. 'Who knows about this?'

'Just my mum and dad.' And Rachel. And Natalie. And probably Johnny too now. They didn't seem the type of married couple to keep secrets.

'Owen?'

'I . . . I don't know. I don't think so.'

'You don't *think* so? What does that mean?'

'Dan! Jeannie!'

They both looked up at the same time and saw a man striding across the polished floor towards them.

It was Owen.

Jeannie's heart skipped, and the usual relief she felt whenever she saw him spread over her, even at this very inconvenient moment. What did he want? He had a strange urgency on his face, as if he needed to get to them more quickly than hospital decorum would allow.

Dan shifted in his chair. 'We should be getting back to the meeting.'

'Owen was trying to call me last night to tell me something. Was that about your mum booking the wedding?'

'Who knows? We're going to be late. Come on. I don't want to talk about this with Owen.' Dan grabbed at the right wheel and tried to give it a shove, then grunted with frustration when it wouldn't move.

Jeannie felt Dan's frustration, and she turned away so Owen wouldn't see her face as he came nearer. She'd done it: she'd told Dan her shameful secret and given him the truth. And now she could go back to the meeting and commit to helping him through the next few months. Or however long it took. Years maybe. It didn't feel as good as she'd hoped it would.

Owen was right in front of them now, but he hadn't said hello. He hadn't said anything; he was staring at Dan, as if waiting for him to speak first. Jeannie distantly noted that he was wearing a T-shirt and jeans, not a suit, so he couldn't have come straight from the office.

'Hello!' Jeannie forced a smile. 'I thought you had a big meeting today?'

'Change of plan,' he said, then turned back to Dan. 'Dan, have you had a chance to talk to Jeannie?'

Dan was fidgeting with his cannula. 'I think this painkiller's wearing off. Come on, Jeannie, wheel us back in.'

Owen stood in front of him, blocking the way. 'Have you told her?'

'Told me what?' Jeannie asked when Dan didn't answer.

'You want me to tell her?'

'Tell me *what*?' she repeated.

380

Owen turned and Jeannie reeled at his expression. He looked the same as he'd done on their first day here, when he'd been struggling to keep his emotions under a mask of calm. Owen had never flinched at difficult conversations, no matter how many times he'd dealt with doctors, a hysterical mother, a scared fiancée, but he'd always seemed able to handle what was coming. Now he seemed to be scared of what he had to say, but determined to say it.

'What's up, Owen?' she said, a sudden glittering sensation unsettling her stomach.

'Oh, fine!' Dan sighed. 'I was just waiting to get a word in edgeways.' He looked up at them from the wheelchair. 'Jeannie,' he said, 'I know who you are.'

'What?'

'Dan's memory's started to repair itself,' Owen explained.

'How? What brought it back?' Jeannie's heart plunged. Please don't let him remember how badly I hurt him, she thought. Please, no.

Dan glanced up at Owen, then down at his own hands. 'It's complicated.'

'You can say that again,' said Owen, and sat down on the bench next to Jeannie with an exhausted sigh.

Chapter Twenty-eight

Jeannie dug her nails into her palm, trying to fix herself in this new surreal turn of events. Adrenalin had surged through her as she forced out her own confession, but now she was disorientated, as if the finishing line had unexpectedly moved and there was another lap to run.

'When you say your memory's come back,' she began, 'how much do you mean? Have you really had no clue who I was until . . . when? Yesterday? What happened? You just woke up and knew who I was?'

Dan looked up at Owen. His blue eyes were pleading. 'Can we do this after the meeting? I don't want to be late.'

'Mr Allcott's secretary came in to tell everyone he's going to be an hour at the very least – I was sent to tell you.' Owen folded his arms. 'You two need to talk about this. *Before* you start making plans for the next few months. Jeannie deserves to know the truth, Dan.'

Dan said nothing. He dropped his gaze to the ground in front of him.

'All right, I can make it easier if you want,' said Owen. 'Where's the phone?'

What phone? Jeannie's head spun.

'It's in my bedside table.'

'It's not, I can see it.' He reached into Dan's dressing

gown pocket and pulled it out. 'There. The phone.' He waggled it. A whole, intact, fully functional phone.

Jeannie stared. Why was Owen being so brisk – almost mean – with Dan? It was so unlike him. 'That's a new phone. Dan's phone's in the bin, in the café. It smashed.'

'The phone smashed, yes. The SIM card is in there.' Owen nodded towards it. 'I stuck it one of my old phones and suddenly a lot of things I couldn't work out started making sense.' He turned back to Dan. 'Mate, if you don't want to talk about this, then you could just let Jeannie see for herself. Show her the messages.'

'She called off the wedding!' Dan pointed to her, outraged. 'Did you know about this?'

'No?' Owen was thrown off balance temporarily. 'When?'

'She was going to jilt me literally outside the church!' Dan looked as if he was just starting, but Owen recovered himself and raised a finger.

'At least Jeannie's had the guts to tell you, instead of lying to everyone, including their own mother . . .'

'What. Is. Going. On?' demanded Jeannie.

'Oh, for God's sake.' Owen grabbed the phone from Dan's lap and handed it to her. 'Read for yourself.'

Dan started to protest, then stopped.

Jeannie's hands trembled as she took the phone from him. 'What's the passcode? Andrea's birthday?'

'Yes,' said Dan, as Owen said, 'And also Carmen's.'

She entered the numbers as the two men watched, her fingers sliding on the glass. The phone unlocked itself and presented the usual screen. It was perfectly normal, as if nothing had ever happened.

Jeannie braced herself and touched the text messages

icon. She was there in the list of contacts, as were Owen and Andrea and Mark and George Fenwick, but they weren't at the top. That position was blank, no name, just a roaring lion as the icon.

She glanced up at Owen and Dan, not understanding. Owen's eyes were fixed on her; Dan was staring at the ground.

'Read it,' said Owen quietly. 'And look at the date and times.'

Jeannie touched the blank line and immediately the screen filled with long messages. She saw the words *love* and *Africa* and *now* and *leave* and *miss you*. And *mistake*. She scrolled back, to the date of the wedding, and there it was.

I miss you. We've made a mistake. I'm sorry. xx.

And Dan's reply.

I'm sorry too. Can you talk? xx.

And the time? She pulled the screen across: 2.04. Just before the wedding. When she'd tried to call him. When she couldn't get through and had to leave her messages.

So Dan was texting someone else when he missed her calls, and walked into the bus. Texting, talking to, whatever. He was distracted by *someone else*.

She looked up. Her body was shaking so hard she thought her teeth might chatter. 'Can you talk? To who?'

'Carmen. She's the one who sent that package to the house,' said Owen. 'She also sent those flowers, and the postcard to the surgery.'

Carmen. Carmen. The name didn't ring any bells in Jeannie's mind. There had been so many friends, relatives, cousins, aunts, over the last few weeks. No Carmen.

'Can I have that back, please?' Dan held out his hand for the phone.

'Who's Carmen?' she asked.

Dan paused for a long second. Too long. 'She's my ex.'

'*Ex*?' Owen spoke quietly, but his voice had a steely undertone.

'Yes, my ex-girlfriend.' Dan glared at him.

A card turned over in Jeannie's mind. The holiday photograph of Owen and the dark-haired girl she'd assumed was his girlfriend; something about it had made her feel so awkward she'd put it away. 'The photo of you with the donkeys – that girl with the curly hair. That's her.'

'Where did you find that?' Dan asked.

'In your sitting-room box. I assumed she was with *Owen*. And that's her?' She turned back to the phone and flipped to the photos. Dan tried to stop her, then realised there was no point.

Jeannie had never looked through Dan's phone before; he'd always kept it in his pocket. She had to scroll back quite a long way, past photos from their year together, but suddenly there was the girl with the tumbling raven curls, in nearly every single photo. Her and Dan. Her posing on her own. It was clearly a very serious relationship. Carmen with sleepy lions, Carmen in desert shorts, Carmen and Dan dressed in black tie at a wedding. They looked like a real couple, their arms wrapped round each other, eyes locked, body language casual and possessive and relaxed. Carmen had a sexy flash in her dark eyes when she looked at Dan, as if she was ready to devour him once the camera had turned away. And Dan? Dan looked as if he'd be quite happy with that.

Not like us, she thought with a pang, thinking of their cosy, sweet selfies. He never wanted to devour me. Cuddle me, yes. Devour me, no.

She looked up. Dan and Owen were both waiting for her reaction; Owen seemed more anxious about it than Dan did. His dark eyebrows were knitted together and he was leaning forward as if he wanted to comfort her but couldn't.

'And?' Jeannie said. 'Who is she? How come you never mentioned Carmen to me?'

Dan turned his head and stared at the wall for a moment or two, then as Owen drew a breath to start speaking, he decided to make a clean breast of it. 'Carmen and I met at vet school. We went out to Africa together on a charity project and started seeing each other then. We were on and off, for a long time. Her dream's always been to go back to Africa and set up her own travelling surgeries. She's done a lot of work for animal charities out there.'

Jeannie was scrolling through photos as he spoke. She noted Dan was carefully talking about Carmen's professional life whereas the photos on his phone were of a much more social creature. She had beautiful arms, an infectious Hollywood-perfect smile, and was no stranger to a plunging neckline. The contrast between her Latin glamour and Dan's blond Englishness was dramatic, but they made – it was weird to note – a striking couple. A good couple. Her heart hurt in her chest. If she'd looked at his phone just once in their relationship, she'd have known. But she hadn't.

'These photos . . . the last one of you two together was taken the month before you and I met,' she said slowly. 'And you never mentioned her?'

'I didn't want to talk about it. We broke up soon after that, and it wasn't exactly . . . amicable. Carmen had raised sponsorship to get her African project off the ground and she'd almost convinced me to go with her. I'd looked into visas, funding, then Mum wasn't well, and I couldn't leave her on her own. Carmen thought Mum was being manipulative. She didn't understand why she finds it so hard being alone. Why she can't trust anyone after . . . Dad.'

Jeannie and Owen exchanged covert glances, since Dan was frowning into space, revisiting painful memories. She guessed Owen was thinking the same as her: if Dan's worst fear was ending up like his unreliable dad, then this wasn't the way to go about it.

'Did Andrea like her?' It was hard to see Carmen in her leopard-print bodycon dresses and – Jeannie peered at another selfie – quite strident animal rights slogan T-shirts chatting about *Emmerdale* and soft furnishings with gentle tennis-playing Andrea.

'Well, the fact that they have absolutely nothing in common other than their birthday . . . It proves astrology is a lot of bull. No, they didn't really understand each other. Carmen's not as patient as you are; she thinks women should just stand up for themselves. Doesn't get why Mum didn't just kick Dad out first time he hit her. And Mum always worried Carmen would talk me into emigrating, so there wasn't much love lost there.'

Another penny dropped. 'Paris?' Jeannie turned to Owen.

'Yup, and he was in Barcelona, not Paris, when the plane was delayed. Visiting Carmen's parents.' He glared at Dan. 'First and last time you ever make me lie to your mother.'

Dan looked ashamed. 'Yeah. Sorry, mate.'

'So what then?'

'Well, Carmen gave me an ultimatum: go to Africa with her, or break up. We broke up. Then I met you. And it was so, so different. I mean that.' Jeannie saw in Dan's sorrowful eyes that he *did* mean it. 'You were exactly what I needed. You're great company. We never argued. We could go away for the weekend and not have to smuggle four feral cats home. Mum thought you were the best thing ever, and you were so good with her. It felt like a proper life, a family life. It was what I'd always wanted.'

'So was I just a rebound fling that went too far?' She didn't let Dan look away, and refused to drop her gaze either. She needed to see in his face that he hadn't been winding her up, or leading her on.

The Dan Hicks she'd fallen in love with looked back at her, the same handsome, happy face that had pressed next to hers on Brooklyn Bridge for their engagement selfie. But she knew that what she'd seen in his eyes then had been the reflection of the Brooklyn sunset, the champagne bubbles of a crush, the rush of an unexpected infatuation that was just about to peak.

'I proposed because it felt like the right thing to do,' he said honestly. 'Because I wanted that moment to last for ever.'

Jeannie knew Dan was telling the truth. She was grateful for that, even though she knew she shouldn't be. They'd both felt the magic in that sunset. It just wasn't magic that lasted in daylight. 'Did you tell Carmen?'

'I did. She was fine about it. I emailed her so she could process it in her own time. She was travelling a lot, with work. I didn't hear from her, but you did, didn't you, Ow?'

Owen looked askance. Carmen obviously hadn't been as fine as Dan wanted to believe. 'She called me to ask if it was serious. I told her Dan was really happy, and that I hadn't met you yet but by all accounts you were fantastic. And so you know, Jeannie, everything Dan told me about you then has turned out to be true.' He glanced between them, measuring how much more about Carmen Jeannie needed to hear. 'Carmen said a lot of . . . *stuff*, and then she hung up on me. And I thought that was that.'

Dan raked his blond hair with his free hand. 'But then apparently she sent us those flowers.'

'How do you know that?' Jeannie couldn't remember any flowers, and then she did: the sodden box of dead roses and lilies she'd thrown away the first day she came back from the hospital. She felt cold. Carmen had found out where they lived?

'She rang *me* to tell me she just wanted to wish you both all the best.' Owen shot another sharp look in Dan's direction. 'And that she was sending Dan's cards and memory box stuff back to him. I told her in no uncertain terms *not* to, but she ignored me. So I had to go and get it back, didn't I?'

That was the package. Jeannie covered her mouth. The silent phone calls made sense now. The hidden parts of Dan she felt she couldn't know. No wonder something had felt off. He'd been hiding a whole other life inside the one she'd been living.

'I'm sorry, Jeannie.' Owen turned to her. 'I felt like such an arse, going through your cupboards looking for that package, but when you asked me about that photo, I realised Dan hadn't told you about Carmen and if you'd opened it . . .' He shrugged. 'I thought about telling you then – I should have. When I saw she'd sent that postcard and realised that she was actively trying to get in touch with Dan, even after the wedding, I had to do something. So I found Dan's SIM card, and put it in my old phone, and . . .'

He lifted his hands and dropped them, as if he didn't want to say the words. Owen had been forced in the middle of Carmen and Dan and her, from the start. But he'd done his best to protect Jeannie, thinking *she* was heartbroken.

The hospital bustle continued around the three of them as they sat in silence, mentally piecing the shattered moments of the wedding day back together to make a very different picture to the one each of them had thought they'd seen.

Do I feel cheated? Jeannie probed her feelings. Angry? Sad? All and none of those. Their beautiful day had been even more of a sham than she'd known. What if she'd never found out that Dan had been texting Carmen? What if she'd gone ahead with the wedding? Would he have told her? Would Owen? Would it have ended Dan's longest and best friendship?

There was one thing she needed to know, even though she didn't *want* to. Jeannie turned to face Dan. 'Were you talking to Carmen when you walked into the bus?'

'I can't remember. But if it's there on the phone, I must have been. I'm sorry. Truly sorry.' Dan seemed sad, and tired, and ashamed of himself. Much the same as me really, thought Jeannie. 'I never meant this to happen, I swear.'

'Meant what to happen? The accident?' Owen interjected. 'Or Carmen going nuts? Or just being found out?'

'Any of the above.' Dan's voice was exhausted.

'Do you still love her?' Jeannie felt as if she was surfing on a wave of honesty, barely balancing on the tips of her toes, but lifted high enough above this messy situation to see a truth that might just move them all forward over the wreckage of their combined mistakes. She sensed Owen's anxious eyes on her, but she didn't turn her head; she was watching Dan, struggling with the knowledge that the truth would hurt, but he couldn't sidestep it now.

He seemed to be silent for hours; then he spoke.

'I don't know,' he said finally, but that was enough.

Jeannie drew in the deepest breath she could, and let it shudder out. They were quits, as bad as each other. Both in love with the dream of something, not the reality. She thought of Andrea, deprived of her happy-family ending, and felt sorry.

'Carmen must really love *you*,' she said. 'She's moved mountains to keep herself on the edge of your world, even from Africa. She's stopped your wedding, and you walked under a bus for her.'

Owen and Dan both stared at her. Jeannie wondered if they expected her to cry. After everything she'd cried over and seen in the past few weeks?

'Does she know?' she went on. 'About your accident?'

Dan turned to Owen, who shook his head. 'No. I haven't told her.'

'Then I think one of you should call her,' Jeannie went on, more calmly than she felt. 'She's the reason we're here, Dan. The least you can do is let her know you're all right.'

This was what Edith would write a song about, she

thought. The star-crossed lovers smashing up lives around them. So much to write about: the love, the drama, the secrets.

Funnily enough, Edith was welcome to it. Just as Carmen was welcome to Dan.

Jeannie said nothing about the conversation when she and Owen wheeled Dan back to the meeting room, and took their seats as the consultant arrived. She was still trying to process what it would mean. She carried on writing notes in Dan's notebook, as normal, while Mr Allcott ran through the treatment plan, in rehab and then at home, and Andrea cried with relief at the arrangements they'd already made for him, and at the hope in the team's words that Dan would, eventually, inch his way back to where he'd been.

'It's a long journey, Daniel,' Mr Allcott finished up, 'but we're getting there.'

Afterwards, Andrea took charge of Dan's wheelchair 'so I can learn how to use this at home' but Jeannie hesitated at the door, letting them sweep ahead down the corridor. She didn't want to go back to the room quite yet. Would Dan tell Andrea what had happened? Or would she have to? And what about her own mum and dad, waiting in the café?

Owen was also hanging back, as if he wanted to talk to her.

'Can I have a quick word?' he said. 'I need to head off soon, my next-door neighbour's looking after Pete.' His serious expression broke. 'I'm running out of dog-sitters. Pete's going through a phase.'

'Chewing?'

'Anything that doesn't move. Some things that do, too, if they're still for long enough.'

She nodded and they stood awkwardly for a moment.

'I just wanted to say sorry, Jeannie.' He was blushing, a deep red. 'I should have told you about Carmen sooner.'

'No, I should have asked. I should have looked.' A man like Dan had exes, of course he did. She just hadn't wanted to compare herself, for fear he'd change his mind. 'Dan put you in an impossible position, and you were a good friend to him.'

'I don't know how much of a friend I've been, really.'

She managed a sad smile. 'I'd say you were the best man at that wedding in more ways than one.'

Now it was over, there was a hollowness in Jeannie's chest. Such a beautiful wedding, which must have looked so joyful from the outside – but it meant nothing. Not to mention the selfies, the engagement photos, the planning. Everyone had been fooled, including her and Dan.

'How do you think you *know*?' she heard herself say. 'How do you know when it's real? When someone's right?'

Owen didn't answer at once.

I guess it's not about the shoes, Jeannie reasoned, staring blankly out of the long window. Or the dress, or the car or the favours. It's about two people being honest. You don't need a fairy-tale dress to make promises you'll keep for ever. You just need a man who makes those promises feel as natural as breathing. A man who doesn't want to live without you. The ache inside her expanded like a rain cloud, heavy with regret.

She clenched her fists to stop the tears in her eyes. I will find that, one day, she told herself. If Lady Sadie can open her heart to trust people again, I can believe there's something better out there for me.

'Are you crying?' Owen's voice surprised her. It was full of tenderness and concern.

She nodded, not looking at him.

'Don't cry, Jeannie. Please.'

She shook her head, pressing her lips together, and made herself turn her head. 'You were right about being honest. I wish I'd done it sooner. It's always for the best.'

'I'll be honest, then.' Owen's expression had a strange sort of intensity to it, and the dark cloud shifted inside her. 'You just asked how do you know someone's the one?' He paused. 'You know when you're offered the job you've always wanted at the other end of the country.'

At the other end of the country? Jeannie's stomach dropped, and she started to say, 'Congratulations . . .' but trailed off because Owen hadn't finished.

'And you don't want to take it because you want to stay to support a friend in need. Or so you tell yourself.'

There was a long pause as the implications of what he was saying sank in. Owen didn't mean Dan. Not the way he was gazing at her, raw with regret. It was the worst confession he could make – so wrong on so many levels – and it was clearly torturing him to make it.

'But,' he went on, 'Dan is my best friend.'

Jeannie nodded, her eyes not leaving Owen's gentle face. She didn't trust herself to speak. A door had opened, just a fraction, to reveal a bright landscape of wild flowers and rolling valleys and distant music in the air, and now it was closing. It was a surprise, but at the same time she realised she'd always known what was there.

I don't want you to go, she wanted to say, for lots of reasons. But how could she? What good would that do?

Owen blew out his cheeks. 'Life isn't fair, is it?'

They stood looking at each other for a long moment. The next one to speak would close that door to a future neither had expected to find. Jeannie hated it, but Owen was right. The hospital with its strip lighting and daily carousel of fear and relief was a strange parallel universe, where nothing was in your control, including your feelings. Messed-up, contradictory, unworthy, *honest* feelings.

Slowly, Jeannie held out her hand and took Owen's. Every nerve in her body seemed to be in her fingertips as their fingers touched, then their palms, pressing together with exactly equal pressure. She made herself breathe slowly, saving this moment in her heart. Tiny sparks flickered across her fingertips, then down into her wrist. She felt his hand push back against hers, feeling what she was feeling: the click, the rightness. The certainty that there could have been so much more. But she wasn't going to make another mistake.

'You are a good man, Owen,' she said. 'The best.'

'He never deserved you.'

Jeannie's heart swelled. But she saw from the bruised honesty in Owen's eyes that he'd weighed it up and chosen the most decent way. He had to, for himself, and for Dan – and also because he cared about her. Truly.

'Please write a song for me,' he said, 'but not about this,' and Jeannie nodded as the tears ran down her face.

'I will,' she said. 'And I'll keep it for myself.'

Epilogue

Quite coincidentally, Jeannie was in the Four Oaks bridal boutique the day her dress was bought by Lydia Rogers, a dental nurse from Little Larton.

It was the first dress Lydia tried on, and – just as Jeannie had done – she hadn't even taken another off the rails once the rustling tulle petticoats had swirled around her legs and the ribbons of the sweetheart bodice were pulled in tightly, nipping in her waist like a Coke bottle.

Lydia didn't seem to be suffering from any of Jeannie's breathing issues as she stood on the satin-covered platform, smiling like a princess in a carriage and turning to admire herself from different angles in the mirror.

Rachel and Jeannie watched her from the side of the boutique while, on the velvet sofa of helpers, Lydia's mother dabbed her eyes with a tissue, and her bridesmaids emptied their champagne flutes and surreptitiously refilled them, since they obviously weren't going to get to linger much longer.

'This is the dress I've always dreamed of!' Lydia announced, swishing the full skirt. 'I can't believe I found it first time out.'

'You're sure you don't want to try on a few more?' Rachel gestured to the rail of possibles she'd pulled out from the back room. The stream of donated dresses had kept flowing, and under Natalie's general management and a team of enthusiastic volunteer stylists, the boutique was drawing customers from outside the county. It funded the rescue's entire food and care bills.

'Love saves the day!' as Rachel liked to tell everyone. That was also the name of their online boutique.

'More like Longhampton women's eye for a bargain,' was George's less romantic verdict, although Jeannie noted he'd stopped talking about early retirement and started helping Rachel with her puppy farm awareness campaign.

'It's absolutely perfect,' said Lydia, then frowned at her friend, whispering on the couch to another bridesmaid. 'What, Helen? Is there something on the back?'

Helen blushed, caught out. 'I just . . .'

'What?'

'I just . . . Are you *sure* you don't want a new dress?' She shot a shifty glance at Rachel and Jeannie. 'I mean, no offence, but don't you wonder if this one's been divorced or something? Like it might have bad luck?'

'It's from a wedding that didn't happen,' said Jeannie before Rachel could answer for her. 'No one's fault. Just didn't happen. So it's never been down the aisle.'

The wedding party looked at her curiously. Jeannie was still in her duffel coat and scarf; she'd called in to see Rachel on her way to the station. She had a meeting in London with her solicitor to discuss the royalties that were coming her way in the new year, which meant that she could start paying Rachel for Dorothy Cottage instead of working at the vet surgery *and* the kennels in lieu of rent.

Edith and the producers had capitulated reasonably quickly about Jeannie's writing credit on 'I Didn't Know' once she'd sent them the files of her demoing the tune. The meeting with the solicitor was more about planning what to do with the money. Jeannie had no intention of blowing it, but if she was going to write at home with Lady Sadie, she needed recording equipment.

'How do you know that?' Lydia blinked in amazement, as if Jeannie might be able to commune psychically with the wedding dresses.

Jeannie shook her head. 'It's my dress. I didn't get married.'

There was an audible intake of breath from the bridesmaids.

'I changed my mind, and so did the groom.' She smiled, because now it was a story, a narrow escape, not a tragedy. 'The right thing as it turned out, for both of us. So there's no bad luck attached. It's a beautiful dress, and I'm just sorry I wasn't the right bride for it.'

'Are you still with the groom?' asked Helen the nosy bridesmaid.

'No, he's moved back to Newcastle, near his mum. I still see him, though, now and again. We're . . . friends.'

'Did he marry someone else?'

'He's with someone else, yes. The right girl for him this time.' Jeannie heard Rachel snort beside her, and gave her a nudge. 'Anyway . . . I just wanted to say congratulations and good luck. It's your dress.'

'Thank you,' said Lydia. 'Did you just know too? When it's right?'

Jeannie nodded. 'I think you do.'

Jeannie had thought about her dress from time to time as she'd settled into her new life with her dog, and her new job, and her school ukulele orchestra and her friends at the rescue, and wondered if it would get the happy ending it deserved.

She'd hoped it would. Because, although nothing had turned out as she'd expected in Longhampton, she was finally happy.

Jeannie sometimes imagined the life she would be living now if she'd refused to listen to that little voice in her head and gone through with a marriage to a man she didn't know. Would their first Christmas have been spoiled with a special delivery from Carmen? Would she have caught Dan sending flowers on her birthday? Would Carmen herself have appeared on their doorstep? Would she and Dan have divorced; made up; grown stronger; had a child to complicate everything?

Whichever route Jeannie's imagination took, she and Dan usually ended up in a painful place, whereas now her life was simple. She ran George's reception three mornings a week, the kennels' for two, gave ukulele lessons in the afternoons, and wrote songs in the evenings. Twice a day she noticed each minute change in the season as she walked Lady Sadie, the lost soul who'd reunited her with her music, around Longhampton's winding footpaths.

The only secret Jeannie kept now was, ironically, about Dan.

Whenever people asked her if she missed him – not people who really knew her, like Rachel, but well-meaning volunteers like Freda – she always smiled sadly and said, 'A bit.' Sadly enough to close down the conversation. The truth was Jeannie didn't miss Dan at all. She missed the romance they'd had, and the exciting weekends of discovering places together, and that lovely dizzy swoop of falling in love. But not Dan himself. There wasn't enough of Dan beyond that fun for her to miss.

She worried about him, though, and kept in touch to support him as his recovery progressed. Dan was strong and determined to get back to normal, and the wedding insurance had paid for a lot of private therapy – so that was a silver lining, she supposed. Thank God Dan had had the presence of mind – or lurking guilt – to take it out. They'd paid their parents back, and he was welcome to the rest. Andrea had taken charge of Dan's recovery plan, and it had brought them closer in a better way. They spent a lot of time talking, she told Jeannie, in one of their long weekly phone calls. Jeannie and Dan had agreed to give Andrea a condensed version of their truth – that they'd mutually decided it had been a mistake – but she still seemed to enjoy chatting to Jeannie. If it helped Andrea build her new life, Jeannie didn't mind.

If Jeannie missed anyone, it was Owen, and she only told Rachel that once.

'Just do it,' Rachel had said, and Jeannie hadn't felt that was very helpful advice.

And so on the fourth Saturday in May, exactly one year after Jeannie's fairy-tale wedding dress should have been making its triumphant appearance down the steps of Longhampton Town Hall, its original owner was waiting by the railings with a box of confetti.

Lydia had left the date of her wedding at the shop, along with the details for the alterations, and since Jeannie was in town that day anyway to meet a potential new music student, she thought she'd go along to say goodbye, and wish its new owner luck.

In the space of a year, Jeannie McCarthy had learned a lot of unexpected lessons about love – *after* the moment that should have been the end of her story.

She'd learned that you shouldn't mistake falling in love, for love itself.

She'd learned that not all mothers-in-law are nightmares, and in fact you can end up feeling more affectionate towards them than towards their sons.

Most of all, Jeannie had learned that love – unfiltered, unedited, unnerving – was not how it seemed on Instagram. That timing, commitment, humour, in-jokes and pure coincidence played a big part in how things pan out, despite your best intentions. But that it had to start with a click.

In short, Jeannie didn't regret her wedding that never was. It had taught her a lot about herself, and brought her a devoted companion, even if it wasn't the species she'd thought she'd end up with.

Inside the town hall, a round of applause indicated that the ceremony was over, and a few moments later, Lydia appeared at the town hall door with her new husband, Robin Pritchard. She glowed with happiness in the May sunshine. Her blonde head was crowned with creamy roses, his arm was around her corseted waist, and as she posed gloriously at the top of the steps Jeannie spotted Lydia's bright red shoes. The perfect finishing touch.

She looks so happy, thought Jeannie, and she was glad for her – and for herself. It had come full circle, and now she could move on.

She scattered confetti over the newly-weds as they rushed down to the waiting car, and then slipped away.

'That was nice, wasn't it?' she commented to Lady Sadie. Jeannie no longer cared that people thought she was mad for talking to her dog. 'I liked her shoes, didn't you?'

Lady Sadie smiled. She was looking particularly smart in a new silver collar because she had places to go as well.

They walked down Longhampton High Street, past the charity bridal boutique, and the bookshop, and the art gallery where Jeannie had splashed out on a huge painting of the town for her bedroom.

This is a good place, she thought as she and Sadie stopped outside Natalie's café where she was meeting her new student. This is somewhere I can be myself at last.

Jeannie pushed open the door, but Sadie saw him before she did, barking at her old friend.

Pete the cockapoo was now fully grown and sitting up by the table, offering a dainty paw that was far more poodle than spaniel in exchange for cake. His owner was refusing to cut into the cake on the plate in front of them.

'You've got to wait, pal,' he said, clearly unafraid to be caught talking to his dog either. 'We're on a date.'

'I can't believe you're sharing your cake!' Jeannie exclaimed, and Owen turned, caught out.

When he saw her, the smile that spread across his face was shy, and hopeful, and excited, all at once. The chemical reactions in Jeannie's stomach fizzed and crackled, but she told herself to take it easy. No rushing, just tea and cake. And a long, long conversation that would probably never end.

'We've all got to start somewhere,' he said, and pulled out a chair for her to sit down. On the other chair, next to him, was a ukulele case covered in stars.

Acknowledgements

First thank yous, as always, to my amazing, all-knowing, all-everything agent, Lizzy Kremer, and to her colleague Harriet Moore, who always makes me wish I was writing the book she's read. Everyone at David Higham, particularly the wondrous Translation Rights agents who've taken Longhampton to places I never dreamed it would go, and the tremendous Maddalena Cavaciuti, is inspiring. If I wasn't represented by DHA, I'd definitely want to work there.

I'm very lucky to be published by such a dynamic team at Transworld, led by my insightful, patient editor, Francesca Best. It's really exciting to be in the middle of so much creativity and enthusiasm: thank you to everyone for the visible and invisible magic you work to turn the words on my laptop into words in someone else's imagination. It's a thrill that never *ever* dims.

Researching weddings was fun, but researching puppy farms definitely wasn't. I'm grateful to Kate Grundy, who gave me lots of information about the dogs who pass through the doors at Hope Rescue in South Wales, and answered my questions with kind patience. Kate's part of the army of volunteers tirelessly rehabilitating and rehoming the living fall-out from this abhorrent trade. Thank you, Kate; I admire what Hope Rescue does so much, and wish there'll be a day when you don't have to do it.

Acknowledgements

A big hug to my family, who've been more huggable than ever this nomadic year, to my best friend and fellow Nancy, Chris, and especially to my indescribably braw husband, Scott. And a grateful wave to every reader who's emailed me, Facebooked, Tweeted or written a nice review somewhere – it honestly means the world, and I appreciate it very much. Please do keep in touch!

Finally, a couple of special dogs: Miss Betsy and Flint. I've never met two more charming, sweet-natured ambassadors for the Staffie breed, with smiles as big as their loyal and forgiving Staffie hearts. This book's for you two beautiful creatures.

Sunday Times bestselling author Lucy Dillon grew up in Cumbria and read English at Cambridge, then read a lot of magazines as a press assistant in London, then read other people's manuscripts as a junior fiction editor. She now lives in a village outside Hereford with her husband, a Border terrier and an otterhound.

Lucy won the Romantic Novelists' Association Contemporary Romantic Novel prize in 2015 for *A Hundred Pieces of Me*, and the Romantic Novel of the Year Award in 2010 for *Lost Dogs and Lonely Hearts*. You can find out more at www.lucydillon.co.uk, follow her on Twitter @lucy_dillon, on Instagram @lucydillonbooks or find her on Facebook at www.facebook.com/pages/LucyDillonBooks.

How to help stop puppy farming

Puppy farming is a cruel but lucrative operation, and the backyard breeders and puppy smugglers know a lot of tricks to convince buyers that they're above board. Do plenty of research before you start, and always ask these questions:

1. **Who are they?** If the only contact you have is a mobile number, google it, and you might find ads for many different breeds: a big red flag. Stock photos of healthy pups are also used in ads; they won't be the dog you buy.
2. **Where are they?** Always see the puppies at home; puppy farmers will often try to arrange to hand the dog over in a 'convenient' place like a car park. If they don't want you to see where the dog was born, then it's because you'd probably be horrified.
3. **Where's mum?** Putting an illegally imported litter of pups with a healthy adult female can give a buyer the impression that the puppies were born there. But are they suckling? Does the mum look as if she's recently given birth? *Always* see the mother, particularly if you start hearing excuses why you can't.
4. **Does it look right?** Puppy farms aren't always literal farms – it could be a normal family home borrowed to 'stage' the sale. Do the dogs seem anxious? Are they relaxed with their owner?
5. **Do the dates add up?** Puppies should be wormed regularly from two weeks old, and vaccinated no earlier than six weeks, usually around eight, and you should ask to speak to the vet if you're suspicious. Eight weeks is the very earliest they should be leaving mum; illegally trafficked puppies are often separated much sooner, leading to trauma and development issues.

6. **Are they asking you questions?** A good breeder wants to be sure their pups are going to responsible homes, so expect to be grilled on your working hours, garden space, daily routine, family . . . everything. They'll also want to take back the dog if you can no longer look after it. If the breeder is only interested in how you're going to pay, beware.

7. **Is the puppy healthy?** Look out for bright eyes, healthy coat, moist nose (not runny) and wriggly energy. Any discharge, lethargy, dirtiness, anxiety or underdevelopment is a bad sign. 'Teacup' is a big red flag for health issues.

8. **Are any documents real?** Ask to see the parents' health tests, and if appropriate, the Kennel Club papers. But be aware that these are often forged to give a better impression. Check with the breed club to make sure the right tests have been done to avoid passing on genetic problems.

Walking away from a puppy-farmed dog is sadly almost impossible, but by taking a sick dog you're only making way for more neglected puppies, born in disgusting conditions to worn-out mothers. If you have suspicions about backyard breeders, report them to your local council, the RSPCA or the police. There are responsible breeders out there, as well as beautiful dogs waiting for homes in rescue shelters – all the links below will help you find your new friend, without putting money into the pockets of animal abusers.

www.bluecross.org.uk/pet-advice/buying-puppy
www.dogstrust.org.uk/help-advice/buyer-advice/how-to-get-a-dog-responsibly
www.rspca.org.uk/adviceandwelfare/pets/dogs/puppy
www.thekennelclub.org.uk/our-resources/kennel-club-campaigns/puppy-farming/how-to-help-stop-puppy-farming